A Plague on Mr Pepys

DEBORAH SWIFT

Published by Accent Press Ltd 2018
Octavo House
West Bute Street
Cardiff
CF10 5LJ

www.accentpress.co.uk

ISBN 9781786154972
eISBN 9781786154163

Printed and bound in Great Britain by Clays Ltd,
Elcograf S.p.A

~ PART ONE ~

Oranges and lemons, Say the bells of St. Clement's.
You owe me five farthings, Say the bells of St. Martin's.
When will you pay me? Say the bells of Old Bailey.
When I grow rich, Say the bells of Shoreditch.
Pray when will that be? Say the bells of Stepney.
I am sure I don't know, Says the great bell of Bow.
Here comes a candle to light you to bed,
And here comes a chopper to chop off your head
Chip chop, chip chop, the last man's dead.

Traditional Nursery Rhyme

Chapter 1
London, March 1663

Bess Bagwell clung to the seat as a wash of freezing river water sluiced over the side of the wherry. She had to shift fast, to avoid a drenching. And the river was full of the usual detritus: a bloated dead rat, and the scum from the tallow factory upstream. Shuddering, she brushed the spray of droplets off her skirts, and cursed the passing coal carrier as it ploughed past them, and onwards towards the ragged, dockside scribble of Ratcliff.

Ratcliff. It wasn't a place a body stayed in for long. Not if you had a choice. Up the Thames estuary they sailed: the Huguenots, the Jews, the runaway slaves; the dispossessed of all nations. They landed in Ratcliff in drifts, each new wave bringing the stink of poverty to add to the stench of brine and fish.

But Bess was determined to be out of it. Her friend Meg had told her there was a house for sale over the river, so she thought she'd take a look. Flaggon Row, Meg had said. Bess took out the hand-drawn map and studied it, the sharp evening breeze cold on the back of her neck, until the jerk of the wherry and another slop of water over the bow told her they'd arrived.

Bess followed the main street past the King's shipyard, the source of Deptford's wealth, her finger tracing the map. Impressed, she lingered in Deptford village, which was swept and tidy, with broad streets; nothing like Ratcliff with its pitch-roofed lodging houses, ramshackle taverns, brothels and opium dens. No beggars clogging up the passageways, either. She pulled up and re-traced her steps. Being short, she'd nearly missed the sign of the leather bottle for Flaggon Row, which swung above her head.

She turned up the street and scanned the houses. Solid, brick-built affairs for grand merchants. A board nailed to one of them drew her eye.

For Purchase. This must be it.

Lit up in the slanting sunlight, the house was a modest two-storey brick-and-wood dwelling, gabled in the Dutch style, with a steep shingle roof. It was separate from the rest of the row, and as soon as she saw it, she knew it was the one. Even the windows winked, attracting her attention. And they were real diamond panes of leaded glass – not just oiled linen, or cheap stretched-out rabbit skin.

She stopped to take it in. Practical as well as pretty – in its own earth yard with a vegetable plot alongside and hog sty and chicken run behind. Not that she'd keep pigs, smelly animals. Perhaps a herb garden instead; that would be more befitting a lady. Of course downstairs was shuttered, but through the narrow gaps she could see that the former parlour had been turned into a cobbler's shop. A carved wooden shoe still hung over the door.

But that would have to go. Her husband would have his own sign. 'William Bagwell, Carpenter. Sign of the Saw.' Especially now he had a fine new commission. He'd be itching to get hold of a hunk of good oak and start. A set of chairs for Mr Hertford, the judge. Six! With scrolled backs and turned legs. And carved fruit too, if Will had his way. He could fashion them right here, in this workshop.

Touch wood. She put a hand out to the green-painted plank door that opened directly onto the dirt highway, before standing back to look up at the set of wooden steps that led up the outside of the building to a jettied balcony and a neat front door.

Two planks had been nailed roughly across the stairs to stop people going up.

A hasty glance over her shoulder to check nobody was in residence, and Bess hitched her skirts up to her knees and clambered over and up the stairs.

The door had a brass keyhole with a shield-shaped cover that slid over it. An escutcheon.

She said it out loud, 'escutcheon'. Even the word meant quality.

Bess nudged it with her fingertip and it slid smoothly aside. The very sight of it gave her a shiver of pleasure. No barring their front door with a drop-bar again. Imagine, slipping your key into that lock like the gentry!

She walked around the balcony to peer in through the windows. There had once been four chambers, but now one was a parlour with a scrubbed slate hearthstone and proper brick chimney, and another was a cookhouse and scullery with a sluice pipe leading straight out over the Thames. Two bedchambers fronted the road.

How fine it would be, to perch above her husband's workshop, with the wherries and barges, and all the trades of London drifting past her window. Close enough to the city to be good for trade, but far away from the smoke and trouble. Far away from the slave-hunters and the whore-houses.

Far away from her mother.

Somehow being up high, above the ground on this jetty, the wind blowing through her curly hair, made her feel like a queen in a castle.

It was perfect.

It was in Deptford, though, and she knew how Will would feel about *that*.

Lodgings, they'd always had until now. It would be a big step.

Will would try to hedge out of it, like he always did, by not making a decision. But somehow, there must be a way. She had never wanted anything so much. Glancing at the board, she wrote down the name of the seller on a piece of paper. Then she kissed it, a big smacking kiss, as if somehow her lips might seal it as hers.

'I *beg* your pardon, mistress.' The voice was strident, and there was no 'beg' about it.

Bess turned.

'It's private property.' A large, square woman in a wide-brimmed hat was bearing down on her, accompanied by a well-dressed serving girl. 'Private,' the woman repeated, wagging a finger.

'I know that,' Bess said. 'We'll be moving in soon. I'm Mrs Bagwell.'

'Oh.' The woman folded her arms. 'I didn't realise it had been let.' It was an accusation.

'Sold. Yes.' Bess smiled sweetly. 'Just yesterday, Mrs…?'

'Mrs Fenwick. That's my house diagonally opposite – Strand House.' She pointed to the biggest house in the street. 'My husband is head draughtsman at the shipyard.'

'How very nice to meet you, Mrs Fenwick. We'll be neighbours then.'

Mrs Fenwick looked her up and down, eyes assessing the rough broadcloth of her skirt, her old-fashioned stays and well-mended shoes. Bess drew back her shoulders and stood straight, keeping her smile fixed in place.

Mrs Fenwick sniffed. 'I'll call, if I may, once you are established.'

'Please do,' Bess said. 'It's so nice to meet you.'

Mrs Fenwick's mouth tried to smile, something it was obviously unused to doing, and then she strode away, the servant scurrying after her like a dog. Bess watched her go, ruminating. Best to cultivate a woman like Mrs Fenwick; it would be good for Will's business. If I can bear it, she thought.

***

'Here's the address,' Bess said, pressing the paper down on the table in front of her husband. She patted him on the shoulder, which released a puff of dust. Will was a fine figure of a man – tall and blond, with arms muscled from lifting timber, and the fine-boned hands of a craftsman, but his clothes were always full of sawdust and wood-shavings.

He turned and smiled, with an expression that said he was ready to humour her.

'It's on the other side of the Thames, close to one of the shipyards. Big houses all round. A nice neighbourhood. Quiet.'

'Where?' Will asked, standing to pick up the paper, and stooping from habit because their attic room was so low.

'Deptford.' She held her breath.

'Deptford?' he said, throwing it back down. 'We're not living in Deptford.'

'Oh, Will, it has to stop sometime. He won't even know we're there.'

'You don't know my father, he gets to know everyone's business.'

'That's no reason. That terrible brimstone preacher lives just round the corner, and we manage well enough to avoid *him*.'

'Ho, ho.'

'We need never see your father. The Deptford yard is enormous. More than a mile end to end. Just think, you could work there fitting out ships, and you'd never set eyes on him.'

She tugged at his sleeve. 'The workshop's so fine – you should see the workbench. More than eight foot long, and it runs right under the window. You can nearly see the whole shipyard from there.' She paused; she knew his weak spot well. 'And the house will be perfect for your new commission. You won't have to hire a work place again.'

'It's more than we can afford, love, to buy a house.'

'You'll get better commissions though, once people see Hertford's chairs. You should see it! There's room for your lathes and there's already a wall with hooks for hanging tools. Just come and look, Will. That's all.'

Will sighed. 'Suppose looking won't hurt.'

***

In the panelled chambers of Thavie's Inn, Holborn, Will Bagwell lifted the quill and dipped it in the ink. His heart was pounding beneath the buttons of his doublet. The paper before him was thick vellum, as if to emphasise the serious nature of the agreement. Ten years of his wages in a good year. An enormous loan. He wanted to read it again, for it was a lot of writing to take in, in a language that took some fathoming. But they were all waiting.

Behind him, he could hear Bess breathing, feel the heat of her hand on his shoulder. He tapped the nib on the edge of the bottle to shake off the excess droplets of ink; Bess's hand tightened. He swallowed. Just shy of sixty pounds. If he signed this, there would be no going back.

He hesitated, and looked up. Opposite him, the turtle-faced goldsmith, Kite, nodded and narrowed his eyes in a tight smile of encouragement. The notary, an official from the Inn of Chancery in a blindingly white cravat, was impatient, shifting from foot to foot. No doubt he'd seen such an agreement many times.

A deep breath. Will felt the nib touch the paper and suddenly, there it was – his signature flowing across the page. He had no sooner lifted the pen from the document than it was swiped out from under his gaze, and Kite the money-lender was scribbling his name under Will's. Immediately, a serving boy came with a stub of smoking sealing wax, and even before Kite had time to press the metal die into the red puddle on the paper, the notary was adding his witness signature.

It was over in a few seconds and Will's damp palm was gripped momentarily in Kite's wrinkled one, before the duplicate loan agreement and the house deeds were thrust into his hand for him to sign.

'My man Bastable will collect the repayments on the last day of each month,' Kite said.

Will felt dazed. He wanted to turn back time, give the agreement back. But they were all smiling, Bess most of all. Her face lit up the room. She had her fine house now, and he couldn't let her down, could he? But all he could think of was the feeling of his empty purse, like a lung with the breath squeezed out of it.

***

Bess paused in her unpacking. 'Come and look, Will!' she said, pointing out of the window. 'We've the best view in Deptford!' She beckoned him over and pointed downstream. 'We can see the buildings of the Royal Dockyard from here.'

Will stepped over the crates and bags, and slipped his arm around her waist. 'Aye, it is a fine view across over the marshes. I can't believe I'm back here. I spent my childhood staring at those lime kilns at Mill Hill. And look at those barges, eh? Who'd have thought it?'

They stood a moment, each with their own memories, watching the log-jam of traffic go by on the Thames. In the spring sunshine the city in the distance was a panorama of shimmering grey spires. Bess sighed. The East End need no longer exist. The memory of Ratcliff was dark and cold; slimy cobbles and the reek of sewers and a bristle of masts stabbing the sky. She pushed it from her mind. It seemed a million miles away from this lofty house above its own carpentry shop.

'Thank you, Will,' Bess said, reaching up to wrap an arm around his neck. 'Maybe your father will warm to us, now we're near neighbours.'

'Don't count on it. I'm the black sheep, as far as he's concerned because I don't want to be a sawman. And he'll think I'm putting myself above him too; he always fancied a big house like this.'

'I know it's a stretch for us, but once you've got yourself into those yards and you're building a fine ship, it'll get easier. Has there been no word from the Guild yet?'

'No. But I suppose these things take time to process. They have to consider each application and follow up the references.'

Bess frowned. They'd had his papers long enough. Will should be leaning on them a little. But she couldn't be cross for long. 'A new start, that's what it is. Mr Hertford was right, you were wasted in that boatyard in Stepney. Will you start his chairs straight away?'

'Sooner the better. No point being idle. And the new apprentice starts tomorrow, so I can get him started, down below.'

'Jacob, is it?'

'Yes, Jacob. Seems willing enough. He'll live at home, though, so we won't need to provide bed and board.'

'Still, an apprentice. My, we're moving up in the world.' She moved a box of cutlery onto the table, but paused with her hand resting on the back of the bench. 'And how about a set of new chairs for us too, instead of these old benches?'

Will sighed. 'Maybe when Hertford's are done, or I get work

in the yards. We can't afford the wood this month, what with the expense of moving.'

'It's a fine house though, and it makes our things look shabby.'

He evaded her eyes. 'I'll go below, unpack my tools, shall I, love?'

When he'd gone, she looked around with satisfaction. There was room for Lucy, their live-in serving girl, in the little room next to Will's workshop, just behind the still-room. Lucy could have a separate bedchamber now, instead of a truckle in their room. And in time, she thought, a cook could be installed in the spare chamber at the back.

She'd need to persuade Will, of course. But she knew she could mould him. She'd always been able to make him do her bidding. Will didn't like fuss, and as long as he had a place for his precious wood, he'd agree with her just to keep the peace. In ten years' time, with luck and a following wind, this house would be theirs, and Will a master carpenter in the yards, and she'd have servants galore. Children too. Then they'd be safe, and no-one would be able to put them out on the streets ever again.

Chapter 2

They'd been in the house two weeks, and Bess was almost done with hanging out the linens to dry, when she saw the familiar scrawny silhouette of her mother just approaching on the other side of the road. There was no mistaking her mother's razor-sharp profile, the squared shoulders, and tightly tied steeple hat, sticking up like a black signpost.

Bess shoved the washing back in the basket and, hitching it onto her hip, ran up the outside stairs. From behind the window she eyed her mother's progress. Her mother had stopped a moment to stare over the wall at a grain barge trying to force its way through a gap between two flat-bottomed barks.

Nosy crow. Since she'd moved, her mother was always seeking an excuse to call and offer advice. Why, Bess couldn't imagine, as she'd made such a pig's swill of her own life.

Bess turned the brass key in the front door with a satisfying click.

At the sound of the lock, Bess's maid of all work, Lucy, paused to look up from threading her darning needle, with the end of the thread still protruding from her mouth like a mouse's tail.

Bess didn't answer her unspoken question, but shut up the shutters, and put her finger to her lips.

Lucy frowned, squinting her dark eyes at the lack of light, and finally having smoothed the end of the thread with spit, she drew the thread through the needle. Bess moved the stockings she was mending to the opposite side of the table. A pale, rippling sun crept in from the window that overhung the river.

A few moments passed as they sewed in the gloom, until a

sound like a whip-crack made Bess yelp and prick her finger.

She was here already. For who else knocked like that – as if the knock should bring folks back from the dead?

Lucy leapt up, ready to answer the door.

'Leave it,' Bess whispered, shaking her head.

Lucy's eyes widened.

Bess shook her head again. The door handle wobbled and the door rattled in the frame.

The two of them stayed still, frozen in space a moment, but then the knock shook the door again.

'We're not at home,' Bess mouthed. 'Go into the kitchen. The peas need soaking for the pudding.' Then, as an afterthought, 'Don't open the shutters.'

Lucy lay down the needle and bobbin with an aggrieved expression and slouched into the adjoining room. Bess bristled with annoyance to see Lucy had deliberately left the kitchen door ajar so she could see what was happening. Bess stood with her back to the door, holding her breath. Thank goodness Will was out; he'd gone to buy timber from the yard at Rotherhithe.

The knock came again. 'Anyone home?' Her mother's hoarse cockney voice.

Bess stiffened, simultaneously irritated and guilty. On the one hand, her conscience pricked her. Her stomach contracted at the thought that she was ashamed of her own mother. On the other hand, she simply couldn't face her. Her mother was just a reminder of the old days; the days of hunger and humiliation. She didn't want her here, in her down-at-heel clothes, bringing her down in the eyes of the neighbourhood.

The window darkened as a shadow pressed up to the glass. 'Bessie? You in there?'

Her mother always called her Bessie and it both irritated and tugged at her heart. She gripped her skirts, but then she slowly let go as she heard the clomp of boots going down the outside steps. When it was silent she felt a rush of regret, but busied herself with putting away the sewing to keep the feeling at bay. When she was quite sure she had gone, Bess opened up the shutters to let in the light, breathed a sigh of relief, and set Lucy to finish putting up the washing and then prepare Will's evening meal.

It was late in the afternoon and Bess was sewing the trim onto her new pillow cases when there was another knock at the door.

Lucy did not appear.

The knock came again, more insistent.

'Lucy!' Bess called, putting the mending in the cupboard.

Lucy put her head around the corner of the kitchen door. 'Have I to answer the door this time?' she said.

'Never mind.' Bess whispered a curse, then opened the door herself. Mrs Fenwick stood on the doorstep, accompanied by her mousy maid.

'Oh,' Mrs Fenwick said, as Bess swung the door open, 'I was expecting a servant.'

Bess smiled politely at her. 'Lucy's busy in the kitchen. Do come in.'

'Just being neighbourly,' Mrs Fenwick said, staring past her into the room. 'I thought you might need something, Mrs Bagwell,' she gestured to her maidservant to sit on the hard chair by the door, 'though perhaps I've come at a bad time?'

'No, it's not a bad time. Not at all.'

Bess stood aside and Mrs Fenwick sailed in, and after plumping up the cushion, lowered her squat, heavy frame into the best chair. It was Will's chair, and Bess subdued a stab of annoyance.

She was glad she'd put the mending away. Mrs Fenwick was quality. It was written all over her – in the supple leather of her gloves, in the imported French lace on her coif, in the angle of her expensive feather-trimmed hat. Not to mention her air of owning the world.

Mrs Fenwick untied the ribbons of her hat and offered it out into the air, obviously expecting someone to take it from her. Bess obliged and hung it on the hook behind the door.

She hurried into the kitchen, and asked Lucy to bring refreshment.

'What kind, mistress?' Lucy asked.

'I don't know… canary wine? No. I think it's too early. Maybe a posset? No, too hot. Lemon water. Yes, that should be acceptable. Two glasses, no three, she's brought her maid.'

When the lemon water came, Mrs Fenwick raised her eyebrows, 'Have you only the one maidservant?'

'I'm afraid so. Cook was called away.' Bess took a sip of lemon water to cover the lie.

'Unreliable servants. The bane of my life,' Mrs Fenwick said. 'I really don't know how you manage without kitchen staff, my dear. I couldn't manage for one day without mine.'

The maidservant did not flicker. She was obviously used to being talked of in her presence.

Bess smiled and nodded, hoping her inexperience in such company didn't show. She subdued the rising sense of inferiority that arose when she had dealings with people like the Fenwicks.

'Your husband makes these, doesn't he?' Mrs Fenwick said, indicating the benches around the big table. 'So clever,' she said, in a tone that implied he was anything but.

'Yes,' Bess said, bridling, 'but he's a ship's carpenter really. Fitting out officer's cabins. And he makes specialist furniture. He's not really in trade.'

'Really? Is he not related to the Bagwell that works the saw in the yard?'

Bess tightened her grip on her skirt. 'No. No relation. Would you like more lemon water?'

In her hurry to change the subject she hadn't noticed that Mrs Fenwick's cup was still full. Now she'd think her a fool. She put on a bright face. 'Will's waiting for his papers from the Shipwright's Guild. But he's out right now, choosing more timber, for a set of chairs he's making for Mr Hertford.' She emphasised the name, hoping it would impress.

'Hertford? Do I know him?'

'He's a judge. Friend of Mr Evelyn's, from the big house by the docks.'

'Is that so? Mary Evelyn is one of my dearest friends. Excuse me, Mrs Bagwell, but this lemon is rather tart. I wonder if I could trouble you for a nip of sugar.'

Bess scurried to the kitchen. 'Cut me some sugar from the loaf, would you, Lucy?'

'Haven't got none, mistress,' Lucy said in loud, accusing tones. 'You didn't put it on the list. You said, "it's either sugar or salt this month". And salt won. Remember?'

Of course. Lucy was right. She'd forgotten. And now the whole of Deptford would hear those words broadcast abroad via Mrs Fenwick's tongue. *Salt won.*

'What about honey?' Bess asked.

'None of that neither. You said—'

'All right, Lucy. We'll manage.'

When she returned to the parlour Mrs Fenwick was standing peering at some working drawings of chairs; Will had been inking them and left them on the side table.

'I'm sorry, Mrs Fenwick, we seem to be out of sugar at the moment.'

'No matter, would you like me to fetch some for you whilst I'm in town?'

'That would be most kind. But I'm afraid until my husband's

home—'

Mrs Fenwick waved her hand in a magnanimous gesture. 'It's of no consequence; we have an account, and an extra cone of sugar won't be noticed.' She laughed, and put down the rule that she was turning absent-mindedly in her hand. 'I called in because we have a little scheme I thought you might be interested in. An educational project.'

Bess was immediately wary. To her regret, she'd had little book-learning, and feared being caught out and made to look a fool.

But Mrs Fenwick was still talking. '… a charitable venture that I'm sure will be of interest. All the ladies are collecting. We're all agreed, we are open to new blood and we're recruiting now. We'll meet at Strand House, of course.' She looked to her servant, 'I'll send Maudie with an invitation, when we've fixed a date.' Maudie gave an almost imperceptible nod.

'Yes, of course. I'd be delighted.' Bess had somehow missed the part of the conversation that told her what the scheme was about. But she could scarcely believe it. Wait until she told Will! She was going to be invited to the Fenwicks's, to Strand House – the biggest, most impressive stone house in the street.

Chapter 3
One month later

Will had assembled the last of Hertford's chairs, and Jacob, his apprentice, had just begun to sand it, when a hand landed hard on his shoulder.

Will swivelled round to see his cousin, Jack Sutherland.

'Don't creep up on me like that, you fool!' Will said. 'You made me jump. What if I'd had a chisel in my hand?'

'You never hear anything when you're working, anyway,' Jack said, depositing his bag near the door. 'Might as well be deaf. I was just passing. Thought I'd call in. Are those the new chairs for Hertford?' His long-jawed face was red from the wind outside, but his slate-grey eyes held an avaricious gleam.

'They've been a devil to do,' Will said, 'he wanted turned stretchers. There's a hellish amount of work in each of those.'

'When's he coming to collect them?' asked Jack, picking up a chisel lying on the bench and turning it in his bony fingers.

Will sighed, took it out of Jack's hand and replaced it firmly on the bench. 'Don't know. I'll send a note today and maybe he'll come at the end of the week. We could certainly do with the money. How are the children?'

'Billy's got a cough again. He'll need another tincture from the apothecary. It'll cost me fourpence. Blighter always gets these things soon as the weather improves. And Toby needs new boots, he's shot up like an arrow. How much will you get for those chairs?'

'Don't know. Hertford said twenty for the six. I'm robbing

myself, but I daren't charge more, I need more work like his.'

Jack raised his eyebrows, then examined the three chairs standing in the corner. 'That second one's not straight,' he said.

'It is. It's just the angle you're looking from.' Why did Jack always make him defensive?

'And he'll pay you twenty pounds for them?'

'It's not much for all that work,' Will said. 'There's a good three months' labour in those. I've worked my breeches off to get them done in a month. Jacob too.'

Before he could stop him, Jack hitched up his doublet and sat down on one of Will's new chairs, leaning back and sticking out his legs; 'spider legs', Will used to call them behind his back, when they were children.

Will curbed the urge to shout at him to get off. Jack always did what he wanted to do; no point in having an argument. Instead, Will hovered over him, frightened he might break it or scratch the carefully polished seat that had taken him so many hours to do.

'Not bad,' Jack said, shuffling his bottom, his sword scabbard scraping on the edge of the seat.

It offended Will to see him sitting there. His fair hair was shaved to a stubble, so he looked like a convict, and his clothes were greasy, the cuffs of his shirt soiled and dark. Nothing seemed to have seen water, or a buck-tub in a long while. Yet he still had that easy swagger that made him seem like a wealthy man. It was something in his face; the rise of his chin, the watchfulness of his eyes.

'What're you looking at me like that for?' Jack said.

'Nothing.'

'You're thinking you don't like me sitting on this chair, aren't you?'

'No… ' Will was conscious of Jacob the apprentice listening to their conversation.

'Well? They're for sitting on, aren't they?'

'Yes, but... well, it's not quite finished – it's pegged, but still needs glueing. It's not really ready to take any weight.'

Jack smiled, as if he saw straight through Will's excuses. Slowly, he stood up. 'Well, you'd best get it finished then. And straighten it up while you're at it. *You* can see it's crooked, can't you?' He fired the question at Jacob, who flushed beet red, but wisely kept his mouth closed.

'Aren't you working today?' Will said.

Jack wandered away from him, scuffed the sawdust with his boot. 'No. I've moved on from the wool trade. The felt-maker didn't do his job properly, and when some of his cloth was sent back, he wanted to pin the blame on me. Said the wool I supplied was below standard.'

Will made a non-committal grunt.

'I told him where to shove it,' Jack said. 'Anyway, I'm well rid – there's no prospects in wool these days, not with the silk imports from the Indies. No, I'll try my hand at importing snuff.'

Snuff? Well, he supposed it wouldn't last long. Jack had gone through as many different trades as jugs of ale. And whenever he left an employment, it was never his fault. He was a man who didn't seem to be able to stick to anything for long.

'So who's looking after the children?' Will asked.

'Old Mrs Minty,' Jack said. 'Neighbour on the corner. She's two of her own, so an extra three's no trouble. She's got 'em making besoms.'

Jack's children were always being pushed from pillar to post, or bullied into piece work; carving clothes pegs or tying bundles of spills. Since Jack's wife Alison had died giving birth to their youngest, Jack didn't seem to know what to do with them. Though the children adored their father, it must be confusing – his erratic employment, irregular hours, and inability to stick to anything for long.

'Why don't you bring them over on Sunday?' Will said. He couldn't help being sorry for the three little boys. It couldn't be much of a life. 'Bess would be glad to see them, and we could do something nice, maybe go and see the puppet show on London Bridge.'

'That's for babes. They're getting a bit old for that now,' Jack said, 'but anything to please the beautiful Bess.' He always called her that, but the edge to his voice told Will he never really meant it as a compliment.

Will kicked himself. What on God's earth had made him invite Jack and the boys? Though Bess loved the children, she and Jack could not bear each other's company, and it often ended like a cockfight between them. Now Sunday would be ruined, and worse, Bess would be unhappy that she'd have to provide dinner for four more people. Not to mention the expense.

As if to read his mind, Jack cleared his throat. 'With me re-investing, I'm a bit short of change,' Jack said. 'The first shipment won't arrive until next week. I wondered if you could give me a copper or two, Will? I'll pay you back Sunday.'

'Don't know that I've got any change myself, Jack,' Will said.

'I'll look, shall I?' Jack moved surprisingly quickly. He was already feeling through Will's bag on the back of the door. With the age-old sinking feeling, Will was helpless as Jack tipped out the purse and scraped the coins into his hand. 'There, see. You've got a bit of change. I'll take this sixpence, oh and the half-crown,' he said as he stepped out of the door. 'Thanks, coz. Bring it back Sunday.' Jack's voice was already faint as he bounded back into the street.

'Hey!' Will followed him but he was too slow. He threw his hands up in frustration. He'd never see that half-crown again, he knew. Yet somehow he couldn't broach it with Jack. He knew Jack only came to him for money, and Jack knew he knew. But he couldn't accuse him of it; not his own flesh and blood. He'd given Jack money to pay his rent again only last month, even though with the loan, money was tighter, and Bess hadn't had any proper housekeeping money that month. The expense of moving had been more than he thought. Of course he'd said nothing, but felt guilty all the same.

Bess hadn't got work in Deptford either, and when he'd hinted at it, she looked affronted. She was busy making cushions and fancy trimmings for the house. It made her happy, but seemed a damned waste of time as far as he was concerned. Will returned to sanding his chair. You knew where you were with wood. This was where he was happiest; people somehow had the knack of flummoxing him.

And Jack was the worst. 'Don't let him rile you,' he said to himself. He applied more elbow-grease to the chair, but the scrape of sandpaper seemed to have lost its power to soothe him.

'Damn his eyes,' he cursed, flinging the sanding block as hard as he could at the wall. But then he saw Jacob's stare and picked it up again. 'Family, eh?' he said.

***

Jack strode down the middle of the street, dodging the horse muck in between the carts and carriages. He was on his way to the Dolphin in Greenwich, where he was meeting Bastable and Kite. At least now he'd be able to stand them a drink. Poor Will, he was such a fool. Jack had only to squeak, and look at him with sad eyes, and Will would hand over his money. It had always been this way, ever since they were boys.

Jack knew Will felt sorry for him, and guilty, and Jack did nothing to disavow him of this idea. They'd always been unequal – Will was the only son, and Jack was an orphan, taken in because he'd nowhere else to go. Always the poor relation.

It suited his purpose right now to act it. Will, the stupid man, kept trying to level it up. He'd never understood that the world would never be fair, that men would never be equal, no matter how much Will wished for it. The world was uncertain; death could come at any moment. Only this morning he'd heard that the plague, the same vile disease that carried off his family, was rife in Holland – and he intended to squeeze some profit from it if he could. After all, it had taken enough from him.

On the corner of Romney Street, Jack paused and sat on a stool to get his shoes shined by a street boy. A farthing well-spent, he knew. People went by appearances. They never looked underneath the surface – more fool them.

Once his shoes gleamed with polish, Jack slid off his filthy coat and pulled another from his bag. This one he'd bought second-hand a few weeks ago from a stall in the Exchange, and it was a clean navy damask that fastened right to the neck with a row of matching fabric buttons. The same rows of buttons were on the turned-back cuffs, and gave him a business-like air. He stowed his dirty coat in the bag and took out a dark 'tied' wig as was the fashion amongst clerks. After he'd straightened it on his head, he glanced in a shop window. Perfect. A sober businessman looked back at him.

He strolled down the street and into the tavern, taking a place near the steamy window. It wasn't long before the bow-backed Kite stooped under the lintel, with the fawning Bastable, his so-called 'rent-collector' in tow.

'Ah, Sutherland. This is Mr Kite.' Bastable, who Jack already knew from the gaming table, made introductions. Jack had heard of Kite. Rumours abounded about him. A small man with a big reputation. He'd made a fortune out of nothing; built a straw empire on debt and dealing.

'Ale, gentlemen?' Jack asked, flashing the half-crown at them.

They sat, and Jack brought a jug over. It cost him three ha'pence but it was an investment.

'I hear you want a share in this shipment of snuff, Sutherland,' Kite said, jutting his mottled chin towards him.

'Depends on the price.'

'The other investors are putting in thirty.'

Jack kept his face blank. So much. Not a hare's chance of getting that much from Will. He'd have to try another tack. 'What are your outbound goods?' he asked.

'Sheepskin and leather, tin from Cornwall,' Bastable answered.

Kite was silent, scrutinising Jack through hooded eyes.

'Well, since you're trading to the Low Countries, I have another proposal for you,' Jack said. 'It's a little irregular, but I'm sure you'll see that it's an idea that will turn a fine profit.'

Jack knew from Kite's expression that the word *irregular* had slid past him smooth as silk, but the words *fine profit* had stuck like glue.

A few moments later and all three heads were close together, deep in discussion.

Chapter 4

A few days later, Bess spotted Mrs Fenwick on the way to church, and seizing an opportunity to pass the time of day with her, told Will to go on ahead.

'How is your charity work, Mrs Fenwick?' Bess asked politely.

'These things take time,' Mrs Fenwick snapped. And then, face pink with embarrassment, she blustered about how her idea for the founding of a new petty school for the poor had been delayed by the parish council. It seemed from reading between the lines that Mrs Fenwick was having difficulty recruiting, although according to Mrs Fenwick, it was important to have the 'right people' on the committee.

Bess nodded and smiled, whilst thinking, by the time she gets round to it, the children will be grown up and gone. She watched Mrs Fenwick's plump figure hurry away to join her husband in the cushioned box pews.

Bess shivered. St Nicholas's Church was chilly in contrast to the spring sunshine outside, and the Sunday service dragged on. Bess had spied her friend Meg and it made her even more impatient. But no matter how dull, they had to bear it or be fined a shilling. By the end Bess was glad to stand up from her hard commoner's pew, and head for the bright daylight and fresh air. Bess peered over the heads of the other shambling parishioners, to where Meg, a plain, dark figure in a steeple hat, stood on tiptoes, craning to catch sight of her.

'How's your new house?' Meg asked, her round face full of interest, when Bess finally got there.

'Will's only gone and invited his cousin Jack and his three children to dine,' Bess said. 'I've to make three herrings and a bit of bread stretch for six of us. I've sent Lucy on ahead to get started.'

'Give them plenty of bread, that's what I say,' Meg said. 'It was good enough for our Lord, after all.' She laughed and pushed Bess on the arm at her joke. 'Besides, you can't beat simple food. Come on, if you're pressed, let's go, and talk as we walk. How's life in Deptford?'

'Fine. But I'm concerned for Jack's boys,' Bess said. The two women walked away from St Nicholas's, arm in arm, as their husbands, Will and Hugh, strode ahead.

'Why?' Meg asked. 'What's the matter?'

'Poor souls don't know if they're coming or going, half the time.'

'Oh, children don't need much, just firm handling, and God's good word.'

Bess made a grunt of assent. Jack refused to set foot in a church, and, quite apart from the fate of his mortal soul, it made Bess nervous that he was breaking the law.

'How's Will? Any news from the Shipwright's Guild, yet?' Meg asked.

'I can't understand what's keeping them so long,' Bess said, heading for the wall to keep out of the path of passers-by, 'they've had all Will's indentures and papers for months.'

'I expect he'll have to have an interview. Who's sponsoring him?'

'Briggs and Evans from the boatyard at Stepney, but they say that Nicholson is a dry old stick who doesn't like outsiders. Or riff-raff. It'll go against him that we've come from Ratcliff. And … if I tell you this, you must promise not to tell a soul…'

'Tell me. What is it?'

'Will was in gaol once, and I'm worried they've found out.'

'In gaol?' Meg's eyes widened. 'Your Will? I didn't know that. What did he do?'

'Nothing.' She paused. 'He won't talk about it. But I know he was a bit wild, back then. Got caught up in the sailors' riots in Wapping and Tower Hill. Took their side and ended up in Newgate.'

Meg blew a 'whissht' through her mouth.

'You won't tell anyone, will you?'

'Course not. And I can't imagine it.' She glanced at the men's retreating backs. 'Will seems so... so steady. Like nothing ever disturbs him.'

'He just hides it all. Anyway, it was more than ten years ago. Best forgotten. He lives for his wood now, always has a chisel in his hands. Never drinks or dices. Keeps out of bad company. But still, I can't help worrying.'

'If it was that far back, I'm sure the Guild can't know anything. Can't Will's family put in a word? They work in the yards, don't they?'

Bess lowered her voice, took Meg's arm to pause her. 'That's the other thing. His father thought Will being in gaol as a rebel reflected badly on him. He's not spoken to Will since. And they don't like me.'

'Why?'

Bess tried to keep the hurt from her voice. 'They blamed me. Said I was giving him ideas. Causing him to rise up against the King. Owen Bagwell's employed by the Royal Naval Dockyard. For that read the Crown. Will's father doesn't want even the whiff of the Protectorate's views in his family. He can't see that all the great promises the King made are already crumbling to nothing. Now Owen Bagwell's ashamed of Will. Though Lord knows, he's got nothing to get so high and mighty about. He's only a foreman in the yard.'

'Maybe he's just jealous of you.'

'Of me?'

'Of your influence. Because Will listens to you, even though, like all men, he pretends he doesn't. Maybe Will's father knows you want more for Will than just labouring in that pit like him.'

'Will'd die there. He's a craftsman, not a sawman. And he's clever. He needs men under him. I wish I knew someone who'd put in a good word for him,' Bess said.

'Bess?' Will was striding back towards them. 'What's keeping you? Jack will be there before us.'

The two women set off again, walking more briskly. Meg squeezed Bess's arm. 'The Guild'll come round when they see what Will can do. I've never seen a man take pride in his work like Will Bagwell.'

'Aye, wood's in his blood, but he's wasted on furniture. He needs to be a shipwright, get a place in the yards.'

'What about Mr Hertford? Would he help? When he goes to my Hugh to buy his news-sheet, he's always singing Will's praises.'

'I don't think Mr Hertford knows anything about shipbuilding,' Bess said.

'Isn't he friends with Pepys, that man from the Navy?' Meg asked. 'I've seen his name, Pepys, in the broadsheets. Such a strange-looking name when you write it down. Should be pronounced 'Peppis' not 'Peeps'. Anyway, he's in charge of buying for the Navy, from all accounts.'

'Is he? Maybe you're right. I think I've heard Hertford mention Pepys. When Mr Hertford first came about his chairs, I invited him in to take some ale with us. I remember now, Mr Hertford said his wife Edith hankered after chairs like the Pepys's.'

'Well then. If Will's family won't help, tell Hertford,' Meg said, 'and see if you can get him to speak to Pepys.'

***

Jack and his three children, Toby, Billy and Hal, were already in the parlour when they got home. Lucy had let them in, and now Jack was leaning forward in his chair, hunched over a broadsheet, filling the room with the stench of smoke from his long-stemmed pipe.

'What news?' Will asked, sitting opposite him.

'Bills of mortality are up in the Low Countries,' Jack said. 'Four hundred dead this week in Amsterdam alone.' He took another puff of his pipe and six-year-old Billy, who was hanging at his knee, flapped at the smoke and coughed. Bess went pointedly to throw back the shutters and push open the casement.

'Why don't you go outside for a few minutes, boys? I'll call you when the dinner's ready,' Bess said. 'There's a rod and tackle by the door. Catch us a nice flounder. Mind you don't fall in, now. And Toby, keep an eye on Hal.' Hal was the youngest at only five.

The boys jostled to get out of the door, the two eldest wrestling over the fishing rod. 'Be good,' she called, jamming a hat on Hal's blond head as he passed.

'Says here the plague came to Holland from Italy,' Jack said with relish, tapping ash from his pipe into a bowl by his elbow. 'Came from goods brought from the Turkey fleet in Algiers. It's rife in all the infidel countries now.'

Bess shuddered. 'Let's hope to heaven it stays there. And don't be putting the fear of God into those boys; they've no mother to comfort them, Heaven rest her.'

'Well, if they don't hear it from me, they'll hear it from somewhere else. No-one can talk of anything else. They've put the Plague Orders out on imported goods, and it says here they're considering putting guards on the city gates.'

'Hope those orders won't apply to wood,' Will said. 'Timber's hard enough to come by. I reckon it's scare-mongering, that's all.'

'You've not seen Amsterdam. I was there a few weeks back, on the wool run, and it's full of migrants. The harbour area's packed tight with them, like herrings in a barrel. And just as rank, I should think. From Germany, the Norse countries, everywhere. They're talking thousands. And now there's scarce a house anywhere without a "P" for "Pest" chalked on it.'

'Do you have to be so ghoulish?' Bess said.

Jack frowned. 'If it's too bold for your female ears, then take yourself to the kitchen. Besides, we want to talk business.'

Bess looked to Will to defend her; she was unused to being spoken to like that in her own home. Will smiled at her, as if to make light of it, to join them together in some sort of unspoken conspiracy against his cousin.

But she did not smile back. Instead she went to join Lucy in the kitchen. She wished that, just for once, Will would take her side against Jack.

Chapter 5

The promised invitation had arrived at last from Mrs Fenwick. Bess whooped; for if Will was to get more work, it was good to keep in her favour. Though she'd need a new spring gown before then, if she wasn't to be completely ashamed. It would be more expense, she knew. She needed to find out how tight their finances were, and she didn't dare ask Will. So there was only one way to find out, and that was to look at the account books.

Bess waited until Will had gone out, and unhooked the big iron key for the workshop from the corner cupboard. Leaving Lucy to scrub the hearth and trim the candle-wicks ready for the evening she headed downstairs. In passing, she peered into Lucy's room next to the workshop and was rather aggrieved to see the bed all unmade, and a heap of Lucy's clothes in the middle of the floor. Still, a glance into the yard showed the chickens had been fed, and she could smell the ale brewing.

Bess was glad Will was out. He'd gone to speak to a man about making bowls for the Navy; work he would never usually consider, and Jacob had gone with him to act as servant. But now Hertford's chairs were almost done, and Will had nothing else forthcoming. No more orders for chairs had come in, because the hearth tax was hitting people hard. The 'chimney men' were out, calling for their dues just as summer was coming, when the only fires lit were for cooking. They had three hearths here in Flaggon Row that would be taxed, and the crease between Will's eyebrows had grown deeper.

In the workshop, the light filtered through dusty glass, and she inhaled the smell of resin and raw timber. At the plan chest beneath the drawing table, she wiped away a layer of sand and sawdust, and pulled it open. There were Will's working drawings of cabinets and chairs, and on top, the ledger – a thick blue-bound book. Even within the chest it was gritty beneath her fingers.

Soon as she opened it, her fingerprints in the dust were unmistakeable. But this did not deter her. She flipped through the pages until she found the last month's accounts. Will was a tidy bookkeeper, and the columns were very neatly written out in his sloping black penmanship.

It didn't take her long to see that a large sum of money had gone through his accounts. At last, a bill had been settled that was owing. Eight shillings from a boat repair in the Stepney yard. There it was in the book, yet Will had never mentioned it, and there was no sign of it in the money jar upstairs. She turned back and forth through the previous months, looking to see if they owed anything. It was a puzzle.

This was most unlike her husband who was very meticulous about money. In fact he was always telling her how careless she was when she left her purse lying on the table, or did not account for every copper from the gratuities jar. Perhaps it was savings that Will was putting away somewhere.

She went through the entries again, *'lime-wood, pot-ash, rabbit-skin glue'*. Then the large sum of the loan repayment. *Bastable - 16/-* Strange, that seemed larger than she remembered. She flipped back.

Yes. An increase of nearly two shillings a month. A frightening increase. For the first time, the reality of the loan penetrated. She brushed away the uneasy feeling. But it wasn't so bad, she told herself; there would still be six shillings left.

Coal, candles, lye, knife-grinder, horse-hire. Another five shillings altogether.

Frowning, she noted another unusual regular payment. A

shilling a week. A week! So that was all of the payment gone, and not a penny of it left.

Next to the entry was one word. *Tyler*. Who was Tyler? She'd never heard of him.

***

She and Lucy laid out the mid-day meal, and Lucy made herself scarce; she always ate in the kitchen, not in the parlour, Bess had insisted on it, because it was what the rich men's wives did. But the mystery of the missing money still bothered her, until, unable to be still, Bess took out the basket of mending. She had barely begun when she heard Will's returning footsteps on the stairs.

'Back so soon?' she asked. 'Where's Jacob?'

'Gone for a stroll into town as usual, to fetch a pie from his mother.'

'How did you get on?'

'The broker was a tight-fisted bugger,' Will said. 'Six dozen bowls. For only a penny-farthing each. They'll be dull to do, and a lot of work, but Jacob can help, I suppose. He's not bad with the lathe now. When Hertford's chairs are done, there'll be nothing else …' His voice tailed off as he caught sight of his accounts. 'What did you want with my book?'

She put down the breeches she was stitching. 'Don't be angry. I was worried about paying Bastable the loan, and wanted to know how we'd manage to keep Lucy on, now you've no work.'

He blinked, taken aback. 'I'll get some soon enough. You've no skill in figures, and you'd no cause to go meddling.'

'It's gone up, hasn't it? The repayment.'

'We'll manage.'

She swallowed. 'I'm not stupid, Will. I need to know. You never told me you'd been paid for that boat repair. And another thing; I checked and double checked and there's four shillings down every month marked off for Tyler. Who is Tyler?'

Will sat down opposite her, and put his elbows on the table. He rested his head in his hands a moment before looking up.

'It's for the children,' he said, 'Jack wouldn't pay for their lettering, thinks it's a waste of money. But Alison was a great believer in education. She said it was the path to riches. She would hate to think of them growing up with no schooling. If they can read and write, then they'll stand more chance. Make something of themselves.'

Bess felt her throat tighten. 'You're telling me you've been giving Jack our hard-earned money to get those boys schooled?'

'Tyler's a schoolmaster. He goes twice a week. Teaches them numbers and letters.'

'And you didn't think that I might like to have a few lessons with our money?'

'Why, what's the matter? You don't need it, do you? You're fine as you are.'

She didn't know how to answer. She was half proud of him for being so generous to the boys, and she liked the idea of them going up in the world, but part of her was consumed by jealousy that those boys should have the opportunities she never had. Her own reading skills had been gained by an almighty struggle with the only book she'd ever had access to: Joseph Prescott's Bible.

Will was talking still. 'It's not that much. And it will make all the difference.'

'But why won't Jack school them?'

'The opportunity came when he couldn't afford it. After his last business failed.'

'What? The wool?'

'No. The one before, the scrap paper trade. So I said I'd step in to help, with a few coppers to tide him over.'

'A few coppers to tide him over! But this—' She pointed

accusingly at the ledger. 'And Maudie, Mrs Fenwick's maid, came with an invitation whilst you were out. Do you know what it's for? It's for her charity she's organising. To give poor children some schooling! Seems to me we're already a charity, thanks to you – never mind Mrs Fenwick.' She paused, threw her hands up in a gesture of frustration. 'Why, Will?'

'Once they'd started, I hadn't the heart to withdraw it, because I know Jack doesn't hold with it. He thinks the boys should be earning, not learning. But they're barely out of petticoats, and it must be hard with no mother at home.'

She shook her head, 'You're soft. I don't know why you let Jack fleece you the way you do, why he has such a hold on you. I've told you before, he'll bleed you dry, given half a chance. Why do you always fall for it?'

'He's had a hard life. You should have seen him, Bess, when he was only six years old and came to us, both his parents dead, and nowhere to go—'

'Will, for heaven's sake! He's a grown man now. You have to let him stand on his own two feet, not come running to us every time he needs something. I know childbed took his wife, and it must be hard, but he needs to take responsibility. You've got to talk to him, and tell him that we can't afford to school those boys any more. What if we have children of our own?'

The words hung between them. It was a long time since she had raised the subject and it prickled like a thorn. They'd been trying for three years, and nothing.

Will stood up. 'All right, I'll talk to him. He's had a spell of bad luck with his businesses, that's all. He just needs to get back on his feet.'

But somehow Bess wasn't convinced.

***

Will watched as Jacob gave the last of the six oak chairs a loving polish with the duster, and then ran his sleeve over the smooth, satiny finish of the wood. He was clearly reluctant to leave them and go back to making cheap bowls. When Hertford arrived later that day with the cart to take the chairs away, they were lined up in a row, gleaming in the sunlight from the window, the carved grapes and vines on the backs so plump you could almost pluck them.

Hertford was a portly man, with bushy side whiskers and a squashed-up face that looked like it was always about to burst into a grin. 'Mr Bagwell,' he said, 'you've excelled yourself, my man. They look splendid. I hardly dare to sit on them.'

Will could not help smiling, 'Go on, try them out,' he said, 'they won't bite!'

Hertford hitched up his breeches and gingerly lowered his behind onto the seat. One hand stroked the smooth wood where it joined the twist of the arm. 'By heaven, comfortable as anything I've ever sat in. These are a fine set. Even better than the Pepyses's. We were there for dinner only last week, and his boasting over his house was enough to make Edith spit. But wait till we get these round our table. We'll show old Pepys a thing or two.'

Will and Jacob helped Hertford load the cart, his precious chairs wrapped in old blankets and secured by ropes to protect them from being scratched.

Life was good. The sun was shining and he had twenty pounds in his pocket. It was such a relief. He'd pay a lump sum off their loan, just as soon as he could get to Bastable, and put the rest away for a rainy day. He took a silver thru'pence from his pocket and held it out to Jacob.

'Here,' he said, 'a little extra, you polished them up so beautifully.'

Jacob's face turned the colour of a beetroot. 'Thank you, sir. I enjoyed it.'

'You're a useful lad. Let's clear up before we make more bowls.'

He picked up the broom and nudged the sawdust into a pile near the door where Jacob crouched with his wooden pan, his spindly knees sticking out at an angle. Will whistled as he worked, in rhythm with the sound of the scraping bristles on the hard earth floor. It was the tune of a job well done. Jacob emptied the pan into the barrel by the door. He'd roll it to the Rose and Crown later so they could use it on the floor of their taproom.

Will had just swept the other end of the workshop, when the door opened again and Jack stepped through, straight into the pile of sawdust.

'Bloody hell, Will, why do you leave it so near the door?' Jack kicked it with a boot so it flew up like feathers.

Will curbed his annoyance and handed his broom to Jacob, who pointedly swept it back into a pile.

'What's up?' Jack said. 'Wasn't that Hertford I just saw leaving? Did you get that chair straightened out in the end?'

'There was nothing the matter with the chair.'

'Did he pay you for them then?'

Will hesitated, reluctant to tell Jack about the money in the leather purse at his belt. It weighed as much as a cabbage, and with Jack standing there in his threadbare clothes it suddenly seemed churlish to hoard it all for himself. Guilt at his good fortune made his face hot.

Will saw Jack's eyes drift to the purse which was dragging Will's belt askew on one side. Jack slapped his thigh. 'Thought so. Drinks are on you then!' With a swipe, he took up the key that was lying on the bench and tossed it to Will.

Will's hand shot out to catch it without thinking.

'Lock up then,' Jack said, 'they've got sea-oysters on the menu at the Dolphin, and I thought we could go out for a bite to eat.'

You mean, get me to pay for your dinner, Will thought. He'd be strong; refuse to be persuaded. 'Sorry, Jack. Bess made me up some bread and cheese; there, in that cloth. I don't want to go to the tavern today, me and Jacob just want to get cleared up here, get the workshop ship-shape again.'

'It's all right, sir. I can manage,' Jacob said, his long, thin face anxious to please.

'It'd be a waste of good food,' Will said, tightness growing in his chest.

'Aw, Bess won't know if we just nip out for a quick sup,' Jack said. 'And you've worked hard. You deserve it. Surely the beautiful Bess won't begrudge you a decent dinner for once.' He picked up Will's doublet from the peg on the door, and banged at it, raising more dust. 'C'mon.' He held it out for Will to put his arms in the sleeves.

Will knew that Bess wouldn't approve. He should be talking to Jack about stopping paying for the boys' schooling, not gallivanting to the tavern with him. But then again, perhaps the tavern was the ideal place to talk to him about it. It might be easier to broach when they'd both had a drink. Will slid his arms in the sleeves of the doublet, and fastened up the buttons.

He took one last guilty glance at the wrap of chequered cloth which he knew contained the buttered bread and cheese that Bess had made him. 'You have that, Jacob,' he said, with a wave of his hand.

Jacob beamed, but Will's stomach churned with worry. This conversation was going to be awkward.

Chapter 6

Even in the height of the day the Dolphin tavern was dark, and a thick blanket of smoke drowned them the minute they walked through the door, making it hard to see more than a yard ahead. The snuff and tobacco, mingled with the yeasty smell of hops, was enough to make Will's eyes water. When they sat, the fug floated at eye-level. Will ducked his head down to suck in some air.

Jack was impervious to the smoke and ordered oysters and ale. As soon as the oysters were slapped down on the pock-marked table, Jack picked one up between finger and thumb and slurped back the oyster from its gritty shell with a deft flick of the wrist.

Will watched the globs of grey slimy gristle disappearing down Jack's throat, with quiet revulsion. He was nauseous, not because of the food, but because he knew he had to confront Jack.

It could not be a coincidence, could it, that his cousin arrived on his doorstep every time he was paid? Last year, when they'd still been living in Ratcliff, he'd delivered some expensive pear-wood stools to one of his customers, and Jack had already been waiting on the doorstep when he returned. But now enough was enough. He cleared his throat, about to speak, but Jack got in before him.

'Not eating, cousin?' Jack said, waving greasy fingers. 'These oysters are bloody good, get them whilst they're hot.'

'How's it going with the snuff business?' Will could not think how to begin.

'All right.' Jack made a grimace and shook his head. 'But it's hard work, and truth be told, the stuff's so perishable, you have to shift it quick. And it's dangerous, being so costly. I'd to tackle two thieves on my own last night. Buggers were hoiking a sack of it out of the gate, brazen as you like. I ran after them, and one of them nearly ran me through with his rapier.'

'Were you all right?'

'I saw them off.' He patted his sword hilt. 'I can handle myself. But I don't know if I'll stick at it for long, though Lord knows, I need the coin. Toby needs a new pair of breeches; his are more hole than cloth.'

'Aye. Bess was mending a pair of his the other day.'

'If he had new, he might be able to get work as a messenger boy – help me out a bit.'

'How old is he now?' Will asked, knowing the answer.

'Seven, going on eight. Old enough to be earning his keep.'

'Doesn't he look after the others?'

'They'll have to look after themselves. But no-one will give him a second glance in those breeches. In fact I was going to ask you if you could give me a loan, just until next week. It makes me ashamed to see a son of mine in such a state.'

'I was going to ask you about their schooling. You see, if Toby's going to be working—'

'I wouldn't need much. A pair of breeches would only be a few shillings.'

Will swallowed and shifted uncomfortably in his seat. 'Thing is, Jack, we're not so well off ourselves right now.'

'But you've just been paid,' Jack said reproachfully. 'Twenty pound, you said, for Hertford's chairs. It'd take me a year to make that, selling snuff, the rate I'm going, and meanwhile my little lad's running ragged round town.'

Will doubted if Toby was as ragged as all that.

'Sorry, Jack, it's all spoken for,' Will said. 'We've got debts. The house loan … and I owe the wood merchant. I had to get the oak for those chairs on tally, and now I've been paid, the woodman'll want his money – and with interest. I've put in a bid to be making pews for St Catherine's, so if it comes off, I'll need to buy in some more good oak for that. With the imports of wood slowing, the price of oak's gone up. Times are hard for us all. And I promised Bess she'd have a new suit, for her outings with Mrs Fenwick. They're going to be doing some sort of charity work.'

'Charity work?' He laughed. 'She's a drain on you, that wife. She looked well-dressed enough last time I saw her. *She's* not got holes in her clothes, has she? Come on, Will, I wouldn't ask if it was for me. But it's for Toby. What would my Alison say if she saw my lads now? She'd turn in her grave, that's what.'

Will looked miserably at the oysters in their greasy shells. Jack knew exactly how to get to him. He knew how Will loved those lads because he and Bess had none of their own.

'Go on, Will,' Jack said, with a hand on his arm. 'Just a few shilling.'

'I promised Bess I wouldn't. We agreed if you asked I'd to say no.'

Jack pushed his chair back from the table. 'So you've been discussing me, have you? Soon as you married her I knew there'd be trouble. She fancies herself too much as a lady.'

'She doesn't. She just wants me to get on, that's all. To make something of myself. And she's always been good with my customers, Bess.'

'Yes,' Jack said. 'Always a bit too good with the tongue, your lady wife. I wouldn't let any wife of mine lay down the law like that.'

'She's a good wife,' Will said, 'you just don't know her well enough.'

'I know her well enough to know she has you under her thumb.'

Will hated it when Jack talked about Bess this way. He

swallowed and took a deep breath, 'Sorry, Jack, but we all have a living to make, and I can't—'

'So that's the way it is.' Jack threw down his oyster shell with a clatter and stood up. 'You're too mean to help your own cousin,' he said in a voice designed to be heard. 'Who would have thought it, that you'd see your own nephew go barefoot in the street?'

Jack always did know how to exaggerate.

With a great waft of air, Jack unhooked his cloak from the back of the chair and swung it over his shoulders. Striding past the other tables and chairs, like some sort of Roman emperor, he flung open the door. It slammed shut behind him and a gust of wind and dust blew in.

Will stood but he was too late to stop him. The men at the next table glared at him with disdain. Will sat back down. The oysters were congealed on the plate in front of him. He prodded his knife into one and wondered whether to try and eat it. He sighed, rested his elbows on the table. He'd better try. He knew he could not leave. After all, with oysters a shilling a pint, somebody would have to foot the bill.

Chapter 7

The next morning Bess was sweeping the stairs and worrying about the fact that Will's talk to Jack had been fruitless. He hadn't said as much, but she guessed, by the way he had turned the subject, when she asked him about it. Still, maybe things would look up now Hertford had collected his chairs and she could ask Will for a little more housekeeping.

'Mrs Bagwell!' A loud, breathy voice made her look up and brush the hair from her eyes. Mrs Fenwick was approaching from across the road, all feathers and floating fichu, waving her plump arms to get her attention.

'Morrow, Mrs Fenwick,' Bess said, flapping her hand in the air to dispel the dust.

'Mrs Bagwell! Had you forgotten? Today's the day! The rest of the ladies I've recruited are at my house. We're all waiting.'

Bess clapped a hand to her mouth. Today? She flushed. 'Oh. No, I'm coming, I just had rather a busy morning. I'll just wash my hands, I hadn't realised time had gone on so …'

'Maudie will let you in,' called Mrs Fenwick as she sped away.

Bess hastened inside, her face hot with embarrassment. She thrust the broom under the stairs, and tidied her hair into coils with her fingers. She'd completely forgotten. What would Mrs Fenwick think of her?

She threw on her Sunday frock and a clean coif, topped with her best hat, and hurried up the street towards the docks. Mrs Fenwick's house was on the edge of Flaggon Row, close to the quayside — a solid stone house with a porticoed front door and an impressive number of chimneys. Bess arrived there out of breath and pink with exertion. Maudie the housemaid looked at Bess's glistening brow with disapproval before showing her into a lofty parlour.

There, a group of three other women, all in fashionable hats, eyed her over their cups. The echoing chamber with its ornamental plaster ceiling of lacy stalactites made Bess feel exposed, like a servant. She slunk to the only available chair. Maudie, tip-toeing on soft leather soles, brought her a steaming cup on a silver tray. The china was so hot she had to juggle it between her fingers to stop from burning herself, and the brown liquid inside gave off an unappetising odour of burnt cork.

'So glad you could come, Mrs Bagwell,' Mrs Fenwick said, and the other ladies dipped their heads, murmuring pleasantries in carefully modulated voices. 'Now then, we have decided we will all make a contribution first of all, and then when we go around with our collecting boxes, they will rattle convincingly.'

A contribution? Bess had brought nothing. Ashamed, she shifted in her seat, took a sip of the brown liquid. It was scalding and bitter and burned her tongue. Tears sprang to her eyes.

'The coffee not to your liking?' Mrs Fenwick asked.

'No, it's lovely. Just a little... it's just hot,' she finished.

The other ladies were drinking the ghastly stuff, so after blowing on it a while, Bess tipped the liquid down her throat in one gulp so she didn't have to taste it.

Meanwhile, another of the ladies, Mrs Evelyn, was passing out the boxes.

The box gave her a tight feeling in the chest. She'd seen a box like this before, in Ratcliff, when the wealthy wives came round do-gooding at Christmas. And she remembered the horse-faced lady who opened it up and distributed one measly copper with a superior and benevolent air. The copper that was too little to do anything useful: too little to feed a family or to get her and her mother out of the stinking pit of a hovel they used to live in. Other people's charity. It made her want to spew.

She gripped the box on her lap as the ladies reached for purses and reticules and plopped their coins into their boxes. *Deptford Christian Education Fund*, Bess read on the label glued to the top. She took it and saw there was a slot for coins, and a string for carrying it. The other ladies ooh-ed and aah-ed as if they were being given a gift. Somehow they reminded Bess of caged birds, all preen and feather, chirruping to each other.

How foolish she was. She hadn't thought to bring any money. Now they were all looking at her, and she was caught – between becoming one of the charitable, who she despised, and the indisputable fact that she would soon be in need of charity herself. The room seemed to grow smaller, as they assessed her, judging. Is she fit? Is she one of us?

'I'm sorry, but I seem to have left my purse at home,' Bess said.

'Yes, I do believe Mrs Bagwell had completely forgotten us!' Mrs Fenwick said.

The others simpered and giggled.

'No, not forgotten, just I had a deal of work to do, and with Will—'

'Never mind.' An older woman with heavy eyebrows scurried over to Bess and pushed a half-sovereign in her box. She gave her a complicit smile. 'I'm Mrs Gordon. You can pay me back next time,' she whispered.

Oh no. Now she was in debt again. And for half a sovereign. Mrs Gordon smiled at her again in a maternal way, but Bess felt the weight of that half-sovereign and longed to throw the whole box out of the window.

'This time next month, I expect these boxes to be full,' Mrs Fenwick announced. 'Then we can begin our good works. There's a room in the old sail-makers that should do for a school. We'll need to equip it properly. There'll be so much to buy! Mrs Gordon has volunteered to teach although we'll need others. Bible instruction, writing, rudimentary calculation.'

'What about providing a meal?' Bess said, thinking of her own hungry belly when she'd been young.

'Oh no,' Mrs Gordon said. 'The society is about education. We need to educate the poor, so they can make better choices. What a funny little thing you are!'

Choices? Bess wasn't aware that there had been any choices.

'It's hard to think when you're hungry,' she said. 'Or at least I should think it is.' She felt her face grow warm. The others smiled to each other as if she'd said something amusing.

'We will give them food for the soul!' Mrs Gordon declaimed.

'Now, we will need some tables and benches for the little ones to sit on,' Mrs Fenwick said, pacing the room, before she turned to look pointedly at Bess. 'Your husband's a carpenter, I wonder, would he …?'

So that was it. They didn't want her to be part of their cosy group at all. They thought they could get Will to make their benches.

Seeing her expression, Mrs Fenwick said, 'Of course we'd buy the wood, but as it's a charitable enterprise …?'

They were expecting Will to work for nothing. And of course he couldn't possibly. Although Hertford's chairs had paid well, Will had still to pay the woodman, and the house loan, and Lucy's wages. The demands for payment crowded into her mind. They would have to count every penny if they were to pay their dues this month. But then, Mrs Fenwick didn't know that. Bess'd been careful to hide their fragile financial security from the Fenwicks. 'I'll have to ask him,' Bess said. 'He's extremely busy and I don't think he'll—'

'Splendid,' Mrs Fenwick said, as if she hadn't spoken. 'Mrs

Bagwell will ask her husband to make the benches.'

***

Bess looked down at her mending, wishing she had company. High summer, and yesterday the longest day of the year, so Will had worked late on the bowls and started again as soon as the sun peeped over the horizon. But she knew for a fact it was like paddling upstream. There would not be enough to pay Bastable if he didn't get bigger commissions. He had no name for his skills in Deptford yet. Perhaps she should consider working again, as she still had not fallen with child. When she married Will she'd given up taking in sewing, which was the only acceptable accomplishment for a lady. She refused to be reduced to going into service. From the kitchen she heard the sound of Lucy drubbing the laundry – the slosh of water and suds.

They'd lose Lucy soon too, if things didn't look up. She'd go without rather than lose Lucy. In this world you were either a master or a servant, and Bess was determined to be the former.

The post came, and Bess went down to the workshop to see if there was any news from the Guild. The sight of Will churning out cheap bowls made her sad. When they'd married she had loved him because of his craft. The way the chisel sat comfortably in his hand, the way he could carve and sculpt lilies and acanthus, scrolls and arabesques; such sinuous curving shapes from a rough hunk of wood. There had been something solid and reassuring about Will's ability to turn firewood into beauty. And now he was showing Jacob how to make cheap scrimshaw.

Will's face grew grim as he opened the first of the letters.

'What is it?'

'It's a cancellation. The pews for St Catherine's. And I've already bought the wood.'

'Oh no. Can you use it for something else?'

'If I get an order, maybe.'

'Did they give a reason?'

'Lack of church funds.' He gave a hollow laugh. 'Jack says business is slow everywhere. Even the King's in hock. They say he's had to borrow money from the French. Jack told me he's so hard-pressed he had to ask his little cabal of friends at court to fund our Navy.' He sighed, stabbed the letter down on a spike. 'I'll just have to hope someone else needs a set of benches.'

'Ah, well … strange you should say that …' She explained about Mrs Fenwick.

'She wants me to do it for nothing?'

'I know. It's brazen cheek. But still, it could be useful to curry favour with the Fenwicks.'

'Don't know how we'll manage the loan this month, with that commission gone. The bowls are just pin-money.'

'Something will turn up,' she said, 'you'll see.' She gave him a brief hug, but could tell he was not convinced. 'Will you do the benches for Mrs Fenwick?'

'I can't afford to do work for nothing.'

'What about Jacob? Can't he do them?'

'We'll see.'

With Will, that usually meant no. She sighed.

As she went back up the stairs, her mind churned over the possibilities. Perhaps Hertford might speak to Pepys, as Meg had suggested. Pepys was a man who'd risen from lowly beginnings as a tailor's son, to make of himself something great, so perhaps he would have some sympathy for Will. She should get Hertford to talk to him.

Bess took off her apron. Well, there was nothing to lose in trying, and no time like the present. Will would be busy with Jacob all afternoon; she could hear the hiss of the spindle on the lathe.

Bess dressed in her finest Sunday dress of tabby damask with a clean white cloth at her neck and a straw hat with a wide brim to keep off the sun.

He might think her impertinent, she knew, to call on him unannounced; but Hertford was a mild-mannered gentleman of cheerful disposition, and from what she could see, fond of Will. Maybe Meg was right, and a word in the right quarter would grease the wheels and get Will into the Guild. But she'd leave Lucy at home. Lucy had made a friend of Maudie, and she wasn't sure she could trust them not to gossip. And she daren't risk word getting back to Will. He'd think her meddlesome again.

Chapter 8

Bess's mother, Agatha Prescott, shuffled closer to the jetty with the rest of the queue for the ferry downriver. The boat from the other side was approaching, but there was a press of people, and everyone wanted to make sure they had a place.

Agatha clutched her bag to her chest. It was weighty, because it was full of earthenware jars of pickled preserves; an excuse to call on Bess.

'I have far too much,' she'd say, feeling the prick of her conscience and knowing that in fact these were her only jars, and she'd scrimped and saved for the sugar to make them, especially for Bess.

The last time she'd called, Bess had been out. Or so it seemed. Agatha didn't like to admit it to herself, but she could have sworn blind she'd seen movement behind the shutters.

Agatha craned her neck as the approaching ferryman leapt off to rope the boat to the mooring post. But wasn't that her Bessie, sitting up front, near the prow? It looked like her, small and buxom, in a big straw hat. As she stood, the sun caught her face; her slightly pouting mouth, her chin up like she owned the world. No mistaking her now, but she hadn't seen her mother in amongst the crowd, and she was obviously going somewhere, all togged up in her Sunday best.

Bess had that determined look which usually meant trouble. Oblivious, she hurried past without even a glance. It hurt, but Agatha felt a stab of pride at her daughter's upright carriage and bouncing black curls. Bess was smiling, and she looked a proper lady in that hat. She probably hadn't even seen her.

Should she call out? She opened her mouth, but the name was stuck somewhere between her heart and her throat. She'd be interrupting. It would feel awkward. She was just another of the drab and dusty crowd and her daughter was rising above her, out of her reach.

Feeling guilty, she followed, head down, concealing herself amongst the passengers from the ferry making their way back into the city. She kept well back as Bess hurried up Cannon Street, past the furrier's on Bearbinder Lane, and finally knocked at the front door of an imposing stone-built house in Whistler's Court.

No back door for her, then. A bent old servant in gold braided livery appeared to open the door.

Anxious not to be seen, Agatha nipped into the narrow, flagged alley that led to the well-appointed coachyard. Neatly painted stable doors; the flags all swept and tidy. The cobblestones slippery and polished under her feet. She hawked and spat down on them. Widowhood was hard. She lived in a cramped attic room with two other Irish families now. Even the horses in this part of London were housed better than she was. It was a pretty pass when even the blooming stables felt too good for a body, Agatha thought.

Curbing her anger, she returned to the alley to wait.

***

Bess smoothed her hair, but then looked over her shoulder. She had the prickling sensation she was being watched, but could see no sign of Will or Jacob. Shaking off the feeling and taking a deep breath, she tugged at the bell-pull. Hertford's ancient manservant answered it, and a few moments later, Hertford himself came huffing to the door, a puzzled look on his face.

He glanced over her shoulder, obviously expecting to see Will. 'Mrs Bagwell,' he said. 'An unexpected pleasure. Are you alone?'

'Quite,' she said. 'Lucy's washing today.'

'Is Will all right?'

'Faring well, thank you. But I am concerned about him, and I have a little favour to ask, if you don't think it too impertinent.' She put on her most charming smile.

'Sounds intriguing,' Hertford said, beckoning her up the smooth stone steps and through his polished front door. 'You had better come in.'

He stood aside and gestured her through with a small bow.

A few moments later and she was sitting in Hertford's panelled parlour, on one of his upholstered chairs and telling him about Will's attempts to get into the Ship's Carpenter's Guild. 'You know Will, he's far too much pride to ask what's happening,' she said. 'But he's been waiting so long, and it doesn't seem fair. They've got all his apprenticeship papers; had them months. I wondered if you could put in a word for him, with your friend Mr Pepys.'

'Does that mean I might never get a matching table for my chairs?' he asked, his eyes twinkling.

'Oh no, sir. I'm sure he'd love to make another piece for you.'

'I was only jesting, my dear. Though truth be told, I will be sad if I were to lose my favourite joiner. He has a great eye, your husband.'

'I'm sure it would make a difference, Mr Hertford, if you could make a personal recommendation.'

'I'll see Pepys the day after tomorrow. Our wives are friends. I'll see what I can do.'

'That would indeed be kind, Mr Hertford. And I hope you don't mind me being so forward as to ask ...' She rose, ready to leave.

'No, my dear,' Hertford said, standing. 'I have great respect for Will. He's a talented young man.'

'And the workshop is quiet this week sir, if you wanted that table ...' She paused at the door, feeling uncomfortable that their need must be so transparent. 'And sir ... Will thinks me too outspoken. So I beg you, Mr Hertford, please don't say anything of our conversation to my husband. He would be angry if he knew I had interfered.'

He winked. 'I can see you have his interests at heart. My lips are sealed. Now, don't hurry away, I insist you take some refreshment.'

***

In the alley opposite, Agatha twisted her body back and forth to relieve her aching back. Bessie had been in that big house for a good quarter hour. Finally the door opened and her daughter came out, all smiles and dimples like she'd been given good news. She glanced up and down the road, and Agatha retreated like quicksilver into the alley.

Quick, but not quick enough.

'What are you doing?' Bess marched over and stood before her, hands on hips.

Agatha fumbled in her bag for something to do, though she knew it looked foolish. 'Nothing. Just passing. And I was about to ask you the same thing.'

'Don't twist it round to me. You were spying on me again, weren't you?' She sighed. 'Why can't I go anywhere without thinking you'll be watching me? It's unnatural. Other people's mothers don't follow them around like this.'

'Other people's daughters invite their mothers to visit, and don't pretend to be out when they call.'

Bess coloured, but kept her chin up. 'I don't know what you're talking about.'

'Yes, you do. You think you're too good for me, now you live

~53 ~

in Deptford, and you're visiting the likes of him. And you walked straight past me; I was trying to catch up with you. I saw him, the gent who came to the door. What were you doing there? Does William know where you are?'

'Of course he does. He's... he's just a friend of Will's, Mr Hertford. He had some chairs made and I was... I was... delivering the bill. Anyway, it's none of your business.'

Her defiant look made Agatha suspicious. She didn't believe it, though the excuse sounded plausible enough. She tried a softer approach. 'I brought you some pickle, love.' Unclasping her bag, she reached in and drew out one of the pots.

'I don't want your pickle. I just want you to leave me alone—'

She tried to push the jar into Bess's hands. 'Please, take it, I made far too much and—'

To her horror, Bess stepped back, and the jar slipped. Agatha fumbled to grab it, but it was too late; it escaped from her hands and crashed onto the cobbles. A splatter of brown went up Bess's skirt.

'Now look what you've done,' Bess said. 'My best Sunday gown. Drunk again. You're an embarrassment.'

'I've not touched a drop. I told you, I'm part of the mission now, and—'

'I don't care if you're supping with the Archbishop of Canterbury himself,' Bess said, eyes like knives, 'I don't want you calling uninvited. And I don't want you telling people my business, or following me place to place.'

Agatha stepped back. The violence of Bess's words shocked her.

'Just leave me alone.' Bess turned and stalked away.

Reluctantly, Agatha dragged her eyes from her daughter's

back. She'd been a bad mother, there was no doubting it. The worst even. The shame of all those wasted years still made her squirm. But those days were gone.

She stooped to scrape the broken jar out of the thoroughfare and into the gutter. Bess hadn't believed her. Why should she? Agatha stood a moment before venturing onto the main street. She feared to see Bess again. She was dry, and respectable as any goodwife now, though it was a struggle. The devil was in the drink, right enough, and she was mindful of his tricks. But maybe the simple fact was that Bess couldn't see it. She couldn't see she'd changed. To Bess she was still the same sad, drunken bedlam-case she used to know.

***

Bess hurried away. She didn't want her mother in her life. Was it so bad to want to break free? Forge a better future for herself? Nevertheless, she had a bad feeling in her stomach.

She had to wait at Old Swan Stairs for a wherry to take her across the river, because one had only just gone. She stared into the brown murk of the Thames. Her mother's life was a disaster she didn't want to follow. She blamed her for this feeling of being on edge all the time, though if she was honest, it was scarcely her mother's fault. The illegal gin distilleries of the Ratcliff docks had proved too great a temptation to a woman whose husband beat her blue. Early on, Bess had vowed never to touch a drop. Even the smell of liquor made her shudder.

Bess stared across the Thames with unseeing eyes. She saw instead the dark interior of their house in Ratcliff. The final panicked night-time scramble to escape the fury of George Allin's fists still gave her cold sweats. The terror that her mother was so drunk she might crumple under her father's onslaught and never stand up again; and after – the blood pounding in her ears as she dragged her mother, stumbling and breathless, into the old barn that served as a church, and slammed home the bolts.

Four nights they spent on the bitter cold flagstones, four nights with her mother alternately raving for a drink, railing at Bess, or praying for forgiveness every time there was a service. Finally, some do-gooders from the church pressed on her mother a few coins to get her out from under their feet and rent a room. Desperate for money, her mother toiled door to door, offering to take in sewing again, though in reality, her hands simply shook too much.

'Here,' she said, 'you do it.' And she passed it to Bess.

Instead, her mother settled on delivering Bible tracts for the church, and laying out the dead for a small fee. But at fourteen years old, Bess was bewildered when her mother came home not more than a month later and proclaimed she'd reformed. And remarried. To Joseph Prescott, a Congregationalist preacher of all things.

'But you're already married!' Bess had said.

'He knows.'

'And he doesn't mind?'

'It's the truth. How could he mind the truth?'

'It's bigamy. And it's too quick. You hardly know him. What if *he* finds out?' She could never bring herself to call George Allin 'father'.

'He won't find me. I'm Mrs Prescott now. Married in the sight of the congregation, and the Lord. And before you ask, I'm quite sober.'

But word was, Allin was still searching for his wife and daughter. Not through love of course. For revenge. George Allin had never had a loving bone in his body.

Bess had been glad to become Bess Prescott. It was simpler than being Bess Allin, apart from having to endure the strange religious views of Joseph Prescott. She'd met Will at church, and Will knew nothing about Allin. He thought her the respectable daughter of Joseph Prescott, preacher. Two years later Prescott had died, and Will, in all seriousness, had asked Bess's mother for her hand.

Bess softened at the memory. Dear Will.

The movement of the queue towards the shore awakened her from her memories. Bess watched the wherry creep towards the landing stage. She was Bess Bagwell now, respectable, and wife of the best ship's carpenter this side of the Thames. She drew her shoulders back. Hertford would talk to Pepys, and she and Will would be coming up in the world.

She didn't want anything to do with her former life. It was over.

As the wherry took her downstream the flow of the water calmed her, though the tide on the Thames was running fast, so when they came to shore, the side of the boat rebounded from the jetty with a jerk. Bess swayed, cursed, and grabbed the hitching post to avoid falling. Stepping off at the Deptford Stairs, she deliberately turned her face away from the eyes of the beggars clustering at the quay.

There are more today, she thought.

She hitched up her skirts to step over the boggy patch by the jetty. It was the King's fault. These days London seemed cut in half, with the rich getting richer and the poor getting poorer. She sidled past the outstretched hands, avoiding getting too close to them.

A tug on her skirt. She wrenched the cloth free and walked on. The tugs became more frantic, until she was forced to look back, annoyed.

Immediately, she hesitated. It was a little girl, no more than her nephew's age – maybe seven or eight. Her hand was held out, and her eyes challenging and determined. Bess knew she must walk on. She couldn't afford to give. But seeing her mother had reminded her of that feeling. The feeling of being an irritation like a flea, or worse, of being invisible, not a person at all. This girl was fighting back. She paused, and the girl let go of her skirts.

'I may regret this,' Bess said aloud, finding the smallest coin she could from her pouch.

She held it out and the girl's fingers closed around it. The girl backed away, bobbed a hurried and awkward curtsey, and headed slowly back towards the stairs, disappointment shouting from every step.

Bess tracked her progress. She knew what it felt like to hope, to imagine that the coin might be silver, instead of a trader's leather token or a copper farthing. And how the disappointment ate into you day after day.

'Wait!' she called. She took out a gold angel and held it, aloft, pinched between finger and thumb. It sparked in the reddening evening sun. *Your last chance,* she thought. *After today my purse will probably be empty.*

The girl stared incredulously, but didn't approach.

'It's alright,' Bess said. 'I can spare it.' But she couldn't, and already she was chiding herself, because she didn't know how she'd explain it to Will. That the girl had pricked her heart, and she'd given her more than half her housekeeping.

Too late. Like a starling snatching a crumb, grubby fingers swiped the coin from her hand. The girl was running now, in a blur, dodging between the passers-by, her blackened bare feet kicking up beneath her skirts as she pelted away. Not a word of thanks, or even a look back. Bess watched her go with the unsettled sensation that she had been taken for a fool.

Coming up in the world was all very well, but she knew that other world so intimately, it was always there, like a monster waiting beneath the bed, ready to grab her by the legs and drag her down.

Chapter 9

Will eyed the letter warily. It was sealed with hard red sealing wax, not the usual soft sheep's grease. Could it be a writ? He hoped not. Could it be about the fact that he had pretended to be out when Bastable called a few days ago for the loan money?

Will turned it over to look at his name, penned on the front in a florid and flamboyant hand. He glanced up to see Bess watching him out of the corner of her eye as he cracked it open.

'Good news?' she asked, from the corner where she was shelling peas.

He read the signature. 'From Mr Samuel Pepys,' he said, bemused. 'What can he want?'

'I've no idea,' Bess said, lifting the bowl from her lap, and setting it down on the floor.

'He's in charge of the Navy Treasury, I met him once in the yards when I went to try to see my father. We had a conversation about timber ... Saints alive. He wants to see me on Friday. At ten.'

'Is it about the Guild?' Bess stood up to come and read over his shoulder.

'He doesn't say. Just that he would like to meet me to talk of "a matter of mutual interest". What do you think it means?'

'I don't know. Mutual interest could be work, couldn't it?'

'It seems peculiar. What would he want me for?'

'Because you're a fine carpenter. He'll want you for a ship I expect. Or the yards. Or maybe he's jealous of Hertford's chairs. You'll go, won't you?'

'I suppose I shall have to, if I want to get any peace.' He

smiled at her, and she squeezed his shoulder. She was pleased, he could tell. And life went much easier when Bess was pleased.

***

On Friday a heat-haze shimmered over the river and the July sun beat down on his hat. Will took his time locking up, methodically checking the workshop was secure. He refused to be chivvied, even when Bess laid a hand on his arm.

'Hurry,' she said, 'we don't want to be late.'

Will shook her off. She fussed too much. Talked too much and fussed too much.

They caught a wherry with no trouble, and walked towards the city, with Bess ahead all the way, hurrying, tilted forwards as if she couldn't get there quick enough. At the end of Thames Street they turned sharp left into the broad thoroughfare of Seething Lane. The jumble of the Navy offices loomed ahead, a cluster of red-brick houses, and tenements, and behind those some imposing stone mansions, like cliffs rising out of the sea of carriages and horses.

Will slowed. His distaste for any kind of authority made him wary. Since the letter came, Hertford had called in to his workshop to say how much his wife, Edith, had liked the chairs, and when Will told him about the letter, Hertford confessed he'd arranged the appointment. He was sure Hertford meant well, but Will'd been a little embarrassed. He didn't really want to go begging to Pepys; it was demeaning.

'Come on,' Bess clucked at him as he caught up, and passed him his doublet from the bag over her arm. 'Smarten yourself up, Will,' she said, 'someone might be looking.'

Will wiped a hand across his damp forehead and shrugged himself into the sleeves. It was devilish warm, even in his shirt sleeves. All this fuss for Pepys. What did it matter which suit he wore? But Bess had made him wear his winter best suit, because it was 'good quality', even though the day was as hot as a roast dinner.

'That's better,' Bess said, smiling at him, though her eyes were anxious. 'Now you look like a gentleman.'

'A gentleman that's trussed up like a chicken,' Will grumbled.

'Whist. You look fine. Just tell him how you were in charge of the whole yard at Stepney, and stand your ground.'

'But I wasn't. I was just the joiner.'

'Good as. Tilford was so drunk half the time, the men looked to you, you know they did.' He acknowledged this was true by a tilt of his head. 'I'll come up with you, and I'll be waiting outside his office. Embrace me for luck now, whilst we're out of sight.'

Will looked down at her expectant face, and softened. He was lucky to have such a wife, who cared so much for how he did. She'd dressed in her best clothes too, the dark blue damask with the ribbon-trimmed bodice nipping in her waist, and a fetching bonnet over her hair. She looked so trim and neat, though she was probably just as hot as he was. A wave of love for her made him hug her tight.

'You'll be late.' She pushed him away with a smile, and he took her arm to walk her formally down the long driveway and around the side to the Navy buildings.

Close up, the scale of the place was even more intimidating, but Will braced himself, and when a liveried servant, resplendent in gold braid, showed them up a long flight of stone stairs, he retained his hat to show he was a gentleman. Outside Pepys's office was a chair in the corridor, so Bess whispered, 'Go on. I'll wait here.'

The servant knocked and immediately the door flew open. Mr Pepys bustled into the corridor, all lace jabot and flapping wig.

'Ah, Bagwell is it, Hertford's man?' he said. He seemed to

take up all the air in the corridor. Will doffed his hat, preparing to bow, but Pepys had caught sight of Bess sitting there, eyes round as coins, and immediately held out a plump hand to her. 'Come in, come in, the pair of you.'

'Me?' She stood, blushing red, but taking the hand he'd offered her.

Pepys led her into his office, and Will hastened to follow behind.

'Sit down, sit down!' Pepys said, assessing them both with bird-like eyes, whilst flapping a cuff over the leather chairs in front of him as if there might be dust there. They sat, but Pepys was already running on. 'My friend Hertford says you're looking to get into the Ship's Carpenter's Guild.'

Will was painfully aware of all the clerks in the room. The scratching of pens had stopped, while they eavesdropped on their business. But Pepys didn't wait for an answer to his question. 'Well, I'm afraid he's sent you here on a fool's errand – though I'm in charge of the victualling of vessels, I have absolutely no jurisdiction over the yards themselves. The person you need to speak to is Nicholson, he's the one who has the say-so over the Guild.'

'Yes, sir, I did write to him, but received no reply—' Will tried to explain.

'Ah well, I expect he'll reply in due course. He's a very busy man.'

Will nodded, but Bess gave him an irritated shake of the head, and leaned towards Pepys. 'Too busy to reply after six months?' she said.

Will turned and shot Bess a warning look, but too late. She'd already stood up, and with a start he saw his wife's hands were actually on Pepys's desk. Mr Pepys's eyes widened, and one of the clerks turned to openly stare.

'I know I speak out of turn,' Bess said, in her loud, clear voice, 'but a better shipwright you couldn't find anywhere in London, than my Will. He's a good draughtsman, and he can carve figureheads too. One he did was a—'

Oh Lord, thought Will, please, not that tale. 'Bess, Mr Pepys doesn't want to know all that—'

'But I do,' Pepys said, sitting back in his chair. 'Let her tell me. She's doing a fine job of speaking for you.'

Will felt about as big as a bug on the floor. And the room was agog, with six heads all turned to hear what Bess would say. Will shrank down further into his chair.

Bess tossed her head, and the ribbons on her bonnet fluttered. 'Not much more I can tell you, sir, except that if it can be made in wood, Will can do it. Mermaids, flowers, even a coach and four. I warrant he could carve it. And he studied hard. What he doesn't know about the lines of ships won't fit on a bodkin. The letter came from the Guild six months past, asking for his papers – for his indentures and so forth, and we sent them all back soon as we could. But since then, nothing. How is he supposed to carry on without his papers, Mr Pepys?' she demanded. 'Even the river men from above the bridge won't give him work without his ship-building papers.'

Two of the clerks exchanged a sly grin. Will felt his face grow hot with embarrassment. 'Sit down, Bess,' he hissed. 'Beg pardon, sir. She doesn't understand business—'

'Maybe not,' Bess said, the colour high in her cheeks, 'but I understand politeness, and the least your Mr Nicholson could do is reply. Will's written to him again four times to ask if he's been accepted into the Guild, and if not, for the return of his papers. If this is how long Nicholson takes to reply to a letter, how long does it take him to build a ship?'

Horrified, Will waited for Pepys to tell them to leave, but

instead he opened his mouth in a huge guffaw. 'Well said, Mrs Bagwell. Six months does seem a long time for him to hold on to your references. Perhaps I'll send a message to Nicholson, ask him if there's been some delay. You'd better come back in a few weeks.'

'Thank you, sir,' Will said, standing, anxious to be out of that office as soon as possible, 'it's really very generous—'

'No, no. Not at all,' Pepys said, still chuckling, and fingering through a leather bound appointment book. 'Call in, let's see, two weeks from now. Friday week. Should have some news for you both by then.'

Bess beamed at him, 'Please give our best regards to Mr Hertford. Will made some chairs for him. His wife said they were every bit as good as the ones in your dining room—'

'Bess!' Will cut her off, with a sharp word, cursing her lack of tact, but Pepys didn't seem to notice. He smiled back at her, eyes alight, one hand patting the soft curls of his wig. He held her gaze a little too long, so Bess had to lower her eyes, and a crimson flush spread up from her throat. The clerks in their dark suits suddenly seemed like black birds of prey, eyes fixed on the little scene unfolding before them.

Will stepped forward stiffly, into the awkward silence. 'Thank you, sir.' He held out his hand, and Pepys shook it, but his eyes drifted over Will's shoulder to his wife.

He whipped his head round. Bess dropped her gaze.

Will turned his head back to Pepys. 'I'll be back in two weeks then,' Will said firmly, gripping Pepys's hand like a clamp to get his attention.

'Oh, yes. Yes.' Pepys finally returned the handshake.

Will turned to go. Bess's face had turned the colour of a brick. A wave of shame flooded him. He was suffocated; had to get out of there. He blundered to the door, and grasped the fat, brass handle. It was slippery in his sweating hands.

'Why don't you both come?' Pepys was calling. 'I'm sure Mrs Bagwell will be keen to hear the news.'

Will whipped round to see Bess backing away from Mr Pepys, with a coy expression. 'Oh no, sir, you don't want me. I don't think—'

'On the contrary,' Pepys said with a suggestive raise of his eyebrows, his eyes fixed on her.

Will blinked. Was he imagining it, or was Pepys being deliberately flirtatious? Why wouldn't the damned door open? He twisted but couldn't get a grip.

'I shall expect you *both*,' Pepys said.

'Well, I…?' Bess turned to Will with a shrug and a questioning look. He glared at her and shook his head.

'Let me help you out.' Pepys pushed past, and the door knob turned easily in his hand. 'There we are,' he said, gesturing for them to go through, in a manner that made Will feel as if he'd been an idiot not to be able to open it.

Will jammed his hat back on his head. When he turned back, it was to see the top of Pepys's luxuriant wig, and his lips fastened tight to his wife's hand.

'I'll see what I can do,' Pepys said, in an intimate whisper.

Will watched Bess extricate her hand and back out of the room. Pepys gave a little wave just before it shut, and the sight gave Will the urgent desire to punch a hole in the door. From behind its solid wall came the sound of the clerks' laughter.

'Well, we've made some progress at last,' Bess said, brushing down her skirts.

'Out.' Will could barely speak. 'Now,' he said, grasping Bess roughly by the arm and hurrying her down the stairs.

'What's the matter? He agreed to help us, didn't he?'

He stopped, turned her to face him. 'I felt a fool. You blethered on, making me look like a half-wit.'

'But Will, I was only—'

'No. No more. I'm tired of your voice. Not a minute goes by, but you must talk.' He strode off down the street, leaving Bess to run after him.

A cry of 'Watch out!' and a blizzard of curses made him turn to see Bess dodging through the traffic to try to keep up with him. His stomach jolted, but he gritted his teeth. Damn fool woman.

When they got home, he threw off his fine doublet and breeches, leaving them on the chamber floor, and after hauling on his leather jerkin and twills, went straight down to the carpentry shop. His anger surged like a tide that threatened to carry him away. Last time he'd been this angry, it had landed him in gaol. He told himself to calm down. A few hours of vigorous planing and polishing relieved the tightness in his chest.

Eventually he sighed and set down the plane. Above him he could no longer hear the creak of boards as Bess went about her chores. What was she doing up there? Maybe he had over-reacted a little. He'd never seen himself as an overly jealous man, but the thought of Pepys's lascivious look, and her blush, was enough to make his temper rise again. He grabbed a wooden peg and hammered it into a joint he was making. It smashed down with such force, the wood split.

A piece of good elm wasted, and it was all Pepys's fault. A plague on the man.

Chapter 10

The next day Bess stared absently out of the window into the wet street beneath, a bowl balanced on her hip, stirring the sour milk into the dough to make bread. What a day to have to go to the bakehouse. It was Lucy's half-day off and she was obliged to make the bread herself, though Lucy had at least left the yeast steeping in a bowl.

Below, the bang of the hammer. She could hear no conversation between Will and Jacob – a bad sign. Will was still grim-faced at her. He had no right to be so angry. She'd got Pepys to write to Nicholson, hadn't she?

She flung more flour into the bowl, and paused as another bout of hammering assaulted her ears. She emptied the dough onto the board, pummelled her fists into the bread, and turned it over with a slap.

Still, how was it her fault, if she was still comely? A glimmer of pride swelled in her chest. It had been nice to be admired. Will hadn't looked at her like that – like he could *eat* her, for years. Where had it gone to, all his passion? These days, Will only had eyes for a nice chair back, or a pedestal table. She paused a moment, chest burning with a lost longing, before she pushed the dough roughly into a dome with her knuckles and draped a cloth over it.

How odd that Pepys had taken such a shine to her, and fancy him demanding to see her again. She wouldn't go. She must let go of these fancies, be a good, plain wife, and abide by her husband's will.

She went to the change jar that they used for every-day

expenses, and shook out a few tokens. Large amounts, like gold coin, Will kept under lock and key in the casket beneath the bed. The change jar rattled with silver coin since Hertford had paid for his chairs, though the amount had dwindled and was even less than she'd thought. And Will hadn't offered her any more housekeeping, despite the fact there was no meat, and the larder was almost empty. She wondered if he had paid Tyler again, and worried that Bastable would be back soon for the loan money. She hoped Pepys would be a man of his word, and find a good position for Will. Quite apart from them needing the money, it might mend the ill-feeling between them.

With change in hand, she threw a shawl over her head, locked the door and hurried along Butt Lane towards the bakehouse. Outside the sky had turned thundery and pewter-grey and threatened a proper storm. Heaven knows they'd had enough – St Swithin must have it in for Londoners.

The low rumble of thunder in the distance made her speed her step. At the bakehouse she got chatting with a neighbour and it was another half-hour before she ran home, dodging through the heavy rain, the hot bread wound in its cloth and stuffed under her shawl next to her stays.

At the bottom of the outside stairs she listened, but could hear nothing. Will must have decided to stop his fettling, and call it a day. Perhaps now they could talk everything over like civilised folk should. She took the stairs two at a time and elbowed open the door, ready to give Will a big smile.

Her face froze. Will's cousin Jack was at the kitchen table and the three damp children were squabbling under it.

'Ah smell that, boys,' Jack said. 'Fresh bread!'

Bess's good humour drained instantly. She reached to put the change in the jar, and was surprised to find it empty except for a few coppers. She looked to Will for an explanation, but he deliberately turned away and dived into the pantry to fetch beer.

'Tear us a bit off, would you, Toby?' asked Jack.

The loaf was whipped from her hands, and in a moment there was only the cob-end left, the rest had been devoured.

'Didn't you have any dinner?' Bess asked.

'Not since yesterday,' Toby said, his mouth spitting crumbs.

'Course they have,' Jack said. He cuffed Toby a sharp clip on the ear without even looking at him. 'That's for telling lies.'

Toby's mouth quivered, but he didn't cry.

Under the table the other two boys fell silent, watching them with wide eyes. The atmosphere was thick and dark, rain drummed on the roof. Will brought the small beer and poured out cups for everyone, smiling to try to pour oil on Bess's temper.

Jack took a long draught. 'We were just passing, and thought we'd drop in.'

'How's business?' Bess asked. She failed to conceal her annoyance. Why he was here in the middle of the day? She prayed they'd go soon.

'I was just saying to Will, I've had a better offer. I'm going into the export business proper. We've got a syndicate. A fellow I know has access to a bigger ship. We'll split the labour, and that way I'll have more time to spend with my boys.'

He ruffled Toby's hair, but Toby shrugged him off, uncomfortable.

'After tonight, that is,' Jack continued. 'Will says you can have them tonight, whilst I go and meet my new business partners.'

So that was what it was about. She was to look after the boys, was she? They'd arranged it without even asking her. Bess turned to Will, who busied himself wiping a spill of beer with rapt concentration. Bess curled her fingers into a fist.

'And who's involved in this new scheme of yours?' Bess asked, unable to keep the tartness from her voice. Somehow every conversation with Jack felt like a boxing match.

'No-one you'd know. Mr Kite and some merchants from the city.'

'Kite the moneylender?' Will frowned. 'He gave us the loan on this house.'

'Did he? He has contacts in Rotterdam. He's processing the snuff in the mills there. Its good quality and very cheap, so it will sell like the devil.'

'What about the quarantine regulations?' Bess asked. 'The Plague Orders you were telling us about? You said nothing's coming in from the Low Countries, not since the pestilence.'

'Ah. That's where it's so clever. There's no regulations for Rotterdam, only Amsterdam. That's why it's such a sure bet. I'm striking whilst the iron's hot.'

'But what if—?'

'It'll be fine. Don't worry, your money'll be safe.'

Your money. She looked to Will, who'd taken a sudden interest in his tankard.

'Have you invested in this?' She pierced Will with her words.

'Sit down, Bess,' Will said. 'Have a drink.'

'I asked if you'd invested.'

'Jack needed a bit more backing to get the wheel turning, and anyway we'll get it back soon, and with profit. It'll double our money, Jack says.'

That was why the jar was nearly empty. It was as if an ice-cold finger pressed on her heart. She put a hand on Will's arm. 'Why didn't you talk to me—?'

'Does he have to ask your say-so?' Jack interrupted. 'Alice never interfered in men's concerns.'

'Then it's no wonder Alice was so miserable,' Bess flashed.

'Curb your tongue, Bess,' Will said, shaking off her hand. 'Have some respect.'

She tugged at his sleeve.

'Just a minute, Jack,' Will said, resisting as she drew him into the kitchen.

'But you promised me,' she whispered. '"No more", you said. You said you'd make Jack stand on his own two feet. And he still owes us from the last time. We're not some bottomless bag, there just to give him a loan.'

Jack's voice called from the parlour, 'If I'm going to cause dissent...'

But it's what you've always done, she thought, at precisely the same time as Will called out, 'No trouble. I'm just fetching more ale.'

Will held up his hands to silence her. 'He's right. Leave it to me. It's only a few angels. It'll be back in our hands before you know it.' And he went back through to Jack.

Bess clamped her mouth shut, because it wasn't good for the boys to hear what she'd really like to say to their father, and because hadn't she given away an angel herself, one they could ill-spare, to that beggar girl?

When Jack had finally left, she had a sudden uncomfortable thought. She went through to the bedchamber and dragged out the locked casket from under the bed. It was suspiciously light. She lifted one end and listened, no chink of coin, no sound at all from within. It was empty.

'You stupid man,' she said.

***

Will sighed. Bess was late to bed, still fussing over the boys who were top to tail on the straw palliasse in the spare room; the one that was supposed to be the chamber for the cook they couldn't afford.

'What possessed you?' she said to him, when she finally got

into bed. 'We'll not see that money again.'

'You never give him a chance.'

'You gave him the money from the casket, didn't you?'

How did she know? He began to protest, 'No, I—'

'I'm not a fool!' she said. 'There's no rattle inside it. I checked.'

'We'll get it back.' He knew his voice sounded sulky and defiant.

Bess propped herself up on her elbow. In the half-light from the street torch outside Will could just make out her face. It was full of disgust.

'Jack Sutherland is hardly the most reliable businessman is he? How many jobs has he lost in the last year? And those poor boys don't know if they're coming or going,' she said. 'And that Toby's turning into a terror.'

'He's just lively. He'll settle soon enough.'

'Why can't Jack meet his cronies in the day? You should have gone with him, to see who these men are. Felons and thieves, knowing your Jack.'

'Rather them than a toad like Pepys.'

'So that's what this is about, is it? You're angry at Pepys, so you think going into business with Jack will make you feel better?' Her whisper grew louder.

'I was ashamed. All those clerks laughing behind our backs…'

'Because I spoke up?'

'No. Keep your voice down! Because you encouraged him with your smiling and your big cow eyes.'

'Is that what you think? That I'm at fault? That somehow because Pepys took notice of me, that I'm to blame?' He couldn't see her face, but he felt the cut of her rage. 'I didn't ask for him to be that way. I was doing it for you! So you'd get into the Guild. Perhaps you would have preferred it if I was rude to him?'

She slipped out of bed, and faced him, dragging the cover with her and holding it to her chest, the sleeves of her chemise pale against the window. Her whisper was penetrating and hoarse, 'I did it for you. Because you're not man enough to stand up for yourself.'

The words hit him like a punch in the guts.

'Is that what you think?' He leapt out of bed and stumbled into his breeches, hitching the braces over his shoulders.

'What are you doing?'

'Getting away from you,' he snapped. Without bothering with a hat or cloak he floundered down the stairs and out into the night air.

Not man enough echoed in his ears.

Behind him he heard Billy's voice calling out, 'Auntie Bess...?' but Will didn't stop.

He loped down the street, splashing through the puddles, along the edge of the Deptford Strond and towards the clinking masts of Middle Water Gate. He only slowed when he had to, when the river slid past his feet, oily and black. There, he leant on a wooden paling, felt the solidity of rough timber under his hands, and let his head hang. Women's moods; he never understood them. But he'd given his heart to Bess, and though she infuriated him, the thought that he'd disappointed her bit deep.

He gazed into the shifting undulation of the water without really seeing it. Bess's accusation that he lacked courage had wounded him. Because he knew it was true; that had she not been there, he would have just agreed with Pepys, and left, with no promise from him or a word of recommendation to Nicholson and the Guild.

Bess had a forceful streak he didn't understand, as if she was goading him all the time, and the more she pushed, the more evasive he became. When she did that, he felt himself turning to water, but he couldn't help it.

He re-played the scene in his mind; Pepys's lips pressing onto the back of Bess's hand, his slightly lascivious smile. Will's whole chest felt hollow so he had to place both hands there and press them to his heart.

'You're an ass, Will Bagwell,' he said to himself. He remembered his own obsequiousness and cringed. She was right. He should have spoken up, made it clear to Pepys that he was in charge, not Bess.

He pushed himself up from the fence, and taking in a deep breath of brackish air, headed up in long strides past the Powder House towards Deptford Creek. Perhaps Jack was right, and Bess was too unruly. But then again, Bess and Jack were always like baited wolves, circling and snapping at each other.

Bess had never understood about him and Jack; why he found Jack so hard to refuse. When Will was only twelve his father had impressed on him that Jack had lost his parents, so he must be kind, and look out for him. Any hint of unkindness to Jack, and his father's belt came out. Now looking after Jack was a pattern that was hard to break. Besides, he felt mean-spirited if he denied him. He'd known him all his life. He was like a brother. And today, he thought ruefully, Jack had been at his persuasive best.

'You'll double your money, easy,' Jack had said.

And what a relief that would be. He'd been carried away with it. With the thought it would pay off Kite and the debt would be gone.

The loan was like a tourniquet; he felt it every day; squeezing, cutting off the blood.

'Nothing ventured, nothing gained,' Jack had said. So he'd emptied the casket too, as well as the coin in the jar. Ten pounds. What was left of Hertford's money added to their little emergency fund. The money that by rights should buy wood for his next commission. But there was no commission in sight, and he gambled that Pepys, curse him, might come up with something.

The thought of all that gold made him catch his breath. And he hadn't realised Kite, the moneylender, was involved in Jack's new venture. They already owed him for the house, and now more of Will's precious coin would be going into Kite's pocket.

But still, Bess shouldn't be querying his judgements on business, and if he wanted to invest in Jack's snuff trade, then why the hell not? It would be all right. If snuff was as lucrative as Jack said it was, the loan would be paid off by next year and then they'd both be rich men. Trouble was, he wasn't sure if he wanted to be rich. Peace was all he wanted. Peace and a lump of wood in his hands.

Chapter 11

Bess slept badly. She heard Will come late and climb into bed, smelling of wind and water and his favourite tobacco. He rolled until his back was towards her, and did not reach to wrap his arm around her waist as he usually did. When dawn came, even though it was Sunday, he was straight out of bed and down to the workshop before she had a chance to offer him something to break his fast.

The three little boys appeared as soon as they heard noises at the table.

'Aunt Bess,' Toby said, 'Hal's wet the bed.'

'Didn't,' Hal said, scowling, 'it was Billy.'

'Liar,' Billy said. 'Anyway, only babies wet the bed.'

Hal burst into tears and pummelled at Billy with his fists and his worn-through boots.

'Cry baby!' Billy taunted, dodging the onslaught.

'Hush up, all of you,' Bess said. 'Sit up on those stools. There's no harm done, Hal. Sheets can be washed.' She held him in an embrace and kissed the top of his head, before grabbing a muslin kerchief and applying it to his face. 'Now sit quietly there or I won't bring you any oatmeal and honey.'

Soon the boys were supping on their week's supply of oatmeal, soaked in milk. Three fair heads all lowered in concentration: Toby's like a thick thatch, Billy's fine and fly-away, and Hal's still all baby curls. Almost like angels, except they were thin as weasels, all of them, and it made her heart ache.

'Was it true what you said, that you'd had no dinner yesterday?' she asked Toby.

Toby kept thoughtful blue eyes on his bowl, obviously unwilling to contradict his father, and no doubt recalling his sore ear.

'We don't get dinner every day,' Billy said, scraping his spoon around his bowl. 'Only on the days Father remembers.'

'What do you do on the days he doesn't?'

Billy shrugged. 'Find stuff. Round the markets, anywhere we can.' He wrinkled his snub, freckled nose. 'Long as it's not mouldy. Toby says not to eat it if it's mouldy or rank. Even if I'm *very* hungry.'

When they'd done eating she went down to the carpentry shop. 'It's the Sabbath. Won't you come up and get ready for church?' she asked Will. 'And there's three little boys upstairs, and I don't know what to do with them. When's Jack coming back?'

Will looked up. 'You know Jack. He didn't say. Noon?'

'What will I do with them after church?'

'I don't know. Get them winding wool for darning. Anything. I have to work. Can't afford not to, Sabbath or no Sabbath.'

'Can't they sweep shavings for you?'

'I can't have them in here. They're not old enough. Too many sharp chisels and knives.'

'What about Toby? He could sweep.' She was stubborn. Inside, she blamed Will for his foolishness with money, and for having suddenly been saddled with Jack's boys.

Will looked up, but his eyes didn't connect with hers. 'Go on then. Suppose you could send Toby down later. But you'll have to look to his brothers.'

The boys were fractious and rowdy in church and Will kept nudging her to shush them.

'You're right,' he said when they got home. 'Best keep them occupied.'

She nodded, with an 'I told you so' expression. Five minutes later peace reigned. The swish of the broom from below was soothing, and now Toby was out of the way, there was nobody to squabble with Billy. She got the two younger boys making spills from old receipts which were kept on an iron spike. They had to roll the paper, then glue it with a dab of flour-and-water paste. Hal's were like fat sausages, all drifting apart at the seams, but Billy was painstaking and his were neat and sturdy.

They're good boys, she thought to herself, with a surge of affection; they just need proper managing.

But by noon there was no sign of Jack, nor by bedtime. By the next day, they were worried and the boys were getting restless, wondering where their father was. Finally she sent Will to see if he could find him.

The news was not good. 'He says, can we keep them a few days?' Will was sheepish. 'Says he's got meetings set up with his investors, and it's crucial he's not interrupted.'

'And what about us? Is your work not crucial?'

'Don't make a fuss, Bess. After all, we have money in Jack's business. It's in all our interests that it should succeed. If you had work, I might not have invested. But I need to pay off that loan. Kite's tightened his demand again – he wants an extra fourpence a month as his loan fee.'

'So I'm to blame, is that what you're saying?'

'Just ride with it a while, won't you, Bess? I know what I'm doing.'

***

The boys looked so forlorn when they heard their father wasn't coming to fetch them home, that Bess couldn't do anything but hug them fiercely and tell them they'd have a lovely stay.

Five days later, though, and their sad faces made her angry.

Jack was taking advantage. If she had work, then he wouldn't be able to do this so easily. It was not that she didn't love the

~79~

boys, but she hated the way Jack manipulated them all. Her and Will, and his sons. Now he was due to return, and they were fractious and unruly, expecting him any moment.

A walk would tire them and make them less troublesome. Fresh air would do them all good, and she could get groceries on the tally-slate again, and peek in at Baxter's, the glover, to see whether there was any chance of being taken on.

Will's words, that it was her fault they were in debt, had wounded her.

She picked up the collecting box for the Educational Fund and took it with her. At the last meeting, she'd been ashamed of how empty it was, and guilty because she still owed Mrs Gordon her half-sovereign. Today, she'd try a bit harder.

Fortunately it was fine, because the boys had no cloaks. When she went to collect Toby from the workshop it was to find him whittling a spoon out of a piece of lime.

'Look, Aunt Bess!' he said, holding it out.

'He's done well,' Will said. He ruffled the boy's hair. 'We'll make a carpenter out of you yet! Now run along with Aunt Bess, and perhaps by the time you get back your father will be here.'

***

They took a wherry upstream, and alighted at Blackstone Stairs. Bess breathed a sigh of relief. Baxter's was close to the fashionable Exchange, in a street of exclusive shops. Bess gave Toby instructions before she went to the door. 'Now play quietly, and don't sit down in the street. Toby, keep an eye on the little ones. I'll only be a quarter hour, if that.'

She'd left them only a few minutes before she turned to see them sitting on their bottoms on the dirt road, playing toss-jacks with a few scraped-up pebbles.

She sighed. Too late now. They'd be filthy already.

Baxter's was a better class of establishment. The door tinkled in a refined way as she opened it, not like the clang at Hutchinson's, where Meg worked. Bess gazed around the room with interest, noting the polished floor, the good quality painted wall-hangings, the fine embroidered drapes at the window. Probably Dutch, she thought, brought in before the pestilence.

Each pair of gloves was on display in an individual glazed cabinet. The brass on the locks gleamed, and under their glass covers the gloves glowed like jewels. Shaped silk and satin in pinks and blues, embellished with ribbons and rosettes. She peered through the glass but couldn't even see the stitching, and the men's cuffs were beautiful French creations, with lace and embroidered flowers and birds. These were the sort of gloves designed never to be worn, but only to be carried for show by rich aristocrats. The quality made her both envious and uncomfortable.

'Yes,' said a voice from behind the counter. Behind him, shelves and shelves of the cheaper gloves, neatly parcelled in calico, formed a white wall. The man looked her up and down with contempt, obviously thinking she could not afford to shop there. In that single defensive moment, she knew instantaneously that a woman with no prior references would have no place in his shop.

'I'm collecting,' she said, sticking out her chin. 'For the Deptford Christian Educational fund.'

He wrinkled his nose. 'Wait,' he said, as if speaking to a servant.

He opened the drawer under the counter and brought out thru'pence. 'Show me your box.'

She held out the box and he read the words in the side. Satisfied she was genuine and not a beggar, he posted the coin gingerly through the slot, before wiping his fingers surreptitiously on his breeches.

Bess turned and made for the door. Her face was hot as coals. She'd thought she'd gone up in the world, but Baxter's was a reminder that she hadn't gone far enough.

She twisted her head this way and that, searching for Toby and his brothers, but couldn't see them. The spot where they had been playing was empty. Around the back of the shop she caught sight of a window and peered in.

Rows and rows of girls sewing. This must be Baxter's workforce. She stared in wonder. There were dozens of them, in well-organised ranks, each girl focusing on one task. A hard-faced woman shooed her from the window with an angry gesture.

'Toby?' she called, peering up the alley again by the shop.

No sign of them, the little vagabonds.

The hubbub of voices and the grating of a knife grinder drew her to the next street where a country market was in progress, with stalls of vegetables, dilapidated chickens trussed to a post, and trestles full of punnets of strawberries. She had barely turned the corner when Toby shot past her, holding something tight to his chest.

'Toby!' she shouted, but he didn't stop, his face taut and red with exertion.

Running after him, and clearly breathless, was a long-boned youth in a striped jerkin and felt cap. He skidded to a panting stop in front of Bess. 'Did you see a boy run past?'

Bess shook her head.

'Christ alive! Third time this week. I'd swear it was the same lad. Need to nail my pies to the counter, he's that quick. I thought I was a runner, but he's that nippy, by the time I realise, he's half-way to Bow.'

Bess pinned a concerned smile to her face, as the pursuer wiped his forehead, and punched at the crown of his cap in frustration before walking away.

A tug at her skirts and Billy appeared. 'Did Toby get caught?' he whispered.

'No,' she said, curbing her crossness. 'Where's Hal?'

'Over there.' He pointed to where Hal was staring, thumb in mouth, through the bars of a rabbit cage, at the coneys that were shortly to be someone's dinner.

'I was hungry,' Billy said earnestly, looking up at her through sandy-coloured lashes. 'I always am.'

'But I would have given you dinner. You just had to be patient. Why didn't you do what you were told?' Billy lowered his eyes and stared at his feet. 'Stealing's wrong,' Bess said. 'Didn't your father teach you that?'

'Father says, "as long as you don't get caught." And Toby's quick as a fox, he never gets caught.' This last was stated with some satisfaction.

'It's still wrong, to take something that belongs to someone else, without paying,' she said as she bustled him over to the rabbits to drag Hal away. 'Come on, let's go and find Toby.'

'Will you beat him?' Billy was pulling her back, fists gripping her skirt.

'Beat him? No, of course not.'

'And you won't tell Pa?' Now he did look scared.

'I don't know. It depends on how good you are for the rest of the day.'

'Don't tell him.' His eyes were pools of fear.

'Then be good,' she said, feeling guilty as if she was taking advantage of him. They found Toby sitting on a low wall near the wharf. The pie was roughly divided into three portions, side by side. Toby flapped a hand over it, to keep off the buzzing flies which rose from the dung in the road.

The two boys fell on their shares and all Bess could do was watch as the pie disappeared.

'Oh,' Toby said, crestfallen, 'Did you want some? It's just we always—'

'Never mind,' she said. 'It wasn't much, though, that pie. Not for three growing lads. Let's see if we can get you something else.'

She stopped and opened up the lock at the bottom of the collecting box. Carefully she extracted the thru'pence she'd just been given. Mrs Fenwick need never know. She'd fill it again, and besides these were poor boys who needed food, and here was the means to get it.

At a roadside stall, she bought salted fish and some breadcakes. As they passed the dockyard on the way to the ferry she couldn't help but notice the skeleton of the King's warship under construction in the dry dock, and it gave her a lump in her throat to think that her Will, with all his skill and experience, was excluded from these yards. She hoped Pepys had spoken to Nicholson by now, and would have good news next time they went to see him.

Once they'd disembarked from the ferry, they sat on the shore and Bess arranged the food on a cloth. The boys were soon poking sticks into the mud, and skimming stones across the water. Though the sky threatened rain again, Bess took off her shoes to let air get to her bare feet. She let the delicious cooling breeze soothe her ankles, and leaning against a breakwater, closed her eyes. She imagined those first brave souls who had gone from just up the river in Redriff, all the way to the New World. *Mayflower* they called the ship. Rather them than her.

'Mrs Bagwell!'

The voice made her jerk upright. She looked behind her but could see no-one. The call came again. It was coming from a private wherry, even now being rowed downstream.

The figure, dressed in voluminous white shirt, and a burnt

orange waistcoat and breeches, waved his feather-trimmed hat, causing the boat to rock dangerously from side to side.

'Oh! Mr Pepys!' She stood up and gave a hesitant wave. Then realising with horror that not only should she have curtseyed, but that her feet were bare, she fumbled to draw on her shoes, hopping from foot to foot. Pray God he hadn't seen.

'I've news! Thought I'd save you the trip as I was coming to the yards. I'll come ashore,' Pepys shouted, grinning broadly and pointing at the jetty down river.

Now was her chance, to push Will forward. 'Not here!' she called back. 'Come to our house. Sign of the Saw, Flaggon Row.'

'Splendid!' He waved his assent, and she stuck her feet into her shoes.

'Boys, hurry, we have to get home.' She bundled all the food up in the cloth and tied it, and pulled the boys from their game.

'Told you we wouldn't get any dinner,' Toby said. 'It's always the same.'

'You will,' Bess said, 'but we have to eat it at home. Come on. Here, Toby, you carry it and I'll take Hal.' She thrust the bundle into Toby's hands and hoisted Hal onto her hip. Breathless, she hared up the road. Mrs Fenwick was just getting into a carriage and paused, mouth open, to stare as she pelted past.

'Hell's breath,' she cursed, but there was no time to stop. She burst in through the workshop door. 'Quick,' she shouted, 'tidy yourself up. Mr Pepys is on his way.'

'What?' Will was holding a polished wooden beaker and a sanding block.

Why didn't he move? 'Mr Pepys. I just saw him on the river. He's coming here, to our house. Give Lucy some coin, and tell her to fetch some wine.'

Still Will didn't move.

Frustrated, she threw up her hands and shouted, 'What's the

matter? He'll be here any minute!'

'There's no money in the jar.'

'Then get it on the slate – the vintner'll loan us some if you promise it back tomorrow. And for heaven's sake, get a suit on.' She didn't wait to see if he did as she asked, just hoped the instructions had gone in. This would be Will's big chance to impress Pepys, if he could take him into the workshop, show him his carving. And a glass of wine might sweeten their visitor.

She thrust the boys up the stairs and into the house, and was just about to go and tidy herself up, when a different voice called out, 'Hello?'

Oh no, not now.

Cousin Jack was on the threshold, leaning in.

Chapter 12

Bess wished she could shut the door in Jack's face.

'Toby?' Jack called, 'Time to go.'

'But we were just about to have our dinner!' Toby was reluctant to relinquish the cloth bundle on the table.

'No time. Gather your brothers together,' Jack said, 'I can't hang about all day. I've got to go to St Paul's. I'm meeting someone.'

'Billy's on the chamber pot,' Toby said mutinously.

There was no time to argue with Jack, though she would have loved to give him a mouthful for leaving the boys so long. Bess straightened her skirts and snatched a clean white coif from the drying rack in the kitchen, just as the door squeaked open again and Will appeared, his shirt streaked with brown dust from sandpapering.

'Did you get the wine? He's on his way,' Bess said, peering out of the window. 'Go and get changed.'

'No, there wasn't time.' Will banged at his breeches making clouds of dust. 'And no sheep's eyes, this time, d'you hear me?'

'Go on with you,' Bess tutted at him, as she cleared pots from the table, and put the room to rights, making it fit for visitors.

'Wine did you say?' Jack asked Will, 'Why? Who's coming?'

'Nobody,' Bess said, at exactly the same time as Will said 'Mr Pepys.' They glared at each other.

'Mr Pepys, *the* Mr Pepys?' Now Jack's eyes lost their impatience and took on an intent expression. He sauntered over to the table and sat himself down.

Bess pursed her lips. 'Toby, fetch Hal and Billy. It's time to go.' She shot Jack a look, wagged her head at Will and hissed, 'Get rid of him.'

A sharp purposeful knock at the door silenced them all. A pause whilst they all looked at each other, then Bess, realising Lucy hadn't heard it, hurried to open the door. 'Welcome, sir,' she said, smiling and dipping her head, 'do come in.'

Pepys ducked under the lintel, and peered around the room. Bess saw he was carrying an ornamental pair of gloves like the ones in Baxter's, with lace-edged cuffs and hanging ribbons.

He cast his gaze round the room. 'Charming,' he pronounced, with a surreptitious glance at Bess.

'Do take a seat,' Jack said, immediately standing to shake Pepys's hand.

'Oh … this is my cousin, Jack Sutherland,' Will said.

'He's just leaving,' Bess said. 'These are our nephews,' she said, waving an arm at the children who were all agog at Pepys's flamboyant attire. 'We were looking after them.'

Jack sat himself back down, at the table next to Pepys. 'Yes,' he said, 'I have some business in the city. I'm a snuff importer,' he said.

For less than a fortnight, thought Bess.

'I've the best snuff in town, so they say, though I wouldn't like to brag. Isn't that so, Will? Of course, I'm the one with the head for business in our family.'

Bess frowned at him. 'Jack, didn't you have an appointment to keep at St Paul's?'

'Not for a while yet, I've time for a glass with you all. Did you say there was wine, my beautiful Bess?'

'If you'll excuse me, I'll just fetch it from below.' And Will made a hasty exit. Bess put on a nonchalant air, shaking out a clean linen cloth for the table, though she knew Will would be running up the street to his wine-merchant friend to beg a flagon from his cellar.

'Father,' Billy said, appearing at Jack's elbow, 'are we having our dinner here?'

'Hush, lad,' Jack said sharply. 'We're busy. Take your brothers into the back chamber. Go on – hurry up.'

'But, Father—'

'We'll dine later. Now go, or you'll feel the back of my hand.' And he turned his attention back to Pepys.

'Lucy?' Bess poked her head around the kitchen door and Lucy emerged. 'Get a cloth. Our wine glasses need a polish.'

But Pepys had lost interest in Jack's description of his special aromatic blend of snuff. Instead, Bess was aware of Pepys's gaze on the back of her neck as she took down the glasses from the shelf, and passed them to Lucy.

'Come sit by me, Mrs Bagwell,' Pepys said.

Bess dared not refuse, but she spread her skirts decorously about her feet, and was glad she'd found time to tuck her kerchief well into the front of her bodice.

Jack was pressing Pepys. 'Our floral snuff is a very good price,' he repeated, and threw out facts and figures about the cost of the tobacco and the grinding process, and how his particular blend was a cure for any number of ills including the great pestilence. Bess could not find the space to interrupt him, and besides, she was mightily perturbed by Pepys's foot, which had nestled beside hers under the table. Even now, his stockinged leg pressed against her skirts. Was it accidental, or not? He seemed to be listening to Jack, but then just as she'd decided it meant nothing, a finger trailed across the back of her hand.

She leapt up as if scalded. 'I'll just check on the children.'

In the back chamber she smoothed her blushing face, and tucked her kerchief more tightly across her bosom.

'What's the matter, Aunt Bess?' Hal asked. 'Is it that man? I

~89~

don't like him. He smells funny.'

'Shh. It's the hair oil on his wig. He's a very important man. He's come to see Uncle Will.'

'When will he be going?'

'Don't know, my little man. Soon, I think.'

Hal let out a long sigh and returned to where Billy and Toby had cleared a space on the wooden boards and were playing at soldiers using their spills as swords.

The bang of the outside door alerted her to Will's return.

Bess hesitated. She pressed her hands to her cheeks to cool them. Will would spot her discomfort straight away. What should she do? It would be rude to rebuke someone of Pepys's status, yet she felt she would have to, if he persisted. And Will would be furious.

Settling her breath, she went carefully back to sit with them, though she did not meet Mr Pepys's eyes, and was careful to guide Will to the space between her and Pepys.

Lucy had laid out the glasses, and Will uncorked the flagon of wine.

Jack was still monopolising the conversation, but by now Mr Pepys was beginning to look glazed. He pushed his wine aside, though Will drained his. Finally when Jack showed no sign of allowing Will a single word, Mr Pepys stood and said, 'Why don't we walk up to Redriffe, Mr Bagwell, and we can talk as we walk? That is if your wife doesn't mind?' Again, that too-long stare.

'A fine idea.' Bess leapt on it before Jack had a chance to reply. 'You can show Mr Pepys your workshop as you pass.'

Lucy retrieved his hat from the peg where Bess had put it, and passed it to him.

'Good evening, Mrs Bagwell,' Pepys said, with an elaborate bow, 'it has been such a pleasure.' He cocked his head on one side, smiling.

Was he teasing her? She gave a small nod and brushed down her skirts, to cover her embarrassment.

'I'll make sure to send you some samples then, Mr Pepys.' Jack rose to his feet and planted himself in the doorway. He extended a hand to Pepys, who had no choice but to drag his eyes from Bess and take it.

Jack held Pepys's hand a moment too long, but finally Will and Mr Pepys were out of the door, and she let out a great sigh of relief. She sent up a prayer that Will would get some advancement from Pepys at least.

'Not what I expected at all,' Jack said. 'Mean, if you ask me. I offered him a fair price, and he turned it down. Can't see a bargain when it hits him between the eyes. Lord knows how he got to be in charge of ships' supplies. What does he want with Will?'

'I've no idea;' she lied, 'something to do with the yards I expect.'

'He's taken a liking to you, though, hasn't he?'

'I didn't notice.'

'Will won't be happy. Pepys's tongue was almost hanging out.' He laughed, but it was a laugh that made her uncomfortable. He stuck his head around the chamber door. 'Come on boys, time to go.'

'But, Father—' Billy's voice, protesting.

'Enough of your lip.' Next moment he'd grabbed Billy and pulled him bawling from the room. Toby and Hal followed, their faces sullen. They couldn't wait for their father to return, but now suddenly, they looked reluctant to be in his company.

'Bye, Aunt Bess,' Toby said.

She saw Billy glance over to the table where the bundle of herring and bread was still wrapped in her apron.

'Wait!' she cried as the boys were chivvied through the door and onto the wooden steps. She waved the bundle towards Jack.

'You forgot their dinner,' she said.

'No time,' he said. 'We'll get something later.'

Later, she knew, for a hungry boy, could be a very long wait.

***

It was almost dark by the time Will returned from his walk with Pepys. Bess had lit the candle lantern above the door, but at the creak of the wooden steps outside, she put down her embroidery, anxious to hear how it had gone. His smile lifted her heart.

'What news?' she asked, reaching for his cloak as he shrugged it off.

'He's spoken to Nicholson, and I'm promised a trial as a ship's carpenter on the new carrack, the *Mercy*.'

'Oh Will, how marvellous!' She went to embrace him, and he opened his arms to her. After a moment the truth of what he was telling her hit home. She pushed him to arm's length, 'On a ship? I'd thought to have you working here in the yards at Deptford. Where does it trade to, this ship?'

A guarded look came over Will's face. 'I think to Bergen, and other towns of the old Hanseatic League. A three-month tour, Pepys said.'

'Three months?' She flopped onto a stool. 'You'll be away that long? What is it carrying?'

'Barley, soap, salt. Onions from Kent.'

'I must lose my husband for a few onions?'

'I've been away before, and it never worried you. I was away for weeks on the *Evangelina*.

'But we were younger then. Time's running on and I want us to try …' She almost said, 'for a child' but she bit it back. 'I mean, I'd hoped we could build a life here – a more stable life. With the shipyards so close by and all.'

He came to put a hand on her shoulder. 'Beggars can't be

choosers, Bess. Especially not now we've got this loan to pay off. And you were the one who was so keen for me to speak to Pepys.'

'But I didn't know then it would take you away from home for so long.' She wrapped her arms around his waist, and rested her head on his chest. The ties of his shirt pressed into her cheek, but his heart thudded a reassuring rhythm. 'When will they send for you?'

'Pepys said it might take a month or more. The Guild committee are being awkward. Likely it will just be an assistant carpenter's post, but at least it's a start. And in any case, the ship is offshore and in quarantine right now.'

'What?' She stepped away and rubbed her hand over her forehead. 'You're telling me you're to be carpenter on a ship that's just come back from the Low Countries?' She did not say the word 'pestilence' but it hung between them just the same.

'I'm lucky they had a vacancy. Come on, take cheer. Money will be coming in, and once I've got my sea legs back, it will be well-paid, better than making bowls.'

'Hertford said he might want a new table.'

'Did he? When was this?'

She realised her mistake instantly. 'Oh … I don't know, just something he said in passing.' Fool. She must learn to guard her tongue.

'Well, one table will hardly keep a household, will it? And the *Mercy* is a fine ship.'

She knew he liked the honesty of the sea, the huge timbers, the giant pulleys, the fact that every part of a ship was a floating forest, functional as well as beautiful, and that it all had to work perfectly. He was skilful, her husband, a draughtsman who could apply the practical techniques to match, but it made her a little jealous, his love of ships. She should be pleased for him, yet she found herself resentful.

'Where's Jack?' Will asked.

'Gone. Those poor boys have had no dinner again.' She told him about Baxter's. 'So if I'm to work, I'll have to find piece work.'

'You won't need to, when I'm taken on,' Will said. 'Come, let's celebrate with that wine. I can pay our neighbour back as soon as I get my first purse.' He poured them two glasses.

She raised her glass to his and they chinked rims. No wonder Pepys had drunk so little, the wine was bitter. And even more bitter was the fact that asking Mr Pepys for his help had all been her idea. She couldn't help wondering if Pepys was sending her husband so far away on purpose.

Chapter 13

Will was glad he had real work at last, and he couldn't wait to get on board the *Mercy*. His first proper position as a carpenter at sea. He'd been a sailor briefly on the *Evangelina*, a merchant ship carrying goods to France, and he'd got a taste for it; the fact that wood could be shaped to form something so enormous, so beautiful and so intricate. Working with wood was his first love, though. He'd been sad to lay off Jacob, but couldn't keep him on, now he'd be at sea.

He needed his sea-boots soling, so today Bess accompanied him down the main street to the cobbler's. He glanced fondly at her as she bounced along by his side, with the occasional hop-skip to keep up. Now he was going away, they had drawn a veil over their differences, and the thought of being absent from her kindled his affection.

On the way they were stopped by Mr and Mrs Fenwick who told them they were about to dine at Sayes Court, the Evelyns's grand house set in its own newly lawned gardens.

'Now don't you forget this month's meeting, Mrs Bagwell,' Mrs Fenwick said, wagging her finger at Bess. 'We've raised seventeen pounds already for our little cause. We'll soon be needing Mr Bagwell's benches.' She simpered at Will.

'Whatever I can do to help,' Will said politely.

'And we've just had the most pleasant conversation with the King's navy treasurer, Mr Pepys,' Mrs Fenwick said. 'He passed by our house not five minutes since, and stopped to give us the time of day.'

'Mr Pepys came to us a few weeks ago.' Bess said. 'He's a

friend of ours. Will's going to sea in a fortnight, and it was Mr Pepys who arranged Will's position on the *Mercy*.'

Will couldn't resist a smile.

'Oh.' Put out, Mrs Fenwick glanced to her husband, who just nodded his head up and down like a simpleton. 'How do you know Pepys?'

'He's friends with Mr Hertford, the judge. Will made his dining chairs,' Bess said.

Mrs Fenwick looked as though she'd swallowed a lemon. 'Come on, James, we'll be late for dinner.' She tugged on her husband's arm. 'I wish you safe passage Mr Bagwell.'

'Arrogant woman,' Will said when she'd gone. 'Don't know how you stand it.'

'Because we want their business, that's why.'

They walked on, quicker now, passing by Deptford Shipyard on their way to the ferry. Past the conglomeration of timber sheds and storehouses with their red pantile roofs, past the upright scaffolds of timbers for ships in dry dock, past the houses for petty officers and the surgeon's house with its sign of the staff and snakes.

'My father's in there, somewhere,' Will said, pointing over the fence.

Bess nudged him, 'Look. There he is.'

'Where?' Will leaned over to look.

It wasn't his father, but Pepys. He was bent over a great tree trunk, his backside facing them, in his burnt orange breeches. Several other men in the uniform of dock-workers – canvas breeches and rough doublets – stood around him.

'What's he doing?' Bess said.

'Measuring for planks, I think.'

'You'd think he'd have the men do it for him, a man like him. And they don't look too pleased. Just look at their faces.'

'They always hate it when the masters interfere.'

Will tried to walk on, but Bess stayed his arm. 'Let's wait for him, exchange a few words. It's good to have friends in high places.'

'I've not even got on the *Mercy* yet.'

They were about to walk on, when Pepys stood up and caught sight of them. He waved at them, a curious little jiggle of the fingers.

'Here he comes. Smarten yourself up.' Bess brushed a speck of sawdust off his sleeve.

Pepys walked over to the fence. 'Ah, Mr Bagwell. And Mrs Bagwell too,' he said. 'What a delightful day.'

'It is that, Mr Pepys.' Bess gave a small curtsey.

'I've just got a new folding measuring rule. Neatest contrivance you ever saw. Here, Bagwell, take a look. A fine piece of craftsmanship, eh? Look at that brass inlay.' He passed it through the fence to Will.

Will admired the rule, which was indeed a good one and would have cost at least a week of his wages. He wouldn't mind one like this in his toolbox. When he looked up Pepys was smiling at Bess.

He tensed. She saw his expression and burst out, 'We're on our way to get Will's boots done. He'll be away on the *Mercy* soon.'

Will took her by the arm and squeezed, hinting they should leave.

'We are so grateful,' she continued, ignoring him, 'though of course I'd rather he was well away from the Low Countries. Our cousin tells us there's pestilence there.'

'Well, Mrs Bagwell, it's but a start. I'll see if I can't do a little better than that for him soon. But I'm sure there's nothing to worry about.' Pepys leant on the fence, his gaze fixed on Bess.

Will was uncomfortable. It was as if he was shut out of the conversation.

'Thank you kindly, sir, we'd appreciate it.'

'Not at all, not at all. It's a pleasure. Do drop by my office, and we can talk further.'

They exchanged pleasantries whilst Pepys looked Bess up and down as if she were a cow at auction. In the end Will had to almost drag Bess away with a sharp tug at the elbow.

'Don't start at me – I know,' she said, once they were out of his earshot. 'But what was I expected to do? Ignore him?'

Will knew that 'yes' was not a reasonable answer, so he kept quiet.

***

Two weeks later, Will and Jack sat at the table, tankards of small beer before them. 'Just came by to wish you *bon voyage*,' Jack said, leaning back so the chair tipped dangerously on two legs. 'So Pepys delivered the goods, I hear.'

'A three-month tour. On the *Mercy*.'

'I wouldn't like to leave my wife all that time,' Jack said. 'It'll be November by the time you're back. A woman on her own... well...'

'Bess will manage fine.' Will passed Jack a plate on which rested some left-over cheese and the last of their dried meat.

'I was thinking more about Pepys.'

'What about him?' A clanging bell of alarm was already ringing in Will's head.

'Seemed to me, he was making a play for her.'

Will shook his head. He clenched his fists under the table. No. Not that again. He tried to be casual. 'He'll have bigger fish to fry, a man like him. He moves in Court circles.'

'He's sending you away though, isn't he? Wouldn't be surprised if he was to call on her.'

'She wouldn't entertain him.'

'He's a wealthy man, Will. Has a lot of influence. But I could keep an eye on her for you. What do you say she has the boys for me, whilst you're gone? That would keep her busy, and deter any … well, any callers. And I could collect them each night, check all is well.'

Will was silent a moment. The tightness in his chest was twisting, like wringing a cloth. The thought of Bess alone with Pepys made up his mind for him. 'Would you do that, Jack? But coming here would be out of your way.'

'True. But a boon to me too, to know my boys were well cared-for. You'd have peace of mind knowing Bess was… well, occupied… and I would be free to deal with earning back our investment.'

'Well, I—'

'Good, that's settled then.'

***

Bess struggled up the steps and lowered the basket to the ground to drag it in through the front door. Whoever would have thought a few scraps of fabric could be so heavy?

Bess was elated. She'd called on her friend Meg, who had suggested Bess should try out for her father's shop, Hutchinson's, to see if her stitching was fine enough for them. So now she had a basket full of unsewn gloves. She hoped Will would be pleased she'd taken it upon herself to help out with their finances in this way. If it worked, they'd be able to keep Lucy. But her good humour died when she saw Jack and the boys in the parlour again with Will.

'If it isn't the beautiful Bess,' Jack said lazily. 'Will's telling me about his new position. Pepys did well for him, hey? Though I shall miss having him about.'

Or rather you'll miss his hand-outs, Bess thought, as she took off her hat and hung it on the peg. 'How's the snuff trade going?' she asked.

'Dandy. It's quite a business now, with the return exports we do. We're expanding. We've taken over a cellar in Blackfriars. You'll soon get a fine return on your money.'

Will smiled expectantly at her, but she could not share his good humour.

'What do you export?' she asked, aware she was being sour, but unable to help herself.

'This and that.' Jack waved his arm expansively. 'Tallow from the wool trade, condiments and other small goods.'

'Jack's had a fine idea,' Will said, 'for while I'm at sea. He thought you could have the boys over to keep you company. After all, he's busy now, what with a snuff mill in Rotterdam to watch over.'

'You know I'd be glad to see them anytime.'

'Good, I thought you'd say that. Jack will bring them over each day before he goes to work.'

At this, Billy came running over to join the conversation. 'Every day? You mean we can come to Auntie Bess's house every day? And have proper food and everything?'

'Well why not?' Will ruffled his hair. 'Auntie Bess would be glad to have you, wouldn't you?' He looked to Bess, and said, 'It will help until I get paid. We get paid in arrears, you see.'

Hal tugged at her skirts. 'Me too! Let me come too.'

'Wait.' Bess felt as if she were glued to the floorboards. 'Have I understood you right, I'm to have the boys here every day?' It was all happening too quickly round her, and she didn't seem to have any say in the matter.

'We thought twopence a day,' Jack said.

'For each of them?'

'They're family,' Will said, with a shake of his head.

Twopence? Was he jesting? Her expression must have showed her incredulity. 'But I've just got piece work. From Meg's father,

Mr Hutchinson. I'm trying out for a position there. I thought you'd be pleased. Sixpence a load.' She pointed to the overflowing basket by the door.

'They can help. Or you can do it in the evenings,' Will said. 'It will keep you busy.'

She caught the flick of his eyes to Jack, and Jack's knowing smile.

Busy? What did he mean? She was going to be busy enough. She struggled to take it in. 'But how can we afford it? What about their food, and all the things they'd need?'

'They don't eat much, do you, boys?' The boys glanced silently at each other. 'And I'll come for them after dusk.'

'It's a long way for them to come on their own, crossing river all by themselves. And what about the fares for the ferryman? We need to think it through for a day or two, draw up an agreement,' she said.

'No need for that,' Jack said, 'after all, we're family, and I trust you with my boys.'

But I don't trust you, were the words in Bess's head.

Chapter 14

They had to catch the evening tide, so it was late, almost nightfall, when Bess and Will arrived at Custom House Quay in Barking, the old wool quay, where boats left for France and Holland. Bess sent Lucy to wait by the coach stand whilst she said goodbye to her husband. The wharf was busy with longshoremen, and drinkers from the taverns on the shore. A lone star winked in the dark above the silhouette of the three-storey Customs House, with its octagonal staircase towers. The *Mercy*, a four-masted carack, was idling with the other tall-ships in the deeper waters of the channel. When his tool-box and bag were loaded into the tender, Will pressed a kiss hard onto Bess's lips.

'Take care, wife,' he said. 'Think of me. I'll be missing you.' His voice was husky, and it tugged a cord deep inside her.

'I will. Stay safe. And promise you'll write me a proper letter, not just one of your three-word notes.' She gave him one last tight hug before they called him on board. The cool moisture of his lips on hers lingered as she lifted her hand to wave.

The row-boat that took Will out to the *Mercy* looked like a walnut floating in the vast estuary. It gave her a peculiar untethered feeling, the sight of him so small and far away.

She watched until the men dissolved into dark shapes, melting into the hulk of the big ship. It made her catch her breath, and she placed a hand to her chest to settle her heart. She felt the loss of him already, and for a moment she regretted even talking to Pepys. If she hadn't, her dear Will would still be at home in his lovely workshop, making tables and chairs.

When there was nothing more to see but inky shapes in the

blackness, she turned to walk back towards Lucy at the wharf. There, hired carriages stood waiting to ferry the families of the sailors back from Barking to the centre of the city. They were about to board when she glimpsed a familiar figure further down the wharf. She stared a moment, unsure, then said to Lucy, 'Don't let them leave without me.'

She turned and hurried down the quay. 'Jack!'

He turned sharply, and the youth who was with him stopped heaving crates, until Jack said sharply, 'Get them on board. Quicker the better.'

'I didn't know you'd come to see Will off. Where were you? Did he know you'd come? Where are the boys?'

Jack did not look pleased to see her, but then he never did. Truth be told, she was always a little scared of being on her own with Jack. He was a man who liked to laugh at others' expense. He delighted in putting people down with his caustic tongue, though he'd not take that from anyone else, and it made him unpredictable. Today she barely recognised him.

'You look smart, cousin,' she said.

He was wearing what looked like a clerk's suit, and under his hat, a dark wig tied up in a sash. He examined her with an assessing eye. 'I didn't come for Will's sake. I'm here on my own business. That's the *Lily Allen* over there. He's gone then?'

She swallowed. The words made his departure seem real. 'Yes, not a quarter hour ago. I take it I'll be minding the boys tomorrow, like you said?'

'They're with Mrs Minty. My man Fletcher will drop them off in the morning, about seven bells.' He gestured to the pot-bellied youth behind who was loading crates into a tender. Bess glanced over; Fletcher was ill-shaven with ears too big for his head and an insolent manner about him.

'Pack them some playthings to keep them occupied, won't

you? I've still got my piece work to do.'

'Yes, yes,' he said impatiently. 'I'll see to it.'

'Is this your snuff?' Bess pointed.

'No. Exports.' He moved to stand in front of them. Something about this suggested he was hiding something. Fletcher grasped the top crate, and balanced it on his heavy stomach. As he lumbered towards the boat she heard the chink of bottles.

'What's in the crates?' she asked. 'Wine?'

'Yes, wine,' Jack said.

'Well I hope it's making a good profit. It's our money you've got in those crates!' She laughed lightly.

'Ah, the beautiful Bess. Always greedy for more.'

She bridled. 'I don't know what you mean.'

'Just a figure of speech. Your money's safe with me.'

A boy ran up and skidded to a stop before them; a boy Bess had noticed earlier, a weasel-faced beggar loitering under the sconces by the tavern. She'd feared him to be a pick-pocket and given him a wide berth.

'Mr Sutherland!' he said, panting for breath. 'The customs men. They're coming this way.'

Jack turned to shout orders to Fletcher. 'Get everything on board. Quick as you can. Fetch the others.' To Bess, he said, 'You've held me up. We need to catch this tide.' He called to Fletcher, 'Don't cast off without me, I've papers for the Master. You can row me back afterwards.'

She was forced to stand back as another four men elbowed in front of her to load Jack's cargo aboard. Something about Jack's furtive disappearance when the customs men were coming triggered a warning in her mind.

All at once, the quay emptied. Behind her, the post-boy called for final passengers for the carriage to the city, and Lucy was frantically gesturing at her from the door. She ran to catch it and climbed in. As the coach rattled away from the quay, iron wheels ringing on the cobblestones, she turned to look back through the window. She could see nothing but the black spires of ships yet to sail, and a moon floating above like a hole cut in the sky.

At Thames Street they climbed out of the carriage and headed for the ferry home. Home. The word seemed odd now Will had gone. There was no ferry yet, so they had to wait.

Across the glimmer of the river, her eyes were pulled towards Ratcliff, to the smudge of houses where she'd first met Will, when he'd just been a jobbing joiner in a small boatyard. A twitch of nostalgia for the coarse friendliness of life on the other side of the river made her shift from foot to foot. She remembered pushing her mother away, and the hollow of guilt swelled. She doubled over, clutching her ribs to relieve the emptiness. Lucy stared at her, as if she'd lost her mind.

When the boat came, she sat with her back to her past.

She could not bear to turn and look.

~ PART TWO ~

I can get no remedy against this consumption of the purse:

borrowing only lingers and lingers it out, but the disease is incurable.

Shakespeare - Henry 1V Part II

Chapter 15
Six months later - February 1664

Agatha Prescott leaned over the body of Alfred Hastings, tailor – a young man, white-skinned and fair, with a powdering of freckles. He was too long for the table and his feet poked off the end, pale as milk, and still soft. Too young, Agatha thought, as she rolled him quickly over to wash his back with vinegar infused with lavender water.

'There, my love,' she said, her breath white in the cold air, 'that'll keep the flies away and make you smell sweet.' She saw nothing odd in talking to corpses. After all, who knew how long they could hear for, once they'd passed over?

Agatha drew the bundle of dried herbs from her basket and crumpled them in her fist until the tang of thyme filled the room. Since being widowed, as well as layer-out, she'd taken on the position of searcher of the parish, one of the women who examined the dead for the cause of their death.

She coughed. The chamber reeked of smoke, for she'd made Hastings's woman douse the fire. Chill was best, as far as corpses were concerned. Still, it was a mystery why this one'd gone. A newly-wed couple, and him just dropping over by his cutting table, with half a pair of breeches still to stitch.

She ran her eyes over him; felt his chest again, his long limbs. Smooth as marble, but with the cold, gooseflesh feel of the dead. She gave him a slap with her palm, the way she slapped bread-dough. 'What do you think you're up to, eh?'

It was a death with no obvious cause. She liked to be certain what she was telling the authorities. It was an important responsibility, reporting for the Bills of Mortality.

She stood back to scrutinise him. He didn't need to be cut and padded with herbs, like the rich ones did. Just his mouth and nose closed with thyme to stop them sinking, so he still looked decent when his poor distraught wife came back to look. Agatha liked to make them look peaceful, even handsome, if she could. It was her duty to do so. This one had been a looker, she could tell. He'd be buried that night, before the flesh could rot. She pushed the herbs into the man's mouth and clamped the jaw shut, tying around the head with a muslin bandage to keep it there until the stiffness set it firm. With effort, the veins standing proud on her sinewy arms, she pulled the tailor straight on the table.

Praise God, I've still my strength, she thought.

She gazed down on him. Must be the same age as her Bess's husband, William. Agatha pondered Bess and Will. Bess had married for love, and at first Agatha couldn't help wishing Will was richer. But the thought of them growing richer gave her a desperate feeling. She missed Bess, and the thought that she would no longer see her daughter hurt.

Now they'd moved away to Deptford and plain woodwork wasn't good enough for him. Oh no. Will wanted to be an artist in wood, Bess said.

An artist. Pff. Agatha blew out her disgust through down-turned lips, and tore at the herbs with a venom, then pushed a plug of it into each of the man's nostrils and sealed them up with beeswax warmed over the candle.

Heaving the man's shoulders off the table, she dressed the tailor in his half-shirt, and breeches cut open for the purpose, and put the boots back on his feet.

'That's better, now. You look like a proper gent.'

Funny how a man didn't look dressed until he had his boots

back on. Then she combed the corpse's hair.

'You're a mystery, you are,' she said to him. 'Don't know why you wanted to up and die, and leave your poor wife grieving so. Night, night.' Her breath stood in the air like a ghost. Was this what a ghost was, the last of a man's air? She tutted at herself for such ungodly thoughts, and covered him over with the cerecloth, so he would be fit for visiting.

'Stopping of the stomach,' that's what she'd tell them. His insides felt hard, and though that could merely be the rigor setting in, it was all she had to go on. There were always unexplained deaths – it was part of the mystery of God – the giving and the taking away.

Her mind drifted back to Bess. Life was short, she knew that now. And it could be lopped off at any time. Like this poor tailor. One minute cutting out breeches, the next, cold and gone. It was more than a month since she'd last tried to call on her daughter. The door was always locked. She'd even had to leave her New Year gift – a plum pie – on the doorstep.

Perhaps it had pricked Bessie's conscience. The thought of her daughter filled her with longing. She'd left it a few months, but she'd not give up. Maybe she could catch her unawares. After all, blood was blood.

***

The next day, Bess placed a sprig of winter greenery in the best glass vase, and laid the table prettily with a linen cloth and her best cups and pewter plates. This week Mrs Fenwick's ladies were meeting at Bess's house, and Lucy had been scrubbing and polishing for days to get it ready until the windows gleamed, and the whole place smelled of beeswax and lavender.

She'd persuaded Lucy to take the boys out, but as luck would have it, on the day, the sky split and delivered a downpour that bounced knee-high off the road. Lucy was reduced to hustling them downstairs to the workshop to get them pinning gloves for Hutchinson's. Their high-pitched protests were still audible as the ladies bustled in, exclaiming about the wet and shaking off their hats and cloaks.

Once Lucy had hung everything, and after a few complaints from Mrs Gordon about how inconvenient it was to meet in an upstairs room because it affected her bad hip, they were finally all seated around Bess's table, and Lucy disappeared below. Despite their work, Bess was conscious of the lack of feather cushions on the chairs, the cheap tallow dips instead of proper wax candles, and the fact that her cups were thick, practical earthenware and not the new 'china'. The fire blazed cheerfully though, and the air began to reek of steam and wool.

'What an interesting view,' Mrs Gordon said, rubbing a finger on the glass and peering out of the window. It seemed to dismiss the rest of the house as being totally unworthy of comment.

She returned to the table and set down her collecting box with a thud. Mrs Fenwick weighed the older woman's collecting box in her hands, 'Well done, Mrs Gordon.'

'It's mostly silver,' Mrs Gordon said, flapping her hand dismissively. 'I went around the Exchange this month, to appeal to my husband's businesses there.'

Mr Gordon was a mercer, selling imported cloth in the fashionable part of the Exchange, and he owned two shops – both of which were so expensive that Bess couldn't even afford a set of hair-ribbons from his counter.

Bess undid the brass catch and slid open the top of her box. She knew her box was only quarter-full again. Folk in Deptford were not so well off that they could spare much, and as well as dipping into it herself, she'd found herself too busy to go knocking on doors further afield. Last time they'd met, just after

Christmas, she'd pressed a half-sovereign's worth of coins into Mrs Gordon's hand. The money had come straight out of the collection box, so it had depleted her takings still more.

'What I owe you,' she'd said.

Mrs Gordon had frowned at the odd collection of change, then ostentatiously dropped it into her box.

Today, Bess was even more reluctant to pour the contents of her box onto the table for Mrs Fenwick's inspection.

Oh no. Practically all leather tokens, except for one solitary silver thru'penny piece which looked paltry beside the other women's heaps of glinting coin. And she knew where that one had come from – from Hertford where she'd called earlier in the week.

'I've been rather busy,' she said, as an apology. 'I've been helping out a friend at the glover's, whilst Will's away.' She tried to make it sound like a diversion rather than a necessity. She wished Will had not taken on another three-month stint at sea.

'You need to hire another girl, then,' Mrs Gordon said. 'I can recommend my girl's sister. She's looking for a post.'

'I'll ask Will,' Bess said, knowing they couldn't afford another girl, and she'd do no such thing.

Below them, the noise of the boys quarrelling.

'I did not!' Hal's voice.

'You did. He did, didn't he Billy?'

'Ow!' A wail like a dog in pain.

'Excuse me a moment,' Bess said. 'I'll fetch refreshment.'

She shot downstairs and poked her head round the door. 'Auntie Bess,' whined Billy, face red and tearful, 'Toby stuck me with a pin!'

'Did not,' Toby said.

'Just keep quiet, the both of you,' she hissed. 'Or there'll be no dinner. Lucy, just get them out of here.'

'But it's raining—'

'I don't care. Just for an hour. Those are my orders, Lucy.'

Back up the stairs, shielding her hair from the wet with an arm across her head. In the parlour, Mrs Fenwick tallied the coins, heaping them into neat piles.

The noise of the door below, and silence. Breathing a sigh of relief, Bess went to bring refreshment. By the time she'd returned, Mrs Fenwick had brought out a damp parcel, cut the string with the scissors from her reticule, and unwrapped a bolt of white cotton.

'I thought we could make cover-alls,' Mrs Fenwick said. 'I have a pattern book with the sweetest pin-tucks around the bodice.'

'Who are these for?' Bess asked, fingering the clean, white fabric.

'Why, for the children of course.'

'You mean, the children in the school?' She had a momentary vision of Billy and Hal glowering at each other.

'Of course. Our children. The ones we will be educating.'

'Are they going to get dirty?'

Mrs Fenwick gave a tinkling laugh and looked to the other ladies, who simpered back. 'No. It's not to keep the dirt from them, but to prevent it rubbing off on us! It will cover up their dirty clothes, and keep them clean. And I'm determined to endow them with a sense of pride.'

It was then Bess realised. They would be treating the children like playthings; like dolls to be dressed up, not real children like Jack's. Not ones with hungry bellies and cold hands. How would these women cope with the infections; with the lice-infested hair? They had no idea what life was like for those children. No idea at all. But she held these thoughts back.

'How much did it cost, the material?' she asked.

Mrs Fenwick smiled. 'Mrs Gordon arranged for her husband to

allow us a special price, seeing as we were buying so much. Only six pence a yard.'

Bess stared at the fabric. It was just an ordinary cotton, like you could buy on any cheap market stall. Six pence a yard. She could barely believe it. There must be yards and yards of it. That many sixpences would feed a family for a month! Not only were they making useless aprons, but they were giving the business straight back to Gordon's. Hard-earned pennies were going to this ... to this game. For that was what it was – a game designed to keep these idle ladies busy.

'I really think we should concentrate on necessities first,' Bess said, 'like perhaps giving the children a slice of bread each morning.'

'Bread? Oh no, we're not feeding them. We'd be inundated with all sorts of undesirables,' Mrs Fenwick said.

'And we don't want to be a workhouse,' Mrs Gordon agreed. 'The cover-alls will send the right message. Clean bodies, clean minds.'

'We shall teach Latin and Greek, and Bible studies,' Mrs Fenwick said.

'But we'll need pencils first,' Bess said, 'and nibs, and ink and paper.'

'Well, we'll all have to make a little more *effort* with our collecting then,' Mrs Gordon said, looking pointedly at Bess.

She was about to retort when there was a sharp knock at the door. Her first thought was that Lucy was back, with the boys. Bess rose and drew open the door a crack, but the wind whipped it open. A splatter of rain whooshed into the room, along with a dark billow of cloak and a smell of wet fabric and something sharper; more medicinal.

Bess's mother pulled the bedraggled hat off her head and shook it, sending drips over the polished wooden floor. 'It's pissing cats out there,' she said.

The words fell into the silence like stones.

Bess hurried over. 'Can't it wait?' she whispered in her mother's ear. 'I'm busy right now.'

Her mother ignored her. 'What a day!' She thrust her wet cloak, reeking of what smelt like camphor, into Bess's arms, then rubbed her damp hands together as she headed for the seat where, until a few moments ago, Bess had been sitting. Bess hastily moved the white cotton onto the sideboard out of her mother's reach. Agatha settled herself down into the chair and leant her elbows onto the table. The fabric of her woollen sleeves was worn threadbare, and the sight of it made Bess shrink with embarrassment.

'I came to tell Bessie there'll be war with the Dutch, sure and certain. The broadsheets are full of it. The Dutch whipped our men shamefully in the East Indies. Then they hung the St George flag beneath their own, and made a solemn oath they'll be masters of all the world.'

The other ladies leant away from the table, but stared in fascination. It was no wonder. Her mother's face was lined and creased, and her hair hung limp and grey from its straggling bun. It was as if poverty itself had walked into the room. Beside her, the other women were plump and shiny, in their taffeta and velvet, their silks and furs.

'"Sovereign of all the South Seas" they're calling themselves.' Her mother wouldn't meet her eye. Damn her. She knew Bess couldn't ask her to leave without appearing rude before the other ladies.

'Is your husband in the Navy too?' Mrs Gordon asked, with a sidelong glance at Mrs Fenwick.

'No. I'm widowed. But I like to keep myself informed, and I like to look in on Bessie, see how she's doing.'

'This is my mother, Mrs Prescott,' Bess said, finally, in as neutral a voice as she could muster.

'Mrs Fenwick,' Bess's neighbour replied. The others mumbled their names too.

'Pleased to make your acquaintance, I'm sure. What are you collecting for?' Agatha asked, tapping a fingernail on the nearest box. 'Mission, is it?'

'The Christian Educational Fund,' Bess said. 'But we were just finishing, weren't we, ladies?'

'But we haven't yet discussed—' Mrs Fenwick began, but Agatha immediately interrupted.

'Education, you say? I'm a Mission woman, myself. Do you know it? Based at St Peter's on Aldgate. We work with no-hopers. The drunks and the destitutes, and the street geese that hang around the Exchange. It's good work. Saves many a soul from sin or damnation.'

'Is that so?' Mrs Fenwick said, weakly. 'And how do you do that?'

'Bible instruction. My late husband's idea. We read the most important passages to them, teach them how to cast evil aside, to ignore priests and preachers and please God alone. Education's alright, but it's just for this world. We care about the next. No point educating a body if they're to be sent to eternal damnation, is there?' She cast her eyes contemptuously over Mrs Fenwick's elaborate fur-trimmed gown. 'Wealth and finery is all very well, but it won't save your soul.'

'I so agree,' Mrs Fenwick said smoothly. 'But think how it would be, if these children could read the scriptures for themselves.'

'Oh, but we have thought,' Agatha said. 'And it would lead to nothing but trouble. They'd think they could go somewhere – be someone. And we all know that's an illusion, don't we?' A thump on the table. 'Because those higher up would never stand for it.' She let out a throaty cackle.

Mrs Gordon glanced uncomfortably at the other women, but Mrs Fenwick's eyes were transfixed.

'Ma—'

'Hush now, Bessie, I'm talking.' Agatha leant further forward, and whispered, 'But no matter how high up you are, death levels us all. I work with Dr Harris, scribing the Bills of Mortality, and just before I came here, I had to attend one of the young King's merry gang, a man who'd died in a duel. Stabbed, and terrible case of the pox—'

'Ma, I don't think the ladies—'

'All I'm saying is, I could almost smell the brimstone as I laid him out. I said to myself, "I know where you're going, fella-me-lad, and it's not up." If someone had only caught him early, told him what to do—'

The other ladies darted anxious looks at Mrs Fenwick. She, on the other hand, showed no intention of moving, but was avidly taking in everything Agatha had to say. 'The pox, you say?'

Mrs Gordon's cheeks turned a mottled pink, and she rose to her feet. 'Beg pardon, Mrs Bagwell. You were right. We were just leaving.' Her voice was imperious and cold, designed to cut through steel.

Still Mrs Fenwick didn't move. Agatha carried on as though Mrs Gordon had not spoken. 'Been a searcher nigh on five years now, and death's nothing to fear, it's what comes after. The flesh rots but the vapours of the dead fly forth and the gates of Heaven open, or the gates of Hell drag you down. I've seen it with my own eyes, watched the soul sucked under. Terrible, to see, it is.'

Bess stared. Her mother was deliberately being provocative. She was acting a part, curse her.

'Mrs Fenwick!' Mrs Gordon took her arm and almost hoisted

her to her feet.

'Oh. Yes.' Mrs Fenwick stood, assumed an air of righteous indignation. 'Excuse us, but we must be going. We'll see ourselves out.' Her manner was a snub, and Bess knew it.

She hastened to fetch their cloaks, silently, like a servant. Mrs Gordon whipped her cloak from Bess's hands without thanks.

Bess stiffened; she couldn't bear to see how these women looked down their noses at her mother, but she also longed to be one of them. On their side of the divide, not on her mother's.

As soon as they were out of the door, she turned on her mother. 'You did that on purpose!'

'What?'

'You look like a vagrant.'

'It's raining out there.' Agatha shrugged, folding her arms defensively.

'You interrupted my meeting.'

'They were going anyway.'

'No, they weren't. You put them off. All that talk about death and corpses and women of the street.'

'It's not my fault people keep on dying, is it? You can't turn death off, like the faucet at the village pump. Folk need laying out. And those that are still of this world need my help.'

Tears of frustration pricked at Bess's eyes. 'You knew exactly what you were doing. "The gates of Hell"... how could you? They'll laugh at me. It was embarrassing.'

'Nonsense. If they can't take plain-talking, they're not worth fretting over.'

'You don't understand, do you? I want... better. Better than...' She nearly said *better than you*, but stopped herself in time.

'I know, love, I'm not blind.' She reached across the table to cover Bess's hand with her own. 'But it hurts me to see you grovel to those harpies.'

Bess withdrew sharply and, pushing her chair back, leapt to her feet. 'They're my friends, and you insulted them.'

'Friends? They treated you like a servant. Real friends would like you for yourself. I've done you a favour. If they can't take a bit of plain talk then you're well rid.'

'And whose fault is that? You don't want me to rise in society. You can't bear it and you just find a way to drag me back down again.'

Her mother got up slowly, her expression shocked. 'Is that what you really think?'

Bess faltered. She did not know. She just wanted to hurt her and she didn't know why.

'If that's what you truly believe, then I'll go.' Her mother dragged her soaking cloak from the hook.

'I never asked you to come.'

'I know that.' Her mother fastened her dripping cloak and shouldered her bag. She pulled open the door and a squall of rain spattered the floor. She did not look back as she clung to the rail, to stop from slipping on the wet treads. It took her a few minutes to negotiate them with her bad hip, but Bess did not go to help.

When she'd gone, Bess stood a moment, hearing the insistent battering of rain on the roof. She felt hollowed out. She wished she could talk to Meg. She was the only friend who she could confide in. But instinctively she knew that Meg would not understand or approve of the way she was behaving. Meg had always set great store by respect for your parents. But then she hadn't had parents like George and Agatha Allin.

Two hours later Lucy returned, with the boys shivering and soaked through. Their shoes were full of water and had to be stuffed with paper and stood on the rack above the fire to dry. Lucy said nothing but cast Bess a look of reproach that cut her to the quick.

Chapter 16

Bess gripped the basket of this week's piece work between her knees, and balanced the collecting box on top, spreading her cloak over both to keep them dry. She wanted to show Mrs Fenwick how much she had collected from the workers at Hutchinson's. It might make up for last week's disastrous meeting, the one where her mother had ruined it all.

The Thames was sullen and grey, the surface mottled by the play of the wind which had the bargemen hitch up their collars and pull down their caps. A splash of icy water made her gasp and shudder.

Quick-footed, she hurried off at Deptford Stairs and dodged through freezing rain, avoiding the gutter which swilled with a stinking soup of horse droppings. Everywhere the aroma of damp horseflesh and wet woollen cloaks. The once clean houses were splattered up to the windows with mud, and women dragged up their sodden hems in a vain attempt to keep them from soiling their shoes.

As soon as she was in the house, she handed her wet cloak and dripping bonnet to Lucy, who gave a grimace. 'I've kept 'em occupied,' Lucy said, indicating the three boys at the table, and a pile of cutlery. 'Grinding and polishing. But it means I'm behind with the dinner.'

'No letters?' She was hoping to hear from Will.

'Not yet. Your shoes, mistress.'

'Here.' She prised off the filth-encrusted shoes and passed them over. Lucy sighed, held them at arm's length, and disappeared to the scullery. Lucy was right to frown, they did not look like a lady's shoes any more. And still no letter from Will. She'd written to ask him what to do about the loan money they owed.

'Auntie Bess!' Billy shouted. 'Look how many we've done.'

Bess examined the knives on the table. 'You *have* been busy,' she said, smiling.

'What's for dinner?' Hal said.

'Faggots. Lucy's making them.' She handed Toby the pot of grease, and a knife for the grinding wheel. The younger ones were rubbing away at the pewter spoons with sand and polishing rags.

'I like polishing,' Hal said.

'It's better'n pinning gloves,' Billy said.

'Well, it's back to pinning tomorrow,' Bess said. 'We've fifty to do this week.'

Groans.

All these long months that Will had been away, the workshop below had been cold and empty. Bess missed the cheerful sound of Will hammering, and the sound of the 'chip, chip, chip' of the chisel. Worse, Will still hadn't been paid, and the few pence from Jack barely compensated her for feeding the boys, let alone all the other expenses that children incur.

The loan had already got behind in the first few months, and when Will was home on Christmas leave he'd laughed easily, and told Bess not to worry because the Master was pleased with him, and he was to be taken on for another voyage on the *Mercy*. Money being tight, he couldn't turn it down. So off he went, and she was darning holes on holes in her stockings now, not to mention that her winter woollen dress was bald at the elbows and cuffs, no matter how hard she brushed it.

She'd grown to dread Jack's visits. He overstayed his welcome, and ignored the children. She hated his swagger and his way of staring at her too long and too often. Gone was his ragged unkempt appearance; instead he looked prosperous, like a man of means. She glanced at the boys. It pained her that they still wore dirty jerkins and holed shoes. So wherever Jack's new-found wealth was coming from it hadn't trickled down to them. Or to her.

She was just musing on this when a movement on the street outside the window caught her attention. Bastable the loan collector, in conversation with Mrs Fenwick.

God's breath, that was all she needed.

Mrs Fenwick's strident voice, '*Such* a good cause, Mr Bastable.'

Bess stood at the window and smiled as Mrs Fenwick thrust her collection box at his chest. Bastable retreated, protesting he had no change of his own, and strode towards Bess's house with a determined air. Mrs Fenwick, eager to convince him, hurried in breathless pursuit.

Even Bastable couldn't escape once Mrs Fenwick got going. It was like trying to stop a geyser. Mrs Fenwick had been ill over the winter with a bad throat and chest, and it had stopped her from talking. Still, she'd been well-recovered at their last meeting, and she was making up for lost time now, thought Bess.

Bess rubbed the steam from the glass, and reluctantly dragged the stone jar from the top shelf. She tipped it out onto the table, then rattled it to catch the last few tokens.

Oh my Lord. Not enough. Not nearly enough.

No sign of Will's pay from the Navy this month either. Fifth month in a row. She cursed the Navy Treasury and that charlatan, Pepys. Hurriedly, she raked the coins off the table into her hand as the rap came, pointed and insistent.

'I know you're in there, Mrs Bagwell. So it does no good pretending you're out.'

Damn. His eyes were as sharp as his nose. She'd better face it. He'd be back tomorrow if she didn't.

'Who is it, Aunt Bess?' Toby's expression was worried. 'Is it bailiffs?'

'No,' she said, 'no need to worry.'

Hurriedly, she emptied the contents of the Deptford Christian Education Fund box onto the table, and scraped the coins into her hand.

The knocking started again, rattling the door in its frame.

'I'm coming,' she shouted, counting the coins. 'No need for such a racket!'

Less coin in the box than she thought. Hutchinson's hadn't donated much at all, the pack of measly dogs.

She dragged the door open, blinking through the mist of rain.

On the threshold, the oily-haired Bastable fingered his rent book and regarded her with his narrow-set eyes. 'No excuses, this time,' he warned.

Bess half-closed the door behind her, so that Lucy and the boys couldn't hear their conversation, and pulled her shawl tighter round her shoulders. 'Sixteen shilling and sixpence,' Bess said brightly, holding out the coins and looking him straight in the eye. 'See, I have it all ready.' She thrust it into his hand.

'Mrs Bagwell, that's not what it says in my book, and you know it.'

'Are you sure?' Bess put on her most innocent expression. 'I paid last month. You stood right there and I counted it into your hand.' She smiled at him, smoothing down her dark skirts over her hips. Just then she saw Mrs Fenwick hovering by the gate with a collection box hung over her arm. Oh Lord. Guilt made her face hot.

She turned her attention back to Bastable who was separating the coins on his palm, to count them. Frowning, he shoved them into his satchel, and extracted a pristine notebook.

'Look.' He raked his finger down the column of figures, and

talked slow, as if talking to a child. 'A month's arrears, it says here. December you only gave me twelve shilling, so there's four and ninepence still owing.'

'Is there?'

'You know there is. It should be sixteen and nine. And this month's is sixpence short. There's only sixteen and thru'pence here.'

'Are you sure? I don't know how that happened,' Bess said.

But Bastable wasn't to be side-tracked. 'There's the month's loan on the four and ninepence too, which is an extra thru'pence. Five shillings plus the sixpence from this month.' Her head reeled, trying to keep up with him.

'Your payments are always late, Mrs Bagwell. Always some excuse. You know I have to tell Kite—'

'Don't be hasty,' she said. Kite would tell half of London they were in debt, then where would they be? She sought to placate him, 'It's like this, Mr Bastable... My husband's still at sea, and his pay has been held up somehow. Like all the sailors. We find ourselves temporarily in difficulty. Temporarily, I assure you.' From the corner of her eye she saw Mrs Fenwick was now within earshot. She hurried on, 'The Treasury will pay soon, unless they want another riot. I'm sure of that. So if you could just see fit to letting us have another month...?'

'No. Not possible, I'm afraid. I know you've been a good customer in the past, but I can't risk my employment.'

Mrs Fenwick was now standing right at the bottom of the stairs, hearing every word.

'I'll give you a day,' Bastable said, pocketing her coins. 'I'll come back tomorrow evening, same time for the rest. Of course, like I said last time... If you don't manage it, I could always come in, we could settle it that way, if you'd prefer...' He smiled at her, and raised an eyebrow.

She drew herself up, glared at him coldly, summoning the

gentlewoman she was determined to be. Pray God Mrs Fenwick hadn't heard. 'Do not insult me. I'll have it. Tomorrow.'

'Shame.' Bastable closed his book with a regretful shake of his head, before his voice took on a hard edge. 'If you don't have the shortfall by then, I can personally guarantee that Kite'll have you out of here quicker than a ferret from a pipe.'

'Good day, madam.' He barged past Mrs Fenwick, who was open-mouthed at the foot of the stairs.

'Mrs Bagwell,' she called, 'how's your collection going?'

'It fares well,' Bess said, 'more than last month.'

'I'll take your box then, Mrs Bagwell.'

'Sorry. Can't stop to talk, the children are calling.' The box was empty. She went indoors and shut the door firmly behind her, knowing it was impolite. But not before she heard the click as Lucy finally closed the kitchen door. She'd seen her raid the collecting box, and no doubt heard every word.

'We weren't calling you, Auntie,' Hal said, accusingly.

Bess sank down on a chair, her forehead in her hands, suddenly overwhelmed. Will had no idea what it was like trying to keep this household going. No idea at all.

And he could do nothing, stuck at sea. Debt was like sinking in quicksand. The more you struggled, the deeper it got. Where was she to find a whole pound before tomorrow?

She could think of only one way out. Pepys would be able to get Will's pay moving, surely?

It was cheek, she knew, to expect an audience with such a great man, unannounced. But she'd done it with Hertford, and it had worked, hadn't it? But Pepys was not so open as Hertford. He had a way of turning everyone's questions away with banter, so you couldn't get to him, no matter how you tried. And Jack had certainly tried. But with Pepys, the cheerful bluster hid something else, something sad and dark.

She quashed the squirm she felt in her chest at the thought of Mr Pepys. She'd go first thing in the morning.

Chapter 17

The Seething Lane offices were fugged with the treacly aroma of pipe smoke, and the black-and-white tiled floor in the downstairs vestibule was slippery with wet, as Bess and her entourage arrived, for she'd had to bring Lucy with her as chaperone, and they had three damp children in tow. Bess's pattens slid and skidded as she tottered across the marble floor, with Hal clinging to her skirt.

A swimming sensation in her stomach. It was uncomfortable, this world of men. Officious-looking clerks in polished shoes, their sheaves of papers clutched to their chests, dodged past each other, frowning at the women as if their very presence was an insult.

They found a bench in the vestibule, opposite a door marked East India Company, and sank onto it with relief. Toby and Billy fidgeted, and tried to snatch each other's caps. Lucy held Hal on her lap, with her back to the other two boys, though Bess had told her expressly to mind them.

She turned to Toby. 'When I go in, look after Hal and Billy, and don't move,' she said, 'or there'll be no dinner.' It was risky leaving the boys there all alone; heaven knew what they might get up to. But she couldn't bring them in to Pepys's office with her, could she?

'Yes, Aunt Bess,' Toby said, eyes wide at all the bustle.

When Pepys eventually came, they nearly missed him, as he came shooting past from a side door, with his boy hopping to keep up, and his cloak flapping drips of wet over the marble floor.

'Mr Pepys!' Bess tottered after him, unsteady on her pattens.

He turned at the female voice in this house of men, and his face broke into a smile.

'Begging your pardon, sir, but I wonder if I might have a word…'

'Splendid! Mrs Bagwell, isn't it? How can I please you? Come upstairs and we can talk there…' His words drifted out of earshot as he beckoned her up the stairs with a crooked finger. He obviously expected her to follow.

'Lucy!' she called as she hurried in his wake.

Lucy leapt up, pressed Hal down onto the bench next to Toby, and trotted after her.

Up the curving stair and along the corridor. Pepys pushed open a door and held it wide for her to enter. She hitched her skirts, hoping they did not show the damp and went inside. He shut the door firmly behind him.

'My maid Lucy…' she began.

'She can wait outside,' Pepys said, with a wave of his hand.

Bess did not have the temerity to object. She followed him through another door into a small closet-like room, darkly panelled, and smelling of tobacco and the dry odour of old books. The walls were lined with shelves upon which rows of heavy ledgers were stacked in teetering piles.

His boy was already there, preparing ink and quills, and heating scarlet sealing wax over a spitting candle flame. Pepys ignored the boy and indicated the only cushioned chair, which happened to be behind his desk. It felt disconcerting to be there, facing the door, in a strange reversal, as if she were interviewing him, for some sort of servant's position. She glanced down, embarrassed, only to catch sight of her dirty pattens which had oozed mud onto the glossy floorboards.

Pepys perched on a high stool opposite her, and smiled, his eyes glittering with good humour. 'A mighty fine way to start the day, good wine and good company. Except, of course, I lack the wine.'

'Shall I fetch some, sir?' the boy asked.

'No! Get along with you! It was a jest, that's all. But go and see if Hewer's got any errands for you. Hurry up. Now Mrs Bagwell, it's good of you to call,' he said. 'I meant to write to you to thank you for your hospitality that time in Deptford, but as you can see, I seem to be drowning in correspondence these days.' He gestured to an overfull basket of letters on his desk. 'Tell me, how is your husband... William is it? How is he doing on the *Mercy*?'

'Well enough. He's on his second tour. I heard from him by letter a few weeks after he first embarked, but nothing for the last month. The *Mercy*'s been requisitioned by the Navy for quarantine duty, to accompany English ships back to Amsterdam or neutral waters, the ones that have no papers. He says the pestilence in the Low Countries cannot be imagined. He hears every day of more men lost to it. The whole city of Amsterdam is in mourning. I worry every day that he's sailing into those waters.'

'I'm sure he is at no risk, my dear, it's carried on the miasma of hot air, not water.'

A knock on the door, and a tall drooping clerk, with limp fair hair, brought in another basket of correspondence.

'What? More?' Pepys made a gesture of good-humoured frustration at Bess, as if to say, *see what I have to deal with*. 'Go through it, would you, Hewer? Anything from his Majesty, with a royal seal, set that to the side, and anything from the Earl of Sandwich – oh, and anything with handwriting like a wandering spider – that'll be from my father, about my brother Robert and what to do about his disastrous affairs—'

'Very good, sir.' Hewer backed out with a bow.

Pepys turned back to Bess. 'Now, my dear, you were saying, your husband—'

She stood up, ready with her prepared speech. 'To speak plain, sir, as I said, the last letter I had from him was in January and no payment had come to him then for the previous voyage, and by consequence, none to me. He's on his second tour now, and I have care of his cousin's children—'

'The boys that I met? Fine-looking lads.'

She steeled herself to persist. 'Yes, sir, they are, it's just that... well, I wondered why his pay was so late coming.' She decided to be frank. 'I can't manage, not without his pay.'

'Cash flow difficulties, is it? Well I'm sure I could arrange a loan—'

'Oh no, Mr Pepys!' Not another loan, merciful heavens. 'I'm not here to beg favours. I thought that as the *Mercy* was requisitioned by the Navy, you would be able to... to *remind* the person in charge of payment—'

'Ah. To remind them. I see.'

He was smiling. She didn't see why he found it amusing. It was clear he didn't grasp the seriousness of what she was saying.

'I meant no offence, sir. I'm simply asking that monies be paid where they're due.'

'Do sit down – sit down, my dear madam, no need to worry. I'll ask the compting department to look into it. I'll admit there have been some delays of late, the remit from the Treasury ...' He waved his arms in a vague expression of apology, then took hold of one of her hands in his.

Another knock at the door.

Pepys let go, and leapt up to open it a crack. 'What is it now?' he snapped.

There were muffled whispers, as Pepys argued with his clerk. Finally she made out the words, 'Stave him off a while ... Just a few more minutes.'

Pepys came back in the room looking harassed. 'I'll give you my own purse,' he assured her. 'It wouldn't do for you to lack any necessities.'

'No, I beg you—'

She'd hoped Pepys would say the lack of payment was a mistake, and take her to the paymaster there and then. But she should have realised he was too great a man to have direct contact with the lowly clerks in charge of sailors' pay.

An undignified tussle ensued where he tried to force a pouch of coins into her hand, but she kept her hands fisted behind her back. He was teasing, almost embracing her in a bear hug when the door swung open again, and Pepys leapt backwards.

'He won't wait, sir.' Hewer cast long-suffering eyes to a speck of dust on the wall.

'Get out,' Mr Pepys hissed, pushing him back out and closing the door again. 'I'm afraid business calls.' He smiled sadly, shaking his head.

'I beg your pardon for interrupting. It was most good of you to see me without an appointment.'

'The pleasure is all mine.' He reached out a chubby finger and stroked her gently under the chin. 'Perhaps you will call in again... I'm most anxious to know how you fare.'

An involuntary shiver snaked up her spine. So transfixed was she by this crossing of the invisible boundary between them, all she could do was swallow.

'Mr Pepys...' she said hesitantly.

'Come again in a few weeks,' he said hoarsely. 'So I'll know if the problem has been solved.'

He grasped her by the hand again and pressed his lips there. They were warm and moist as a sponge.

A sharp knock.

Pepys leapt to the door, as two men in outdoor cloaks jostled to get in.

'Gentlemen, have a care,' he cried, 'Mrs Bagwell is just leaving us.'

***

Bess hurried away from Seething Lane as if drunk, with Lucy and the boys in her wake. Pepys was certainly pressing his affections on her, though it was something she could scarcely dare countenance. At Flaggon Row she'd thought maybe she'd imagined it, but now she was sure. Fending off Bastable was one thing, but a man of Pepys's stature, quite another. Her mind wrestled with the implications. When she'd married Will she had thought it would be simple; he'd get work as a master carpenter in the yards, and she'd have his children and be happy as a lark.

But neither had happened. Living in Ratcliff had made her used to thinking of rich men as prey, but now it seemed she was the one being hunted.

Pepys had tried to push a purse on her, and fool that she was, she'd refused it. Had she lost all reason? But by instinct, she knew taking payment would mean a debt. And a debt of the worst sort – one that wasn't a clear transaction. But still, he had been willing to part with his money on a word from her.

'Did you see Mr Pip?' Toby asked, running to catch up with her.

'Pepys, yes.' She was distracted. To have a patron like Pepys was good for Will, but she wasn't at all sure it would be good for her. To cultivate Mr Pepys's interest in Will's welfare could not be done, it seemed, at least not without the risk of fanning Mr Pepys's fire.

When they got to the public stairs to the ferry, she handed over the last coins in her purse. All across the water, she thought what to do. Time had run out. Bastable would want his money. She'd have to pawn something.

The noon bells clanged out from all over London. With a sudden realisation she remembered it was Wednesday. Half-day. The pawnbroker would shut at one o'clock. If she had to go home, she'd be too late.

She craned her neck, as the ferry inched towards the shore, willing the waterman to row faster. As soon as it touched the bank, she leapt out. 'Lucy, take the boys home. I promised Bastable his dues today, but he's a wily dog, so keep the door locked and the shutters closed until I get back.'

'But, mistress, what about cleaning the steps—'

'They'll have to stay dirty for once. I've got to go, there's no time for arguing.'

If she ran, she might just make it in time.

Chapter 18

Bess raced along the riverside path dodging past the stevedores from the yards heading for the taverns, and the muffled-up women puffing back from the shops with their laden baskets.

She burst in through the pawnbroker's door, blinking as her eyes grew accustomed to the cave-like interior. Loans such as these were illegal, but everyone turned a blind eye to that. She ducked to avoid catching her hair in the collection of assorted parasols and walking canes dangling like stalactites from the beam above.

Pritchard the pawnbroker was on his way to the door, key in hand. He was swathed in a woollen scarf, with a knitted cap pulled down over his bald pate. 'We're closed,' he said.

'It's urgent,' she said. 'Please, it won't take long.'

'What have you got?'

Bess propped one elbow on the counter, removed her gloves, and tugged at her wedding ring. With one last twist it slid over her knuckle and she placed it carefully, significantly, on the counter. Mr Pritchard pressed his palm down over it, as if he expected her to change her mind and drag it back. His eyes glanced down at her hands, registering something like pity.

Bess forced a smile onto her face. She'd have to harden herself, if she was to get enough for Bastable.

'You sure you want to pledge it?'

She pushed back her shoulders. 'My husband's pay's been held up, that's all. I'll be back for it soon enough.'

'Won't be worth much, for all it will hurt you to part with it,' Pritchard said, rolling it to and fro in his palm. 'No, can't give you much.'

Bess was ready for this, it was what pawnbrokers always said whenever anyone brought anything in, and she recognised it as the usual pattern of bargaining. She smiled her prettiest smile and prepared to charm him. She opened her mouth but he cut her off.

'Wedding bands are common,' he said, going round behind the counter, 'and people don't like to buy them second-hand. Bad luck, see.'

'It's gold, though, Mr Pritchard, not brass. And look at that chased design around the centre.'

Pritchard squinted at her as he jammed in his eyeglass. 'We'll see about that,' he said. 'No good soft-talking me, though. You wouldn't be here if you didn't need the money.'

'My Will's never been niggardly. Feel the weight, it's heavy. Probably cost him a half year's wages. More, even.' Bess leant a bit nearer and flashed her eyes at him, tried a bit of blether. 'You wouldn't begrudge us a little celebration would you? It's his birthday. I was going to ask my maid Lucy to make him something special; not every day a man gets to be thirty, now is it?'

'Maid is it now? You're not so rich you don't need to be in here though, eh? Stop your chatter then, woman, and let me have a good look at it.'

It hurt to be back in a place like this. It made her heart beat fast under her stays. She sucked in the fusty air that smelled of polished metal and second-hand shoes, and blew a strand of hair from her forehead. Unable to be still, and anxious for it to be over, she tapped the counter as she waited.

Pritchard took a bubble of glass from a drawer and peered through it, turning the ring over and over. She already felt naked without it.

'It's nothing special,' Pritchard said. The words pierced her.

'The scrolled design on the outside is worn. And I can't do much with this engraving. What's it say? Not your names, is it?' He pointed with his fingernail at the scratched letters running around the inside of the ring.

She didn't want to tell a stranger what the words said, the words of love that Will had chiselled there himself. *'Veritas, Fide et Amore.'*

Truth, fidelity and love. She watched Pritchard decipher the inscription. He looked up and caught her eye, gave a derisive laugh.

Bess shook her dark curls, as if to shake off his opinion, and pulled back her shoulders. 'I'll buy it back,' she said, 'don't you worry, as soon as my Will gets paid.'

'Aye, well it's only worth the weight of the gold. I'll go fetch my scales.'

Mr Pritchard pushed through a curtain at the back of the shop, and as soon as he'd gone Bess slumped. Other people's dingy cast-off belongings crowded in; the smell of dust, sweat and poverty. By the door was a rack of worn clogs. Times were bad if people were pawning these, Bess thought. She'd be mortified if she had to go barefoot again like a beggar.

She turned her attention back to the counter, her eye drawn by a wooden cabinet. Will would love that. It oozed craftsmanship, with the rollback top cleverly constructed from slats of wood. He'd made a similar one himself, just after they were wed.

Bess rolled back the slatted cover. Such a sweet mechanism, so nicely made. She slid it back and forth and glanced inside. She paused with it half-open. The cabinet was full of rings like hers, all sitting on a pad of faded, balding velvet.

It was like looking at a row of marriages; all of them poor, all of them losing the last of what had joined them together. She shut it hard as if it burned her fingers.

'Five shilling,' said Mr Pritchard, re-appearing from behind the curtain, 'that's all I can give you.'

Not enough to pay the rent and have any over. Not enough for Lucy's wages. Bess stiffened and held out her hand.

'But it's worth an angel at least!'

'Six shilling.'

'Then I'll take it home again,' she said.

Mr Pritchard shook his head. 'I guess your husband won't be getting his birthday dinner after all. But I intend to have mine, so if you don't mind ...' He held up the key.

Bess hesitated. Pritchard was right. She thought of Will, all those miles away on the dark, thrashing ocean, and how it would feel to have no familiar home to come back to. It was only a ring after all. And one good thing – with all the others in that cabinet, it may not sell straightaway.

'Add an extra sixpence then,' she said, 'and it's a deal. Go on, be a dear, Mr Pritchard. Call it a birthday gift.'

A thin smile appeared on his face. 'You'll run me out of business.' He wagged a scolding finger at her. 'And, if you don't mind some advice, you might be wise to purchase one of these.' From under the counter he brought out a string, threaded with twenty or so rough brass rings. 'Saves questions, see. I can let you have one for thru'pence.'

Thru'pence! The wily dog. But she could see he was right.

'Will you take these for it?' She pointed to her gloves.

He nodded and counted out the money for the ring into her hand. Unlike Pepys's purse, this was a loan she understood, where the agreement was clear on both sides.

The door opened behind her, letting in a draught of freezing air.

'We're closed,' Pritchard bellowed.

Mrs Fenwick ignored him and bustled in, muffled up to the

ears in fur.

Hastily, Bess reached out her hand for the brass ring that Pritchard held out to her and slipped it on.

'Mrs Bagwell, well I never,' Mrs Fenwick said, shutting the door on Maudie as she was about to enter. A wooden collecting box dangled from Mrs Fenwick's arm.

Bess folded her arms, pushing her brass-ringed hand out of sight.

Mrs Fenwick's broad nostrils flared as if she could smell the money changing hands. 'Thought it was you when I looked through the window, so I just popped in for a word or two. You've been avoiding me, I fear.'

'No, not at all. I've just been rather busy.'

'We're closed, madam.' Pritchard tried again.

'Your maid never seems to answer the door,' Mrs Fenwick said.

'I'm minding my nephews, you see. Sometimes we don't hear the knock.' Bess was aware of Pritchard hovering by the door with the key; all ears.

Mrs Fenwick put a gloved hand on her arm. '*So* nice to meet your mother.'

Bess shifted her gaze away in embarrassment.

'But I need your collection box. I didn't take it the other week. And we missed you at our meeting. We were expecting you, and you didn't come.'

Bess hadn't dared go with an empty box.

Mrs Fenwick continued, 'The new school is nearly ready now.'

'Is it? Already?' Bess said. 'That's good news.'

'But we were counting on your husband for our benches.'

'I'm sorry, Mrs Fenwick, but William's still away at sea.'

'Oh dear. How inconvenient. I think I'd better ask someone else. It's been six months or more since he said he'd do it.'

'No, I'm sure there's no need for that. I know he started them, and as soon as he's back, they'll be finished.'

'Can we expect you this week at our little meeting?'

'I'll try.' Bess forced a cheerful expression.

'You haven't abandoned us for your mother's mission work?'

A big sigh from Pritchard.

Bess reddened. 'Such a winter, we've had. I hear you were poorly.'

Mrs Fenwick took the bait. 'Do you know, the physician quite despaired of me? Said he's never heard such a rattle in anyone's chest, and the cough! I thought it would never end. My physician said—'

'So nice to see you, Mrs Fenwick, but Mr Pritchard here is waiting to shut up shop, and I've an appointment in town. I'll talk to William about your benches, and give our best regards to your husband.' And Bess made good her escape and plunged into the street.

Once outside she inhaled, filling her lungs with fresh air, grateful for the scouring cold after the dust and gloom of the shop.

Through the window she saw Mrs Fenwick hold her box out to Pritchard. Trust her luck, she thought, that Mrs Fenwick should come in after her. Once word got round that you were going down in the world, you just went down the quicker.

Thank God Will wasn't here to see that brass ring. She must buy the real one back as soon as she could. And well before Will's next shore leave.

She stood a moment turning the unfamiliar ring on her finger, quashing the disturbing feelings of guilt that were swirling in her chest.

***

That evening Bastable came to the door and it was with great satisfaction that she could hand over the loan money.

'Told you I'd get it,' she said.

'Shame,' he said. 'Sure you don't want to keep it? Buy yourself a nice trinket? I could come in, and we could settle it that way—'

'Go to hell.'

'No call to be rude.' Bastable pocketed the money and she stood over him to check he wrote it correctly in the book. 'See you next month,' he said. 'And by the way, the loan fee might increase. Kite doesn't like awkward customers.'

She shut the door in his face.

***

The next day she went in to Hutchinson's to see if there was any chance of extra work. After the bitter chill of the air, Hutchinson's was warm, the windows grey with steam, but she managed to persuade Mr Hutchinson to give her a small parcel of gloves to sew. It might pay Lucy's wages. Once you lost your servant everyone knew you were sinking, and the only alternative was to take in lodgers. But she didn't like to bring anyone into the house without Will's say-so, and it would be a sign of their ailing fortunes. No, she'd keep their troubles behind closed doors. After all, she had her pride.

When she came out of Hutchinson's, her ears tingled. She tucked the parcel of gloves under her arm, and drew her collar up around her neck. A shadow; a darkening of the light.

'Bessie!' The hand on her shoulder made her almost leap out of her shoes. She turned to see who was behind her.

Her mother's wrinkled face peered out from under her black hat. Bess shook her head with impatience. 'Were you following me again?'

'No. I was just taking this to the clothes stall on Cheapside market.' Her mother held out an embroidered summer shawl.

'Look. From a woman who died in childbirth. One of the relatives gave me it. They were grateful for how I laid her out. But the silk's too thin for this cold weather – flimsy thing. Thought I could get a few shillings whilst I wait for summer.' She took Bessie by the arm as if to hug her. 'It's good to see you, Bessie. Let bygones be bygones, eh?'

Bess stepped away but not in time to avoid her mother's cold dry skin brushing hers. She did not smell any drink on her breath this time, but the thought of her mother's closeness to all those dead bodies repelled her. Her mother was greying now, and there were wrinkles round her lips. It took her aback. She was old. She'd never realised it before.

'You well?' her mother asked.

Bess squirmed under her penetrating gaze. 'Managing,' she said. Her mother could always see through her. 'How's it going ... what you do?' She couldn't bring herself to say the word 'searcher'. It stank of death and plague.

'Same as always. People die, and that's the fact of it. It's better than what I did before, you know that. Better than the doxy shop. And I never go near the gin house these days. I thought you'd be in the family way by now, seeing as you're settled.'

'Will's gone to sea,' she blurted, 'so the prospects of it are slim. And I'm looking after Jack's children.' Her bitterness was a surprise even to herself, but her mother saw it and frowned.

'Come on. Let's take a walk in the New Spring Gardens and you can tell me. I've time to spare.' She took Bess's arm, and for once, Bess let her. They walked in through the big iron gates, past the circular shrubbery with the fountain, now frozen and motionless, and into one of the close walks. There were few other people about, the weather being so cold. Above their heads, the trees bristled black and bare-branched.

'Best keep walking, or we'll freeze,' Agatha said.

Bess was thinking of Mr Pepys, of how he'd touched her under the chin, his eyes asking the question she didn't want to answer. She turned to look at Agatha, 'So it's all over now, is it, you don't see them at the doxy shop?'

'I'm through with all that. Though it put bread on the table. Searching is better.'

'It's not respectable, though, is it?'

'Work's work. Being a whore was work. Whoever says it's not, has never tried it. And the shame was in other folk's eyes, not what I felt for myself. Same with this – people might think it's something to be ashamed of, but not me. I feel proud. I can walk tall, look anyone in the eye.'

'But all those dead bodies—'

'My Joseph reckoned laying out the dead's a holy calling. I don't know about that, but I do know that once you see death every day you start to understand life. Joseph said I'd to hearken to the will of God. Though it seems mighty strange God would've chosen an old wreck like me to do his bidding. He must be hard up for choice, is all I can say.'

'Will and I don't hold with all these sects. What's wrong with the plain old Church of England?'

'Everything, Joseph said. Too much authority and not enough charity. And too hard on sinners. You should try the Congregationalists. Come to our meetings.'

'They're charlatans, Mother, everyone says so.'

Her mother's face tightened, but she said nothing.

Just then a pair of gentlemen in riding boots and flat-topped beaver hats strolled by, followed by two boy servants walking stiffly behind in their silver-braided livery. Bess and her mother stood aside as was the custom of the poor, to let them pass.

Bess watched them go past, the two serving boys stepping like soldiers. 'Did you ever have a fancy-man that was a rich man,

Ma?'

'In my time, yes. When I was younger.'

'Was it… I mean… what was it like?'

Her mother gave her a sharp look. 'They've the same down below as everyone else. What do you think? Everyone's got the same body under their clothes. It's what's in their heads that makes the difference, whether they treat you like dirt off their shoe or whether they treat you like a lady. What's this about?'

She shivered, folded her arms. She did not dare mention Mr Pepys. They walked on in silence a moment, the stillness only broken by the distant rattle of wheels. Finally Bess stopped. They'd reached the corner and needed to retrace their steps.

'Would you do a favour for me, Ma?'

'Depends. Seems the only time you'll talk to me is when you want something.'

'That's not true. It's just…' She sighed. 'I don't mean to be so… so short-tempered.'

They walked in silence a moment. 'What is it? What's this thing you want me to do?'

'Would you look to Jack's children for a few hours of a night? I need to get my sewing done, and Will's cousin Jack, well, he likes to keep me talking.'

'Is that all?'

'If you're there, you can talk with him whilst I do my piece work. I've got work for Hutchinson's, and money's a bit tight.' She explained about Will's pay, but not about going to see Pepys.

'Will you let me over the doorstep?'

'It's hard, Ma. I don't want to remember… I mean—'

'I was jesting, love. I know you don't want to go back there. We've both memories we'd rather forget. What time did you have in mind?'

'Dusk, about lighting-up time. You could come back with me

now, meet Jack's boys, see what you think.'

Agatha paused. For a moment Bess thought she was going to refuse, but then she said, 'I'll come. Times must be hard if you need to pawn your wedding band.'

'I didn't—'

'That brass one doesn't fool me. Too loose. You're holding it on. Besides, I've worn a few like that myself. But it never bodes well. You'll need to get it back soon as you can. Men don't like it, see. To them it's your shackle, and once you've lost it, they think you could be up to anything.'

***

'Bess?' Jack didn't bother to knock, but just came in as usual, with Fletcher following behind.

He stopped dead. There was an older woman sitting at the kitchen table, with what looked like a Bible opened before her, and his three boys sat round her, unnaturally quiet, drawing with sticks of lead on an old news sheet.

'Pa!' Hal was already up and drawing him towards the table.

He shook him off. 'Where's Bess?' he asked.

'You must be William's cousin. Jack, is it? I'm Mrs Prescott, her mother. She said, would I hand them over. She's in the back bedchamber, doing her piece work.' She stood, as if he might offer a greeting.

He ignored her. 'Bess?' he shouted through the door to the bedchamber, but it remained shut. He masked his irritation. If she was in there, she should come out. It was only polite. He knocked.

Nothing. He pushed on the door, but it did not give. Locked, then.

'Maybe she's fallen asleep,' the woman said, in an overly helpful tone of voice. 'She works hard, my Bessie.'

Jack turned away, leant over Toby's shoulder and snapped the

Bible shut. He'd imagined sending Fletcher home with the boys, and a pleasant conversation with Bess in front of the fire, and now here was Bess's mother acting as chaperone.

Jack stared at her mother, at her lined face, at the shabby black bodice, something cast off from the old king's time. She looked like an old moulting crow. There was something about her – something he recognised in her long nose and dark eyes.

No. He couldn't remember.

'Leave that drawing now, boys,' Bess's mother said. 'Your father's waiting.' She turned to Jack, and looked him up and down; a slight air of disapproval in her features. 'She's that busy with her work and these children, I'm not surprised she needs her rest. And there's this week's money owing, so I hear.'

'I've got no small change today. I'll bring it tomorrow. Besides, they help her with the pinning, and they do it for nothing too.'

'It's not hard labour, that. You wouldn't want her to turn your children away, would you?'

Foul old baggage. Why did she have to interfere? 'But it's all money, isn't it? Money my lads are making. Come on, boys, let's get you home.'

Fletcher gave a wag of his head towards the door and the three boys rushed under his arm and outside.

Jack followed the boys down the outside steps, his mind racing. A vision had just come to him – the same woman, but dressed in a garish low-cut bodice in one of the stews across the river. Well Christ be hanged; this woman was Allin's wife, he'd swear it. Skinny bitch, she was, but looked older without the painted face. Allin used to own one of the bawdy houses before he invested his takings in ships, and his wife was the one who persuaded the girls into the whorehouse. He'd used the place himself, once or twice. Nice plump young girls, Allin had. When they were too old, the word was, he shipped them off as slaves to the plantations. White slaves were worth more.

Allin's wife didn't like the trade and tried to get Allin to stop, but she'd not a hope in hell. Allin always got his way. He threatened he'd put her and his daughter on the next ship unless she did his bidding. He was mighty sore when they disappeared. Took it personal. Since she'd gone, his bawdy house had lost popularity and closed down.

He could swear it was the same woman. It didn't fool him that this woman was dressed in sombre black.

Jack frowned as he watched the boys darting after Fletcher. But his mind was on the woman he'd just met. If she really was Allin's wife, then he'd hold that information close to his chest. Allin had moved into the shipping trade, and he was still a powerful man. You could never tell when such knowledge might come in useful.

***

Bess counted out her coppers and tokens. The money from her wedding band was gone, and there was just the pittance from her piece work. She sighed, wondering whether to keep Lucy on, or if they should eat pease porridge again. Though the children were only with her in the daytime, it seemed Jack never fed them in the evening, so the money she did have, had to feed four of them.

Every morning they were waiting shivering on her doorstep, filthy and stinking of snuff, and every evening at dusk they were clean and well-fed as she or her mother pressed the ferry money into their hands. She made them work, but having the nights free was the only way she'd get time to herself to finish the sewing she needed to do.

Once or twice she'd thought to keep the boys there and teach them needle skills. At least then they'd be more use. Though Toby and Billy resisted it as 'girl's work'.

'What do you do in the evenings?' she asked them.

'Pa goes out and we mind the house. Keep the door locked against thieves and that,' Toby said. 'There's all sorts in our house now. Pa says we'll soon move somewhere bigger.'

Billy tugged at her sleeve. 'Aunt Bess, we have to measure snuff—'

'With a big scoop! And twist it into paper. Then it goes in big boxes.' Hal stretched his arms out wide.

'You don't,' Billy said. 'I end up doing it on my own. Hal makes a mess, and *you're* always sneaking out.' He glared at Toby.

'Toby, you're too young to be out at night,' Bess said.

Toby just shrugged.

But it made her wonder. If Jack could afford to move somewhere bigger, then he could certainly afford to pay her more. Trouble was, with no man to back her, making him do it would be like pulling teeth.

***

A few days later she heard from Will. She hugged the letter to her chest, then kissed it, before dancing round the parlour. He'd be home at the end of March with a fair wind, and then, thank goodness, maybe things would return to normal. Jack's boys would go home, and once Will was paid, perhaps there'd even be a sum to put away in their money chest. Things would get better. They had to. This was just a temporary setback. Once the loan for the house was paid, they'd be established.

Chapter 19

The lower deck of the *Mercy* tilted and heaved.

'Come up, sir.' A pull on Will's sleeve.

'What is it?' Usually Will spent his time below deck, as assistant master carpenter he was responsible for supervising repairs and reconstruction; leaks in the body of the ship. Two planks needed a splice and pegging. But today something in Robin's face made him stop his peg-whittling to follow him aloft.

'There, sir.' His assistant joiner pointed. 'Is it fish?'

'Don't know, Robin.' Will stood on deck with the rest of the crew staring through the drizzle at the dark shapes on the water.

They had just rounded the bluff of Vlieland but dare not go much further into Dutch waters. Behind them was a Dutch vessel they were escorting back to Holland, and another English vessel, the fighter, the *Pulcinello,* bringing up the rear. The Dutch vessel was under English escort and was limping home, a cannon-hole in one side and their crew riddled with the pestilence.

Will was glad there was a good deal of clean sea air between him and them. It wasn't legal, what they were doing, and the Master knew it, but the alternative was to let the boat drift into English waters, and although escorting an enemy vessel was in contravention of orders, it was in the spirit of the law, if not the letter of it, and the English would thank them for sending the disease back where it came from.

Now there was this – some sort of problem in the waters ahead. Rocks? But there shouldn't be rocks here.

'What do you think it is?' asked the sailor next to him, peering through the misty air. 'Could be a shoal of something, I suppose.'

'Hasn't anyone got a "scope"?' Robin asked.

They squinted into the swell. From above them, the order, 'Ready about!'

'Small craft,' the shout came from the rigging, 'fishing smacks.'

'What the devil—?' The sailor stared as the *Mercy* ploughed onwards.

Up close, the water ahead was littered with vessels of all shapes and sizes – dark bulbous shapes moving on the water.

'God's truth! Are they mad?' the sailor said. 'They're right in our path! If they don't get out of the way we'll mow them down!'

'Lower the topsail!' came the cry.

Around him men scurried to reef the sails, and slow their progress.

Ahead, there was scarcely a yard of water without some sort of craft. Every sort of vessel was there, all bursting with people, with bundles and with livestock. Some seemed to be making slow progress in a direction away from the port, some just bobbed helplessly on the waves. Around the craft bumped an assortment of ownerless objects – hats, boxes, a dead chicken.

A row-boat ahead of them, only fit for the river, and oarless, drifted, the people crammed together so it resembled some multi-headed gorgon. A pig squealed, its scrabbling trotters held tight to stop it plunging into the sea. The boat was precarious, too low in the water, weighed down by trunks and bundles and too much humanity.

Two old men in flat-brimmed hats, miraculously still on their heads, steered a raft made of an old cart, by paddling it with their hands. Behind them huddled women and children, the women in mourning, their faces white and ghostly, their eyes wide with terror. What struck Will the most and sent a chill down his back, was that these people were silent.

'Down sail!' came the frantic cry, and suddenly they were drifting themselves, caught in the tide, surrounded by hundreds of makeshift boats. Boats made of planks and barrels, long flat canal barges. Will could only stare at the extraordinary sight. The Master of the ship was giving orders on the top deck to hoist sail again, but nobody near Will moved. They were all staring at this floating city.

Half of Amsterdam must be here, thought Will.

Just as he had this thought, on one of the larger fishing boats there was a sudden burst of commotion. From the boat came a piercing scream, then cries and flailing arms. A fight had broken out. The boat rocked, tilting back and forth. And then, without warning, the people pushed a woman into the sea. A woman in skirts that would drag her under.

Shouts and curses. Moments later someone threw what looked like a baby in the water, and a young boy. A man on board punched another man in the head before leaping overboard after his family.

He dived under the water and surfaced spluttering, his face contorted with grief. The fight was in earnest now, with more toppled overboard. It was as if they'd all lost their reason.

Will rushed along the rails, along with the other men to see what was happening. He elbowed his way into a gap between two other sailors and peered into the grey-green water below. Salt stung his eyes. They were a quarter mile out from land, and there was nowhere to swim to. Even if they could swim.

In the water, he saw the woman's head bob up for a gasp of air, then sink under the swell.

'Hebt genade!'

There was no mistaking the cry. The young man, his white shirt ballooning in the water, blood staining the side of his face, splashed desperately towards another boat, but it was already over-full and a man with a low-brimmed hat and ragged beard pushed an oar into his face. He jabbed so hard that Will heard the crack as the young man's head jerked backwards. Immediately he sank. Moments later he floated face-down in the water. Of the baby, there was no sign.

The sea was filled with the black dots of heads and the white thrash of arms. The other boats, instead of going towards them, started paddling away as fast as they could. Those still floundering in the water fixed their sights on the *Mercy* and called out with what breath they had left.

It was all confusion. Will could make no sense of it. All he could do was stare.

Right in front of him the woman was struggling to keep her boy's head above the water. He was about Toby's age from the look of him, his dark hair plastered to his head.

On the boat nearest to them a man cursed them, and threw his boot at them, and soon the rest in the boat followed. A clog smacked the boy in the cheek and his mother tried her best to shield him as she hauled him out of range.

Will couldn't believe what he was seeing. Anger rushed up through him like a red hot river.

'Throw ropes!' Will shouted, tugging a coil free of its moorings, and passing the end to Robin. But wet, it was too heavy for them to manhandle on their own.

'No.' A midshipman wrenched the rope from his hands. 'Leave it. Word is, they've the pestilence, we can't risk it.'

So that was it. The fact took a moment to sink in, before he shouted, 'We can't leave them to drown! Not women and children.'

'They're Dutch. Their own people won't help them.' He shrugged. 'Why should we? God's bringing his vengeance on them. Sinners. Amsterdam's full of heathens and sinners.'

'And if they have the plague, they'll die anyway,' Robin said, matter-of-factly.

Will leaned over the rail. The woman and her boy were moving less in the water now, overcome by the icy suck of the sea and the dawning realisation that no-one would help them.

On the original boat, the fight was over. Folk huddled together, dark figures, stiff as statues; the boat drifting like an island.

Will ran to where a rope ladder was cleated to the deck. There was no sign of the anchor watchman, so he released the catch and heaved it over the side. It hit the water with a splash.

The woman with the young boy saw it. She was dark-haired, like Bess, and still afloat, on her back, dragging her son with her, inch by inch towards them. She fixed her gaze on the ladder, but she was tiring and her arms were barely moving.

'Come on!' yelled Will.

At the same time, the ship lurched into motion, and a bow-wave swamped over her. She tried to call something, but then her face dipped silently below.

'No,' groaned Will, gripping the rail.

He could see a shadow, just a murky smudge beneath the water, and her floating dark hair, spread out like on a pillow. And then she was gone. She did not rise again.

The boy frantically searched the surface for his mother, oblivious to the rope ladder dangling behind him.

'Take the rope!' Will cried, willing him to see it.

But the boy was swimming in circles now, his mouth opening and closing in a call Will could not hear. Another wave made the boy swallow water and then emerge a moment later gasping for air.

'The rope!' Will shouted.

But around him the sailors were making ready, and he and Robin were alone at the rails. Above them the sails unfurled with

~153~

a crack of canvas.

Will heard the noise and his heart skipped a beat. At the same moment, the boy saw the rope ladder and reached for it; his hand, small and white, struggling to get a grip on the floating rung. His head and neck were out of the water. His neck was disfigured by a red chancre, big as a fist.

The sails billowed into the wind and the ship lurched away. Will was helpless to do anything. The ladder whipped out of reach, and the rung ripped from the boy's slippery hand.

Will gripped the freezing rail as the ship ploughed through the flotsam of people and debris as if they were icebergs, not boats with people at all. Screams and the crack of wood. He ran to the back of the ship.

The boy's head disappeared under the foaming wake.

'Come on!' he cried. But he knew it was no use. The further away they went, the bigger the expanse of ocean. He wiped the screen of drizzle from his eyes. Soon he could see nothing but a grey haze.

He thought of Bess and the boys, safe at home, and the thought of them made him dig his fingernails into his palms.

***

That night, he and Robin talked low and quiet in their hammocks. They'd left the Dutch vessel they'd been escorting. Left it there, surrounded by the floating town, and now both English ships were glad to be away back towards England and the safety of London.

'What was the Dutch vessel carrying?' Will asked.

'Herring, cats' skins, anchovies. The herrings were starting to stink already.' Robin's mood was sombre.

Will thought back over the last few days. When the Dutch trader had no papers, they had captured it easily. The men on board were all ailing or dead, and the rest had taken the tenders and left the plague ship to her fate. Those that had been on board came back gaunt and white with shock at what they'd seen.

Will knew that they could have brought the pestilence back with them. So now in the dim, flickering glow of the horn lanterns, the belly of this ship felt like the bowels of hell, as if they were waiting below for the Devil himself to make an appearance. Everything looked changed.

'It felt mighty odd just leaving the ship stranded there, and all those boats blocking their passage.'

Robin was silent a while, the creak of his hammock the only sound.

'They say a flock of strange birds was seen over the city, and that was the start of it,' Robin said, eventually. 'Black birds, big as eagles.'

'Probably crows. People believe anything. The bo'sun thinks God made tiny flying dragons and snakes and infected the air of Amsterdam. He says if you breathe the air there, you breathe them in, and then big purple swellings like snake-eggs grow and cover your body.'

'Sounds mighty strange,' Robin said, 'but who knows. I'd not take chances.'

'But watching children drown—'

'We were right to keep well away. Still, it must be desperate bad to make folk take to the sea like that.'

Will made a grunt of assent. 'It didn't feel right, what we did.' He meant, what they'd failed to do.

Robin's hammock stopped creaking and he turned his head to look at Will. 'Could be safer at sea, where the clean air is, and away from the stink of the city. And if it was me, and people were dying round me like that, just like them I'd want to leave.'

'Fear's a mighty strange thing. That they'd rather take their chances on the sea than in the city with the pestilence.'

'Ask me, the city's gone crazy. Tainted in the wits. Perhaps bo'sun's right and it's a punishment.'

'I can't get over the fact we just left them to drown. And us on a ship called the *Mercy*. Did you see that boy?'

Robin didn't answer, but Will knew he'd heard him.

When Will slept, he dreamt he was that small boy thrashing in circles, calling for his mother.

Chapter 20

Bess was counting the coins that Hutchinson's had just paid her for sewing gloves, when Toby burst through the door, breathless, cheeks pink with excitement, 'Aunt Bess! Nanny Prescott! The *Mercy*'s come in! Grandfather says he saw it coming up the Thames.'

'What?' Bess had no idea the *Mercy* had docked. March, Will had promised her and it was already the middle of April, and she'd almost given up hope. She handed the skillet she was drying to Lucy, and looked to her mother.

'Where?' Agatha asked. 'Are you sure?'

'Grandfather knows all the ships.'

Bess wiped her hands hurriedly on her skirts, shoved all the coins into the money jar, and clutching it to her bosom, ran out of the door and down the steps. She'd thought to have more warning.

'Bess!' her mother shouted, but Bess didn't stop.

In a panic, she burst through Pritchard's door. She emptied the jar onto the table with a clatter.

Pritchard shook his head impatiently.

'I know it's not enough,' she said, panting, 'but please, I—'

'You're too late,' he said. 'If it's about that ring, I sold it just this morning. A young sailor came in, looking for a gift for his sweetheart.'

The shock was a physical pain like a hammer blow.

'No.' She couldn't believe it. 'But you said it wouldn't sell, you said—'

'I'd forgotten it, but he picked it out of the others. Right taken with that inscription he was.'

She felt it like a kick in the ribs. She started to scrape the money back into the jar.

'I can sell you another,' he said.

'I wanted that one,' she said. Tears pricked her eyes, but she blinked them back and took herself out of the shop so that Pritchard wouldn't see how much it hurt. Another girl would be wearing her ring. The words that Will had chased so beautifully, just for her, would be wound around another girl's finger.

She'd been wearing the brass one all this time, which didn't matter when Will wasn't there to see it. But he'd fashioned the gold himself and it had taken days of labour. Panic wouldn't help. Whatever would he say? She'd have to keep her hands out of his view and pray he wouldn't notice.

***

It was mid-afternoon by the time a hired cart rumbled up Flaggon Row and came to a halt outside their door. Toby rushed upstairs to fetch Bess, and everyone hastened out to greet it. Will already had Billy and Hal on his lap, and was grinning wildly. The sight of his smile removed Bess's apprehension. He was glad to be home.

He stood the two boys down when he saw her, and leapt down to embrace her. He stumbled and almost fell into her.

She laughed. 'Careful,' she said.

'Sorry, not got my land-legs back yet,' he said.

He looked strange and familiar all at the same time. She could not stop her smile which meant she could not speak. She reached out to hold him – how good to feel his firm-muscled back under his doublet, his bristled chin against her cheek.

He pushed her away to arm's length. 'You look different.'

'No, it's you. You look thinner. Older.'

'Did you get my letters?'

'Yes. I read them over and over. Nearly wore them out. Mine?'

'Some. In batches when we got to port. The last was in February. The one about Hal cutting himself on the shears.'

'It was Toby's fault,' Billy said.

'Never mind that now,' Bess chided. 'Help Lucy take Uncle Will's bag upstairs.'

Billy and Toby grabbed one handle, and Lucy the other, and strained to lift it. The bag was heavy with seawater and stained with salt. Will and the carter meanwhile heaved down his carpenter's box.

'Fetch the workshop key, would you, love?'

As she reached the key from the hook, she saw the brass ring on her finger, and it jolted her. She must try to keep her hand out of sight, until she could find a way to explain. A few minutes later and the workshop stood open, and Will and the carter lugged Will's box of tools inside. She watched Will tip him, and then help the carter turn the horse. They went inside, and Will sat unsteadily on one of the stools near the bench.

'I missed the smell of this place,' he said. His voice was shaky, she could have sworn it was full of unshed tears.

'Oh, Will,' she said, and went to put her hands around his waist from behind. 'I missed you too.'

'Needs cleaning though. Just look at those cobwebs.'

'Sorry, there wasn't much time for that, what with the boys—'

'Uncle Will—' Toby appeared at the door.

'Not now, Toby,' Bess said.

'Aye. Give us a few minutes peace, would you,' Will said, gruffly. 'Why don't you take the others down to the harbour? See if you can find the pie man.' Will fished in his pocket and brought out a copper.

'Whoop!' Toby was off like a whippet, and Bess laughed at the excited squeals coming from the other two outside.

'Give me a kiss, wife,' he said, throwing off his hat, 'I long for some civil company.' His lips lowered to hers, but almost immediately he drew away.

'What is it?'

'Nothing. Just the jitters. I've been at sea so long, and I can't quite believe I'm back. I think part of me's still stuck on that ship.' She reached to put an arm around his neck

'What's that you're wearing?'

She pulled away, knowing instantly what he meant.

He had hold of her hand now and was staring down at it. 'That's not my ring.'

'I know, I lost it. I lost weight and then I was out with the boys and...' She floundered. 'I must have lost it on the shore somewhere.'

'Have you been back? Searched everywhere?'

'High and low. No sign of it. So I had to have something. My mother gave me a brass one. I keep hoping I'll find it one day.'

She tried to move away, but he gripped her tight. 'But it was real gold, melted down from my mother's. And I engraved it specially.'

His frowning face pierced her with guilt.

'Have you posted a lost notice?'

'No, not yet—'

'Someone might have picked it up. Why didn't you write and tell me?'

'You'd enough worries on that ship, I thought—'

'You should have told me. It's valuable. You should have put out a notice.'

'I will,' she said, knowing she wouldn't.

Will let go of her arm and stood up, his face dark.

If she told him she pawned it because his pay hadn't come, it would sound like an accusation. And he'd be angry she had chosen to pawn that, instead of something else.

She tried to placate him. 'Come up into the house then, and I'll pour us some Malmsey wine. There's a drop left in that old bottle.'

'In a few moments. I just want to stay here a while, put out some tools.' He paused, glanced out of the door. 'And I'd hoped to be just the two of us.'

'Ma's been helping me with the boys, so's I can get my gloves made.'

'But you don't need her now, do you? Not now I'm home.' He evaded her when she reached for him. 'Get her to leave us in peace, would you?'

She pulled him to her, insistent, her hands around his waist. 'This is the end of it, is it Will? You're home now?'

'Go and pour that wine. There'll be time to talk later.'

***

When she'd gone, Will let out a long sigh. Bess was lying about the ring. Why? If she'd pawned it, why not just tell him? But then again, he daren't tell Bess he'd been offered another stint on the *Mercy*. He didn't want to sour his homecoming. And truth be told, the idea of it was something he didn't want to think of. This world and the world at sea were impossible to reconcile. One; a phlegmatic liquid world of salt and damp, where days blended and bled into one another. Here, a world earthy and dry, the hard weight and grain of obligations, of dates and coinage and responsibility. He ran his hand along the edge of the oak stool where he sat, and winced. His fingers were cracked and sore with salt-water.

He unpacked his tools. To see his chisels lined up on the bench cheered him. His hands still shook though, as if palsied. He didn't want to go back to sea. Especially not to the quarantine ship. The vision of the plague-ridden waters of Amsterdam still haunted him. No, he hoped that Jack's business would be doing well, and he'd be able to concentrate on more decorative work. Figureheads perhaps, or panelling for the new great houses he'd seen as they sailed up the Thames. There might even be work for him closer to home, fitting out ships' cabins in the King's Yard.

He stayed in the workshop until the six o'clock bell. By that time he'd swept the floor, and was feeling more stable on his feet, though the walls still swam if he turned too quick. Bess's mother had shouted goodbye to him through the door, and now he could hear footsteps above of Bess and Lucy and the boys, and the noise of the scraping of chair legs. He should go up. But it was the first time he'd been alone in months, and he felt the relief of it ease the tension in his shoulders, un-knot the tightness in his chest.

'Will?' Bess's tentative voice calling from aloft.

Reluctantly, he left the workshop, closed the door and locked it. When he got upstairs he found the table scrubbed, the wine flagon out, and the boys washed and sitting up ready for Jack to collect them.

'Jack's late again,' Bess said. 'What shall I do?'

'Is he?' Will sat down. It was so good to be still.

'Can we eat with you, Uncle Will?' Toby looked longingly at the bread.

A savoury smell of frying fish made Will's mouth water. He didn't want to wait for his meal. 'Yes, lad, I dare say. Sit down all of you. Bess, go and see if Lucy can make it stretch.' It felt good to be master of this ship, to have some control again.

Bess's lips tightened and her face turned expressionless. 'I'll go see how it's doing,' she said sharply, hurrying away to the kitchen. He admired her small waist and her full figure as she went. She'd put on a clean neckerchief and a clean coif, since he arrived, and she looked bonny as springtime.

When she returned, he could tell she was put out by the boys being at the table, but he couldn't deal with trouble – not today.

'Let us say grace,' he said. '*Sanctificet nobis victum qui cuncta creavit.*' Let He who created all things bless our food. Anything other than ship's biscuits was a blessing.

'Amen,' Bess said.

'Amen,' the boys mumbled after her, before three pairs of hands snatched for the bread.

He'd just pulled off his own hunk of bread, when the sound of heels rang on the outside stairs.

Bess threw up her hands. 'What did I tell you? That'll be him now.' She flung open the door, looking as if she was ready to give him a mouthful, but instead she stood back. A fine gentleman in a long, glossy periwig strode in.

Will stared as the boys immediately leapt up from their stools.

'Pa!' Billy cried.

It was only then that Will realised it was Jack. At first he was too taken aback to speak. This new Jack sported a fine embroidered waistcoat of blue damask, and with it, a figured velvet doublet, and a pair of wide Rhinegrave breeches. In his luxuriant dark periwig and lace cravat, he looked like a parody of King Charles himself.

'I heard you were back,' he said to Will, ignoring his sons and settling himself on a stool.

Will stared at Jack's red-heeled shoes with the silk-ribbon ties. What foolish footwear. They wavered before his eyes.

'Your father came and told me the *Mercy* had docked,' Jack continued, helping himself to bread, 'so I came myself instead of sending Fletcher.'

'Now Will's back, you can settle your dues, Jack Sutherland,' Bess said.

'What dues?' Jack said easily.

'Four weeks money it is now.' Bess gave him a meaningful look before glancing to Jack. 'I've fed them most nights too,

~163~

because you don't seem to think boys need feeding.'

Will frowned. 'Is that right, Jack?' He'd suddenly grasped what Bess was saying.

'Must've slipped my mind,' Jack said. 'But it's easily remedied.'

Bess simply turned and went to the kitchen.

A moment's pause whilst Will waited for the kitchen door to shut. 'Everything all right whilst I was away?' Will asked.

'With Bess you mean?'

'Yes. No callers, were there?'

'No sign of Pepys here,' Jack said.

Will exhaled.

'Though the boys said she'd been to see him once at his offices.'

'What for?' Will kept his tone light.

'Don't know. The boys had to wait in the hall, isn't that right, Toby?'

'What, Pa?'

'You waited in the hall while Auntie Bess went to see Mr Pepys.'

'Yes. We waited *ages.*'

'Probably something innocent enough,' Will said, his shoulders tensing.

'Like what?' Jack said.

He heard himself snap, 'I don't know! I'll ask her. And is she right, Jack? Do you owe us?' He had an urge to smack Jack in the teeth.

Jack threw up his hands in a shrug. 'I was busy. I just forgot. Business… you know. How was it on the *Mercy*?'

Will shook his head. The weight of the house seemed to press down on him. 'Bess says it's a month's money you owe us. Rumour on board ship is that the pay from the Navy will be delayed again, so we need every last penny.'

'Hell, don't look at me like that. You should be pleased I'm so busy. You've got a stake in the business too, don't forget.'

'Is there any payout yet to investors?'

'No. Too early. I'll bring the money for the boys tomorrow. Besides, Bess has had her use out of them for making gloves. She should be grateful.'

'But, Jack—'

'The boys will be with me from now on. I've work for them. We're expanding our exports and we've an urgent order to complete.'

'Aww. Packing snuff again, Pa?' Toby asked.

'Ugh.' Billy made a face. 'Makes me sneeze.'

'You'll do as you're told, or feel the back of my hand,' Jack said.

***

When Bess got to the kitchen it was hot with fishy smoke, and Lucy was flustered, trying to make scraps of herring stretch to feed them all, and when finally it was all on plates, she burst out, 'Mistress Bagwell, I need to tell you… I'm giving notice… when I first came I thought you'd be getting more staff, but it's too much for one girl…' She tailed off.

'Oh no, Lucy.' Bess's spirits sank. She should have seen this coming.

'Sorry, mistress, but I'm done. I'm run ragged. It's a big house, with all the hearths, and the laundry, and what with Mr Sutherland with all them little ones in tow, it's just too much. And there'll be dust from the shop now Mr Bagwell's home. I'll be going, end of the week.'

'But Lucy, how will I manage without you?'

Lucy dropped her gaze; pouted. 'I've got work with Mrs

Fenwick, on the Strond. She wants a kitchen-maid. Two shilling a week.'

'Mrs Fenwick. Oh.' She braced herself. 'The food's getting cold. Please take it through.'

'Yes, mistress.' Lucy grabbed the plates and ducked away through the door.

Bess followed and set the other plates on the table with a heavy heart. The few ragged bits of greasy herring, and flaccid pickled vegetables in brine looked sad and forlorn.

No servants. It was the first sign of sinking. And Lucy was going to Mrs Fenwick. Her business would be all over the servant's kitchen in a trice. Mrs Fenwick would find out all their secrets, and they would be a laughing stock.

She stood as the boys fell on the food like dogs, cramming it into their mouths. They did not even pick up the cutlery. Suddenly Bess could not bear it any more. Jack sitting there looking like a king, when she'd scraped and saved to feed his children. And now she was to be left with no help. She snatched her bag from the hook and dragged open the door.

'Where are you going?' Will's voice called after her, impatient, but she didn't stop, just ran down the stairs.

Chapter 21

When she returned it was almost four hours later, and Will was sitting on the outside stairs watching for her. He said nothing, merely opened the door for her to enter.

His silence was such that she felt it more cutting than his questions. He didn't ask her where she had been, nor did she tell him she had walked up and down past the Fenwicks's house, and past the Evelyns's house, the rich houses of the town, looking in through their candle-lit windows with her heart bitter and full of envy. 'I needed to clear my head,' was all she said.

'I know you don't like Jack, but there's no need to make it so abundantly obvious,' Will said. 'He's family, Bess. It's not much of a homecoming, this ... this bad feeling. I know he can be a bit awkward, but that's just his way.'

A bit awkward? 'He's here too much. He treats me...' how could she put it, '... like he owns me. I don't like it.'

'I asked him to keep an eye on you. Just to make sure you were all right.'

'He makes me uncomfortable. That's why I asked my mother to come and help me.'

'I thought you'd done with her?'

'I know. But it's different when you're away. I'm a woman on my own, and she's family. I can rely on her.'

'Well, that's how I feel about Jack. And at least he's still speaking to me.'

Bess sighed. She knew how much it hurt him that his father had rejected him.

After a pause, she sat down opposite him, and reached for his hand. 'I don't understand why your father keeps it up. He should apologise.'

'Him? Never. He's always in the right. He had our future all planned out, me and Jack. Working in the yard.'

'It's Jack who should be working in the yard – it might steady him a little,' Bess said.

'Can't see him in the sawpits, can you?' Will said. 'Not in that rig-out he was wearing today, at any rate.'

'You're worth ten of Jack. Don't know why your father puts up with him. Jack goes to the Old Oak to drink with him you know, after he's left here. Makes the boys sit outside in the dark. Makes my blood boil.'

'Yes, that sounds like Jack.'

'I don't know what your father sees in him. He seems to favour him more than you.' Bess realised what she'd said too late. Will's face immediately shut off.

'Let's not talk of my father,' Will said, and the subject was closed.

She watched him take up the key to the workshop and heard the click as he went out. Moments later she heard the rasp of the saw. Should she go after him? No. She didn't know what she could say.

When dusk fell and she went to fetch a taper from the bedchamber, her throat constricted at the sight of the bed where the boys used to sleep. Just a few discarded dirty underclothes remained. The house was forlorn. Lucy had packed her serving box, Jack and the boys had gone, and now there was just her and Will. Everything had changed in a day. Even Will. It wasn't just that he was thin – he looked deflated, as if he had been eaten away from the inside.

She'd thought he would take all the burden from her shoulders.

But now she sensed a shrinking in him; a shying away from responsibility. She'd need to tackle him about money, about insisting the Navy paymaster paid him. And he wouldn't want to hear it. Not now. Not after the bad feeling over her wedding ring.

Yet do it she must.

***

Just before curfew Will came back upstairs and Bess watched as he tackled the stack of unopened letters that had come whilst he was away. He sifted through them with a lacklustre air.

'Did you notice his suit?' Bess asked, still unable to get over Jack. 'It must've cost ten guineas or more.'

'I'll sort it out with him – the money I mean.' Will dragged a smaller pile of mail towards him.

She watched him open and discard the correspondence with growing frustration. His face paled by degrees until the last letter caught his attention and he read it twice before he groaned and pushed it aside.

'Anything about pay?' she asked. 'It's just that Bastable—'

'I'll deal with it in the morning.' He cut her off.

'If we don't pay Bastable this month we'll—'

'I said, I'll go and see them tomorrow.' He got up from the table. 'I think I'll turn in. I can't wait for a proper bed again.'

Bess watched him go. It wasn't supposed to be like this, his homecoming. She felt a gulf between them, an awkwardness that hadn't been there before. Give him time, she thought to herself.

But that night he tossed and turned until he finally got out of bed. She thought he was going to the closet, but when he didn't return she found him poring over the letters again.

'What is it?'

'It's my papers. I've only a few days' shore leave. I've to be back on another ship on Friday.'

The words hit her like a fist in the stomach. She clutched the table with both hands to steady herself. 'So soon?'

'The *Salvation*. The carpenter got another position so there's a vacancy.'

'Is it a better ship?' She did not tell him she had been to see Pepys again, to ask if Will could be promoted to another ship – one that wasn't sailing into plague-ridden waters. Pepys had kissed her hand, and complimented her in a teasing way, but she had impressed upon him what a good husband Will was, and how faithful, and he had seemed cowed by her declaration of such moral decency. He'd promised her a bigger ship for Will than the *Mercy*. 'Is it bigger then?' she asked.

'No. Same size,' Will said, 'but newer. I signed for it, but now this. A letter from the Navy office. There were rumours of this, but I never thought they'd dare. The pay's been held up again. We'll get paid after the next voyage.'

Bess felt as if the breath had been knocked out of her. 'They can't do that! What will I do with you gone, and no money from the Navy? And we've already lost Lucy.'

'Manage, like you always do. At least the boys will be out of your way. You can do more piece work.' He gestured at the basket of cut-out gloves by the door.

'How long this time?'

'Another three-month passage.'

A wave of despair. 'Please, Will, isn't there another way?'

'Not if we want to keep this house, no. We shouldn't have taken it on.'

Bess tensed, feeling his unspoken criticism. 'Things will even out, once you're paid.'

'It's not as simple as that. They're saying we didn't pay by the due date this month, so Kite's increased the amount.' He pinned her with a look of accusation, picked up another of the letters and shook it at her.

She took it from his hand and read it, painstakingly, for her reading was slow. When looked at in black and white, the loan figure had hardly decreased at all, and the monthly amount they'd to pay was much more. Was it her fault, because she'd refused Bastable's advances? Bess's stomach dropped. They couldn't lose the house. Where would they go? And if the loan was still outstanding and Kite reclaimed the house, then it would be debtor's prison for Will.

Old fears rushed up, threatening to overwhelm her. A vision of coach wheels rumbling past, splattering her with filth as she begged for alms on the pavement, the sight of her mother, red-eyed and bleary from drink, taking a leering man into her chamber. She thrust the letter back to him. 'Where this time?' She could hardly speak. 'Where are they sending you?'

'Same. The quarantine run.'

'It's safe, isn't it? I mean, you don't come into contact with anyone—'

'It's work. And we need the money.' Will turned his back on her. There was a bitterness in his voice, and something about the way he began to order the letters into neat piles bothered her.

'I don't like you going to the Low Countries. Jack says on Allin's ship they throw men overboard if they find tokens of pestilence on them.'

'Then Jack doesn't know what he's talking about.' Will busied himself folding and stacking the letters again.

Chapter 22

After work, Agatha hurried up Flaggon Row, pressing forward against the wind and limping a little because her hip ached. She carried a basket stuffed with cinnamon twists on her arm. She'd enjoyed minding Jack's boys for Bess. They called her Nanny Prescott, and she'd learnt that a few sweetmeats and a tale or two about gruesome deaths were enough to earn their affection. Nobody else seemed to have time for them, even Bess. And certainly not their father.

Agatha gave an involuntary sniff. A wastrel of a father Jack Sutherland'd turned out to be; always late, and never feeding them properly. Fortunately they had her, Nanny Prescott, to put them right. She loved the squirmy feel of Hal nestling on her knee, thumb stuck in his mouth, even though he was growing gangly and unruly like a proper boy, instead of an infant. And Toby, he'd soon be a man, with a sly look of Jack about him, but stubborn, like her Bessie. And scrawny Billy, always the one people forgot, but always the first to look in her bag for treats. She was looking forward to seeing them, and after a day with the dead, who said not a word, it would be a blessed relief to be bombarded with lively chatter.

She would ask Bess how William had fared at sea. He'd looked so thin and pale when she saw him yesterday, like a proper ghost.

At Bess's door, she gave a sharp rap, but anxious to be out of the weather, bustled straight in as usual.

Bess started and turned hurriedly from a letter she was reading. 'Ma,' she said, looking surprised to see her.

'Where's William?' Agatha asked. 'In the workshop already?'

'He wanted an early start.'

'The boys out?'

'No. They're with Jack. Helping him pack snuff by all accounts.'

'When will they be back?' Agatha asked as she dumped her bag and unbuttoned the frogging on her cloak.

'They won't be back.'

Agatha paused. Something in Bess's manner disturbed her. The basket of gloves was untouched by the door. 'What do you mean?'

'I'm not to mind them anymore. It's a relief really. It will give Will and me a chance to have a bit of time together. He's to go to sea again soon, so we won't need you, Ma.'

She couldn't make sense of the words. 'Not need me? Why? Are they not coming here at all?'

'Seems not. So we don't need any help.'

'But I brought cinnamon twists.'

'Sorry, Ma. They're not here.'

'But when will I get to see them?'

'I don't know. Jack didn't say. But you might as well go home. There's nothing for you to do here.'

Agatha bridled. 'So that's it, is it? I'm just dismissed, like a servant?'

'No, Ma. You know it's not like that.' Bess heaved the glove basket onto her hip. 'It's just I've all these to do, and no-one to help.'

'Pass me the pins then,' Agatha said, holding out a hand as she sat down.

'No, Ma. Will and I need time on our own, time to organise our lives without anyone else interfering.'

'Interfering? You didn't think I was interfering when you needed me to mind those boys night after night.'

'I'm grateful, Ma, of course I am, but—'

'But you've no use for me anymore.' She stood. 'I understand. I'm supposed to just disappear at your convenience.' She picked up her bags and clasped them to her chest. 'Never a thought for how I might be feeling, or those boys. It's always what suits you.'

'That's not true—'

'Yes it is. For months I had to follow you to even catch a glimpse of you. I wasn't good enough for you, though I raised you, kept you safe all those years from that devil Allin. And how did you repay me?'

'But, Ma, I was only—'

'Don't make excuses. You wouldn't even let me across the doorstep. Not until you wanted something, that is. Then when you needed help I was supposed to just drop my own life and pander to your bidding.' The smell of the cinnamon from her bag drifted up to her nose. 'Well, I've news for you, Bessie,' she choked out, 'I won't be coming here again, not even if you paid me. Though chance of it would be a fine thing.'

Rage carried her out of that door, down the steps. So fast she felt she might fall, with her chest burning, and her breath coming in short gasps.

'Ma!' Bessie yelled. Behind her the door banged shut in the wind.

But Agatha kept going. She loved those boys. Bess had no right to keep her from them. How dare she? She'd helped her all this time, and now she was just being cast off like a used coat.

She'd go to Jack Sutherland herself, ask after them. They'd be missing her, with only that cold fish of a father to love them. The rejection cut deep. Bessie didn't need her. She'd only wanted a free minder for the boys.

Well she'd not get her help again, not even if she begged her for it.

***

Will was getting ready for his next voyage. He picked up a chasing chisel and wrapped it in baize before sliding it to the bottom of his tool chest, and then ran his thumb over the keen edge of his draw-knife. Blunt. He re-applied it to the whetstone. Afterwards, he oiled the saws against the salt of the sea, and repaired the handles on his hammers before wrapping them. Preparing his tools was one way of soothing his anxiety. He surveyed the neat row of the tools of his trade with satisfaction, before stacking them neatly into his tool box in their proper order.

Bess insisted on coming with him to see the *Salvation*, so that she could see where he would be berthed when the ship sailed in a few days' time. He was to have a few more days on shore, on day duty, whilst the crew did repairs and fixed up anything that needed repairing. They travelled by hired cart, an expense they could barely afford, so he could bring his box. Bess feigned good humour, but he could tell from her face she was still annoyed he had to go to sea.

On the wharf, it was blustery, and the cargo of bales of tobacco, and sacks of wheat swung from the gantries, the ropes and pulleys arcing their dangerous loads over their heads. Two burly vintners rumbled barrels noisily down the quay to a waiting dray.

'Stand back, Bess,' Will said, shielding her from a passing barrel. 'I'll find the Master, tell him I'm here, and see what needs to be done.'

Bess gripped his arm, overwhelmed by the size and bulk of the ship. 'Introduce us, won't you, Will? I want to meet this Master that's responsible for the safe passage of my husband,' she said. 'It's a very precious cargo.'

Her sudden concern touched him, 'All right. But then you must leave me to my work. It's no place for a woman here – too dangerous.'

At the plank he asked the bo'sun where they could find the Master.

'Below decks. You our new chippy?' He tilted his head towards Will's tool box, now standing waiting on the edge of the quay.

'Yes, name's Will Bagwell. And this is my good wife Bess.'

'Turner. Pleased to meet you. There's a lot for you to do, we've been a few months without. Hope you've packed a good plug of baccy, and plenty of vinegar for washing – don't want you to go the same way as the last one, do we now?' He winked at Bess.

Will's stomach sank. Bess's ears never missed a trick.

'Will, what does he mean?' she said.

'He just means… best take precautions, that's all.'

'Was that what you meant?' demanded Bess, fixing calculating eyes on Turner.

'Don't worry, missy, we've been quarantined more'n a month. Nobody else on board has shown any sickness or tokens.'

Will watched Bess's face tighten. That's torn it, he thought. He braced himself.

'You knew!' she said to Will, in disgust. 'And you kept it from me. The last carpenter died of the pestilence. Don't tell me I'm wrong, because I'll soon enough find out. Why didn't you tell me?'

'Whoo.' Turner fanned his face, enjoying Will's discomfort. 'Looks like you're in the fire, son.'

'How could you?' Bess grabbed Will's sleeve to draw him aside, and spoke through a tightened jaw, 'you said it was safe. You said the other carpenter had found a better position.'

'Now come on, Bess…'

'You do me wrong, Will Bagwell,' she said, her eyes glittering with anger and indignation. Her hand shot out to push him hard in the chest, forcing him to step back.

He took hold of her wrists to quieten her, but she fought him off with slaps.

'Look, Bess,' he said, trying to still her, 'this is why, woman! Because I knew you'd make a fuss. But work's work. If you want to stay in your precious Flaggon Row, I can't turn it down. And Turner said it, didn't he? There's been no signs since. I didn't want you to worry.'

'No signs? I'll give you signs.' Before he could stop her, Bess bent over his tool chest and with surprising strength she gave it an almighty shove.

The echo of its scrape along the flags resonated a moment before the box teetered on the edge of the wharf. No-one moved. It was as if the deed could be reversed if no-one drew breath. Then slowly it toppled, and with surprising grace, slid out of sight.

A dull sucking sound, more like a swallow than a splash.

Will thought his heart must have stopped. But before he could think, he heard his own cry of anguish as, like a wild beast, he threw himself in after it. The cold water closed over his head and instinct made him surface, gasping for air.

He caught a momentary glimpse of Bess's face, her eyes wide and shocked, her hand over her mouth. Wet had splashed a dark stain up the front of her gown. But he didn't think, just took a gulp of air, and dived towards the bottom. The water was deep there, and foul, and no matter how he struggled, forcing his hands through the murky brown, he couldn't feel any solid object.

The weight of his boots dragged on his ankles. He kicked but they wouldn't loosen. When he thought his chest might cave in from lack of air, a pair of hands grabbed him under the armpits and hauled him to the surface. More hands dragged him over the stone flags and dumped him on the quay. Thumps and slaps at his back. Almost immediately he vomited. His hair was plastered to his face, his nose stung with water. He squinted, seeing discarded sailors' boots and dripping legs. He wiped the filth from his eyes to face a gawping crowd, but no sign of Bess.

The humiliation of being forcibly dragged from that sewer of dark water was total. The Master and many of the crew had all come to witness how the new carpenter's wife had buried his tool box at sea, and he had thrown himself in with his boots on, and almost drowned. Will endured it, being the butt of their ribald laughter, feigning a cheerful face, but inside he seethed. The fact that he was soaked to the skin and smelt of stagnant river water and vomit did nothing to help.

Turner was one of the men who was dripping, having jettisoned his boots and leapt in to save him. Someone else lent Will a dry jerkin so he could walk home in a modicum of comfort.

'Good job Donnelly died,' Turner said, winking. 'You'll be needing his tools now.'

Will could not bear to think of it. Using a dead man's things. It was like some sort of omen. He wouldn't touch those tools. Nor could he stomach boarding a ship where he would be a laughing stock.

He had no idea what had happened to Bess, nor did he care. At that moment he never wanted to see her again. The walk home was a walk of humiliation and inside him, the anger boiled.

When he got home there was no sign of her. Perhaps she dare not return.

Years of collecting, years of fettling and making – all gone in a few seconds. It made him want to weep. Not to mention his reputation. He didn't know what he would do to Bess when she came back. Shaking with anger, he peeled off his filthy clothes and threw them down in a heap on the chamber floor. It struck him that he did not know which he'd loved the more: his tools, or his wife.

***

A sluice with water from the ewer, and a good scrub with soap removed the worst of the filth. Will dressed hurriedly in a dry pair of breeches and clean shirt, and threw more of his clean clothes into a canvas carry-all. He was anxious to be away and out of the house before Bess returned. He had no plan but to be away from her.

In his mind he could still hear the sound as the Thames swallowed his box. It gave him a physical pain that made him moan out loud.

He locked the door after him, noting with bitter satisfaction that Bess had not taken her key. He needed a drink, and not just ale; he had never felt this much in need of oblivion in his life. The shame of it still ate into him, the looks of all those sailors pointing and laughing.

The Dolphin was busy, with men talking and gesticulating over the hubbub, long-stemmed pipes in hand after their day's work. Once he'd got his hands on a double measure of rum, Will slunk into a corner. He had no desire to come across anyone from the *Salvation*, hence his choice of a tavern in town. A deep swig from the thick glass, and the rum burned its way down his throat, springing water to his eyes. He'd been sitting only a few minutes, the fiery warmth in his throat, when a familiar voice reached his ears. Jack.

He'd no wish to see his cousin now. He'd have to explain what he was doing here, he – who usually hardly touched a drop. Jack would know instantly that something was the matter. Will slid further into his seat, pulled his slouch hat lower over his ears, took another large glug.

'I need labels for a thousand bottles,' he heard Jack say from the booth behind him.

'Not a ha'porth chance. I can't do that many in less than a fortnight,' a gruffer, cockney voice replied. 'It takes time to set up the press, and time to print and then to shear the paper. You're asking a lot, Jack Sutherland.'

'If you can't do it, I daresay I'll find someone else who can—'

'I'm not saying that. Just saying, I'd expect a bit more, if I've to do it in a hurry, like.' Will struggled to hear what was being said over the clank of tankards and the swell of conversation.

'Four pound's what we agreed,' Jack said. 'The boom's now. No point in waiting till they're all dead, is there? Take it or leave it.'

'Five'd be more like it.'

'I said four. D'you want my trade or not?'

A loud sigh. 'Where shall I deliver the stuff to?'

'We're in the derelict old cloisters, under where the Benedictines used to be, on Blackfriars. I've taken on more workers for the bottling, so I'll need the labels as soon as you've got them. Keep it under your hat, though, where we are. We've had trouble once already and had to move.'

'You got glue?' the cockney asked, 'I've a contact at the tannery, if not.'

'No, don't need it. Got someone boiling up glue already.'

'What's in it anyway, this stuff?'

'Ah. Secret recipe,' Jack said. 'But don't worry, I'll save you a couple of bottles, just in case. Let's hope you won't need them, eh?'

Will was confused. He was hoping for a good return on the money he'd loaned Jack, but surely he'd said his new business was in snuff? What was all this talk of bottling and labels? Snuff usually came in paper packets. Probably some illegal still that Jack had – wouldn't put it past him, to find Jack was trading liquor on the side. Will drained the last of his rum, and his head was muzzy, but the pain was still lodged in his chest. He needed another, if he could only sneak his way to the counter without Jack seeing him.

When he stood, he was more unsteady than he thought, and he wavered on his feet, trying to avoid bumping into another broad-beamed man at the bar. But he misjudged, and knocked hard into his elbow. The man's pipe flew from his hand, skittering to the floor, where its long, chalky stem snapped into three pieces.

'Watch where you're going, can't you?' the man cried, stamping out the burning wad of tobacco where it had landed, in the sawdust.

'Beg pardon,' Will said, stooping to pick up the pieces. 'May I buy you another?' His words felt thick as leather in his mouth.

'You should be more careful,' the man said. 'You nearly sent me flying.'

Will was just about to apologise again when Jack appeared between them, 'Causing trouble again, are we, cousin?'

'It was an accident,' Will said, acutely aware of the broken pipe dangling in his hand.

'You always were clumsy. You having another?' He glanced at the glass in Will's hand. 'I'll have the same.'

Clumsy. Yes, that's what his father always called him too. Will got two more glasses and a new pipe of tobacco for the man he'd knocked, but the smell of the rum made him queasy. Meanwhile Jack had made space for him at his table. There was no sign of the cockney gentleman Jack had been talking to earlier. Will slid into place opposite Jack.

'Your last night of freedom, is it?' Jack said, 'I heard rumours you'd got passage as carpenter on the *Salvation*.'

'Who'd you hear that from?'

'Can't remember. I know a lot of folk in the shipping trade. Word just gets round. When I've built up my business, and bought my own ship, there might be work for you, dear coz.'

Will stared into the dark liquid in his glass. 'I don't need work.'

'What's up? Had a row with the beautiful Bess?'

'We did have words, yes.'

'Thought so. You can't keep her under control, that wife of yours. What's she done now?'

Even as he said the first words, Will knew it was unwise to say anything to Jack, but somehow he couldn't stop himself. It was as if his thoughts would consume him, if he didn't tell someone. When he had blurted it all out, he caught the triumphant glitter in Jack's eyes.

'You need to teach her a lesson,' Jack said. 'Father said she was an uppity wench. And you're too soft. I'd have cast her out by now. What she needs is a good beating.'

Chapter 23

Bess walked up and down the river bank twisting the laces of her bodice in her fingers. Even before that box had hit the water she'd regretted it. How could she have been so foolish? But it still rankled that Will had known all along he was about to risk his life on that plaguey ship and hadn't seen fit to tell her.

His expression kept coming back to her, his horrified disbelief as he saw all his most prized possessions plunge to the bottom of the river. If that box ever shifted with the tide, some mudlark might find it, but it was clear there was no retrieving it now. And the cost! What would it cost him to replace it?

She paced and paced, cursing her quick temper, and hardly seeing the passing wherries or barges, nor noticing the men hurling their ropes onto the decks, or the women in low-cut bodices hanging around the entrance to the docks. It was dusk when she finally plucked up the courage to go home. It had been a terrible, foolhardy thing to do. She would have to beg Will's forgiveness, and offer to replace everything. She didn't know how, but she'd do it somehow.

The house was in darkness. She got to the top of the stairs and then remembered – she had no key. She hadn't thought to take one, expecting she and Will would return together. When she walked through Deptford, she saw Will's father's house was lit by candles. She wondered if he'd gone there, or decided to spend the night aboard the *Salvation*. If so, she could hardly blame him.

She tried the door. It was open. Thank God.

In the gloom she caught movement, 'Why are you sitting in the dark?' she called out, in as normal a voice as possible, though her heart was throbbing hard behind her ribs.

She caught the distinctive peaty smell of rum. As she got closer, she realised it was Jack, not Will, sitting there at the table. He was finely dressed, complete with the long, dark periwig.

'What are you doing here?' she snapped. She did not want him here in the house this night. 'Where are the boys?'

'He came home with me.' Another figure materialised out of the shadows. Will's voice was choked.

In Will's hand was a cane, about two and a half feet long, thin, like a horse-whip.

'What—?'

Will raised it above his shoulder uncertainly.

Jack leapt in, 'No!' he shouted, grabbing Will's arm, and the thing whistled through the air. 'Give me that.' He took hold of the switch and tried to pull it from Will's grasp.

Will's eyes registered only confusion.

'Let go,' Jack panted, keeping his grip.

Will tried to speak. 'But you said—'

Next thing she knew, Jack had raised his fist and brought it crashing into Will's nose. Will reeled backwards and fell over a chair, sprawling on the ground.

'Don't you dare try that again,' he said, with a glance at Bess.

Will still had the cane in his hand now and raised it against Jack. His eyes were dazed, and blood poured from his nose.

'Stop this!' she cried. 'Have you turned raving mad?'

Both men turned to her, but she hid her head in her hands, half-expecting another blow, but instead she heard a crack and another.

She looked up. Jack threw the broken pieces of the cane out of the open door.

Will took a wild swing at him and connected with his eye.

Jack staggered back, clutching his wig to his head and holding his eye.

Bess jumped between the two men. 'Enough!' What the hell was happening? None of it made sense. Why were they fighting over her?

'He was going to beat you. What kind of man beats his wife, like that?' Jack said.

'It's none of your business,' she said. 'Just leave us alone.'

With sudden venom Jack kicked out hard and caught Will on the knee. And then he was gone, leaving Will groaning on the floor.

'Are you all right?' She knelt beside him.

He pushed her hard so she sprawled on the ground. 'Get out of my way.' He stumbled away into the bedchamber and slammed the door.

Chapter 24

Jack was fizzing when he got home. A good fight made him feel alive. He bounded upstairs and checked that Mrs Minty had put the boys to bed. Sure enough, they were sleeping in a huddled heap on the mattress. Tired out from bottling probably. It would do them good; toughen them up.

He dragged off his wig, shook it, and put it on the newel post of the stairs. In the cupboard he found a flask of rum and poured himself a generous slug. A restlessness made him unable to sit down. His mind kept returning to Bess, and her face when she thought Will was going to hit her.

He would have too, if Jack hadn't stopped him. Will was a fool. He just did whatever Jack told him to do. Bess didn't deserve a fool like Will.

He pushed the thought away. From a box under the window he extracted his maps and notebooks and spread them out on the table. His house was long and narrow with windows only front and back, so even though there was a bright moon he had to burn two tallow candles to get enough light to see by. Under the smoking candles, he mapped out the snuff trading route and then calculated how many crates of bottles he could fit in the hold as export to Holland. Snuff would only be one half of the trade. His medicinal elixir the other.

In the current climate, the other half could make his fortune. One man's misfortune was another man's profit, and in Holland the bad luck was everywhere.

He drained his rum, savoured the burn at the back of his throat, and sat back. He'd need much more investment first if his idea was to make maximum return. Of course he'd told Kite and Bastable he already had the wherewithal. They thought him already set up. A big investor would be better – Pepys would have been ideal. He imagined for a moment casually telling Kite he had the great Navy man Mr Pepys backing him. The thought brought a warm glow.

He told himself to be realistic. Will's money was the best he could hope for, and it was already spent.

Jack began to fold away his maps. Despite all his efforts to flatter Pepys when they'd met, the man had shown no interest in his business. The only thing Pepys had been interested in was Bess. And according to his boys, she'd been to see him whilst Will was at sea.

He wagered that Will had no idea she'd been there.

Again, Jack let his mind rest on her; on her oval face with its clear complexion, her slightly pouting mouth, her habit of twining her soft dark ringlets in her fingers.

He remembered her reaction that time at Flaggon Row when Pepys touched her hand under the table. The slight startle, the way her eyes jerked to Pepys. Pepys himself had stared ahead as if his hand were separate from his thoughts. But Jack'd seen the flush stain Bess's cheeks pink, and the way she leapt up in a flurry.

Of course, she didn't pay Jack any attention, because she thought he hadn't seen. So he'd tightened his jaw and swallowed the desire to pulp Pepys's face with his fist. How dare he? Bess was Will's. And what was Will's was his. Sooner or later.

The rolled-up map hung in his hand.

Jack poured another rum and downed it, ruminating. Of course he'd always found her attractive – her figure shapely as a bell, and that single-minded determination. What Bess wanted, Bess got. And he'd loved to have seen Will's face when she'd shoved his tool-box into the Thames. Poor Will. He couldn't tame a firebrand like Bess.

He on the other hand...

It hit him like a sudden shaft of light. It would be the answer to everything. The boys already treated her like a mother. He put the maps away and let the chest lid bang down.

He didn't know yet how it could be achieved. Will would have to give her up first, and he wasn't the sort to be fickle. And she'd an unsavoury history that he'd have to ignore; the daughter of a whorehouse madam, and that snake, George Allin.

Or perhaps instead of ignoring it, he should bear it in mind. It might provide just the leverage he needed.

A house by the Thames, and a wife that would look to his boys. Flaggon Row and Bess; that would suit them all nicely.

Chapter 25

'Forgive me,' Bess said, kneeling by the bed and placing her hand lightly, tentatively, on Will's shoulder.

It had been a week since they had spoken, each of them moving around the house like a spectre to the other, invisible, silent and cold. Will turned, still sleeping, and reached his arm out to her as he used to. There was a purplish bruise over his nose and his lip was still a little swollen. It clutched at Bess's heart to see him so trusting, until his eyes snapped open, and he stared at her, as if he had only just seen who she was. His brown eyes searched her face.

'Why?' he asked, after a long moment. His voice was full of compressed emotion.

She knew exactly what he was asking. 'I must beg your pardon. I know it was wrong of me. I was angry. Angry that my opinion counted for nothing.'

'You shouldn't have done it.'

'I know. It was madness. But I was afraid of losing you. Lately I seem to be...' she searched for the words, '...losing everything.'

'But I thought it was what you wanted,' he said, propping himself on his elbow, 'that I should go to sea and make something of my life. I can't be a ship's carpenter without my tools.'

'So what will you do?'

'Carry on turning bowls and platters, I suppose, with the few tools left in my workshop. Until I can afford more.'

She rubbed his shoulder through his nightshirt, longing to hug him, but not daring to break their fragile truce. 'You won't go to sea?' She dare not mention the *Salvation*.

He sighed. 'No, Bess. It sailed. They took on someone else.'

'We'll have money coming in. I went to Hutchinson's. They've been satisfied with my work so Meg's persuaded them to take me on as a permanent worker, stitching gloves. I start Monday.'

He turned to look directly at her. His eyes showed his disapproval.

She shrugged. 'I want to help. To make it up to you.'

'Oh, Bess.' He shook his head sadly.

'And maybe we'll get some return from Jack's business, you know, from your investment.'

'Maybe.' He reached to touch her face. 'Why did he hit me?'

She leaned her face to his hand, surprised at the tenderness of his touch. 'I don't know. Because you would have taken the rod to me, I suppose. Who knows what goes on in his thoughts? He's like gunpowder – unstable.'

'I don't understand him. He wanted me to beat you. It was his idea. He kept talking of beating you, like he wanted some sort of revenge.' He sighed. 'But then suddenly he was stopping me. It doesn't make sense.'

'Nothing makes sense with Jack.'

'A beating's all we knew when we were children. My father … well, never mind all that.'

She put a forefinger to the bruise. 'Does it hurt a lot?'

'No. Other things hurt more.'

The unspoken image of the tool box on the quay hung between them.

'I wish I could undo it. Go back in time to standing on that wharf.'

'I'd be on the *Salvation* by now if you had.' He paused. 'Heading for plaguey waters. I missed you, Bess.'

She let herself be drawn into his arms. They clung to each

other then, and their lovemaking was hot and urgent, as if they were the last people alive. Afterwards she couldn't help hoping that this time – this time she'd be with child.

***

Will treadled the lathe, turning a new chair leg with a badly weighted chisel, feeling all the time as if he was shrinking, becoming less useful all the time. He worried that folk were talking about him – the man who'd lost his tools into the Thames. The customer with a broken chair leg told him he'd seen the *Salvation* sail, and Will was torn, feeling he ought to be with them at sea, though it was the last thing he really wanted. And now Bess would be working like any common wife. He'd wanted better for her. The thought that he couldn't support her dented his pride. Just repairs now. That was all he was good for.

Indeed, word must have spread quickly, for a servant from Deptford Boy's School came later in the week to ask if he made platters; goods any raw apprentice could make. He looked at the chit and shook his head, and wished Jacob was still with him, but he'd laid him off, thinking he would be at sea, and a good thing too, for they could no longer afford him. The prospect of such dull work made him want to throw down his chisel, but he sighed and began the labour, for how would they pay off Kite's confounded loan, else?

He applied his boot to the treadle again, hearing the hiss of the string as it turned the spindle. When the chair leg was done, he turned to the school order. The order was for the cheapest platters. Hard-woods like oak and elm were in dwindling supply because so many had been used for ship-building, shoring up the Navy against the fear of war with the Dutch.

He was forced to use lime-wood and old patterns, and he itched for close-grained timber and something intricate or substantial to do.

And there was the added worry that Bess was not telling him the truth. Jack's accusation that she'd visited Pepys rankled. All week he'd waited to see if she'd mention it, and she didn't. But as he worked, the rhythm of the pole-lathe soothed his ill-temper, so he could almost forget.

***

Bess was working at Hutchinson's now, so she never went back to Mrs Fenwick's for her meetings. Besides, she hadn't managed to collect any more money, and she was afraid if she did, she'd be hard-pressed not to take it herself. She tried to call on Mrs Fenwick one evening to explain, but when Bess knocked at her door, Maudie opened it and told her Mrs Fenwick was out. A patent lie, as she'd seen her enter her house not ten minutes earlier.

She tried again. This time it was Lucy who answered the door.

'Lucy!' She was pleased to see her.

But Lucy stood up tall in her starched cap. 'Who shall I say is calling?'

'Don't be foolish, it's me.'

Lucy looked down her nose. 'I'll ask if she'll see you.' A few moments later she returned. 'Mistress is not at home.'

So Bess handed the empty box over. She asked Lucy to send her apologies, but she'd no longer be collecting for the Christian Educational Fund as she was working. A few days later, a note arrived saying they would not require Will's benches after all.

Will was dumbfounded. 'But I worked for months in my own time on those benches. What do they expect me to do with them now? Are they not opening a school after all?'

'I don't know. I haven't seen Mrs Fenwick. She won't open the door to me.'

'What is it, Bess? What's going on?'

'It's just, I gave them their collecting box back. I can never fill it. I've no time to be collecting for their foolish fund.'

'Oh Lord, Bess. We can't afford to be on the wrong side of Fenwick. I was hoping he'd recommend me for work in the yards.'

Chapter 26

As the hot months of the summer passed, Will's work became even duller and more predictable, and Will more morose. The talk of war with Holland did little to ease the tension that gripped the city, and folk were hiding their gold, not spending it. The platters earned little, and it was with some trepidation that Bess felt compelled to write to Pepys again, urging payment of the Navy wages, though she never mentioned it to Will. It was with great relief that finally Will received some payment from the boy's school, though it barely covered the payments on the loan, and with no work for Will on board ship, they were no better off.

Bess felt Will's dissatisfaction, and their lack of money like a pin left in a gown, a constant small irritation. And since Lucy had left them, she had no time to visit the children; not with the cooking, the laundry, the brewing of ale in the stillroom, the making of milk into butter and cheese, as well as her work.

It shamed her, the struggle to keep house. She used to set great store by appearance, and had a liking for fine things, but now she was never without apron and coif, always in her old slippers. As she put his supper before him, she wondered why Will hadn't noticed she had become so drab. Lately she'd caught him gazing out of the window, as if there was something out there calling him.

'Come on,' she said, slapping him on the shoulder, 'let's go out.'

'Why?'

'I need some air. We both do.'

'You look tired,' he said.

'There's a lot to do, now Lucy's gone.'

'I wondered if you were …' He let the words hang.

'No,' she said shortly, grabbing her hat from the hook. 'And don't say it.'

'What?'

'That there's something wrong with me,' she whispered, as they walked down the stairs. 'Other people can't help falling with child. Look at Jack's wife, Alison, she had three one after the other, and would probably have had a dozen if she hadn't been taken from us.'

'I haven't seen Jack for months,' Will said. 'I don't much feel like seeing him either. Not since he punched me in the nose.'

'No surprise there. It's because he knows we have no money. Soon as your pockets are full, he'll be back.'

'But he doesn't need us now, does he? He looks well-to-do.'

'Thanks to the likes of us. You invested in his business, didn't you? You should go and see how it does.'

'I suppose so. I didn't feel like seeing him. It will be up to me, to mend it, if I know Jack. He never was one for apologies.'

'Do that, and then find out how his business does.'

Will didn't answer. He was squinting into the sun, his attention hooked by a group of men in shirt sleeves, approaching from the other direction.

Bess's stomach tightened into a knot. 'It's your father,' she said.

'Cross over,' Will said, 'go up the back alley.'

'Will, wait.' His father called, and Will looked so taken aback to hear him speak, that he actually stopped.

Bess grasped his arm and stood by his side as the group of three men approached. Owen Bagwell was still tall and broad, despite his age, his mahogany forearms scratched with tattoos from his earlier life at sea. But his face was lined, like wrinkled leather, and scored into permanent discontent. The men behind him were hard, muscled men; one short and stocky with a neck like a bull, the other taller with arms dangling away from his body. All three wore sailor's knitted caps despite the summer heat. They stared at Will with undisguised curiosity.

'I was coming to see you,' Mr Bagwell said to Will, when he got within talking distance. 'I want a word or two.'

'Wonders will never cease. To what do we owe this honour?' Will asked.

Mr Bagwell turned to Bess. 'I hope you're pleased with yourself. Throwing away good tools. They still jest about it, d'you know that? You made me a laughing stock in the yards; a man whose son can't keep control of his wife.'

The men behind him stifled smiles. Bess saw Will's face flush, and opened her mouth to protest, but Will cut across her. 'Stop exaggerating. That was months ago. And if you've come to insult us—' Will steered Bess by the arm ready to leave.

'Hear me out.' In one stride, Will's father put his bulk in their way. 'Jack says you're not getting much work. And never let it be said by anyone that I wouldn't help my own son.' He glanced around and puffed out his chest. 'There's a vacancy just come up at the yard, for a sawman's mate. I've put you down for it.'

'If he's man enough,' the shorter man whispered to his friend.

Will's father turned and gave him the eye so he closed his mouth.

Bloody Jack again, Bess thought. What business was it of his?

'Who said I needed work?' Will asked. 'We don't need any assistance. Not from Jack, or you, or anybody else.'

'He's told you before. He doesn't want to work in the saw pits,' Bess said.

'I don't want your opinion,' his father said, swiping Bess with a glare. 'Jack's only trying to help. He's got a good business head and he's done well for himself. When he comes in the yard he looks like a proper gentleman, but he's still not above buying us all a round in the Oak of a night. When do you ever do that?'

'I've been at sea, Father. Or have you forgotten?'

'Forget? From what I heard, you made a proper cock's gizzard of it. Jack says you couldn't stomach it. But now's your chance, Will. To get straightened out, get something regular.'

Will raised his chin. 'Not if it's in the pits—'

'Above earning a day's wages for a good day's work, are you now?'

'No, Father, it's just—'

The shorter man turned to the other, whispering, 'He'd rather piddle about with bowls for a farthing apiece.'

Bess ignored this slur. 'Mr Bagwell,' she said, 'Will's a craftsman. His work is sought after all over London. I don't know what nonsense Jack's been telling you but he's—'

'It's not Jack that's the problem, it's *her*.' His father jabbed a finger in Bess's direction. 'She's made you want more than you were born to.'

'Gawd knows why,' the taller man hissed in his friend's ear, 'because from what I've heard, she's only half out of the gutter herself and—'

Will made a sudden step forward, 'I heard you. Don't you dare speak about my wife like that.'

His father held up his hand, 'All right, all right.' The taller man retreated. 'Look, William, I'm trying to encourage you.'

'Encourage me?' Will's laugh was bitter. 'Ha. Control me, more like. Your idea of encouragement was to beat it out of me.'

A pause. Owen Bagwell tightened his fists, and the atmosphere darkened. 'You're a fine one to talk,' he said. 'You ungrateful sod. You black the eye of your own cousin, and throw our help back in our faces.'

'Jack punched me first,' Will said.

Owen Bagwell curled his lip in derision. 'You were always useless in a fist fight. Never thought any son of mine would be a coward. Or frightened of hard work.'

At the sound of a muffled snort, Mr Bagwell swivelled to his friends, who hurriedly masked their smiles.

He turned back to Will to put in the last thrust. 'Turn me down, would you? Then I've had enough.' He spat in the dirt at Will's feet. 'I'll not offer again. I raised you, but you're no kin of mine.'

'I don't need you!' Will shouted.

His father cast him a look of contempt and the three men swaggered away, back down the street.

'I don't need you,' Will whispered again, almost to himself. 'I've *never* needed you.'

Bess was silent as they walked, following Will as he strode towards the wharf, and the green fields of the tenter lot. The argument with his father hung over them both, like a bad smell. Finally Will stopped, staring out over the field of sheets, pegged out to dry in the breeze.

'I don't know what came over me,' Will said. 'I should've taken it. We've no money, and I've no commissions coming in, and no money for this month's payment.'

'No,' Bess said. 'You're better than that.'

'But I need some sort of work, God knows. If we get evicted, he'll have won, and I don't know if I can bear it. He just … well, he always makes me feel so inadequate.'

'I hate the way he compares you with Jack,' Bess said. 'But if Jack's doing so well, there's all that money you invested in his business.'

'I hit him. I can't believe I did that.'

'And he hit you. I don't know what that was all about. Bedlam fools both of you. Anyway, Jack looked prosperous enough last time we saw him in his fancy outfit. Forget your father. You must ask Jack for our investment back. Go tomorrow. He's had it long enough, and there must be a return by now.'

They stared over the sheets in silence. They both knew the chances of him clawing anything back from Jack were slim.

Chapter 27

The next morning, Will put on his felt hat against the sun, and set off to Blackfriars. He strode quickly, in the shadows of the overhangs, persuading himself the visit was his own idea, not Bess's. He should mend it with Jack, and try to retrieve his investment. He'd heard Jack tell the man in the tavern that his snuff business was based under the Benedictine Priory, in the old cloisters. Jack had never invited him to visit, but Will didn't see why he shouldn't – after all, Jack had called in on him uninvited often enough. Of course Will had been drunk that night in the tavern, but he was sure he'd remembered rightly what Jack had said.

Last time he'd seen the old Benedictine monastery it had been a weaving shed, full of fleeces, and stinking of sheep. Now it was full of chattering girls. The noise was like gulls at the seashore chasing after fish – such a screech and clamour.

It took a moment before he realised it had been turned into a ribbon factory. He paused on the threshold, wincing. It was this foolish new fashion of be-ribboned breeches that had stormed the city. He'd never wear them. It was ludicrously impractical, to have his breeks festooned with ribbons; stupid loops that would catch on everything you passed, and trip you up.

He picked his way between the rows of girls who were hunkered on the ground, weaving on tiny hand-held looms. There was not an inch of floor space between them as they passed their miniature shuttles through the long strands. So much labour, and all for what? It was just more of the Popish madness that had taken over the city since the King had returned to Court. When people were starving on the streets, the manufacture of ribbons was like an insult.

He scanned the scene for Jack, or any sign of snuff manufacture, but could smell nothing. The light poured in rainbow streams through the stained glass – through gaudy scenes depicting the Virgin Mary and the Lamb of God. He was surprised these had survived Cromwell's purge. Will spotted an arched stone doorway, and manoeuvred his way past the shelves of brightly coloured bobbins, each wound with silk thread: amber, damson, scarlet, gold and blue.

Spotting a man, obviously a supervisor, he asked for Jack Bagwell.

'Below,' shouted the man, above the cacophony, 'in the cellars.'

Will headed for the stone stairwell that the man was pointing out. The spiral stone steps led down into what must have been a crypt. Before he had reached the bottom a foulness drifted up to his nose, a smell of something dark and oozing, stagnant like pond-water. At the pit of the flagged stairs he paused, his eyes adjusting to the gloom. Brass sconces lined the walls, lit by smoking flares, and in this murky light squatted two huge wooden vats, standing on what had once been the flat, flagged tombs of some nobleman. Behind them, ranks of long tables glimmered with glass bottles. A gaggle of rough-dressed beggars were hammering in corks with wooden mallets. The place was enormous – just as big as the ribbon manufacturer upstairs, but the contrast couldn't have been greater. Heaven and hell, he thought.

But before he could step into the chamber, a small grimy figure leapt up to him. 'Uncle Will!'

'Billy!' He lifted him up and swung him round, feeling the lithe lightness of his flying limbs.

'What's all this?' he asked. 'Where's the snuff?'

Toby appeared at his shoulder. 'Snuff comes in from the ships, and the bottles go out. We never see the snuff no more. It's too damp here. Come on, Billy'll show you what we do.'

Will followed him to a table. Grinning at his uncle all the while, Billy picked up a glass bottle and dunked it into one of the vats. Will peered into the liquid which was cloudy as it came out of the vat. 'What is it?' he asked.

'Secret recipe,' Toby said, 'but I can tell you.' He put his hand round his mouth to whisper. 'Just water. But we have to add the dye. Look, it's over here.'

Will followed, bemused, as Toby took him to a smaller vat where a viscous green liquid that smelled of copper was boiling over a fire. 'One drop in each bottle,' he said, 'to make it green.' He squeezed a pig's bladder into the liquid, sucked up a drop, and carefully held the dropper over the bottle until the bead of green plopped into it. 'Only one drop, the old man says, because it's expensive.'

'But what's it for?' Will asked.

'Ah,' Billy said, coming up behind them, 'Toby, show him the labels!' They passed a long rank of tables, full of workers bottling, and then at the end of the row Billy turned right into another smaller chamber where wooden boxes were stacked high, and there was a choking smell of boiling glue. Another group of youths were pasting labels onto the jars. Right at the end, little Hal was engrossed in stirring a dribbling glue-pot with a stick.

Will picked up a jar. '*Pestdrenk*,' he said, 'what's that?'

'It's foreign,' Billy said.

'Plague water,' Toby translated.

'Where did you spring from?' Jack was suddenly in front of him, and not best pleased to see him, judging by his expression.

'Morning, Jack.' Will felt the heat of embarrassment under his collar.

'What do you want?'

'I saw my father and …'

Jack continued to glare, arms folded. 'Boys, get on with your work. Billy, you're supposed to be watching Hal.'

'I was just passing,' Will said, 'and I came to apologise… I remembered someone said your snuff works was here. What's this though?' He held up the bottle.

'Who? Who said I was here?'

'The man in the Dolphin. You ordered these labels from him.' He waved one before Jack.

'I don't like visitors. And if you've come to apologise, you took your time.'

'Sorry, Jack. Let's forget it, eh? You're family. It's not right for us to be falling out.'

'You hit me.'

'I know. I didn't mean it. I was angry and upset, and I wasn't in my right mind.'

'You gave me a black eye. It made me look like a wastrel. It's no good for business, looking like a prize-fighter. It cost me. And I don't want you in here, you'll get in the way.' He took Will's arm and tried to steer him back towards the stairs.

'This isn't snuff, is it?'

'It's a little side-line,' he said, pulling impatiently on Will's sleeve. 'Something I send out after importing the snuff.'

'So what is it?'

Jack looked around, as if afraid someone might hear him. 'It's herbal medicine. Very efficacious against all manner of diseases.'

'Like the plague,' Toby said, looking up from his corking. 'Isn't that right, Pa?'

'We can talk somewhere else if you like,' Will said. 'I'll stand you a dinner, if you can loan me a coin or two to do it. I don't like bad feeling between us.'

'Wait whilst I leave instructions, then.'

A few moments later and Jack was ready.

Will shook up the bottle in his hand, watched the sediment settle to the bottom. 'You're exporting this remedy to Rotterdam, where the snuff comes from?'

'It's very profitable,' Jack said, 'Come on.'

'More than snuff?'

He sighed. 'No use sending an empty ship back, is there? And there's a monumental demand. People want to buy something to guard against the pestilence. D'you know how bad it is in Rotterdam? A hundred and forty reported cases of the plague. And that was just last week, and with this summer heat ...'

'Does it work?' Will held the liquid up to the light to scrutinise it.

'Course it works.' Jack was sulky. 'It's full of health-giving herbs and sedative powders.'

'Then how did you afford to buy the ingredients?'

'I have my contacts. And I got it on credit.'

Behind them, one of the workers in a sacking apron was openly staring.

Will said nothing. Maybe Toby was wrong, and the green stuff wasn't just dye. But something about it didn't feel right.

At the same time, he noticed that Jack was wearing another suit he'd never seen before. A yellow embroidered vest showed underneath his fashionable long coat, and there were matching ribbon roses on his shoes. He looked like a well-to-do man. It was this that needled him, Jack's peacock appearance, when he couldn't afford to buy Bess even a ribbon for her hair.

'Are we going to the tavern or not?' Jack asked.

'What about the boys?'

'Fletcher'll keep an eye on them.'

Will didn't answer. His father's voice came back to him, that he was lazy and afraid of hard work. Standing before Jack in his finery, his cousin who had never done a day's hard work in his life, but got his children to work in such filthy conditions, Will felt something hard and sharp well up inside.

Finally Will spoke. 'I'm glad you're doing so well, Jack,' he said, failing to keep the sarcastic edge from his voice, 'because I came to ask about my investment. You said a few months, and it's August already.'

'It's safe,' Jack said.

'Maybe so,' Will said. 'But if you've enough for another new suit, I'm sure you can give me an advance on my share of the profits.'

'Investors will get a pay-out after the Dutch pay me for the next consignment.'

'Bess and I aren't prepared to live on promises any longer. Especially, as you're so keen to tell my father, money's tight for us lately.'

The barb registered, and Jack looked away. 'Don't be a fool. I haven't any ready coin.'

'There's no hurry,' Will said, leaning up against the wall. Anger stoked his determination. 'I can wait. In fact, I'll wait here until you fetch it. I'll need it to pay for our dinner.' This was a trick straight from Jack's own repertoire.

The youth with the big ears had moved within earshot and was listening intently. 'Let's talk about it somewhere else. Not here.' He pulled the youth to the side. 'Fletcher, keep an eye on the boys will you? I've got to go out.'

'Sir.' The youth gave a desultory bow.

Jack bustled Will out of the cloister and up the stone steps. As they got half-way up, another man, equally well-dressed, but with a bullish expression was on his way down.

'Do I know you?' the man asked coldly, squinting over his narrow nose at Will.

'My cousin,' Jack said. 'Come to take me to lunch.'

'We said, "no visitors", Sutherland.' He made it sound like a warning.

'I know.' Jack gave Will a hard push. 'We're going.'

Will stumbled up the twisting stone stairs. At the top, Will paused, struck again by the contrast between the rainbow colours of the weavers above, and that dismal pit below.

'Who was that?' Will asked. 'I didn't catch his name.'

'George Allin. It's his ship.' Jack steered him past coaches and sedans and down the main thoroughfare towards Threadneedle Street.

Will pressed Jack again for an advance. 'I'm not going home until I have some coin,' he said.

At the compter's, Jack went inside, but was gone only a few moments before emerging with a small pouch of chinking coins.

'There, two pounds. That's all I can give you until the ship docks again in ten days' time. You haven't got children to feed. Now, let's eat.'

Jack started to walk away towards the tavern on the corner, but Will clapped him on the shoulder. 'About the snuff, Jack …'

Jack turned. 'What of it?'

'How do you get past the quarantine restrictions? Rotterdam's closed off now for trade.'

'Where'd you hear that?'

'When I was going to go on the—' He nearly said, the *Salvation*, but stopped himself. 'From a neighbour.'

'We've never had any trouble.'

Will moved aside as two gentlemen pushed past them. 'I mean, people wouldn't want snuff from an infected port, would they?' He dropped the words softly, but kept eye contact.

Jack gave him a hard stare back. Will felt something shift between them.

'Infected snuff wouldn't sell, would it?' Will insisted.

Jack's mouth twitched as if he was swallowing a stone. 'The snuff's clean. But you won't mention Rotterdam, or Mr Allin, to anyone, will you?' he said. 'It's strictly within the family, understand?'

'Wouldn't dream of it,' Will said, then casually, 'at least not as long as Kite's loan's paid each month. But a word in Mr Pepys's ear, and I'm sure he'd want to investigate—'

'You wouldn't.'

'So it's not clean,' Will said. 'I thought not.'

'If you want that loan paid, I'll see to it,' Jack said tersely.

Will could not help feeling a surge of power. The first time he'd ever had his cousin on a back foot, and it felt good. So many years he'd been the one bullied into Jack's way. Now the boot was on the other foot. He was elated. But under the elation was a new uncomfortable feeling. He'd forced Jack, and now he was the bully.

'The Dolphin?' Will said, holding up the purse.

'No,' Jack said, sulkily. 'I need to get back, see what Allin wants.'

***

With the purse of coins jingling in his hand, Will stopped at St Paul's church, looking for a daily maid to hire. The loss of Lucy had hit Bess hard, and he wanted to smooth things between them, prove himself as a good provider. In the gloomy interior of the church there were several young girls, shuffling from foot to foot on the hiring dais, holding up their references. He chose a short, gap-toothed girl called Mary, newly for hire from Shoreditch. She looked about fourteen years old but sturdy, and her face was open and willing. After that, he walked to the cutler's market on Chiswell Street and chose some new chisels from Jenck's – beauties, with oak handles and steel shafts. And on a whim, he bought Bess a tortoiseshell comb.

By the time he got home, Mary had already called at Flaggon Row, and assured Bess she'd be back early in the morning, ready to lay the fires. Bess was thrilled, and she was even more delighted with the comb. It was a long time since he'd given her a gift, Will realised. He told Bess that Jack's snuff business was thriving, doing so well that Jack'd offered him an advance on his share of the profits.

'Well hogs might fly,' Bess said. 'He's finally stuck at something, would you believe it?'

Later, when he lay in bed, he couldn't get comfortable. He thumped the bolster and closed his eyes, but soon they were wide open again, seeing Jack in his fancy breeches and high-heeled shoes. Jack said he'd make sure their loan was paid. It was both a relief and a thorn in his conscience.

The next morning Bess had the new comb fastened in her hair, and she looked so comely with the loops of ringlets fastened to the nape of her neck.

'We'll still need your glove money a while, Bess, if we're to keep Mary,' he said to her.

'I know,' she said. 'I don't mind. I like working with Meg. It's been nice these last few months to have company whilst I sew, even if Mr Hutchinson is a sour old stick.'

Will found an offcut of limewood, intent on carving something decorative, but he couldn't settle to it. The new chisel was an unfamiliar weight in his hand. He set it down again and replayed the conversation with Bess in his mind. What he'd said about Jack's business wasn't an untruth, but it wasn't exactly the truth either, and it needled him. He'd done nothing wrong, except ask for his money back, but it still niggled at him, like a paper-cut on the thumb, never quite forgotten.

What if the authorities were to catch up with Jack? He was clearly trading illegally. Somehow Allin must be sneaking his ship between ports where the pestilence was rife. And he, Will, was encouraging it – deliberately turning a blind eye for profit. He didn't feel happy in himself; a moment's lust to pull one over on Jack, and he was already in deep. Deeper than he felt comfortable.

In the middle of the morning Bess arrived, full of smiles, to say that her new maidservant, Mary, was a godsend. She'd already finished what Lucy would have taken a whole day to do. Will tried not to be annoyed at the interruption to his thoughts.

'And are these new?' Bess said, pointing to the chisels.

'Yes, yes.' He was distracted.

But worse than that, he was fairly sure that the remedy Jack was peddling was useless. He felt sorry for all those desperate Dutchmen who handed out their savings for Jack's promise of a cure, only to find the remedy made no difference at all. Toby had said it was water. Just water and dye. It couldn't be right, could it, to prey on other people's misfortune?

He remembered the scene on the water outside Amsterdam. Now the plague was spreading, and if it was that bad in Rotterdam, and ships were flouting the rules, what was to stop it coming to London?

A cry woke him from his reverie. Bess was clutching her palm and beads of blood spattered into the dust.

'What have you done?' Will said.

'It just slipped.'

'I've told you before – don't touch my tools. Let me look.' The wound was deep but clean. Will gave her his kerchief to tie round the cut.

When she'd gone back upstairs, he picked up the chisel where it had dropped on the floor, and wiped it on his breeches. A scent of danger hung in the air. Perhaps it was the sight of blood. He gathered up the rest of the new chisels and pushed them all to the back of the cupboard. He wasn't superstitious, but couldn't help feeling the taint of Jack's money; that those chisels had brought him bad luck.

Chapter 28

At the sign of the Glove and Bobbin, the heat of the day, and the sheer number of women stitching, sucked all the air from the room. Bess lifted her dark curls away from the back of her neck and dabbed her kerchief there to dry it. She put down the pair of warm gloves she was stitching, to lick the end of the cotton and thread the needle.

Fur gloves in August! Mr Hutchinson had them preparing winter stock; manufacturers had to be in advance of the season. She had only just picked up her needle again when the shop door flew open, then banged shut so hard it juddered in the door-frame. All the women shot upright to attention.

Mr Hutchinson, Bess's employer, strode past clutching his black hat, with an expression icy enough to freeze a hot posset, even in this heatwave. Hutchinson was a man with Puritan leanings, no sense of humour and a cutting tongue. Everyone wondered how he could possibly have produced a daughter as sweet as Meg.

Hastily, Bess lowered her head, looking down at her embroidery as if it was of extreme interest. They all held their breath until the door to his office clicked shut.

'Looks like the meeting with the moneylender didn't go too well,' whispered his daughter Meg, grimacing. 'That scoundrel Baxter's taken all our trade. I don't know how he makes so much stock. He's only the same number of girls as we have.'

'It's a sweatshop.' Bess dismissed it with a grimace. She sewed a few more stitches, then said, 'But his gloves look French. And he's efficient, I'll say that for him. I looked in his workshop.

He makes each girl do only one task. They get good at it, and then it's quicker, and he turns out more gloves. If he wants to keep up, your father could do the same.'

'Sshh. He'll hear you. We've always done it this way,' Meg said, her pale eyes full of worry. 'Father says that customers like the fact that each pair is "lovingly wrought" by one person.'

'Lovingly wrought? Maybe that used to be true. But not now. We have to keep up with the styles coming from France.' Bess looked down at the white kidskin gloves with the fur trim. 'These are old-fashioned already, let alone by Christmas,' she said.

'Why do you always want to change things?' Meg asked.

'I don't. I just want to move forward, that's all. Onwards and upwards. If cutters did all the cutting out and the lining, and embroiderers did all the embroidery, like at Baxter's, it would be quicker. Your father needs to move with the times; he'd make more stock then, and turn a bigger profit.'

Meg coughed loudly and stared at her with meaningful eyes, but Bess barely registered it. Instead, she picked up the offending pair of gloves. 'And these are too plain,' she said, stabbing them with a forefinger. 'He needs to look at what Baxter's doing. Ideas have changed. Your father's designs look as though they're stuck in Cromwell's time.'

'Bess!' hissed Meg.

Bess froze. She heard the tap of Mr Hutchinson's boots as he came to stand in front of her. He leaned in until his face was inches away from hers. 'Would you like to repeat that, Mrs Bagwell?'

She flushed under his gaze. 'I was just saying, sir, that gloves with be-ribboned cuffs are selling well, so maybe Hutchinson's could take advantage, and make some too.'

'Like Baxter, you mean?' His expression was sour. 'That man is an insult to the trade. Papist foolery. Flash instead of substance.

His gloves are ill-finished. No wear in them at all.'

'Father,' Meg put her hand on his arm, 'she didn't mean any harm. It was well-meant. She was just wanting to help.'

Mr Hutchinson leaned over the cutting table. 'I don't need help. I need staff who do my bidding.' He turned to Bess. 'You've got far too much to say for yourself, Mrs Bagwell, and I've had enough. Pack up your things.'

Meg looked to her father with wide eyes. 'You mean she's to go?'

Mr Hutchinson's words were clipped. 'I thought she was the wrong sort of girl from the first day, but I took a chance because you have a foolish affection for her. Her stitching is not up to standard.' He turned to Bess. 'Your employment is terminated.'

There was a collective inhalation from Meg and the other women.

The wrong sort of girl. Bess knew she should not speak, but she couldn't help herself. She wanted to lash out with the only weapon she had. Her tongue.

She stood up to her full height of all of five foot two inches, and braced her shoulders. 'Whilst we're on home truths, Mr Hutchinson, there is nothing wrong with my stitching. But the reason your business is losing money is because you don't listen to us.' She swept up a limp chamois leather glove and thrust it in front of his chest. 'Who do you think buys your winter gloves?'

Silence.

'We do,' she said. 'Women. Any one of us could tell you what will sell. Meg here has told you over and over that the new Court fashion's for ribbons and rosettes, but no. You make us blanket stitch, or sew on buttons instead. You won't even listen to your own daughter.' She threw the glove down on the table.

Hutchinson's face reddened to the colour of a plum. He opened his mouth and said something, but Bess was already moving, picking up her bag, as if carried on a wave of her own words. She caught a glimpse of Meg's scandalised face.

'Sorry, Meg,' she said, squeezing the arm of her best friend, before she turned the brass handle, yanked the door open, and burst into the street.

Once outside, she realised she was breathless, and a lump like gristle seemed to have solidified in her chest. She took herself back under the overhang of the house next door to catch her breath.

'Oh Lord, that's done it,' she said aloud.

Her blether and blarney. It always got her into trouble.

Bess walked blindly down the street, letting it sink in. It took about a quarter hour before she stopped wanting to punch Hutchinson in the face, and began to convince herself she never really wanted to work for him anyway.

Will would be cross when she told him she'd lost her work. He'd shake his head sadly, and tell her she should have kept her thoughts to herself, but he'd do it with that resigned expression – the one that meant her outspokenness was a trial he had to bear only too often. Dear Will, he knew her so well.

She shivered. *Pack up your things.* Mr Hutchinson's voice echoed in her ears. She'd heard the same phrase over and over in her life. And here it was again.

Turning, she stuck up two fingers at the shop. She'd get other work at a better place. There must be many other glovers who would need a girl with her experience.

Baxter's. It was worth a try. After all, she knew now that their elegant shop front was just that – a front. And nothing like the cramped rooms at the back.

***

'Do you want the good news or the bad news?' Bess asked, as

Will came in through the door, smelling of heat and wood.

'Don't know. I expect you've decided for me anyway,' he said.

She took a deep breath. 'Well, the bad news is that Hutchinson was laying off workers, and I'm the first.'

'What? Wait a minute whilst I get my bearings.' Will sat down, took off his hat, wiped the sheen of sweat from his brow. 'He can't do that. What grounds?'

'Hutchinson's is losing money to Baxter's. Hutchinson's designs are too old-fashioned and he's too stubborn to learn from his competitors.'

Will sighed. 'You didn't tell him that, did you?'

'No. Course not.' But she couldn't prevent the heat from rising up her cheeks.

'Oh, Bess.' His face creased into the disappointed expression she dreaded. 'What about Meg? What did she say?'

'She took my side, but he wouldn't listen.'

'It's one thing after another. First my tools, then this. Just when I think things are on an even keel, you throw another stick between the wheels. Only now there's Mary's wages too. Did he give you any notice?'

'No. He said—'

'No notice?'

She shook her head. He used to hate her working. Now they were both reliant on it, and she knew it rankled him.

'This good news of yours, well, it'd better be good.'

She went to lay a hand on his arm, stroke the thick corn-coloured hair where it was tied back in a black sash. 'There's no good news. Except this,' she kissed him on the lips.

He did not respond.

'Come on, it's not that bad; I can always try another glover's.'

'Tomorrow?'

'Tomorrow,' she said, and pressed a hand against the curve of his backside.

'Get away with you,' he said. But she knew he was worried because usually he would have kissed her and pulled off her coif to twine her heavy dark curls in his fingers.

Chapter 29

The following Sunday before church, Meg was waiting for Bess in the churchyard. Autumn leaves had gathered and caught around the hem of her dark skirts. Of Mr Hutchinson, to Bess's immense relief, there was no sign.

Will, seeing Meg waiting there, her face taut with worry, tipped his hat to her, but knowing the situation, he left Bess to talk to her friend alone.

'I'm sorry.' Meg put her hand on Bess's arm. 'Nothing I can say will make Father change his mind. I tried every ruse I could, but nothing worked. He'd lose face with the other staff, see, if he had you back.'

'It doesn't matter. I'll find something else.'

'Have you tried Baxter's?'

'First place I went,' said Bess. 'No vacancies. And Will still can't get work in the yards in Deptford.'

'Did you ever go to Pepys?'

Bess's face grew warm. 'Yes, he was the one who found Will a shipboard position as a carpenter's mate.' She paused. 'It didn't suit him. But now Will's invested in a business of his cousin's – you know, I told you – he went in with Jack. Jack Sutherland. It seems to be doing well.'

'Sutherland? Oh. Is it a snuff business? Father used to get his snuff from a man called Sutherland, because it was cheap, but to be frank, he says the quality got worse and worse. Sutherland seemed to be in some difficulty and asked my father for a loan, but he refused him. Father says he has a bad reputation in business. That Sutherland's not your Jack, though is it?'

'Your father must mean someone else. Jack's snuff business is doing very well, from what I can see.' Bess felt her reply turn frosty.

'I didn't mean to imply—'

'Will trusts him. They were brought up together.'

'Oh.' Meg did not speak any more.

At the lych gate Bess stopped. Neither of them knew what to say.

'I must go,' Bess said. 'I've a new maid, Mary, she needs supervising.'

A brief pause. 'I'll write, arrange a time to meet,' Meg said, avoiding Bess's eyes.

'Yes, do.' Bess said.

Meg hurried away down the path through the graveyard. Bess watched her go. How quickly a friendship could be broken, she thought.

***

Whenever the messenger boy came with the damp wadge of post, Bess pounced on him, hoping for good news – a better commission for Will, or news of some bespoke carpentry work in the yards. She even hoped for news from Mr Pepys. But as the months passed, and no news came, she feared he must have forgotten her. That idea was both welcome and unwelcome. It was always good to have friends in high places.

'Bastable's not been for his money again,' she said to Will, as she helped Mary fold his clean shirts. 'It's been months. Do you think he's ill?'

'No,' Will said, soaping his hands in the washbowl. 'I must've forgotten to tell you. It's paid in advance now. Jack sorts it out, from the business.'

'Really?'

'It's an arrangement we have, because of the loan we gave him.'

Mary paused on her way to the bedroom with his pile of clean shirts. Bess shooed her on her way with a gesture and waited until she was out of earshot. 'Seems foolish, doesn't it? We've loaned money to Jack, so we can pay off a loan from Kite. All that coin, floating invisible in the air. I liked it better when we counted it from the jar.'

'It's just trade. Everyone does it.' He dried his hands.

She picked up on his defensive tone, and sought to soothe him. 'Well, I suppose that's one less thing to worry over. And how does it do, the business with Jack?'

'It does well enough,' Will said. 'There's more money in that than carpentry, sad to say. And I'm thinking we might have to let the workshop if we're to stay here.'

'Let it? Who to?'

'I don't know, do I? All I know is that it's making no money and it could get us a pound a week. Jack knows someone who wants a place to store some things.'

'What, and have strangers right underneath our feet?'

'You want to keep Mary, don't you? And it seems more sensible than me making bowls for the rest of my life.'

'No, we're not doing that. You'll get a commission or another shipboard post soon, I just know it.' She went over and put her arms around his waist. 'Is there no sign of any profit from Jack yet?'

'Stop asking me. It's all you ever do.' He pulled away, ran his hand through his hair. Bess looked up at him, frowning. His reticence was odd. She knew they were still struggling with money because Will had pawned his Sunday hat for a candle-lantern, so when the skies were dark, she might have 'more light to sew'. It was obviously a hint she should find more sewing work. She couldn't help wondering if Jack's boys were still getting their education, but Will kept his account book in a locked cupboard now, so she couldn't find out.

Jack was a wily fox. Odds were, he was trying to profit from them somehow. Meg's words had lodged in her mind too. About Jack being bad in business. The thought of Meg made her sigh. She'd been curt with poor Meg when she'd only been saying what Bess knew herself.

'Better check with Jack though,' she said, 'that our loan's being paid.'

'Stop hounding me, woman.'

She went to help Mary put away Will's shirts. She didn't trust Jack, and the fact that Will was in business with him made her uneasy. 'It wouldn't hurt just to check,' she called again over her shoulder.

Her words were met with silence.

To have strangers underneath them, that would never do. And it would signal straight away they were struggling. Word would travel fast they were taking in lodgers.

And as for the idea that Will would have nowhere to work, ridiculous. Wood was his passion, his life. Will without his carpentry was like a tree with no branches – inconceivable. It would turn him into a nobody. She couldn't bear that. She wanted her Will back; the man brimming with enthusiasm over a nice piece of oak, the man who stood at the window with his ale in hand and pointed out exactly how every ship that passed was built. She had to do something.

As soon as Will had gone downstairs, Bess took up paper and pen and wrote a hurried note. Quickly, she sealed the letter with a blob of wax and gave it to Mary.

'Take this to Mr Pepys at the Navy Offices,' she said, blowing the wax dry. 'Look for the sign of the ship, on Seething Lane.'

'Yes, mistress.'

'And, Mary, make sure it goes direct to his hand. He's a busy man, and I don't want it hanging on his desk for weeks.'

As soon as Mary had gone, she regretted it, but it was too late now. She would have to be careful, because she knew what Mr Pepys was like, but she couldn't think what else to do. She was doing it for Will. He need never know.

She had barely got started on supper when Mary was back.

'He wrote this directly, mistress, said to bring it straight home.'

The letter was not even sealed.

5th September 1664

Tomorrow at my office. Two in the afternoon. I shall expect you with pleasure.

Samuel Pepys

Seeing his flamboyant handwriting sprawling across the page gave Bess a wave of hope, but then a prick of guilt. His writing was so different from Will's sober, practical hand.

Quickly, she ripped the message in two and pushed it into the kitchen fire until it flared and settled into ash.

Chapter 30

The next day she dressed in her finest blue dress, and announced to Will that she was going to meet Meg at the Exchange. 'It's her half-day,' she explained, hoping he would not ask any questions.

'I'll walk with you,' he said. 'Mary can get on with clearing away the dinner things. Besides, I've made so many wooden trenchers, if I have to see another, I'll break it over someone's head. I miss Jacob; it never seemed to bother him.' He grabbed his hat. 'I'll take a morning off; I could do with some air.'

Oh no. The last thing she needed. 'But Will, you'll hate it. It's only silly women's business,' she said, trying to deter him. 'We want to shop for trimmings.'

'Will you ask at the glover's in the Exchange about work?' She didn't answer, but he carried on anyway. 'I'm glad it's Meg you're meeting. I didn't take to Mrs Fenwick and Mrs Evelyn and those other women, cancelling an order like that. And nobody seems to want their blasted benches. What a waste of good wood! Tell you what, I'll walk with you as far as the Exchange,' he said, 'and we can talk as we go.'

It was a glorious autumn morning, and Bess had to clamp down her hat with her hand against the breeze.

'What's the matter?' Will asked. 'You're quiet today.'

'Nothing,' Bess said, as they approached the broad colonnades of the Exchange.

Of course there was no sign of Meg, and Bess was forced to hang around the fan stall for a full fifteen minutes, knowing full well that Meg wasn't coming.

Will hovered impatiently by her side, as she picked up a

tortoiseshell-handled fan, with a painted scene of St James's Palace. He scanned the upper galleries. 'It's not like Meg to forget,' Will said. 'What time? Are you sure she said the Exchange?'

'Of course I am,' Bess said, closing the fan with a snap. 'I wouldn't be waiting here otherwise, would I?'

'All right,' Will said, holding up his hands, 'no call to be short with me.'

They waited a little longer under the suspicious and watchful eye of the stall-keeper, before Bess could bear it no more. 'She's not coming, so we might as well go home,' Bess said, her stomach churning, all the while picturing Mr Pepys glancing at the gold timepiece hanging from his waistcoat and wondering where she was.

'Shame to waste the ferry fare,' Will said. 'Let's take a stroll to the bridge, wife, whilst we're here.'

Bess was quiet. Half past two! What would Pepys think of her? She would have to write to apologise to him, as soon as Will's back was turned.

'Look!' Will said. 'There's Meg after all. She's just coming.'

His words made Bess's heart plunge. He must be mistaken. She'd made it up, about Meg's half-day. But no, coming down the thoroughfare, basket on her arm, was the familiar dark figure in her steeple hat. Oh my heaven. In the whole of London, it was the very last person she wanted to see. Lady Luck was playing some sort of evil jest with her.

Meg had spotted Will, and was already up on tiptoe, waving. Bess felt her face flame.

'There you are,' Will said, when Meg got to them. 'We waited at the Exchange, but thought you must have been delayed.'

'Delayed?' Meg's forehead creased. 'I suppose I am a bit late. I needed some bread, but the baker's wife would keep me talking. I promised Hugh that I'd only be a few minutes. Have you seen him?'

'No,' Bess said, forestalling her. She touched Will on the arm. 'It's all right, Will, Meg's here now. You can leave us to our women's business.' She prayed he'd leave.

'I didn't know Hugh was coming,' Will said, stubbornly. 'Bess never said.'

Meg was frowning even more now. She'd obviously realised that something wasn't quite right. 'We dined with Hugh's uncle; he's up for the Fair. But I needed a few things, and now Hugh's gone ahead to the bookbinder's. Well, I'll be getting along or he'll wonder where I've got to. And I promised father I'd be back at work by three. Bess, we must arrange something.'

'You'd forgotten, hadn't you,' Will said, smiling. 'You were supposed to be meeting Bess today. At the Exchange. Two o'clock.'

Meg took a step backwards. 'Was I? I'm sure ... I don't remember—'

'It was only a tentative arrangement, it doesn't matter,' Bess said hurriedly. 'Perhaps we'll see you at church. Come on, Will.'

She pulled Will away, leaving Meg looking after them in the street.

'That was kind, Bess, saving her embarrassment,' Will said, as they threaded their way back towards the embankment and the ferries. 'She'd obviously completely forgotten.'

Bess didn't answer him. She just remembered Meg's puzzled face, and a slithering, wormy sensation of guilt that she couldn't dispel.

She wrote an apology that afternoon to Pepys, claiming a headache had prevented her from leaving the house. When she handed it to Mary, Mary said, 'To Mr Pepys? Again?'

'If you please, Mary,' Bess said, in a low voice. She didn't want Will overhearing her from the workshop. Mary sighed. Seething Lane was a long walk.

Bess could barely concentrate, wondering if she'd spoilt the chances for Will. But sure enough, a reply came back straight away.

If you are recovered I can receive you at the same time tomorrow.

Pepys

***

The next day she hurried across the gravelled pathways to the Navy buildings on Seething Lane. Will would be horrified if he knew she'd arranged to see Pepys on his behalf. But what else could she do? It was her fault she'd lost her work at Hutchinson's, and only today they'd found out Will's plan to export platters to the Low Countries had been stopped. There were new laws on trade with infected ports and even wood was not exempt.

The long corridors, the narrow wooden stairs with their gleaming banisters, were all designed for men of importance, not women like her. She flattened herself to the wall as a dark-robed clerk bustled by, weighed under piles of ledgers.

At her knock, Pepys hurried her in, whisking her into a small closet-like room out of sight of the main office.

She got the impression he didn't want her to be seen. 'Ah, the lovely Mrs Bagwell,' he said, raising his eyebrows at her. 'How do you fare today? Headache gone?'

'I'm quite well, sir,' she said. 'It passed, and I'm none the worse for it.'

'Then you'll be able to go to Bartholomew Fair. Word is, it's the biggest yet. They say there's a juggler who can swallow a sword. Do sit, my dear. Did you come by sedan? No? You walked? Then do take the weight off your feet. I'll call for refreshment.'

He leaned out of the door, clicked his fingers and called to someone in the outer office. 'No interruptions,' she heard him hiss.

He turned back into the room and quietly shut the door. Something about the way he did this made Bess's throat tighten. She had read the signals, and knew the game was on – she must tantalise him enough to get what she wanted, but not give in to him.

'Now what can I do to help?' he asked, pulling up a chair and placing himself so their knees were almost touching.

She moved her legs to the side. 'My husband Will. I spoke to you before about him. I wondered if there was the possibility of him joining another ship. One not bound for Holland. You see, the pestilence makes him uneasy.'

'But I hear his work is much in demand. Didn't we give him an order for bowls ...?' He began to open a ledger.

'Yes, sir, you did.' How could she explain that these were far beneath his skill? 'But he was hoping for more complex work in the yards or on board ship. He's a time-served craftsman. But Nicholson is still refusing him permission to join the Guild, and we don't understand why.'

'Ah yes. That little problem. I think I know where the difficulty lies. Your husband has a father who works in the yards, does he not?'

'Yes, Owen Bagwell. He's a sawman. But he's nothing to do with the Guild.'

'But it seems he has influence in the yards. The men respect him, and he's told Nicholson that if they take on his son, he will call on the sawmen to stop work.'

'You're telling me that Will's own father is blocking his appointment?'

'It would seem so. The best thing I can advise you to do is to repair this dispute with his father. Nicholson sets great store by Owen Bagwell, so I've heard.'

'Owen Bagwell is a bully of the worst kind, Mr Pepys.' She stood up, shaking her head. 'I can scarce believe it. The blaggard! That he should treat his own son so. Will said his father wanted to keep him down, but this? Well, it beggars belief.' The unfairness of it made her sit back down. She pressed her forehead into her fingers, before looking up. 'Is there nothing we can do?'

'This has come as a shock, Mrs Bagwell. Bess. I may call you Bess, may I not?' Mr Pepys reached over to pat her on the knee. 'Of course, sometimes I do small favours for my special friends.' He had taken hold of her hand, and now clasped it between his.

Bess looked down at it, hardly seeing it. In her mind she was seeing the face of Owen Bagwell as he shouted at Will in the street.

'I can count you as one of my *special* friends, can't I?' Pepys said. His thumb was moving over the back of her hand, stroking it. He leaned in towards her. 'Ladies who do me special favours can rely on me to have a word in the right ears.' He winked.

He was propositioning her. There was absolutely no doubt about it. His hand was moist on hers. Her thoughts had fled, her mind blank. She could not think of a suitable rejoinder.

'A feel of your bubbies, and I'll talk to Nicholson.' He leaned in towards her, took hold of her shoulders.

At that moment there was a loud rap at the door, and Pepys shot back in his chair.

'Later,' bellowed Pepys at the door.

But the door creaked open and a scared-looking fair-haired lad appeared with a tray, set out with a tall earthenware jug of small beer and some matching brown goblets. 'Beg pardon sir, but Mr Lawson's here to see you, sir. He won't wait. I've put out another cup.'

The lad slid the tray onto the desk as quick as he could and slipped out of the door, leaving it gaping open.

'I'll be going,' Bess said, pushing herself up from the leather chair, and attempting natural conversation. 'I won't keep you from your business, Mr Pepys. But please, if you could just talk to Nicholson and explain that—'

'Ah, Pepys! About this latest report ...' A broad-shouldered man in a flapping cloak – presumably Lawson – barrelled past Bess as if she didn't exist. He thrust a large document with dangling seals into Pepys's hands.

Bess took the interruption as a signal to slide away. She headed unsteadily for the stairs, her shoes tapping unevenly on the wooden boards, but stood a moment, swaying, leaning on the banister. The ground below seemed a long way down, and for a moment she felt she might faint. She took a huge breath of air, and putting the back of her hand to her forehead, realised it was clammy with sweat.

Will's own father was sabotaging his career. And there was only one way to get him to stop, and that would be to apply pressure from above; from Nicholson, or some other big-wig at the Shipwright's Guild. Pepys had said he might help, but only if...

Bess tidied her hair and shook out her skirts. She was no stranger to the idea of a trade. She'd watched the trulls of Ratcliff exchange money for 'favours' over and over again in the bawdy-houses and alleys. But she had thought she'd moved up beyond it. Stupid. Of course the oldest trade was the same here as everywhere else, just in finer clothes.

'Can I help you, mistress?' An elderly clerk had paused on his way up the stairs.

'No, I'm just leaving,' Bess said, hauling her thoughts back to order.

She put her shoulders back and gripping the banister, tottered down the stairs. Will would be waiting at home, all innocent, with no idea that he would never get work in the yards as long as his father was there. The thought made her want to go straight to Owen Bagwell and kick him hard where it hurt. Except it would do no earthly good, she knew that.

She'd have to go above him; that was all. And if Pepys wanted her, Pepys would have to pay.

Chapter 31

Will locked the paper in the cupboard and pocketed the key. Yet another letter from Kite increasing the charges on the loan for the house. Almost double. He paced the workshop floor, his fingers pressing into his temples.

He shouldn't have tried to bully Jack. He'd tried to stand up to him when he was a boy, but it never worked. Jack had always found a way to turn the tables and make everything Will's fault. He hoped Jack was still paying the interest on Flaggon Row now it had increased. If not, what would he do? But the increase had to have something to do with Jack; it was too much of a coincidence otherwise. He squirmed, like a fish on a hook.

He'd have to go and see Jack again. He sighed and took off his apron.

As he sat squashed into the wherry travelling upstream from Gravesend, with the wind in his face, he could not help but crane his neck to see into the royal dockyard. They were building a new gun battery in case of a Dutch invasion. The sight of all the industry, the huge hulls in the dry dock, from which he was excluded, gave him a physical pain. Their progress was slow, for on this stretch of twisted waterway, the traffic was always more, and they were obliged to crawl past the East India Company yards at Blackhall.

He was taken aback. The enormous wet-dock where a whole fleet could lie in wait for the tide or the weather, was full of warships.

A bad sign. Perhaps war with the Dutch was imminent.

If there was war, maybe the plague in Holland would have

abated, and the whole plague-water quackery would be finished.

But no, once he was in the Benedictine's place, the smell on the stairs and the chink of bottles soon disillusioned him. At the back of the crypt, where the air was dankest, he finally found Jack, busy noting down the numbers of crates stacked against the walls.

'Will,' Jack said. 'Managed to get that wife of yours under control yet?'

'We had another letter from Bastable,' Will said.

'Ah yes.' Jack didn't stop writing.

'The loan repayment's doubled. It's unreasonable.'

'Not at all. More people are moving into London, and the price of housing is going up.'

'Have you got some sort of agreement with Kite and Bastable?'

'Bastable's got a stake in our business,' Jack said with a shrug, 'if that's what you mean.'

'What's Bastable got to do with it?' Will followed Jack's lead as he counted more full bottles into the crates of straw. He picked up one of the bottles and rolled it in his palm. It was clammy in the fetid damp of the cloisters.

'There are about forty shareholders,' Jack said. 'Did you think you were the only one? Bastable's amongst them. And Kite. He put up the money for Allin's purchase of the ship. You said you wanted the interest on your loan paid, so I just passed it over each month. Unlike you, Bastable knows to keep his mouth shut.'

'I won't say anything, I swear. Just tell Bastable to put the repayments back to what they were.'

'Sorry, coz. Can't be done.'

'Why not?'

'We need the money. It's spoken for. We're buying another ship.'

'But that's extortion!'

'You should be pleased. It's an investment. You'll get it back with interest.'

'But we can't afford it. You know we can't. Bess has lost her work, and with no trade in wood because of this damned Dutch plague—'

'You won't be calling it that when we've made our fortune.'

'But another ship? Surely you won't be sailing through the winter months?'

'Have to. Even in tall seas. Too many investors like you, wanting their cut. Another six months,' Jack said, 'then perhaps there'll be a payout. Sales are slower with winter coming. There'll be more demand in spring.'

In other words, more folk would have fallen to the plague. The thought of it, even the idea of this terrible affliction, made Will's throat dry. He swallowed, rubbed a hand over his perspiring forehead.

'Is Rotterdam very bad?' he could not resist asking, even though he didn't really want an answer.

'It's a ghost town. The River Rotte is thick with people trying to leave. There are more corpses in the streets they say, than living men. They're piled three deep round the Laurenskerk. They stumble there to make their peace with God, and die where they stand.' Jack paused, tightened his pristine white cravat, smoothed his neck where it had been recently shaved. Then his voice took on a breezy tone. 'A mercy we're there to help with our medicine, hey, Will?'

'But I don't want this investment. This is all tangled, I can't keep it straight – what I owe Kite should have nothing to do with this business.'

'On the contrary. It was your idea. You asked me to pay off your loan, in return for ... how shall I say it? Your silence about where our snuff comes from.'

Will turned to face the wall. He was suffocating with a spiralling sense that somehow everything was becoming less and less under his control.

He took a deep breath. 'I want my money back. You'll have to find someone else.'

Jack laughed. 'Can't do that. The money's spent. And anyway, you'd be a fool; the next load is our biggest. Then we'll be rich men and I may be able to buy you out. I'm buying up all the shares I can. I want to own one of those ships at the end of it.'

'A ship? You?' Will couldn't keep the incredulity from his voice. Jack knew nothing of the sea.

Jack shot back, 'Then maybe I'd be able to find you a decent post, seeing as no-one else will.' The sting of Jack's words made him reel.

'I want no part of it. This... this dross.' He hurled the bottle in his hand at the floor. Glass fragments and green liquid splashed over Jack's immaculate shoes and up his ivory hose.

'You shouldn't have done that.' Jack's voice was low and cold.

Will backed away as Jack brushed a fleck of glass off his breeches.

Behind him, through the archway, the noise had drawn some of Jack's workers, who stood like a wall between Will and the stairs. One of them was armed with a club, another had his hand on his sword.

'Better pick that up,' Jack said.

Fear snaked up Will's spine. He did not dare refuse. He stooped to pick up the slivers of glass and the neck of the bottle with the cork still lodged in it, and dropped them back on the table.

'It's all right, lads,' Jack said. 'Just a little accident.'

The men melted back into the other chamber, leaving Will feeling stupid and small.

Jack walked over to Will and stood a little too close. 'Kite's an associate of mine with stakes in my business. It's thanks to me you've still got your house. He hates bad debtors. And Bastable fancies your workshop for his son. He's a smith.'

Will said nothing, but stared at the embroidered buttons on Jack's coat. I'm a coward, he thought. But the thought of losing his home and his workshop was too sobering. Though he had thought of renting out the workshop, the idea of the likes of rough men like Kite or Bastable underneath his home, with Bess upstairs was not a pretty one. Will wanted to leave; the atmosphere between them was thick, like sulphur. But he had to mend this, had to get Jack back to the affable pretence of before. Will made a tiny nod.

His acquiescence seemed to please Jack. 'Just be grateful you're bringing some relief to those poor afflicted souls.'

'Talk to Bastable for me, Jack. Ask him to put the repayments back to how they were.' Will hated the begging note in his voice.

Jack didn't answer.

Will stood a moment, his hands hanging uselessly by his side. Then he ducked his head under the stone archway and headed for the stairs.

His nephews, happily pressing corks into the necks of bottles, grinned at him and waved. He suppressed the urge to drag them out of there. Looking at the dishevelled workers, filling thousands of bottles, their bare feet slipping in the dregs on the cold flagged floor, he couldn't decide if Jack really believed in his potion, or whether he was deluding himself. Did he honestly think his elixir did any good? Was he fooling himself? Did all these others believe him too, that a bit of pond-water and some dye really helped anyone? If so, Jack was more of a fool than he thought.

Will climbed back up on jellied legs. This was why he avoided coming here. To shut it from his mind. Yet what could he do? He couldn't turn Jack in to the constables, because he had three small boys to support. What would happen to them, with no father? But he knew he wouldn't tell Bess what Jack was doing, and that's how he knew it was off the mark. And she'd warned him too, hadn't she? But he hadn't listened.

At the top of the stairs he paused to catch his breath, but had to stand aside as three heavy-set men tried to push past him. They were soaked and their hair was flattened to their heads. His first thought was that it must be raining. But then more men followed; fat-stomached, like merchants, with a rabble of serving men, bristling with sticks and swords. He flattened himself to the wall as they hurried down out of sight, but their rude manner alarmed him. And he'd seen the clubs of Jack's men below.

'Break it boys!' From below, raised voices. Splintering wood. Crashing glass. Shouts.

Every instinct told him to run, but he couldn't. More scuffling and thuds.

What in blaze's name was going on?

His heart gave a lurch. The boys. He had to get them out of there.

He had one foot on the stair when a drove of Jack's ragged workers burst from the doorway, tripping over each other in their hurry to get out. One held his sleeve to his face where a cut gushed blood. The boys weren't amongst them. As soon as he could, Will pushed past, almost toppling as he was on the narrowest part of the spiral. Down the stairs, two at a time.

'Toby! Hal!' he yelled. 'Billy!'

The floor was awash with green liquid and splinters of broken glass. The cloisters were full of noise and fighting men. Two of the men in soaked doublets upended another barrel, and water gushed in a cold waterfall over his ankles. Another was throwing crates to the ground.

Three workers danced behind Jack, their fists up. Jack swiped at the air before him with the jagged edge of a broken bottle. 'No nearer,' he shouted, through a lip thick with bruising.

Will had barely time to take this in when he heard whimpering.

'Uncle Will,' whispered Toby, 'under here.' Toby was trying to drag him by the leg under the table. The three boys were crouching there, backs against the slimy wall, eyes wide with terror.

'Listen to me. I'm getting you out,' he said. 'When I say run, run. Right?'

'What about Pa?' Toby asked.

A scuffle. Will turned to see Jack brawling with one of the men. 'He can take care of himself,' Will said. 'Are you ready?'

He was in time to see Jack slash at one of the men with his bottle. The intruders launched themselves towards the fighting men.

'Out. Hurry.' Will shepherded the boys under his arms and to the stairs, 'Go!' he shouted, pushing them from behind. The two elder boys scrambled up the steps.

Little Hal still cowered back under the table.

'No!' shouted Will, but it was too late.

Hal picked up a piece of broken glass, but let go of it with a cry as blood trickled from a cut in his fingers. The sight seemed to transfix him. 'Hurts!' he whimpered.

'Drop it.' Will reached under the trestle to drag him out, but he was screaming now with fear at his own blood. Finally Will managed to haul him out and, tucking him under his arm, made a run for the stairs.

At the top, they darted between the rows of goggling ribbon-workers who stood back to let them run by. As soon as they got outside and to a safe distance, he plonked Hal onto his feet.

The rain was lashing down, great gouts of water poured from the eaves and jetties of the houses. Toby and Billy appeared at his side, blinking through the rain.

'Let's look at your finger,' he said.

'Fumb,' Hal said. 'Not finger.'

Will tied a hasty bandage around the injured thumb with his kerchief, and made to cross the road, but Toby pressed himself up against the shelter of the building. 'We have to wait for my old man,' he said, his expression mutinous.

'No,' Will said, 'it's not safe. Not with all that broken glass. Let's get out of the rain. Your father knows where we live. He can come and get you when it's all over. It's no place for little ones like you.'

'Huh. I'm not a little one,' Toby said. 'I'm nine. I'm staying here. They'll go, once they've smashed everything. Then we'll start again, like last time.'

Will had hold of the other two boys, Hal and Billy, one by each slippery hand. They were already drenched.

'We'll have to help Pa sweep, like before,' Billy said, 'then carry everything somewhere else.'

'Tell you what,' Will said, 'we can come back later. How does that sound? I'll bet Bess has got a nice dinner cooking.'

'What will it be, Uncle Will?' Billy asked. 'For dinner?'

'I don't know. Something nice. A meat stew, maybe. With big potatoes, and maybe a rag pudding. And a sweet berry pie.' He looked to see if his words had reached Toby's ears. 'But we'll let Toby wait here for his father, if he wants to, and we'll come back to meet him after we've had our dinner.'

It worked. 'Think I'll come too. Just to keep an eye on the little ones for my old man,' Toby said.

'Good idea, Toby. I'll need a hand to cross all those roads.'

So they set off down Thames Street, walking fast, heads down against the rain, because Will hadn't enough money for the waterman. The rain eased as they walked, so they stopped to watch a big coal ship unload its lumpy cargo onto the wharf. The boys wanted to watch the huge derricks and pulleys swinging the sacks of coal. Under the creaking timbers, the navvies laboured, shoulders draped with leather to protect them from the weight of the sacks.

'Those men that came to make trouble,' Will said casually, 'you say they've been before?'

'Before we moved to the Cloisters,' Toby said. 'Used to be under the Merchant 'Venturer's before that. We have to be some place near the river for water, see? One of those girls above must've told on us. We have to keep quiet about where we are, Pa says. Or they come and smash everything up.'

'Why though?' Will asked, though he could think of many good reasons of his own.

'It's the 'Pothecary's Guild,' Toby said. 'They don't like the competition, Pa says.' Will couldn't blame them, especially as their remedies were more likely to effect a cure.

'They don't like it that his bottles sell best.' Billy said. 'People who take the 'Pothecaries' stuff die.'

'How d'you know?'

'Everyone knows. When the *Lily Allen* docks in Holland, the crates are gone within minutes. The whole of Holland's heard of my father,' Toby said proudly. Then he paused. 'He'll be alright, won't he?' His anxious eyes peered up at Will.

'He'll be fine, old chap.' Will spoke with a reassurance he didn't feel, slapped Toby on the shoulder as if he were a man.

'I'm hungry,' Billy said, pulling on his sleeve.

So what's new, Will thought, as he picked up Hal, sat him on his hip, and set off towards Flaggon Row with the two other boys following. Though Lord knows what he'd tell Bess.

***

The rain had stopped, and after the sudden downpour, the sun had come out, along with a stiff breeze, so Bess was hanging out Will's shirts to dry on the back fence. She paused, peg in mouth, as a delivery man leading a dripping donkey halted outside their house. He heaved a sack from the pannier. 'For you, mistress,' he called.

She put down the washing basket and hurried over, stepping over the puddles in her path.

'Apples, from Mistress Stoner,' the delivery man said. 'There's a note in there with them.'

Bess looked in the sack – Kentish pippins. She pulled out the damp note, guilt washing over her. She'd meant to write to Meg to explain about their last meeting, but Meg had beaten her to it.

Apples again, from my uncle's orchard. Hope you can use them, as he always has too many, and there's no demand in Kent. I know it's awkward with my father not wanting us to meet, so I hope this will make amends. And I realise I was uncharitable about Will's cousin. Last time I saw you, you looked harassed, and Will was behaving most strangely. Is all well between you? If you pass by the shop one noon-time, we could walk in the Convent Garden and exchange news. Hoping you fare well, as do I.

Your affectionate friend, Meg

Bess asked the man to help her take them upstairs and wait whilst she wrote a note of thanks. She'd heard Will go out, so she couldn't ask him to help. She wrote quickly, unwilling to think about the whole deception with Mr Pepys, and the fact that Meg somehow thought it was Will to blame for the misunderstanding. She simply scrawled a thank-you to Meg and promised her she would visit soon.

When the man had gone she finished hanging out Will's shirts to dry in the breeze. As she smoothed them over the line, she wondered how she had even thought about deceiving such a good, honest man as her husband.

***

Bess heard the boys before she saw them. She recognised the clatter of their feet up the outside stairs, and held the door open wide for them to come in.

'Guess who I found in the city,' Will said, handing Hal over to Bess. She took hold of the squirming child and hugged him tight. He was soaked through. 'Did you get caught in that rain?'

'Pa's fighting,' Hal said. 'With a bottle. And I hurt my fumb.'

'Is dinner cooking?' Billy asked hopefully.

'Not yet, my little man,' she said, 'but it will be. I'll see if I can find some bread and cheese in the meantime—'

But already the two eldest boys were opening the big press in the larder, and arguing over who should use the bread knife. 'Go and mind them, would you, Will?' she said.

'Look, Aunt Bess, my fumb.' Hal held out his thumb again, tied up in an unwieldy knot with Will's kerchief.

'Oh my,' she said. 'What happened there?'

Will reappeared by her side, bread knife in hand. 'He cut it, on a piece of broken glass,' he said, speaking in a hurry. 'It's a clean cut, shouldn't fester.'

'What's this about Jack and a fight?'

'Jack was having a bit of trouble with some customers. It was getting a little heated, so I brought the boys here. Out of the way.'

'Hal called it a fight.'

'It was just a bit of a scuffle.'

'Oh, Will.' She let out a heavy sigh. 'What was it about this time?'

'They're in competition with him, and they don't like that he's doing so well.'

'Did you call for a constable?'

'It didn't seem necessary.'

'You should have called for a constable. It's intimidation. Those poor boys.'

***

Later that day Bess climbed up the loft ladder to stack Meg's apples under the roof ready for winter. It was hot in the attic and dusty, and she had to be careful not to put a foot between the rafters. Mary followed her up and began to stolidly lay the apples out in rows, making sure each didn't touch the next. Bess followed suit, but she was uneasy. Will had looked on edge, and the boys were over-excited and fractious.

Beneath her, she could hear the three boys helping Will with polishing the cutlery. There was obviously some sort of mock fight going on with the knives, and she hoped they'd be careful and not cut themselves again. She wondered how Hal had hurt his thumb. Trust Jack not to have been watching him.

As if to read her mind, she heard the door downstairs slam, and Jack's voice from beneath her knees. She paused, an apple in hand.

'Shall I go down, mistress?' Mary asked.

'No need,' Bess said. 'It's only Jack.'

'Pa!' The children's excited shouts from below. 'Did you whip 'em, Pa?'

''Course I did. They'll not come back for another roasting.'

Mary held up an apple. 'This one looks—'

'Shh.' Bess brought her finger to her lips. She wanted to hear what the men were saying. Mary shrugged and put the apple to one side, carrying on with her task. Bess didn't move. She sat in the dark, listening, trying to make sense of Jack's words.

'It's put the whole operation weeks behind,' Jack said. 'So I can't spare funds from the profits to pay your loan this month, coz.'

'But you must. We can't pay it. It's double what it was! I told you. Bess has lost her work at the glover's and I've no more work. All my money's in your damn business. We'll be homeless if you don't.'

It was unlike Will to swear.

'I can't do anything,' Jack said.

'I'll tell the authorities you're trading from infected ports.'

'And what good would that do? They'd close us down. And then you still wouldn't be able to pay.'

'Hush now, Bess is upstairs,' Will's voice cut over him, and the voices fell to whispers.

'Why are we whispering?' Billy's loud whisper was fit for the stage.

'Tell you what, here's a farthing,' Jack replied in a low voice. 'See if you can get some ends of sausage from the butcher. They'll be shutting up shop soon.'

The bang of the door again and the voices fell to a low hum. Heedless of what Mary might think, Bess leaned over, ear close to the floorboards. They were hiding things from her, keeping something back, that they didn't want her to know. Was that her own name, in amongst the talk? The thought made her chest tight. It was stifling up here, she could barely breathe.

From below, 'Bess?'

'He's calling, mistress,' Mary said.

'I know.' Bess's voice came out more sharp than she intended. She went to place the apple down on the rafters, but as she reached out, it gave, soft and pulpy in her hand. She held it up to the crack of light streaming through the roof tiles. It was brown, rotten.

'The rest are bad, mistress. I was trying to tell you but—'

Bess dropped it with a thud, and opened up the sack. Even in the gloom she could smell that the apples at the bottom were fermenting. There was the sweet, musty aroma of rotting fruit.

'There must've been a bad one in the bottom,' Mary said.

'Best get rid, then. Save any you can.' Bess crawled to the trapdoor and manoeuvred herself awkwardly down the ladder. The men stopped talking as soon as Bess appeared, and the room was suddenly still.

There were some papers on the table and a quill and ink.

Will hurried to sign his name, Jack tipped a vial of sand over it, shook it to dry it, and hurriedly pocketed it.

'What's that?' Bess asked.

'Paperwork … for an extension to the loan.'

'An extension?'

'Yes. Jack's given us a sort of bridge – a little more time to pay off Kite, that's all.' His gaze shifted away from her. He was lying. The words of Jack and Will's conversation came back to her. *Close us down. Infected ports. Homeless.*

'Meg sent us some apples, but half of them are off. You'll need to bring them down when Mary's done.' Bess's voice was tight and harsh.

'Later,' Will said, still avoiding her eyes. 'I'll do it later.'

Bess took in Jack's bruised lip and what was obviously going to be another black eye. 'What happened to you?' she asked.

'Just a bit of a skirmish. They came off worst,' Jack said, casually. 'Unlike some, I can stand up for myself.' He glanced at Will, but Will was strangely silent.

'What was it about?' she asked Jack directly.

'Some folk who want to put me out of business. They've tried it before.'

'Snuff traders?'

'Rogues and scoundrels.'

She looked to Will for more explanation, but he just said, 'Leave it, Bess. Jack's had enough to contend with.'

But Bess couldn't leave it. She kept on thinking about it for the rest of the day.

She didn't like the air of secrecy. Or the idea of an extension to the loan.

Nowadays their money never appeared as actual coinage in the jar, though Bastable's knock never shivered the door the way it used to.

She was tired of the worry, of wondering if they'd be able to pay the loan, tired of the friction between her and Will; just wanted an end to it.

Chapter 32

At night Bess tried to draw Will into her arms, but he would not have any dealings with her. He pretended to sleep, but she often heard him prowling the chambers at night, the bang of the workshop door as he came and went. Will was mysteriously silent about Jack and what sort of help he was giving them with the loan.

One night, Will was late coming up for supper. Bess went down to the workshop and saw him staring by candlelight at his empty work-bench. His knitted cap was pulled firmly over his ears to keep off the cold, and his shoulders rose and fell in a sigh, before he scraped at the pile of sawdust in front of him, moving it to and fro. She watched him absently gouge a hole in the bench with his drawknife.

'It's past seven bells. Did you not hear them?'

Bess pulled up a wooden stool and sat next to Will, resting her hand on his needlecord breeches. 'Tell me what's going on, Will. I know something's wrong.'

'Nothing's wrong.'

'The other week – what was Jack fighting about?' He swivelled away, so her hand fell to her side. 'You brought those children home for some reason,' she persisted. 'What was Jack doing?'

'He was busy. It was men's business.'

'Men's business, men's business.' She stood and threw up her hands in annoyance. 'That's just an excuse. Why won't you talk to me? I know we can afford a servant and such, but this business with Jack, I can see there's more to it than you're telling and—'

'It's just business, Bess.' He turned back and caught her eyes with a warning look.

'Beg pardon, husband,' she said, bitterly.

'I have to earn a living how I can. I lost my chance on the *Salvation*. And you've no work now, not since the glover laid you off. And I have to do what I have to. Beggars can't be choosers.'

Bess felt the unspoken words though he hadn't said them – that it was her fault he was not at sea on the *Salvation*, earning his keep as a ship's carpenter. Not that they'd seen any money yet from his last stint, like all the sailors. The King's treatment of his fleet was a scandal. She pursed her lips and went back up to the chilly parlour, longing for Will's company but not daring to ask for it.

***

Will watched Bess go, her back straight as a fire-iron, her skirts dragging wood-shavings with her. The *Salvation* was on his mind. Hertford had called in earlier and said she was waiting in quarantine. There'd been two more cases of the plague on board, and such was the men's fear of the disease, that the ill men had been off-loaded, still living, into the sea. He imagined the cold suck of it, the lungs screaming for air. The slow drift downwards, eyes staring sightless into the greenish depths. It could have been him, he realised, thrown overboard to drown. And now the ship was quarantined, becalmed by the disease, not the wind.

'Damn it to hell,' he said, thumping his fist on the bench. Bess and her questions – she didn't want to know what business he was in. It was sordid. Not just Jack, but the apothecaries too; all after grabbing what profits they could reap from someone else's misfortune.

Upstairs, Bess heard the thump of his fist, and wondered if something had fallen. They couldn't go on this way. The promise from Pepys had come to nothing. She'd waited and waited, but no letter came, no promise of advancement for Will. It made her angry, that Pepys could have treated her that way, to try to seduce her, and then to just drop her as if she was of no importance at all. She was determined to keep the pressure on Mr Pepys to do something for Will.

Full of anger she penned a curt note to remind Pepys about keeping his word, and set off outside to find a messenger to take it to Seething Lane. By the ferry she found a link-boy, and, offering him an apple, told him to put the letter through the slot at the Navy offices. The boy took a bite, grinned, and sped away. Her message would be on Pepys' desk by the morning. When it was out of her hands she immediately wanted to call it back. What would Pepys think of her, harassing him this way? He was a big man in the city. The thought of how she was grovelling to him filled her with shame. At the same time, she remembered that moment in his office where she'd seen something softer beneath the bumptious façade of the man. Perhaps this time, he'd keep his promise.

Chapter 33

Will took a bowl off the lathe. Another Navy commission with a pittance of a profit. Everyone knew times were hard for woodturners and so the Navy office had bargained him down. He hoped the Navy would not notice he made the bowls smaller now, to take less wood, but it made him feel guilty.

The swing of the door and a draught made him look up. 'Jacob.'

'Morrow, sir.' Jacob was already blushing, and he looked up at Will through a lock of hair that had fallen over his eyes.

'What can I help you with? It's good to see you.'

'I was wondering ... you see ...' His mouth worked as he chewed his lip.

'Come on lad, get it out.'

'I want to come back, sir. I tried the tannery, but it stinks. Besides, wood's all I want to do. I'd be no trouble, and I know you can't feed me nor nothing, nor spare the wood, but I could live at home and I'd like to just be in here watching like, if you'll have me.'

Will softened at the sight of his earnest face. 'I'm sorry, Jacob, but you can see I'm only turning bowls. It's all I've got. There's not enough work for two.'

'I know that. But all I want to do is watch. You're the best. I went to look at the other masters but none of them have the feeling for it. Please, sir. Don't send me away.'

Jacob's eager expression melted him. 'I suppose so. But I can't give you an apprentice wage, and I can only give you scraps of wood.'

'Yes, sir. I understand.' A huge grin split his face. 'Thank you. I'll get my smock on, shall I?'

Will smiled. 'Best had.'

He set Jacob to making wooden handles for tankards with the small offcuts lying in the corners of the shed. Maybe he could sell them to the pewterer. Having Jacob back in the workshop revived him. It was cheering to have company, and the lad was more than willing. And he loved to teach him, to show his skill, and pass it on.

He was coaching Jacob in the art of turning the sinuous curves of tankard handles when Hertford blustered through the door.

'Can you spare me a moment, Will?' Hertford asked cheerily, shaking the drips off his hat and trying to pull the feather back into shape.

'Course I can,' Will said. 'Come on in, my friend, out of the wet. Jacob's got the hang of these handles now anyway.' He turned to Jacob. 'Take the gentleman's cloak, then carry on, and make another six just like that one.' He ushered Hertford to the corner where two stools were set up next to the plan table where he drew up his designs. 'How are you, Mr Hertford?'

'I'm well. Good to be back. We've been out of town. My wife wanted to take a tour of Italy. And now she has a desire for a small card table, something pretty, perhaps with folding leaves. They have such things there. She finds London rather dull now, and wants to invite her friends to play cribbage in the afternoons. Of course I told her you'd likely be too busy—'

'No, not busy at all.' Will's heart leapt. 'In fact, business has been rather slow. It will be a pleasure.'

'Really? I thought you'd have some work with the Shipwrights Guild by now. Did Pepys not have a word with Nicholson? Is there no work for you in the yard?'

'Yes, I think he did, but I've still heard nothing.' He kept his voice down so that Jacob did not hear him. 'Not that I'm not grateful — thank you for trying for me, Mr Hertford.'

'It's not me you should be thanking, it's your wife; it was her idea.'

'Bess? Why?'

'Oh.' Hertford looked abashed. He plucked at his non-existent beard. 'I wasn't supposed to tell you. Damn it all, I'm no good at keeping secrets. She came to see me. To ask if I'd speak to Sam Pepys, get him to have a word in the right ears.'

Will blinked. He remembered every single meeting with Pepys in excruciating detail. So it was all Bess's doing, not really Hertford wanting to help him at all. He'd thought Hertford had asked Pepys because Will was his friend, but no. It was Bess interfering again. She'd called a favour on one of his best customers – his *only* decent customer. A niggle of irritation burned in his chest, but he tried to be calm, and stood up and went to fetch a flagon of ale.

'Sorry, Will. I think I spoke out of turn,' Hertford said.

'It's all right,' he said, with effort, 'she told me.' Will could almost see the relief flush over Hertford's face, as his worried frown was replaced by his usual cheerful smile.

'You're a good pair,' Hertford said. 'There's many would want a wife who cares so much.'

'Aye,' Will said. But the hot feeling in his throat had not died.

'Still, you're better off on dry land I daresay. It's awkward for shipping with all these regulations. Have you heard about the *Lily Allen*?'

'No.' He was barely listening, searching for the designs in his drawer. 'What about her?'

'Whole crew was arrested. They caught her running without papers.'

Will paused. The name had registered. He turned cold. The

Lily Allen – wasn't that Jack's ship?

Hertford was still speaking, while even Jacob, eager for gossip, stopped his carving to listen. 'Yes. Ignored the quarantine regulations and tried to sneak in via Hay's Wharf in Southwark. Wasn't the crew's fault, was it? They've taken all her cargo and dumped it out at sea. I've heard tell it was snuff. Good thing I get mine from Grimes on Hawthorn Street. He's straight as a die. Wouldn't want to breathe in anything from Holland, not with the pestilence so rife there.'

'You do right, sir,' Jacob pronounced.

Will's mind raced. He tried to scrape his thoughts together, calm the thudding of his heart. 'What of the men who invested in the ship? What of them?'

'Fools. They must have known what was going on, yet they let the crew take the blame. I hope they find them all and give them a good long spell in the clink.'

'Maybe not all of them knew what was going on,' Will said defensively.

Hertford shook his head, leaned back against the wall. 'They knew all right. It's sad, isn't it, Jacob – good honest men like Will, trying to make a living by their own skill and hard work, and then men like that – ready to put us all at risk for money. Doesn't bear thinking of.'

'Terrible, sir.' Will pinned a concerned look on his face, but didn't dare meet Hertford's eyes. He studied the plans in front of him instead.

'I'm glad they've stopped it,' Hertford said. 'They'll catch up with them soon enough. Pepys says they'll be banned from trading again.'

'Good.' He repeated it in case he'd not been convincing. 'Good. That's good.'

Hertford frowned at him. 'You all right? You look a bit… well…'

~251~

'I'm fine. Never better. Jacob, you'd best get those handles finished. Shall I make a sketch for this card table, Mr Hertford?'

But when Will picked up the lead, his hand shook. He sketched out a line, but then put his lead down. He couldn't do it. He needed to find out what had happened to their money. The thought of it, how they were relying on it, made him want to groan. 'I need to think about the design,' he said. 'How would it be, if you called in tomorrow, yes tomorrow, and I'll have the sketches ready. Jacob, would you fetch Mr Hertford's cloak?'

Hertford stood, plainly puzzled by Will's sudden impatience to see him go. 'Well, I suppose—'

'Yes. That's it. I'll do several sketches,' he said, ushering Hertford to the door, 'in the Italian style. It will be better if I take my time, no point rushing them is there, you'll want different designs to choose from … your wife can approve them, and she might want to see a good selection... here's your hat, sir.' He willed Hertford to leave. What if the constables came here? And where was Jack?

'There's no hurry—' Hertford took his hat and let himself be escorted to the door.

'I'll see you tomorrow, sir. The sketches will be ready then, I promise.'

As soon as he'd gone, Will buttoned up his doublet and threw on his cloak and hat. He peered out of the door to check Hertford had gone.

'You going out, master?' Jacob asked.

'Yes, yes. Just go on with those handles.' He was impatient. He didn't tidy his tools, just left them all where they lay, and in a panic, almost ran up the street. The rain and wind whipped at his face, so he had to remove his hat and his hair soon hung bedraggled round his face. His first call was to the warehouse below the ribbon factory. When he arrived, he was in time to see two men huffing up the stairs. One held a lighted taper in his hand.

'Out of my way,' the man said gruffly, pushing past.

Will stood to one side, and let them go. He didn't know if they were Jack's men, or the constable's men. He hurried down the stairs.

When he got to the bottom he stopped, clinging to the rope handrail. The cloisters were in darkness. He took out a flint and struck it, lighting some tinder to get a spill to catch. The tiny flame illuminated what he feared. An empty chamber.

He touched the taper to the wall-sconce and it leapt into flickering life. He lit another and another, progressing through the arched vaults. The vats were there, but no workers, no bottles. No crates. The place had been stripped clean. The only thing left were some labels, clinging damply to the tables and sticking to his boots underfoot. *Pestdrenk,* he kept reading, *Pestdrenk*. The word lost its meaning.

Maybe they'd moved. Yes, that was it. They'd moved somewhere else after the apothecaries had been. But there was no sign of Jack or the boys. He'd have to see if he was at home. He dared not think of his investment, all his savings, because he knew it would lead him into despair. No. Think about finding Jack. He forced one foot in front of the other. He didn't bother blowing out the sconces, just headed out of the darkness into the light.

On the way out, he stopped the weaving supervisor, but before he could say a word, the man held up his hand. 'If it's about Jack Bagwell, you're not the first to come looking, and I know nothing. He left a few weeks ago. Took his business somewhere else. A right blaggard if ever I met one. I'd like to punch his lights out. Bleeding constables tramping through here in their big boots, upsetting my girls. Since then there's been constant coming and going, and no sign of Mr Bagwell.'

Will caught a wherry across the mud-grey river and ran along

Drury Lane to St Giles, the crossroads at which so many had entered life in the city of London, or exited it, on their way to their executions at the triple tree at Tyburn. He hurried up past the parish stocks and whipping post, only had to pause for breath at the churchyard gate. He leant up against it, the very place where prisoners would be offered a sip from the 'St Giles's Bowl', their last drop of ale on earth.

Off Broad Street the houses changed from those of merchants to ramshackle rookeries and shanty dwellings, crammed together as if they'd been thrown there. Will slowed, searching for the right house. He'd only ever been there once before, because Jack never invited him.

This was the place. It backed onto the bear-baiting ring, from where he could hear the shouts of a crowd and the guttural growls of a bear. Jack's house was a thin sliver of a building scarcely eight feet wide, jammed in what had been the gap between two bigger houses. He hammered on Jack's door but nobody answered. He stood back to look at the single narrow window on the first floor, and thought he saw movement behind the crack in the shutter. He pounded again, calling, 'Jack? It's me, Will. Open up.'

Still no answer.

'Jack! I know you're there. I'm on my own. Let me in.'

He was about to go away when there was a noise from behind the door of a bolt being shunted back. A moment later the door opened. 'Uncle Will?' Toby stood there, his face pale, his eyes red.

'Where's your father?'

'They took him. And the landlord was shouting at us, telling us to get out. Said he'd break our heads, if he caught us. But I locked the door and shut him out. But I think he'll be back. He tried to smash in the door.'

'Where? Where did they take him?'

'The Fleet. I kicked them, got their shins good and hard, but I couldn't stop them.' Toby's mouth quivered with suppressed emotion. 'It's the prison, isn't it?'

Just then Billy appeared behind him, holding a crying Hal by the hand.

'It's all right. I'm here now,' Will said, shepherding them into the downstairs parlour. 'Just stay here quietly a moment like good boys.'

'They said Pa's ship's impounded,' Billy said. 'What's "impounded", Uncle Will?'

'It means confiscated. Like when he takes your penny whistle off you, when you make too much noise.' He patted Billy on the head before he made a thorough search of the cupboards. He opened jars and took the lids off pots, but found only a half-used packet of tobacco and some discarded pen-nibs.

'What are you looking for?' Toby asked.

'Did you have another place where you made the potions, Toby?'

'No. Pa said the ship had to come back before we could afford to rent another place. Them 'pothecaries did us good n'proper.'

'Just wait there,' Will said. He strode up the narrow stairs two at a time to the upstairs parlour. There he threw open more cupboards, searched the table, opened drawers, pulling out papers. So many papers. Sheaves of unpaid bills, gambling debts, tallies of money owed. Every one of them a demand, not a single one a payment. Will scanned them all, his stomach sinking. Nothing. No money, nothing to show for his investment.

He dragged open another drawer, and seeing the contents, hurled it against the wall. It crashed to the floor. Just more of those damned labels, *Pestdrenk*. They fluttered down like moths round his feet.

'Uncle Will?' Toby's panicked shout from downstairs.

Will didn't answer but leapt up the flight of stairs to the bedroom. Two mattresses – one was obviously Jack's, the other the boys' because it was strewn with small linens. He upturned the bedding, nearly tipping over a half-full stinking chamberpot in the process. Only straw and dust.

'No,' he groaned. He sank down on the floor, rested his head in his hands.

'Don't be sad, Uncle Will.' Billy appeared at the door. 'They'll let him out, won't they? They always do. Soon as he gets someone to pay his debts.'

Will laughed, but heard the bitterness in his own voice, saw Billy's puzzled expression. He stood up, took a deep breath, brushed down his breeches. 'Come with me, boys,' Will said, rallying himself, 'let's fetch you a few things, and you can come home with me.'

'What about Pa?' Toby said. 'When he comes back, he won't know where we've gone.'

'Then we'll leave a note. Have you paper?'

Toby handed him a piece of paper and a nub of charcoal, but Will said, 'No, you write it. Just say, "Gone to uncle's".' Will didn't want to sign his name to anything, or leave his name or address in case someone came looking for them.

Toby pushed it back to him. 'I'm not much good with letters. Never had the practice, see.'

'Can't you write?'

'Never learnt. Can read a bit though. Nanny Prescott showed us.'

Will groaned. He'd though he'd paid for their education. The betrayal was like a fist in the guts. 'What about Tyler?'

'Who?' Toby's face was puzzled.

'Your tutor.'

'Never heard of him.'

Will closed his eyes a moment, seeking strength. Then he leant on the wax-strewn table and wrote the note himself in hurried capital letters. 'Now, let's pack a few things and go, quick, before the landlord comes back.'

He found some empty hessian sacks by the back door and bundled everything that could be useful inside. The boy's threadbare outdoor clothes, their nightshirts, the dog-eared prayer book. Jack's house seemed to have little comforts; some of the windows were stuffed with rags to keep out the cold.

'We have to take these,' Toby said, dragging out a trunk and throwing open the lid. 'They were his best. He'll leather us if we leave them behind.'

Will gazed down at the new suits of clothes, all velvet and damask, fine horn buttons and embroidery. Even ribbons on the breeches. A pristine pair of leather shoes with gilded buckles. Another with ribboned roses. He bent down and lifted up the top layer to find more heavy velvets beneath. Good Lord, there were at least three suits here. And there was the canary yellow waistcoat he'd seen Jack wearing a few weeks ago. And his periwig. Touching that hair made him nauseous. He pressed it back. 'We can't, Toby. They're too heavy for us to carry.'

'I'll carry them. He was proud of them. Looked like a king wearing them. Clothes maketh the man, Pa says.'

'An' if we don't take them, the landlord'll have them,' Billy said.

Will knew this to be true. 'It's a long way. One of you might have to piggy-back Hal,' he warned.

'I don't mind,' Toby said, stroking the figured cloth of the doublet, longingly.

Will bundled the weight of cloth into a sack. At least he might be able to pawn these. He still hung onto the hope, like a thin thread, that Jack might have saved some money in the compter's, that his savings would by some miracle return to him. But first, he had to broach Bess.

'Let's not mention to Aunt Bess about the ship,' he said as they struggled their way down the street, the drizzle making them squint. 'Your pa'll be out in a couple of days, and it will only worry her.'

'You mean tell a lie, Uncle Will?' Billy asked.

'No, not a real lie. Just a white lie. To save your auntie from worry. We'll tell her it's just a misunderstanding … like a mistake.'

'Will he be out tomorrow then, if it's a mistake?' Billy asked.

'I should hope so,' Will said. He glanced sideways and saw Toby's expression. It was full of a knowing beyond his years and it made Will sad.

Chapter 34

'Our money,' Bess said, 'they can't touch that, can they?'

'No,' Will said.

But he'd kept out of her way in the workshop ever since, leaving her to cope with the boys, and there'd barely been time for a proper conversation.

Another gambling debt, Will had said. Bess couldn't fathom why Jack hadn't bribed his way out of the clink, as usual. Hal didn't understand, and asked when Jack was coming home every hour, and Toby was unruly, refusing to do what he was told.

'You're not my pa,' he kept saying scathingly when she asked him to help.

Bess poked at the fire to try to get more flame. The air was icy, and the heat of the fire barely brought forth steam from the wooden drying horse, dripping with boys' shirts in three different sizes. It was two weeks ago now, and Will had been to visit Jack in prison twice, taking him bread and a few other necessities. He'd returned each time grey and haggard, and snapped at her when she asked when Jack would be coming to fetch his sons.

Still, it would be just like Jack to suddenly appear on the front doorstep, so every time there was a knock, the three little boys were out of their seats like greased lightning. And when it wasn't him, the boys were even more sullen and argumentative. After another week or so, Will set the boys to carving spoons.

'Don't want them to be idle,' he said.

Bess enjoyed seeing them each tie a tablecloth round their waists and set to work. She'd thought at first the boys working was a game, but they were down there long hours, and so was

Jacob, the apprentice. Jack's boys tried hard, but they weren't Jacob. And another thing – Will had given the boys cheap softwood, not his usual oak, and in their unskilled hands the spoons were misshapen and clumsy. Instead of throwing them away, Will had sanded them, and polished them up.

At first she'd thought it was kind-heartedness, that he'd encouraged them, and finished the spoons to give the boys something to be proud of. But when she asked Jacob to show her Toby's one day, he said Will had sold it. His face reddened with embarrassment as he told her. He said Will had sold them all to a market trader on Cheapside, even though they certainly didn't look like the sort of quality that usually came from his workshop.

Will selling shoddy work was something she'd never seen before. And then there was the lack of money. Will denied her and looked furtive whenever she asked for housekeeping money.

The next day there was a deafening knock at the door, and when Bess opened it, there was the angular figure of Bastable. For months, their loan had been paid in advance, so she was flustered to find Bastable on the doorstep, and she knew already that the coin jar was empty. She threw on a warm shawl and ran downstairs to ask Will, with Bastable picking his way gingerly after her in his heavy black cloak. Will turned his back on them both, but she heard him scrape all the loose coins from his pouch. A moment later he strode over to the dusty bowl on the shelf by the door. It was the bowl for the farthings usually reserved for messenger boys.

'Here.' Bess watched him count out the money into her cupped hands.

'It's two ha'pence short,' Will said, curtly. 'Tell him, I'll have it tomorrow.'

Bastable leaned on the door jamb of the workshop, took the fistful of coppers and smiled. 'See Jack Bagwell caught you too,' he said. 'Me and my brother had our eyes on this place, but we can't afford it now. My Edward lost everything. He's gone back to heaving coal. Guess this might be the last time I see you here, too eh? Shame. Make a nice little business for someone this, with the house above and all.'

Bess nodded, but his words lodged in her head like splinters.

'Not so hoity-toity now, are you.' He laughed, a wheezing, mirthless laugh. 'Still, at least we're alive, not like them buggers in Holland,' Bastable said.

Bess retreated fast inside the door and slammed it closed, turning her back on it. Will looked up from his work bench, a sheepish expression on his face.

'Time to tell me what's going on, Will,' she said. 'We haven't a single farthing left in the house. And Bastable seems to think he'll not see us next month.' She advanced on him now, her temper roused, her face hot with rage and humiliation. 'Why's that, Will?'

'Take no notice of Bastable, he's just—'

'He said he'd been caught out by Jack Bagwell too. What did he mean?'

'Bess,' Will placated, 'not in front of Jacob and the boys.'

'Why not? They know their father's in gaol, don't they? What can be worse than that?'

'We'll talk later.'

'No. We'll talk now, or you'll be looking to find someone else to take care of these children, so help me God. Bastable was laughing at us. Laughing, Will! Since when did we become a laughing stock?'

Billy took hold of her skirts and began to cry. 'Please don't shout at him! It's our fault, isn't it? We didn't mean it, Auntie.'

'No, sweetheart, it's not you.' She knelt down and took him by the arms, instantly sorry to have raised her voice. She ran a hand over his head to soothe his grizzling. 'It's just …' She was at a loss to explain, without heaping blame on Will or on Jack. In the corner, Jacob was twisting his work smock and looking like he didn't want to be there.

'Is it because of the ship?' Billy said. 'Uncle Will said we'd not to upset you.'

'What ship?' From the corner of her eye she caught Will's guilty expression.

'Pa's ship. The one that was imp … imp … confiscated,' Toby said, glancing at Will with sudden venom.

She suddenly saw it all. Jack's business couldn't operate without a ship.

When she turned to Will, he was already backing away. 'Our savings.' She choked out the words. 'You put all our money in Jack's ship.'

The pain in his eyes told her everything, but she didn't want to hear it. She went back to the door and swung it open.

'Bess, wait, I can explain …'

But the time for explaining was over. She slammed the door behind her and ran, her feet barely touching the ground. She was at the Thames before she realised it, her face stinging with cold, and her fingers numb. Already the edge of the river was lapping under scales of ice.

She pulled her shawl tighter and pressed her fists to her cheeks to warm them. How could he? Lose all their money and not say a word? Everything fell into place. How could she have been so naïve not to see it before? Will's scrimping and the way he sold those spoons at two for a farthing. Not only had Jack put paid to their future, but he'd somehow saddled them with three extra mouths to feed. They'd worked so hard to come up in the world, and now it was as if the ground had been ripped from beneath her feet.

Oh Lord. If they couldn't afford to stay in Flaggon Row then Will would lose his carpenter's shop. With no real business and no access to the Guild or the yards, how would he make a living? They were sinking fast.

And then she had another thought. Maybe Will had lied to her, and Jack wasn't coming back. All the warmth drained from her. What would happen then? The children – they'd have no place else to go.

~ PART THREE ~

Love never fails to master what he finds,

But works a different way in different minds,

The fool it enlightens and the wise it blinds.

John Dryden

Chapter 35

Bess swivelled to face the city; the chimneys smoked hazy black stripes into the icy air. She'd no money for a fare. Well, she'd just have to walk to the Fleet. She had so many questions, and if Will wouldn't talk, there was only one person who could answer them.

Grim-faced, she strode up the hill to Ludgate, past the half-timbered Apothecaries Hall and the Belle Sauvage Inn with its steamed-up windows, averting her eyes from the crudely painted sign of a naked woman wielding a bow and arrow. For a moment she baulked. Why hadn't she brought Mary with her? The Fleet quarter wasn't the sort of place any respectable woman should walk alone, but she'd been in too much of a hurry to think of that.

She thrust the thought away and pushed on, ignoring the stitch in her side, and the fact that although her shawl was thickly knitted, it was almost useless in this bitter weather. The winters seemed to be getting worse – already there was a rime of frost on the cobblestones.

Once under the arched gate, the smell of the Fleet Ditch caught in her throat. Thick with excrement, the sluggish channel of the river oozed behind the buildings, and the Fleet gateway marked an invisible barrier between the city and the lawless side-alleys and yards of the Fleet quarter. Here, prisoners who could afford the privilege were allowed to live openly, under the so-called 'Rules of The Fleet', but it meant that the streets were populated by cheats, felons and low-life, all intent on getting a little extra from unsuspecting passers-by.

Bess kept her arms pressed tight into her sides to make herself less of a target. If there was one thing she knew, it was that Will wouldn't have had the money to bail Jack out, so Jack would be lodged on the Commoners Side, not on the Masters side.

Ahead of her the iron gate into the yard of the prison stood open. Beyond stood a hulking stone edifice, black with soot, its barred windows even blacker, like unblinking eyes. She joined the queue at a grilled window in the side of the gatehouse, but saw straight away that it was hopeless. She'd wasted her time. Unless she slid a coin through the grille, the warder wouldn't give a nod or a ticket to pass through. What was she going to do now? She wasn't going home again, not now she'd walked all this way. And come what may, she'd confront that scoundrel Jack about what he expected them to do with his children.

She stamped to bring some feeling to her frozen feet as she queued, debating what to do. Finally it was her turn.

'Cold day, isn't it?' She smiled at the warder winningly. 'Must be half-frozen stuck in there all day.'

'Yeh. Don't get off duty until five.'

'I'm after Jack Sutherland,' she said.

'First time visiting?'

She dipped her head.

'Thought so. T'aint a bleedin' hospital; I don't know all their names,' the man said, sniffing, his voice nasal. He was obviously full of a cold. 'If your man's not been able to send you a note he'll be down in Bartholomew Fair most likely.'

'Where's that?'

'Worst place you can be. Down the cellars. It can be rough in there. Sure you want to go in?'

'Yes.' Her answer was firm.

'Penny then.'

The words she'd been dreading. She put on a concerned face. 'Aren't you cold, sitting there in that draught? You poor man. I can tell you're not well. You'll catch your death; you should be at home with a hot posset and a nice warm fire.'

'And beggars might fly.' He sniffed again. 'It'll be full on dark by the time I get off. Always is.'

'Well, we can't have you catching your death. Here – have this.' She was already bundling up her shawl and stuffing it under the grille. 'Take it. It's a good thick one – an extra layer to keep your knees warm.'

'Oh, no. I couldn't do that,' he said, but he was feeling its texture and she could see he was tempted.

'Say no more about it. You need it more than I do, and soon as I've seen Jack, I'll be off home. I won't be sitting out here in this icy wind like you.'

'Well, I don't know what to say. That's so kind. You're right, I feel proper sickly. And if you're sure—'

'You have a care now, and remember to get that hot toddy when you get home. I'll just take my ticket ...'

The man pushed the ticket through, and bent to arrange the shawl over his knees. In that few seconds, Bess took her chance and ran.

A few moments later and she'd shown her ticket and been let into a large quadrangle. She walked stiffly now, her shoulders hunched against the chill, too intent on her purpose to take much notice of the few men playing skittles and the women who followed after her begging for alms. It was so bitter out that most prisoners must be under shelter indoors.

Down the flagged stairs to the lower quarters. Before her was a long, low L-shaped room with high squares of windows letting in a paltry grey light. She put a hand to the wall for support, but withdrew it with a shudder. The rough distemper was moistly warm, packed as the chamber was with prisoners huddled together in small groups.

She started down the long room. Some prisoners seemed to be

working; she passed a group of tailors stitching nightcaps, and a group of cobblers bent over a cobbler's last. Where was Jack? She couldn't see him immediately, so she walked down the long central aisle, acutely conscious of the stares as she passed. She folded her arms across her chest, partly to keep warm, but partly for protection.

A moment's silence, then a wolf whistle. Immediately it was followed by several more, and lewd laughter. Instinct told her she had attracted attention. What a moon-calf, to come here alone. She should have brought Mary with her, or better still, Will. Oh, how she longed for his bulky presence by her side now. Why hadn't she insisted he should come, instead of haring up here on her own? She tried to ignore the noise behind her, and kept walking, head held high. Something touched her on the shoulder and she spun round. A group of unshaven men had come up behind her. When she turned back, ready to scream, she was surrounded.

'You new? Or a visitor?' The tallest one examined her.

'Visitor,' she croaked.

'Who you looking for?'

'Mr Sutherland.'

'*Mister* Sutherland, eh? Never heard him called that before. He's just Fancy Jack to us.' He walked around her, with an assessing look. 'What've you brought him?'

'Nothing. I came to ask him something, that's all.'

'Don't believe you. Folk don't come in here with nothing.' He was close now, and she could see the wear on his coat sleeves, smell the musty scent of old sweat. 'Hold her, boys.'

She'd no time to react. Strong hands threw her onto her back. Her ribs hit the stone floor with a whump that knocked the breath from her. Please God no. Her mouth opened to scream but she'd not enough breath and the sound that came out was a squeak. A hand pressed down on her mouth and her shoulders and hips were clamped to the ground. She closed her eyes tight. Lie still, she thought, and they might not kill me. She felt hands roaming over her skirts, her bodice, even her legs.

A familiar voice. 'What's she got?'

The hands let go. She was suddenly free. She sat up.

A dirty, unshaven Jack was standing over her. 'What the hell are you doing here?' His expression was one of genuine shock.

He turned on the men. 'You stupid coxcombs. You should have fetched me first.' He ran a hand over his hair which was sprouting in dirty yellow tufts, and straightened his filthy cravat.

'Sorry, Jack,' said the tallest man, backing away. 'We were just doing the usual. But she's got nothing. Can you credit it? Not a bean. We never found nothing.'

'Where's Will?' Jack said, hauling her up.

How typical of Jack, not to ask if she was all right, nor to offer any kind of comfort. She stood up tall, summoned a semblance of calm. Looked him in the eye. 'Hello, Jack. Still keeping the same bad company, I see. Tell your "friends" to leave me alone.'

'You can leave her to me, lads,' Jack said. 'This is Bess, my cousin's wife.'

The men swaggered away. 'What a gib-cat,' she heard one of them say. Her legs were shaking, but she hoped Jack couldn't see them, under her skirts.

'I expect you've come to gloat,' he said, turning down his mouth. 'You should have let me know you were coming.'

'I came because I need some answers.'

'It's no place for you. At least Will had the sense to bring me bread and soap. Trust the beautiful Bess. So full of yourself that you've come empty-handed. If you want to talk to me, then bring me something useful.' He began to walk away.

'Aren't you even going to ask after your boys?'

He turned then, sharp, his face still set hard, but she caught the shaft of fear in his eyes. 'Why, what's the matter with them?'

'Nothing. They miss their pa, that's all. And Will won't tell me how long you'll be ... how long you'll be kept in here.'

'Six months. Bloody half a year. For doing nothing. Nothing, I tell you. But I should have guessed those so-called gentlemen would push the blame onto me.'

Six months. Jesus, that long. 'Does Will know? I mean about how long you'll be in?'

''Course he does. But he can't buy me out into the Master's side, or won't.'

'But what about the boys?'

'What do you think? I can't bring them in here, can I? Will said you'd look after them. I asked him not to tell them anything.' He approached her then and pressed a finger into her chest just below the neck. His voice dropped to an intimate tone. 'You care for them too, don't you?'

'Of course I do.' She stepped out of reach.

'So you won't say a word to them either. Because I know what Will's like. He'll be telling them all sorts of tales. Running me down whilst he pretends to have the perfect home – clean sheets and dinner on the table, and making me look like I'm not fit to be their father.'

'He'll tell them the truth. They deserve that much at least. Were you expecting to keep it quiet for six months? Six months, Jack! It's eternity to a child! They jump up every time there's a knock on the door, thinking it's you come back.'

'Do they?' His face lit up.

''Course they do. You're their pa. But I just wish you'd think of them first, before you end up in a place like this.'

'I was doing it for them. Don't think badly of me, Bess. I only wanted them to have a future, one better than mine. Enough cash to make gentlemen of them, that's what I wanted. Speculation and risk, that's how money's made.'

She shivered; the cold was eating through her thin clothes. 'What happened to our money, Jack?'

'You have to think big. It's not my fault.'

'Jack?' Any shaft of sympathy for him evaporated. 'Just tell me straight.'

'Gone. Nothing I could do. The cargo of snuff was impounded. We hadn't earned enough to buy out the ship. The other investors bought us out. I had to let them. To pay my debts.'

'What do you mean, *us*?'

'Will's share. It's owned by Kite now.'

'You're saying our money paid your debts? You used our money and did it without asking us?'

He scraped a boot back and forth on the flagstones. 'Had to. It would've been two years else. Six months for breaking quarantine, and eighteen months in the debtor's yard. And I want to see my boys before they're grown up.'

'Oh, Jack.' She could scarce believe it. She turned to face the wall, stared at the blocks of stone in front of her. 'You've ruined us,' she whispered. 'Ruined us all.'

Chapter 36

Where was Bess? Will paced the floor until, just when he thought he could stand it no more, he heard Bess's feet on the steps. He prepared himself. The boys were already in bed, he'd worked them hard whittling spoons, partly because he couldn't stand waiting for Bess to return.

She came in shivering; he could see her teeth chattering so much she didn't attempt to speak.

'Where've you been? And where's your shawl? You shouldn't have gone out without a cloak.' His worry sounded like anger, but he couldn't bite his tongue.

'Where are the boys?' she asked.

'In bed. Did you go to your mother's?'

'No. Why would I go there?' She threw him a disparaging look. 'She's not speaking to me, remember? She blamed me because Jack was no longer bringing the boys. And now look, they're back here again and there's no Agatha to help.'

'Where've you been, Bess?'

'Where do you think? I went to the Fleet, to talk to Jack, at least I thought if I could get some sense—'

'Oh.' Then she'd know everything. 'There's soup in the scullery. Mary made it.'

'Soup? Is that all you can talk of, soup? Our whole savings gone – everything we were relying on, and you want to talk about soup?'

He dropped his gaze. She'd seen through his attempts to bypass the inevitable.

'What will we do?' she blazed at him. 'We've got his children to feed too. How will we survive?'

'I don't know. I'll find something. Maybe I'll have to try to get work in the yards after all. My father's always wanting me to work in the sawpits.'

'Then he'll have won.' She slumped onto a chair. 'You'll be stuck there – a common labouring man. You'll never get out. He's intent on keeping you down, on purpose. Pepys says your father threatened to get the men to down tools if the Guild employed you.'

'What?' He tried to take it all in. His father. That man again, Pepys. He saw Bess realise what she'd said, and the red flush rise to the roots of her hair. It made him want to shake her.

'Your father's keeping you down, deliberately,' she said, 'didn't you know?'

Will sat down heavily opposite her. 'When did you see Pepys? When did he tell you this?'

Her eyes shifted away from him. 'I went to ask him why you'd got no work fitting out at the shipyard, and that's what he told me.'

The door creaked open. 'Excuse me, mistress, but will sir be wanting—' Mary's head poked into the room.

'No, Mary,' Will snapped. 'And shut the door after you.' As soon as it clicked shut, Will leant forward and lowered his voice. 'You are not to go near that man again, do you hear me? I absolutely forbid it. You had no business ... no business, to go to him with our personal concerns. What will they think of me in the Navy Office – that I send my wife running to them every time there's a problem? Hardly a recommendation, is it?'

'You'd wait forever if it was up to you.' She leapt up away from him. 'You've got no drive, you just want everything to fall into your lap. Well the world's not like that. You have to actually do something—'

'Look at the trouble you get us into with your meddling. What about Hertford? He told me you'd persuaded him to introduce us to Pepys. My best client, and you made me into a fool.'

'You didn't need my help to make you into a fool,' Bess said, in a scathing undertone. 'I wasn't the one who sunk all our savings into Jack Sutherland's ship.'

'And I suppose Pepys made his sheep's eyes at you and you believed every word he said. What did you do with him, eh?' He lunged out of the chair, grabbed her by the wrist. 'What did he make you do?'

'Nothing,' she shouted. 'He's a gentleman. Which is more than can be said for some people.'

'If I hear you've been near him again, I'll—'

'Uncle Will? What is it?' Billy's anxious face appeared around the door.

'Just leave it,' Bess said, wrestling her arm away. 'I was trying to help. But there's no point, is there, when you keep throwing it all away.'

'Auntie Bess?' Billy whined.

'Saints alive. Can't I get any privacy here?' Then she softened, 'Come on, Billy, let's go through. You can cuddle up next to me, you'll soon be back to sleep.' And with one last cold look, she scooped up Billy and went through to the bedroom.

All night long Will waited for Bess, but she didn't come to bed. He knew she was restless in the other chamber, because he could hear her tossing on the boys' mattress, the rustle of straw as she turned.

He wanted to say he was sorry, but she didn't give him the chance. And she was right. He'd been foolish. He should have known that any scheme of Jack's was bound to end in disaster. And a tight knot of pain in his stomach reminded him that his long-cherished dream of being a ship builder was dead. Trodden into the dust by his own father. He brought his knees up to his chest, to stop himself from groaning. He imagined his father's self-satisfied face if he had to grovel to him for work.

And Pepys. He saw again the man's fat lips on Bess's hand.

The thought made him leap out of bed. Still in his night-shirt, despite the rain and wind, he threw himself into his workshop and seized an axe. A pile of Navy bowls were stacked on the workbench.

With a sudden swing, he arced the axe down. The bowls split satisfyingly into two halves. Firewood. That was all these bloody things were good for. Thwack, the axe went, as he struck down on the block over and over in a jealous rage. He'd not do anything for that man.

Above, Hal crying. Then an insistent bang on the ceiling. Bess no doubt, telling him he was waking the whole house. So what? Nothing mattered anymore. He carried on splintering wood.

***

The next morning Bess got the children ready, though they were bleary-eyed with lack of sleep. She sent them down to Will. She'd have to go to Threadneedle Street, and look for something, though she couldn't do much, only piece work, with the children a millstone around her neck. She could hear Will still crashing about in the workshop. Stupid man, it was his own fault. She hoped he'd go out too; try to find some joinery work, or they'd be out on the street by the end of the month. And she couldn't do that to those children. She remembered the cold of winter on the street all too well.

She dressed well and warmly, hoping a respectable appearance might help her cause. On the way out she glanced into the workshop and saw Will staring morosely at his workbench. The children seemed to be squabbling under a table. She sighed, gritted her teeth and walked on through the grey drizzle.

She was nearing the ferry when she saw a lad disembark. He hurried towards her, 'Mrs Bagwell?' he asked, breathless.

'Yes,' she said, warily. She recognised the flat nose and freckles straight away. Pepys's boy, his suit dark on the shoulders from the rain.

'Sir said I'd to bring this to you. If there's a reply could you please write it quick, so I can catch the next ferry back?'

She broke the seal and read, shielding the writing from the rain, which was now coming down steadily.

Because of the defeat of the Dutch in Guinea, Pepys wrote, *there is much talk of retribution against us. I fear there is a need for speedy recruitment, and we know we will need a fleet of at least twelve sail. There is an urgent need of master carpenters. Perhaps there may be a place for your husband there? If you will please to drop by my office on the morrow, we can discuss it then, and I'll appraise you of what I can do.*

'Is there a reply?' the boy asked.

'No. No reply.'

The boy held out his hand, and Bess realised he expected a gratuity. She shook her head. 'I've no change.'

'Mean cow,' the boy muttered, and bolted, scrambling aboard the ferry just as the ferryman cast off.

She stared after him, then pulled out the letter again. It was too good to be true. Just when they needed it most. Yet her heart was full of doubts. She read the words carefully, but it did seem to be an offer for Will. A master carpenter. But it was on a warship. He'd be at war with the Dutch. Not a safe merchant trading ship, but one armed with cannon and gunpowder.

She thought of his slumped shoulders, and knew this could be the saving of him. But he'd forbidden her to see Mr Pepys again.

What should she do? She paced in the rain, the letter becoming blurred as she re-read it over and over. 'Meddling,' Will had called her. Well she was about to meddle one last time.

Chapter 37

Bess brushed the rain off her cloak, grateful for the calm dryness of the Navy Buildings after the battering wind. In her hand she clutched the soggy letter from Pepys. He'd said tomorrow, but she couldn't wait. She tucked a loose strand of damp hair under her coif, determined to be respectable, but to get some sort of promise for Will.

The clerk told her to wait, but she didn't need to wait long. Mr Pepys was in jovial mood as he came out through the door, cleanly shaven and smelling, even from a distance, of lemon soap and pomade. He took her cloak, and ushered her past the rows of clerks and their scratching nibs, and in to his private office. His hand on the small of her back slid downwards to pat her on the bottom in the process. It made her heart lurch under her bodice.

'Just been speaking to my colleague, Pen,' he said, his voice booming in the small room, 'and we have mighty preparations in Chatham. I think perhaps there'll be space on board one of our ships for a time-served carpenter.' He smiled like an uncle offering a child a sweetmeat, and patted her again, this time on the shoulder.

'That's good news for Will,' Bess said, smiling sweetly, but endeavouring to keep the conversation on her husband. 'When can he start, Mr Pepys?'

'Well now … soon, I should think. There are still a few details that need to be, how shall we say, tied up.' He caught her around the waist, so his face was inches from her own, his wig brushing against her cheek.

She took a step back, but her knees hit a stool behind her. This private closet was so cramped, there was nowhere to go. She'd admired his vast collection of books before, but now they seemed like walls, hemming her in. He took hold of her more tightly.

She took on a playful persona. 'Now, Mr Pepys, you're being very naughty. Let go, or I shall have to scream.'

'A little cuddle from my special friend isn't *very* naughty. And you owe me a kiss for finding a position for your husband.'

'Did you speak to Nicholson again about Will joining the Guild?'

'Give me a kiss, and I'll tell you.'

She drew back, still smiling, though a small war was waging in her head. Will's strict instructions that she shouldn't be here, and the tempting offer of work with the Navy.

'Just one,' she said. It would be over, and then Will would have his promotion. She turned her face towards his.

'Let me feel you,' Pepys said, his voice suddenly quieter. He pressed both hands on her breasts, then lowered his lips onto hers, but gently. She'd expected a bruise of a kiss. Instead, his lips lingered on hers, his eyes still open, looking down at her.

She was too surprised to move. He reached a hand to touch her hair, pulled a dark curl loose from her coif.

The game was over. She hadn't expected any tenderness. Between them, a pinch of something real had arisen.

Shaken, she tucked the curl back under her coif. 'Sir, I really don't think you should do this.' She tried to take the moment back to the game by attempting a little laugh, 'If you do this with all the wives, your reputation will be ruined.'

'I don't do it with all the wives,' he said, with what could almost have been regret. 'Only with you.'

She wanted to believe it; the girlish dream that her beauty was such that it had overwhelmed him. She wanted to believe that she was the only woman who this great man desired in this way. But in her heart she suspected that he tried it all too often. With sudden revulsion, at where his lips might have been before, she pulled away, holding out a palm to keep him from her.

'If you care for me, will you help us? I'll be straightforward. We are in financial difficulty, and Will needs this work. I'm a good wife, Mr Pepys, a godly wife, and I only want the best for my husband, as I'm sure your wife does for you. I will bargain for favours with you, sir, but the terms need to be clear.'

'Is that so?' He turned to his desk and shuffled the papers from place to place. Still with his back to her, he said, 'As you know, I have many responsibilities, and I can't always—'

'But Mr Pepys, you asked me to come! And in return you said that there'd be a place for Will—'

'I've said,' he turned and emphasised his words, 'I'll see what I can do. Why don't you come back a week today, and we'll see.' He took up pen and ink, and wrote *15th November* on a chit of paper. 'Give this to my clerk on the way out,' he said.

It was clear she was being dismissed. A wave of anger and bitterness rose into her gullet. She'd paid for the ferry to get her here, and given up an afternoon when she should have been sewing. And all for what? A promise she wasn't even sure he would keep. The 'farewell' stuck in her throat.

***

Will handed over the benches and helped load them up onto the cart, ready to go to St Botolph's church. When the cart clattered off, he looked at the coins in his hand. Nine shillings. Much less than he'd hoped for, but at least he was rid of them. Having them in the workshop reminded him of Mrs Fenwick, and she reminded him of her husband, and the shipbuilding yard. But St Botolph's had made him an offer for these benches and he'd had little choice but to take it.

The loan was bigger now, so large it was like a physical stone on his shoulders, and with Jack's business broken, there was nobody else to pay it. His savings were gone – used to pay Jack's debts. There'd be no payout from any investment. Kite owned all that was left of Jack's share of the *Lily Allen*.

And there was the other thing. The thing he hadn't told Bess. That even if he could pay off the loan, Jack would own half of Flaggon Row, because, fool that he was, he'd signed over half to him. He rued the day he'd done that – the day Jack's business had been smashed up. He hadn't been thinking straight; he thought it would be temporary and he'd buy Jack's half back when the ship came in. Now it never would.

He went back indoors were Jacob and the boys were chipping at the spoons as usual.

'When's Pa coming home?' Billy asked.

'I don't know. When they let him out, I expect.'

He saw a shadow pass the window. Bess was going out again. There she was, with Mary following behind.

He stuck his head out of the door. 'Where are you going? Aren't we getting any dinner?'

She flushed. 'It's on the table. I left you a note. You've just got to butter the bread, that's all.'

'Why? Where you going?'

'Just into the Exchange, the boys need new leather laces in their shoes. You know how it is.'

Mary cast her eyes downwards, away from his questioning look.

'New laces? We can't afford anything new. Not even laces.'

'D'you want their shoes to fall off?' Bess said.

He didn't answer.

'See you later then.' She bit her lip, gave him a wave, and then hurried away up the street, with pale-faced Mary two paces behind.

Will watched them go. Bess was lying. He knew that. No-one went to buy laces in town when there was a stall for them right in Deptford. And he knew Bess well enough to know she never went anywhere on baking day in her best Sunday hat. It was odd. She'd been out last week too, all dressed up, and he'd wondered where she was going, and expected her to tell him, but she'd never said a word. And Mary had looked shifty, as if she didn't want to be asked what they were doing. It could only mean one thing, but Will didn't want to face it. He'd told her, hadn't he, not to go near Pepys.

Perhaps he was being too suspicious.

He went back inside and shut the door, but almost immediately he skidded on something and ended up on his backside.

He rubbed his sore elbow, picked up the offending marble and leapt to his feet. He held up the marble, suddenly angry.

'Sorry Uncle Will,' Billy said, the giggles dying on his lips.

'What've I told you?' he yelled. 'No games in here. Are you half-wits? Jacob, why weren't you watching them? There's sharp tools around. There'll be no dinner for any of you. And you can give me the rest.'

He held out his hands for the pouch of marbles.

'We won't get them out again, we promise,' Toby said.

'Give me those marbles right now.' Will walked over and glowered at him.

Toby jutted out his chin. 'You can't make me. You're not my pa.'

'Whilst you're under my roof and eating my food, you'll do as I say,' Will said, 'unless you want a belting from me.'

'Go on then.' Toby's face was pale, but belligerent like a bulldog, his eyes cocky and challenging.

'Don't, Toby,' yelled Billy.

Will raised his arm, but then he let it fall. What was the point? What was he doing? It was only a marble for god's sake.

Toby's face filled with scorn. 'See. You can't do it. You're too chicken. Pa would've walloped me.'

The words twisted like a knife in the chest. Will didn't trust himself to speak.

Jacob stood like a statue, holding a spoon and chewing his lip.

'What are you looking at?' he shouted at Jacob. 'Work's over for the day. Over, d'you hear? Take your cap and get out of here.'

Jacob scurried to fetch his things and was gone in under the time it took Will to fetch the key. Will strode out of the workshop and turned the key in the door. Too chicken, eh? Maybe the lack of food would change their minds. With heavy feet he went upstairs to eat dinner alone. He buttered half his bread before putting it down. A note was propped against the milk jug,

'William. Had to go into the city for a few things. Have taken Mary. Make sure the boys drink their milk. Bess.'

They were getting nothing. Not until they showed him some respect. And Bess, where was she? Laces be damned. He was uneasy. A wife shouldn't keep secrets from her husband. Maybe he should just ask her; tell her he knew she was lying. But he couldn't imagine her being best pleased with that accusation. He chided himself. There was probably some perfectly sensible explanation. Maybe he'd just wait, see what she said. She'd tell him if it was something important, wouldn't she? But underneath, he heard Toby's words again, *chicken*.

***

By the time Bess returned Will had spent a miserable afternoon in the workshop with no Jacob, and three chilled, hungry and recalcitrant boys. Bess unloaded her basket as though nothing was amiss, and deliberately put the shoe-laces on the table in front of his nose, along with a few other bits of haberdashery.

He picked them up, ran them through his fingers. 'You went all the way into the city for these?'

'These are good and strong.'

'You've been a long while. What took you so long?'

'Where are the boys?'

Will recognised this as an old tactic of Bess's. If she didn't want to answer, she'd just pretend he'd never asked.

'I asked why it took so long?'

'Traffic.' She waved her arms vaguely before her. She soon spotted the remains of the dinner which he'd heaped on the sideboard. 'But nobody's eaten anything! Where are the boys? Is Jack back? What's going on?'

'I forbade them their dinner. They tripped me up on a marble.'

'A marble?'

Even to his own ears it sounded pathetic.

'Yes, they were—'

'William Bagwell. Give me that key at once. At once!' The key lay on the table and both of them pounced, but Bess was the quicker. Within minutes she was out of the door, and he heard her feet clatter down the stairs.

He had the sensation of sinking, as if he was always losing, never quite up to managing his life. She shouldn't be able to do this to him, to make him feel so unmanned.

Chapter 38

Will looked out of the window at the darkening sky. Four o'clock and Bess had disappeared again for a whole afternoon. This time she hadn't taken Mary with her, but had left her bottling winter preserves.

'I'm going to the Exchange,' Bess had said. 'We need some more muslin to cover the chutneys, and for the plum puddings.'

'We can't afford it.'

'We'll have to, or have no puddings or preserves through the winter. And I'll pawn one of Jack's suits while I'm there.'

'It doesn't seem right.'

'We have to feed his children, don't we?'

'Can't it wait?' he said. 'We can go together tomorrow. And if we must pawn something, haven't we anything else? Like that gown you're wearing. It seems a little fine for doing errands.'

'No, husband,' she said, 'I need to look respectable. Besides, we need the muslin now. Isn't that right, Mary?'

And Mary had forced a smile and nod at Bess's sharp look.

Once again, Will felt as if he was on shifting sand. He didn't want to accuse Bess of anything because he wasn't exactly sure what he was accusing her of, but all the same, when the hour stretched into two, and then three, and there'd still been no sign of her return, he left Jacob and the boys working and went upstairs.

'She's not back yet, then?'

'No, sir.' Mary kept her eyes fixed on the pot she was stirring. A smell that was both sweet and sour assailed his nostrils. He sat down at the table, pushing aside cones of lump sugar and pans of dried fruit so he could get his elbows onto its surface.

He watched as Mary dropped a large blob of vinegary mess into a jar. 'D'you know where she's gone?'

'No, sir.'

Still she didn't look at him.

'What was she buying?'

Now she did look up. 'She said muslin, sir. That's what she said.'

'Remember when you went with her for the shoe-laces? To the Exchange?' He persisted.

'When was that?'

'The day she went out in her Sunday hat, like today.'

'I don't remember.' Mary pressed a square of muslin onto the jar, and expertly wound a piece of string around the top. Her face grew flushed and pink under his gaze.

'You'd tell me if there was anything I needed to know, wouldn't you, Mary?'

She looked up. Her eyes met his a moment. 'Like what, sir?'

He felt his own eyes slide away. 'Nothing. It's nothing. Carry on... with the bottling I mean. It's good to have some preserves in the larder. Chutney is it? Looks good.'

He was rambling. He took a deep breath and fled. He almost tripped over his own feet, he was in such a hurry to get out of the door. He couldn't ask her outright. It would be too embarrassing. And worse, if he did, it would be all over Deptford on the servants' tattle-wagon before he knew it. His father might even get to hear of it.

She was an attractive woman, Bess, and lively. When he'd married her he'd promised her the moon – well, at any rate a comfortable living. He'd vowed he'd be in the shipyards within five years, with a gang of men under him. Maybe even Master of the Guild. But where was he now? He stood in the workshop and looked round. A pile of shoddy spoons on the shelf. No decent wood in the store at the corner. Once he'd made chairs and

cabinets, and figureheads, for God's sake! What had happened to
him? What had gone wrong?

A thought needled at the back of his mind. Jack's plague
water. Selling that had been a sin.

Chapter 39

Bess shivered, partly from cold and partly through trepidation. She'd been waiting by the eel stall in the Exchange for a quarter hour. Shrinking into the shadows, she was intent on avoiding anyone she knew who might see her there and ask her who she was waiting for.

She peered over the heads of the crowd, but couldn't see him. Twice before she'd been to Pepys's office and been pressed for favours. But whatever she did, when she let him kiss her or caress her, his assurances so far had come to naught. But Will needed work, and he could supply it. What would they do, else? She would never go back to Ratcliff, and as long as she was in the house, she felt like she was a somebody, not just a nothing. That she'd moved up in the world.

The clocks struck noon, a cacophony of clanging from all over London, and Bess could not help but think of Will. He'd be hearing the bells of St Nicholas, and putting down his plane or his sanding block, and going up for his dinner. He'd find the children in the care of Mary, and another note propped up behind the milk ewer, assuring him she needed more starch.

She'd learnt not to wear her best clothes, because Will noticed whenever she went out in her best clothes, and Mary had let drop that he'd mentioned her Sunday hat. But she'd pawned the hat last week, anyway. She was a good girl, Mary. Bess wished she still had the hat today though, for it was raining and her plain linen coif had soon got soaked into a rag.

The crowd parted politely as Pepys strolled down the alley, walking as if he owned it, despite his rather shabby appearance.

Bess was disappointed; it looked as if he was also in disguise, in a threadbare and sombre suit, more fit for a funeral than the fashionable Exchange. On his head was perched a much-worn flat hat, even now soggy and misshapen with the rain.

'Mrs Bagwell,' he said, doffing it, so water dripped onto his shoes.

'Any news for me?' she asked.

'Patience, my dear. Let us sally forth to dine. A sedan awaits.'

Actually, it was a pair of sedans, the four bearers drenched and surly. She saw Pepys give copious long-winded instructions to his two bearers before he climbed in, with a wave to her. He looked self-important, despite his shabby suit, but she caught the look the bearers gave each other before they set off. The look which clearly said he was a burden in more than one way.

The sedan swayed and moved off in a squelch of the bearers' shoes. She hoped it would not be far. She must only be an hour. Will would be waiting at home, and the thought of him made her stomach roll like butter in a churn. Anxiously, she peered out to see where the bearers were going. Gault's Chop House perhaps?

Today she'd make Pepys keep his promise. She glanced out of the window. This was taking a long time. And there were the city walls! Out through Moorgate, past the Bethlem hospital, and onto the open common of Moorfields. She began to panic. Where was he taking her? She hadn't meant to go so far from the Exchange. And how would she get home?

She tapped on the side of the sedan, but either the bearers didn't hear her through the hiss of the rain, or took no notice. The sedan took a sharp right turn, and suddenly there were houses, and the men slowed. The contraption lurched and hit the ground with a shudder. The bearers, their hair plastered flat to their heads, retreated sharply to the shelter of an overhang, so when she got out only Mr Pepys was waiting there, all solicitous concern.

The Inkwell, the sign said. They dashed in out of the rain, and picked their way past the rickety tables and stools jostling for space in the cramped chamber. The fire glowed fiercely orange from a bank of stacked coals, and the tiny window dripped runnels from its steamy surface. Bess fumbled with the frogging at her throat. She was already perspiring under her wet cloak.

Pepys put his hat on the table; a mistake, for it steamed and gave off a noxious aroma of pomade, sweat and drizzle. He mumbled an apology and shifted it to the floor beside him.

'We'll be quite undisturbed here,' he said, and seeing her struggling with the weight of damp wool added, 'Let me take your cloak.'

'I can't stay long,' she said.

Pepys squashed himself up against her so she had to retreat to the corner, far too close to the fire. She felt one cheek burn hot, and pressed the back of her hand to it. Her palm was straight away roasted.

'I was hoping there'd be some news for us,' she said. 'If not the Guild, then news about getting Will aboard a ship.'

'Ah yes. A little dalliance first.' Both his hands were already on her thighs.

She must be strong, and insist on her part of the bargain. She took hold of his wrists and moved his hands away, but they just latched on somewhere else. She thrust him away hard, slapping at his hands. 'No, Mr Pepys.'

He sat back then, shocked. 'Don't do that. No slapping. Or I shan't feel inclined to give any kind of recommendation.'

'But you promised me. You said you'd find Will something, and we can't go on like this. You said if I came with you here, you'd have good news.'

'So I have.' He pouted at her. 'But that was before you became so reluctant. If you want your husband to have a post as ship's carpenter, then I know a post at forty pounds a year, and I can easily arrange it.' He paused, took a lock of her hair in his fingers. 'But if you don't want it...'

'You know I do.'

'Then I'd expect you to express your thanks in a pretty way.'

A pretty way? The sweat trickled down inside her bodice. The heat made her head swim. Forty pounds. She thought of Will and the three boys at home. She could do this one thing for them. They'd never know. One afternoon and it could turn their lives around. She closed her eyes tight. *Forgive me, Will.*

When she opened her eyes Mr Pepys read the change in them. He tugged her towards him by a lock of hair. 'Ship's carpenter's wife, eh?' He smiled, reached to push the skirts above her knee. 'We'll see what we can do.'

Bess felt the heat of the fire burn on her thighs, but she did not resist.

***

There was no sedan to take them home, and they had to walk. Bess said little. The memory of Pepys's hands, blotched in the firelight, kept revisiting her. Outside, the eaves poured water so they had to skulk close to the walls, and the streets were slick and slippery underfoot. Pepys chattered on, not noticing her reticence, in a monologue about ships, provisions and Tangier. As soon as they got to Moorgate he stuck up his hand to summon a coach. He'd to go to Whitehall, he said, 'to a Committee Meeting about one of the colonies.'

'You won't let Will find out it was me doing the asking, will you?' Bess said.

'Asking what?' Pepys backed into her, concerned with moving himself away from the splash of the wheels.

'About the carpenter's position.' He wasn't listening. She had to make him. Insistent, she tugged him by the sleeve. 'Can we expect them to send him a letter?'

'Oh, I imagine so,' Pepys said. But the way he said it filled her with a deep dread. She was already of no account. She didn't dare even think it. That she'd done *that thing* with him, and it would be for nothing.

A door slam and the cry of the coachman. Bess slumped. The coach was gone, and with it, Pepys – whooshing down the street in a rattle of wheels. He'd just left her, without even a 'fare thee well.'

She stood a moment, until another carriage swept by, throwing up a wall of water that splattered her skirts. It brought her to her senses. She scanned her surroundings.

Fleet Street. She knew where she was, that was no problem; she could find her way home, but the light was fading fast and the link-men were out already with their lanterns.

What on earth could she say? She'd been out far longer than she intended, it was a good hour's walk home, and she'd have a lot of explaining to do. She braced herself.

Starch, that's what she'd told Will. She'd have to go and buy starch.

***

'I fed the children. It's late,' was all he said. But his look was cold.

She put the wrapped block of starch on the table. 'There was a long queue, and then I bumped into Meg and we got talking and—'

'Why didn't you take Mary with you? I don't like you going out alone.'

His stare washed over her mud-spattered skirts. At the same time she felt as if he could see the traces left by Pepys's hands. Guilt uncoiled in her chest, making her throat tight. She could not trust herself to answer. Instead she said, 'There are rumours from the broadsheet sellers. I saw their notices outside the Exchange. Many of them. Plague in London, they said.'

'It's just rumour. Don't talk of it further. The children might hear you.'

'What?' Billy appeared from the bedchamber. Trust him. His ears were always sharp as a stag's.

'Nothing, sweet. Have you had your supper?'

'Yes, Aunt Bess. But it was only bread and cheese. Where were you?'

'Just with Meg from the glover's. We got talking.' The lie slipped out easily but Will's watchful expression made her shut her mouth.

***

That night, Will turned his back on Bess. She was not telling the truth, he was certain. It made him almost sea-sick, a wormy sensation in the stomach that he couldn't quell. All night she'd been fawning over him, too anxious to please.

She hadn't been at Meg's, he'd stake his life on it.

For another few weeks Will watched Bess. He found himself counting the hours she was out, calculating distances and walking speeds, and he hated himself for it. But he couldn't help himself. Twice more she gave him thin excuses for her late return, but then again, everything she did now seemed tainted with suspicion.

When she told him again that she'd met with Meg, a cold, hard lump formed in his chest. He wasn't going to let it drop this time. He'd go to Meg tomorrow.

The next morning as he pulled on his woollen stockings, he said, 'You'll have to take care of the boys today. Jacob will set them to making spoons again, if you ask him. I need to go out.'

'Oh. Is it a commission?' She sat up against the pillows and smiled at him. Her smile made his heart ache.

'No.' He pulled his doublet on over his shirt.

'Are you going to see Jack again?'

'No.'

'Ah, Christmas shopping. It's all right, I won't tell the boys.'

Christmas was just something else he didn't want to think about. The memories were too sweet, so sweet they would burn him. He watched Bess bite her lip when he didn't respond, then pin another smile on her face. 'Well,' she said, getting out of bed and winding her arms about his waist, 'you never know, perhaps there'll be some good news from the King's Yard soon. Some Christmas cheer, eh?'

'And hogs will lay eggs.' He shrugged her off and went through to the parlour to find his boots. She'd polished them, he noticed. Normally he had to remind her. Another sign that she was trying to placate him.

A few minutes later the boots were on his feet and he was striding up past Deptford Strond towards the ferry stage at Water Gate, a beaver hat jammed low on his head against the cold.

***

Will pushed his way through the crowds of well-wrapped shoppers towards the stalls around St Paul's Church. Awnings flapped over them today in case of snow. There was a tingle in the air, and above him, the skies were grey; cloud thickened in layers above the stump of the church tower, its spire truncated by one of the frequent city fires.

Meg's shop, or rather her father's business, was one of the bigger ones, with a stall out front selling news-sheets, chapbooks, and religious tracts. The stall was owned by Meg's husband, Hugh and today it was besieged by people. Will thrust his way past the crowd, but one word kept catching his attention. Plague.

Behind the counter, a harassed Hugh was reassuring people. 'No, there's nothing in today's news-sheet. It's just rumour. The Bills of Mortality say nothing of it.'

'They say it's in St Giles,' a man in a knitted muffler said. 'Best place for it, if you ask me.' A smatter of nervous laughter.

'No, sir, I've told you,' Hugh said to another gentleman, who was waving a paper at him, and protesting, 'there's no foundation to the rumour. If there was, then Stoner's News-sheet would be the first to let you know. We pride ourselves on it.'

'Trouble?' asked Will, smiling at his friend.

'Will, you wouldn't believe it. It comes in waves. No sooner have I seen one lot off, than another bunch arrive.'

'What's going on?'

'Some foolish wag has put about that the plague has reached London. Well, of course it has. It never goes away. They come to me for news of it. But there is none. To hear these folk, you'd think the grim reaper himself was on his way down the road with his sickle and scythe.'

'Don't be so certain,' another man said, overhearing. 'I was in Jonathan's Coffee House this morning, and they say Holland's bad. Thousands dead.'

'Doesn't bear thinking about,' Will murmured as he made his way down the back alley towards Hutchinson's. A twinge of guilt assailed him that he hadn't told Hugh he was going to see Meg. Best if Hugh kept out of it, he thought.

To his relief Meg was behind the sales counter at the glove shop, and not sewing in the back room with the other girls. In her plain worsted dress and brown apron, she looked homely and entirely without guile. She smiled. 'Morrow, Will. What can I do for you? New gloves, is it?'

'No. I was just on my way to the Exchange, and thought I'd

pass the time of day.'

'How's Bess?' Meg said, making a pile of coins on the counter.

'She's fine. Said it was good to see you yesterday.'

Meg froze in counting the coins. 'It can't have been me. I don't think... I mean, I haven't seen Bess in months. You must be mistaken, Will. I was just thinking that I should call, see how she is.' She shoved the coins in her pocket, looking discomfited.

'Are you sure?'

'What is it, Will? Is there something wrong?'

Her earnest face made his throat close up. 'No ... no.' He struggled to find sensible words in a pause that seemed to last too long. 'Oh, sorry, it's probably my mistake. I must have got the wrong person.'

'Shall I call this evening then? I'd like to catch up with Bess.'

'No, not this evening, we'll be busy. I mean to say, we've got a previous engagement.' Previous engagement? What ridiculous words. He didn't know where they'd come from, but only that he didn't want Bess to know he'd been spying on her friend.

'Well. Another time then.'

Meg's face closed. He'd hurt her.

Behind him the bell on the door tinkled.

'I'll be going,' he said. 'God be—'

But Meg had turned away to serve the customer behind him.

Will fled the shop and elbowed his way back through the crowds with Meg's words burning in his mind. His sense of triumph to have caught Bess out had evaporated, and been replaced with a pain that made his stomach clench. His wife. His wife was cuckolding him.

All the way back downstream in the wherry he stared at other men, wondered if they were being fooled by their wives. The man opposite, a merchant by the look of him, in his navy plush suit, with his servant togged out in livery; did he know where his wife was today? He looked so calm.

Will stared. Was he less of a man than that merchant?

He should tell Bess to go. But the very thought of it brought him into a cold sweat.

Chapter 40

Bess hurried past the houses adorned with greenery for the Christmas festivities, deliberately turning her head away from the boughs of holly and ivy with their garlands of red ribbon. Chestnut-roasting braziers glowed on each street corner, as families gathered to gawp at the new displays in the shop windows. Happy families that just made her feel that she and Will were even further out of kilter.

Will had been taciturn and surly this morning, and she felt his suspicion of her like an almost physical presence. He'd gone out, refusing to say where. No letter had come for him about any sort of employment, so she'd been forced to go to the Navy offices again. The encounter had been fruitless and degrading as usual. Curse Pepys. The wily dog hadn't kept his side of agreement, and the thought made her bitter.

Bess skidded and tottered on the icy cobbles, anxious to get home, worried about Will and that Mary would not be taking proper care of the children. When she opened the door, it was to see Will sitting stiffly in the parlour in his best suit. One look at his face was enough to fill her with foreboding.

'Take the children out for half-an-hour, Mary,' he said.

Mary put down the coal scuttle with a clang. 'But I've to do the dishes and—'

'Now. I won't stand for disobedience.'

Bess was un-nerved. Will was never sharp with Mary. She made a great show of removing her gloves as Mary bustled the subdued children past her to put on scarves and hats before shooing them out into the chill.

When they'd gone, the room fell empty and silent. Bess made to go to the kitchen but Will stopped her with an outstretched arm. 'Sit,' he said.

She lowered herself into the chair, her stomach tying itself in knots, a heat rising to her face.

'I went to see Meg,' Will said. 'You weren't there yesterday. Or any of the other times. She says she hasn't seen you for months.'

So he'd been spying on her. Oh my Lord. And Meg would know she'd lied. What would she think? She licked her lips, but for once in her life, no ready excuses came. She dropped her gaze to study the scores and cuts in the table top.

'Tell me where you've been, Bess.' His voice was gentle, hopeful, still waiting for a plausible excuse.

What could she say? She shook her head.

'I need the truth, Bess. Whatever it is, we can't go on like this.'

'I went to... to see Mr Pepys.'

'Pepys?' He groaned. 'I should have guessed. All those other times, was that him too?'

She couldn't answer. How much did he know? Whilst she hesitated, his face seemed to have aged in a few moments, his eyes hollow, his cheeks sunken.

She licked her lips. No sound came.

He stood slowly, deliberately, and reached for a cloak from the hook.

'No, wait... I can explain.' She lunged to take hold of his arm.

'Leave go! What's to explain? You've been dallying behind my back, that's all. I've been made a laughing stock.'

She gripped her nails into the fabric of his sleeve. 'No. It's not what you think. I can explain. We were just... talking. I did it for you.'

He wrenched his arm away, eyes instantly dark with fury. 'For me? You're telling me you did it for me?' he sneered at her. 'That's a jest. If you were doing it for me, why didn't you tell me?'

He took hold of the door handle, but she held onto his arm. 'He promised you work in the yard—'

'Oh yes, I believe you. That's why I'm working in the yard now, instead of making poxy spoons.'

'It's true. I only went to see if I could get you work. Don't go, love—'

But it was too late, the door slammed behind him.

What had she done? She slumped back onto the chair and put her head in her hands. What had happened to them? Her chest felt as though it had been run over by a cart. It was only now that she was certain. Seeing Mr Pepys hadn't been worth it. No matter what he'd been offering her, it wasn't worth it.

She locked the door to prevent anyone coming in, put her head in her hands and closed her eyes as if to shut out the world and everyone in it. She must have been sitting a half hour when she heard feet on the stairs.

Bang. Bang.

She looked up. Someone was knocking at the door. A shaft of hope pierced her. She wiped her face, and flung open the door. 'Will, I'm—'

But the face on the doorstep wasn't Will, and at first she didn't recognise him.

'What's the matter? Has someone died?' the man said. Bess put her hands to her mouth. She recognised that voice.

'Jack? What are you doing here?'

The last person she wanted to see. He was bone-thin and his clothes hung off his shoulders. His once-fine cuffs were threadbare and stained with grime, and his stockings were holed at the knees, showing skin red with cold.

'Where are the boys?' he asked, peering behind her.

'They're … they're out. With my maidservant, Mary.' She didn't want him to come in, but he was already pushing past her and making for the fire at the other end of the parlour.

She followed him. 'How did you …? I mean, when did they let you out?'

'Bribed my way out. Warder's mother has the plague. I promised him a bottle of my herbal plague cure. Wanted to be here at Christmas for my boys, didn't I?'

Bess was aware of her red eyes and the fact that she still felt unsteady on her feet. Will finding out about Mr Pepys had been a shock. She was still trying to take it all in. And now, to make things worse, here was Jack, ready to upset the applecart all over again.

'You can't stay here.' That much she knew.

'Where's Will? There's no noise from the workshop.'

'He had to go out.'

'When will he be back?'

'I don't know. He could be gone a while.' She couldn't prevent herself from blushing, felt the prick of her swollen eyelids. But she busied herself wiping down the table, her mind still in a turmoil.

A smell of damp unwashed body wafted from the fireplace. 'Jack,' she said, pulling herself together, 'would you like to clean yourself up?'

He turned back to face her, and rested his heels on the hearth, swaying back and forth before the fire, surveying her with a blank expression.

'I mean, there's still water in the ewer,' she said. 'Through in our bedchamber. Wash-cloth's on the hook.'

He set off in that direction, but another clatter of footsteps on the outside stairs halted him mid-stride. Mary and the boys. The door burst open, bringing with it chilly air and the smell of the river.

'Look who's here,' Bess said, her voice choked.

'Pa!' shouted Billy, and he rushed to him, stopping dead just before him. 'You smell bad.' He wrinkled his nose.

'Dare say I do. So would you, if you'd been holed up in a damp cellar for months.'

'Was it really bad?' Toby's eyes were wide with excitement.

'Like hell. It was full of felons and murderers. I had to fight them off; it was dog eat dog in there.' Bess had the sudden impression she was listening to another small boy.

'How did you get out?' The boys crowded round him as he sat down, and Hal made to climb onto his knee.

'Get down, you're too big for that now,' Jack said. 'You want to know how I got out? I escaped, lad. Over the wall. Used my fists. Like this.' He held up his fists, mimed boxing. 'Battered the warder – great big bleeder he was, like the side of a mountain. Then I stole his keys from his pocket and let myself out.'

The three boys had gathered round the table now, and Jack was holding court. The sight of it made her want to scream. She'd only just got those boys back on the straight and narrow, and here was Jack filling their heads with all sorts of nonsense.

She'd no time to ponder that, for the door swung open again and Will stood on the threshold. Bess immediately looked away, but not before she'd seen the hard expression on his face.

'Jack?' His expression changed to one of incredulity.

The next few minutes were filled with Will slapping Jack on the shoulder and acting like he was a prodigal son, rather than the man who'd fleeced them of their savings and was now about to take his three sons from the only stability they'd ever known. It hurt even more as he had not a word to say to her.

'Can we wait till after supper to go home, Pa?' Billy asked, anxious for his stomach as usual.

A twisting sensation in her heart. Those poor boys. Where would Jack take them?

'What's for dinner?' Will turned to her, but his eyes were cold.

'Mary'd planned pasties,' Bess said, the prick of tears still behind her eyes. 'I'll go and see …'

She headed for the kitchen door, and was just about to go through it when she heard Jack say, 'I'll need to stay here … you see we can't go home …'

Bess whipped round. 'No,' she said.

'What's happened?' Will said, ignoring her.

'We've nowhere else to go,' Jack said. 'They emptied our lodgings and sold everything off to pay the rent that was owing.'

'No, Will. I won't have it.'

'You'll have what I say you'll have.' Will spoke deliberately, 'You're welcome here, Jack. More than welcome. It's your home too, so stay as long as you like.' At her horrified face, he shot her a look of bitter triumph.

Jack caught the look and smiled. 'Had a spat, have you? Thought there was something in the air.'

'We've not had a spat,' Bess said stiffly. 'Don't be silly.'

But Will's face denied her words.

Chapter 41

Will wrapped the woollen scarf tighter round his neck and speeded his step. He had to get away. He was stifled in the house. As if he couldn't breathe. Or perhaps it was because he still hadn't decided what to do about Pepys. Part of him had wanted to go and punch the fat bastard in the face. But he knew that would certainly finish his ship's carpenter's career – not that it had ever really started.

There'd been an atmosphere in the workshop all day.

'What's wrong, sir?,' Jacob had asked. 'Is it something I've done?'

'No, lad. It's just…' He'd shaken his head, unable to find the words. He couldn't bear to talk to Jacob, and in the end had sent him home.

And now it was the second night Will had to push away Jack's offer of company. He wrapped up warm and headed for the churchyard, his eyes fixed on the sky. He couldn't fathom it – the strange apparition above him. For God had certainly placed that bright comet in the sky, right over London.

He shivered as he sat down and the cold of the tombstone bit through his breeches, but he didn't look away. He pondered on the comet's trajectory, working out angles and ellipses in his head, as if he could make it conform to a ship's sextant, but it seemed to move of its own accord, subject to its own unearthly will.

He had never thought much about his soul before, but now, with that light showing up the shadows of every soul in London, he was humbled. It was no star, he was certain. It was a flaming torch, but dark, moving slowly as if watching them all. What did it mean? Would it suddenly fall to earth and consume the city? It was a sign. It could even be a sign especially for him. He'd sinned, he knew, just as certainly as if he'd made that plague water himself. For hadn't things started to go wrong just as soon as he'd given away their savings?

He'd tried to talk to Jack about it, but he'd dismissed him, blaming the new quarantine laws for their misfortune. Didn't they always say, bad things came in threes?

First the loss of his work, then the loss of his savings, now the loss of his wife.

He'd had no work since he'd gone into business with Jack, selling those potions. Just today, the Shipwright's Guild had sent his papers back unstamped, with no offer of a place in the Guild. His father, curse him, must have the Guild in the palm of his hand.

He shivered. Or perhaps God was punishing him. He'd seen a preacher on the corner of Lombard Street tell them they must repent their sins, for a day of judgement was coming. He used to have no sins to speak of, but now? Well he couldn't help but think of all those dying people in Holland, taking hope from Jack's medicine, where there was no hope to be had.

He got up and walked towards the jutting spire of the church, stamping his feet to keep warm. He hadn't told Bess about the plague water, because he'd thought she'd chide him for turning a blind eye to something so cruel.

But now he was not convinced he knew his wife at all. One thing he did know – he didn't want to look. He didn't want to know what she'd done with Pepys. He just wanted it not to exist, for them to be back the way they were before. But that was impossible. At night they lay apart, each in their own cold, silent shroud of sheets.

God, please God, help me. But the church door was locked. He leant on the walls, pressed his hands to the stones, trying to feel something, to absorb the holiness of those walls, to get some comfort. Things were all stirred up inside him; there was a pressure building, like a boil that needed to be lanced. He had to do something. But what? There were only two things he knew how to do – to carve and shape wood was the first, and the other was to pray. Anything else would be to jump out of his own shoes.

He prayed now, asking God why he was a failure. As a shipwright. As a son. As a husband. And asking him what he should do. No answer came, just the steady burn of the flame in the sky, and the feeling that the flame was burning inside him, eating him from the inside out.

***

That night when Will got back, Jack was sitting by the window, the limp periwig hanging round his face. He was wearing one of his two remaining fine velvet suits, his bony wrists protruding from lace cuffs. Next to him lay an empty flagon of ale.

'Where did you get that?' Will asked, his voice low so as not to wake Bess or the children.

'The Cock Crow. They let me have it on the slate. I went in to ask about work.'

'You'll find something.'

'I already have.'

Will raised his eyebrows in question.

'Your father was in there, and we got talking.' He was looking to Will intently for his reaction.

'And...?' He was wary. Not his father. Surely Jack hadn't got work with his father?

'Your father's helping me out. He saw it was bad luck our ship got impounded. He wants to invest in my business. There's always plague in London, so he can see the sense in it. We'll start small. We won't need a ship then, we can sell directly on the streets.'

Will felt his tension rise. 'Not the plague water again, Jack; please tell me you're not thinking of that again.'

'Why? It's profitable. Your father's got a syndicate of sawmen from the shipyard to back me.'

'C'mon, Jack, Toby told me it's just dye and water.'

'Toby's just a boy. He always gets things wrong.'

'I'll tell the authorities.'

'And if you do, I'll say you were my accomplice. See how Bess likes that.'

'Do it. I don't care.'

'What's going on? You used to be all over each other. Now you act like you want to stick knives into each other.'

'Nothing. We're just tired,' he said.

Chapter 42

'Christmas is coming already,' Agatha said to her friend Margrit, the other searcher, as they sat in Dr Harris's parlour. 'And I worry about Bessie. I just heard that Jack Sutherland was one of the men imprisoned for trading infected snuff. Dr Harris told me. What a bounder. Apparently they've just let them out. But Bessie never let me know, not in all this time.'

'What?' Margrit wasn't really listening, she was in front of the fire, resting her feet on the fender whilst Dr Harris was out, and reading a news-sheet; a piece with a woodcut illustration of three women hanged for witches.

'That explains why there was never anyone in when I called on Jack,' Agatha said. 'I expect Bessie and Will took the boys in, and she deliberately didn't tell me. Can you believe that?' Agatha paused with her finger pressed to the book where she was counting deaths. 'She doesn't want me near them. I'm a bad influence, she thinks.'

'It's a shame,' Margrit said without looking up.

'But I'll find out where they live, now Jack's out. It can't be that hard, and Bessie can't stop me. Though we seem to be busier of late, have you noticed?' Agatha paused in her counting to leaf back through the entries in this week's Bill of Mortality. Something wasn't right.

She checked again.

'There's too many,' Agatha said, running her finger down the list. 'It makes no sense.'

'Terrible,' Margrit mumbled.

'Look at the causes of death – *palsie, lethargie, ague in the guts, sores, ulcers, falling sickness*. And most of them in St Giles, or its scurvy neighbour, St Andrew Holborn. Does that say anything to you?'

'Can you believe it? The youngest was only fourteen.'

'Margrit!' Agatha grabbed the paper from her. 'Never mind about the witches. Listen to what I'm saying. Forty. In only a week. Didn't you say you'd seen a case last week?'

'A case of what?'

'The plague. I'm talking about the plague. Have you seen any other cases?'

Margrit stretched. 'Could have. There was one man who could have had it, here in St Clement Danes. The daughter said he had ulcers. But then he'd gone stark mad, hanged himself in his stairwell. So I wrote it down as death by hanging.'

'Any others?'

'No. Oh … except the woman who died in childbed. She was sick with something, but we thought it was the measles.'

'And the baby?'

'Born dead. It's in the book. *Childbed*, it says for both of them. You don't really think—'

'Figures don't lie. We need to tell Dr Harris. He'll know what to do to stop it spreading.'

A rap at the door.

'You go, Margrit,' Agatha said. 'I'll check these figures again.'

Margrit made no move and the knock sounded again. Finally Margrit put aside her paper and with a loud sigh, went to the door.

'I need to speak with Dr Harris.' The voice from the doorstep made Agatha's blood freeze. She'd recognise George Allin's cocky belligerence anywhere.

'He's out on his rounds,' Margrit said. 'What's it about?'

Agatha tiptoed towards the back door, and pulled at the handle.

Locked. Which way out? The window. She tugged, but it was stuck tight. And too high up too.

Allin's grating voice; 'They say my wife's working for him, Agatha Allin. Or maybe she calls herself Prescott. I want a word with her.'

'There's nobody of that name here,' Margrit said firmly.

'Get out of my way, woman. I'll see for myself.'

Margrit protesting, 'You can't come in here!'

'Hold her, boys.'

The noise of a scuffle, and several pairs of boots.

In desperation Agatha hurried into the back chamber where a corpse lay, fresh from a hanging, and ready for dissection. It stank already. She grabbed the winding sheet and scrambled onto the table, tucking her skirts around her thighs. Hooking the winding cloth over the corpse's rigid feet, she dragged it up over her head, clinging tight to the clammy naked flesh to make herself smaller.

From under the sheet she heard feet on the tiles in the main chamber and muffled conversation.

'What's through there?' Another man's voice.

'The dissecting room, sir.'

'Let's take a look shall we.' The same gruff man. Must be one of Allin's men.

Agatha held her breath. Under the cloth, shadows loomed, passing over the sheet. She heard the men move around the chamber, the clink as they picked up the jars of pickled body parts.

'Ugh. Is that what I think it is?'

'Put it back, Jones.'

A dark shadow over her face. 'God's breath, it stinks. What's he dead of?'

'How should I know?' Margrit said. 'Dr Harris don't like us in here. Could be a hanged man, could be the plague.'

'Plague?'

A pause.

'Let's get out of here.' The boots retreated.

Agatha's chest was about to burst from holding her breath when the door shut. She exhaled.

'Well?' Allin's voice from the next room.

'Nobody there, sir,' Jones said.

'Just a corpse. Rank, it is.'

Agatha let go of her cold sleeping companion, but stayed where she was until she heard the outer door go, and the men leave.

'Agatha?' Margrit creaked the door open again.

She sat up and threw off the cloth.

Margrit squealed and shot backwards. 'You daft bugger. You nearly did for me! I thought you'd gone out the back. Was that him? The husband you're running from?'

'Aye. George Allin. He'd have me transported if he could catch me, and my daughter too.'

'I guessed. I didn't like the way he barged in here without a "by your leave".' She rubbed her arm, 'he grabbed me that tight I've got bruises. And he had two pig-tailed ruffians with him in filthy jerkins.'

'Thanks, Margrit. But if they come again, don't cross him. I've seen what he can do. And it's my fight, not yours. I don't want anyone hurt on my account.'

'Do you think he'll be back?'

'I don't know. But I know one thing, he never gives up on a grudge.'

***

At Flaggon Row a messenger knocked at the door, and Mary opened it. Bess looked out, curious to see who it was, and saw a boy she recognised. Pepys's boy. Immediately she felt a chill, as she reached out her hand for the message. What did he want of her? Then she saw the name. *Mr. Willm. Bagwell Esq.*

She tried to keep her voice steady. 'It's for you.' She handed it to Will, hoping her hand didn't tremble.

Jack looked up from where he was tamping tobacco into a pipe, as Will frowned down at it. Bess was seized with nervousness, but carried on with giving the children their evening Bible lesson. They squirmed restlessly in their chairs, watching the messenger boy who was still waiting, staring cheekily at them in his velvet livery by the half-open door. Bess continued to read aloud from the scripture, under the light of the candle-lantern, stumbling over the text because one eye was fixed on Will. He saw her watching and deliberately turned his back to her, taking the letter to the wall-sconce to read it.

A crackle of paper as he opened it, and sharp look over his shoulder, but she dropped her gaze, pretending to be busy reading.

'Good news?' asked Jack, blowing out a huge cloud of smoke.

'Could be,' Will said. 'Don't know. I've to meet someone tomorrow.' He shot another look at Bess, folded the letter and stuffed it into his breeches pocket. 'Tell him, yes,' he called to the messenger boy, who promptly rattled away down the stairs.

Yes to what? Bess kept on with her Bible-reading, though a terror had seized her that Pepys and Will might discuss her, discuss what she'd done. She felt queasy at the prospect.

Don't be foolish, she told herself. Perhaps it's the work he promised him. But the sweat pooled inside her bodice at the thought of it. Opposite her, Jack was blowing more smoke out of his slack mouth, his eyes fixed on her as if he could almost see her thoughts.

***

Bess couldn't sleep. Snores emanated from Jack, sleeping next door in the spare cook's chamber. She hated having Jack so close, but there was little she could do about it. Will had not discussed Jack's continued residence at their house, not since the night he arrived, and she felt powerless to challenge it. They had no privacy for discussion anyway, for every conversation could be heard by Jack's flapping ears. She seethed in silent resentment.

The letter from Pepys weighed on her mind. She had to see what it said. Careful not to disturb Will's sleeping form, she gently peeled back the covers and slid out of bed. By touch she felt through her husband's pockets until she found the hard edge of the parchment. She pulled it out and tiptoed into the parlour where she lit a rush-light, jamming it into its holder so she could squint at the writing.

Mr Bagwell,

I believe you seek better employment as a ship's carpenter. War ships are being fitted out at Chatham. Please present yourself at the Master Shipwright's office at the King's Yard, Deptford at 12 noon tomorrow, where I will be pleased to meet with you and see what can be arranged. Please send immediate reply by return.

Your servant,

Samuel Pepys

So it was work after all. Pepys was keeping his word. It should have reassured her, but somehow it didn't. Too much had gone on between her and Mr Pepys for Bess to be comfortable about the two men meeting. What if Will should ask Pepys about her? Would he answer him honestly? She didn't know. And war. The word made the hairs on her arms stand up.

Hastily she folded the letter, and was about to creep back into the bedroom to return it, when Jack appeared, grubby shirt dangling over his breeches.

Bess started, guiltily.

'What have we here?' Jack said quietly. 'Is that the letter that came earlier?'

'Yes. What of it?' she kept her voice to a whisper.

'Who's it from?'

'None of your business.'

'And none of yours either, but it seems you like to spy on your husband when he's asleep.' He held out his hand for the letter. 'I could tell him, you know. That you went through his pockets.'

Damn him. He would too. She didn't relish the idea of that conversation. Dully, she handed it over.

Jack leant over the rush-light, and took his time reading it, before folding it and handing it back to her. 'Better put it back,' he said.

She swiped it from his hand.

'Pepys is a powerful man,' he said, 'with a powerful reputation.' He paused, rubbed his chin. 'Powerful reputation as a cuckolder too, eh, beautiful Bess?' He was watching her as she shrivelled beneath his look, unable to escape, breathless, as if her shame was pinned to her sleeve. He knew. He'd seen what she'd done, even though not a word of it had passed her lips.

'You could do better than Pepys,' he whispered. He reached out to touch her cheek.

Startled, she recoiled, put her hand up to her face. Stumbling, she rushed back into the bedchamber and shut the door.

Chapter 43

The next day Will turned Jacob away. 'I'll send for you when I need you,' he said. 'I need a few days on my own.'

'Is there anything I can do?'

'No. I'm sorry. It's not your fault.' He hated the look of disappointment on Jacob's face, and the slump of his shoulders as he walked away.

He braced himself and walked steadily past the dockyard, pulling his collar up against the chill, hearing his boots crunch through the frozen puddles. A light dusting of snow silvered the rooftops and cobbles. His best suit felt too thin, and hung off him. He'd lost weight. He'd worn the same clothes on the day he'd been to see Pepys the summer before last, but then he'd been sweltering in the heat.

He hadn't told Bess anything about the letter. Even Pepys's name gave him a bitter taste on the tongue. His chest hurt, as if too many feelings were bottled in there, like flies buzzing to get out. But no more. Today he'd ask Pepys about Bess, get the poison out and into the open.

From a distance he heard the clatter of chipping and hammering and the rasp of the big saw from the shipyard. It took four men to work the saws, to cut through the massive oak timbers that would form the skeleton of any new ship. Today the sound of it grated. He resisted the urge to look down towards the saw-pits where his father would be working. He'd no wish to draw his attention. He resented the fact Jack had wheedled his way into his father's pockets so easily. Though he was surprised Jack hadn't asked him about the letter – usually he couldn't wait to poke his nose into Will's business. Perhaps a spell in gaol had done him good after all.

Determined, he set his sights on the lath and plaster building that was the foreman's office. His breath puffed out before him in standing clouds as he walked towards the row of damp timber sheds. They stank of boiling rope from the ropery adjoining, and the ever-present reek of sewage from the river. Today the detritus had backed up against ramparts of ice forming on the banks of the Thames, forming an unwholesome slick. It didn't make his stomach feel any better.

Before entering, he paused a moment to collect himself, steel his resolve. Once he'd asked Pepys about Bess, he'd have to live with the answer. His palms were sweating, despite the cold. He wiped them on the seat of his pants, and was about to knock when the door opened.

'Ah, Bagwell, my good man! I saw you arrive!' Pepys was beaming. He waved his servant away and ushered Will inside, to a room illuminated from one end by the greenish light from the river. On the shelves around him were miniature models of ships, uncared for, and gathering dust. How could he bear to leave them like that? It was sheer carelessness.

'Glad you could come,' Pepys said. 'I've just the position for you. It's a shipboard position, on the *Garamond*. Look, I've the plans here—' He was already unrolling a large scroll covered in ink sketches of a large warship.

No. That wasn't why he'd come. 'That's very good of you, sir, but I didn't want an on-board positio—'

His protests were in vain, Pepys was rushing on. 'But we are at war. We need all able- bodied men. It will suit you perfectly, my man. She's standing at Chatham right now, but I said if you agree we can sort out a month's trial contract straightaway—'

'But, sir, I hadn't planned to go to sea, it wouldn't be fair on my family. I've a cousin see, and his three boys that live with us and then there's...' He swallowed. Why couldn't he get the words out? Why couldn't he say Bess's name?

'You are worried about being away from...?' Pepys fiddled with the lead weights that were to hold down the plans. It seemed he could not say Bess's name either, but it hung in the air between them, a solid presence that had grabbed hold of both of them, as if by the wrists.

Will watched Pepys's hands shuffle the weights; those soft white hands that had never made anything in his life. Plump fingers and carefully manicured nails. Those hands might have touched his wife. A rush of something seemed to almost lift him from the ground.

His words came out ragged, 'Did you touch her?'

Pepys's eyebrows shot up. He blinked, surprised.

'Did you touch my wife?' He took a step forward, belligerent. Pepys backed away.

'She... she...' Pepys's mouth worked, and he shook his head, but his eyes were unfocused, as if remembering, before they flickered, seeking escape. Pepys could make no words come, and in that moment Will knew.

It was as if he'd been slit open.

He slumped against the table, his head hanging down. His anger deflated, like a bagpipe losing air, his body turning flaccid in the space of a heartbeat. Tears of humiliation burned his eyes. He brought up his forearm to his eyes, felt the sting of the rough sleeve. He cursed himself. He should have hit him. Why didn't he? Now Pepys would think him weak.

He took a deep, shuddering breath. Bess. His Bess. With that man.

Pepys fussed over his pens and ink, deliberately ignoring him, until he cleared his throat. 'I can see fit to giving you a little extra from Navy coffers,' Pepys said, his voice quiet and measured, 'to purchase the tools you may need.'

It was a gesture, he realised, of compensation. This was the moment. The moment when he should throw it all into Pepys's face. But Pepys's solid figure and authority cowed him. What good would that do? To make an enemy of Pepys? Finally he pushed down through his palms and slowly raised himself from the table, punch-drunk with the thoughts rampaging around his head. The sooner he got to sea, the better. He'd be further away from Bess. Further away from everything.

'Do you want the position?' Pepys asked, in a voice devoid of emotion.

He would not let Pepys see what it had done to him. He'd retain his pride. It took a monumental effort to look him in the face.

'Yes. Very good, sir,' Will said, 'I accept.'

There. It was done. And Bess could do nothing about it. A sudden hatred for her sprang up, filling him with cold fury. Maybe he'd die at sea. Then she'd be sorry.

'The papers are here,' Pepys said, indicating where he should sign.

He stabbed the nib down on the paper and scrawled his name. And simply to show he did not care, he said, 'Why don't you walk back with me, and I'll have my wife give us a little supper.' He cast the words down like gauntlets.

'I don't think...' Pepys was doubtful.

'I insist,' Will said. 'It is the least I can do, after such a generous offer. My wife will be very glad to see you.' The trace of sarcasm still sounded in his voice.

***

Only five more days until Christmas, and Bess was helping the children to make Yuletide decorations from pieces of greenery they'd found earlier in the woods out towards the marshes. Holly and ivy, bay branches, scarlet-stemmed dogwood, and the red beads of hips and haws from the hedges. They were sitting at the table tying the sap-scented boughs with ribbon, and decorating them with curls of wood, like ringlets, tied in bunches, that they'd saved from the workshop. She was impatient with the boys, for she was on tenterhooks, knowing Will had gone to see Mr Pepys.

But it was Jack who was first back through the door after his meeting at the yard with Will's father. He was still thin as a greyhound, but his skin had lost its pallor and was now ruddy with cold. The children jumped up, excited to see him, but he ignored their clamour.

'Will's not back yet then?' he said to Bess.

'No,' Bess said, trying for normality. 'You didn't see him at the yard?'

'I saw him pass. His father saw him too. I won't tell you what his father said about him.'

'Don't bother, I can guess.' She left him to the children then, and went to help Mary with the evening meal. It was a ham hock, well-stewed, so she'd be able to use the left-overs for broth. In the kitchen the fire glowed red, and the room was filled with salty steam.

She didn't hear Will come in. The first she knew of it was when Jack poked his head round the door and hissed, 'He's back. And he's brought a *guest* with him.' The way he said 'guest' made her instantly wary. She dried her hands on a towel and pushed open the parlour door.

Her stomach dropped. Will and Mr Pepys both turned to look as she entered. Pepys's face was flushed, his expression apologetic. Will's face showed no expression at all. It was this that chilled her the most.

'Fetch Mr Pepys some small beer, Bess, and lay an extra place for dinner,' Will said, as if ordering a servant.

No. Pepys couldn't be staying. She looked to Will to protest, but he turned away, rattled more coal from the bucket onto the fire, and the three men sat down. Pepys began to tell them about a meeting he'd arranged at Court with Lord and Lady Sandwich, and their plans for the new navy. Bess hurriedly cleared the greenery from the table and brushed it down, trying to catch Will's attention.

'Aunt Bess, can we go out?' Billy tugged at her sleeve. 'There's icicles on the railings, we want to get some.'

'Yes,' she said, distracted, looking at the men's backs, 'but only if you wrap up warm.'

'Save us some supper!' Billy shouted. The boys tugged scarves and caps from the hooks and were out of the door like rabbits from a hole.

'Don't bring any icicles inside,' she shouted after them, 'and stick together!'

Something was wrong. She just knew it. Pepys staying. Oh Lord, what was she to do? Hastily, she went through to the kitchen, and gave Mary instructions to stretch the amount of ham by chopping more onions and adding more stock. With fumbling fingers she unstoppered the barrel to pour the ale into a jug, all the time hearing Mr Pepys's plum-like tones regaling Will and Jack with tales of the sinking of Dutch ships. She tilted the barrel to get at the dregs. Oh no, the ale was cloudy and smelled sour. Never mind, it would have to do.

When she got back into the parlour, Jack turned to her, 'Good news. Will's got a position on board the *Garamond*.'

'What?' She wasn't sure she'd heard right.

Will didn't meet her eyes. 'You'll be pleased, I dare say. I'm to sail with the warship *Garamond*, soon as she's ready. Mr Pepys has it all arranged.' The words were barbed, designed to hurt.

She glanced to Pepys, and he gave her a look that was both too hot and too long. She felt colour rise to her face and made a great fuss of putting out the table linen, ashamed to see it was still stained from the children's previous encounter with a lamb stew. She hurriedly placed a jug of ale over the offending marks. She couldn't think, her emotions heaved in her chest like the sea, and all the time Jack was observing the scene – leaning back in his chair as if the whole situation was vastly amusing.

Supper was a torment. She couldn't catch Will's eye, but on the other hand, Mr Pepys's eye was always ready to catch hers. He was sending Will to sea, when she'd specifically asked him for work in the yards. To sea, and to war.

She pushed the food around her plate with the spoon, for the ham had no savour in her mouth, and the smell of the ale made her retch. She dare not leave the table in case she became the subject of their conversation, so was relieved to hear Jack say he was going into business again. It wasn't snuff, this time, but trust Jack – he had some cock-eyed idea of making herbal medicine.

'I need investors like you,' Jack said to Pepys, 'to get it off the ground. There'll be much profit in it.'

'Much profit eh? And how is it—'

Bess was shocked to see Will speak over Mr Pepys to berate Jack. He seemed angry. 'Forget it, Jack. You're not at the stage yet where you need investment. Why you've barely just got out of—'

'It's never too soon,' Jack said, glaring. 'Now, Mr Pepys, I've heard tell we could be in for another tide of the pestilence. Best be prepared.'

'It's just rumour,' Pepys said, 'best not to heed it.' He was looking from Will to Jack. The atmosphere had suddenly become icy between them.

'I'm telling you, they falsify the Bills of Mortality,' Jack said.

'The searchers are corrupt. They get paid to keep their mouths shut, everyone knows that. There's been far too many deaths in St Giles, and no proper explanation.'

'The searchers are not corrupt!' Bess said. 'Why, my mother works in that capacity and—'

'I'm not sure it's a wise investment,' Will said firmly, cutting over Bess as if she had not spoken. 'You're taking too much risk. If the rumours are false, then there'll be no profit in it. None at all.'

'We'll talk about this later,' Jack said.

'Oh, don't mind me,' Mr Pepys said. 'This stew is good.' Bess sensed some undercurrent between Will and Jack that she hadn't seen before, and the meal continued in stony silence.

When it was done, Pepys said, 'Mr Bagwell, I'm sure your good wife would like to see the plans for the *Garamond*. Why don't you walk over and fetch them?' He rummaged in his satchel. 'And, er... Bagwell, here's a shilling. You could stop off for some wine on the way. This ale's ... a little ripe.'

'Oh, I'm sorry, sir,' Bess said, 'it's just we weren't expecting—'

'I'm sure your husband will get us some fresh. After all, we will need to toast his new position.'

Will nodded.

'Will—' She tried to catch him by the sleeve to draw him aside, but he shook her off; cut her dead.

Will turned to Jack. 'Come with me. I need to discuss a few things with you.'

'I'd rather stay here,' Jack said, settling back in his chair. 'I want to talk to Mr Pepys. And besides, Bess might need help with the children.'

'It sounds like your cousin wants your company, Mr Sutherland,' Pepys said.

A silence. Jack scowled.

Will heaved Jack by the arm, 'You're coming with me. And Mary will come with us to take care of the boys. Bess doesn't need them under her feet.' Still he didn't look at her.

A dawning realisation made her blood seem to stop in her veins. He couldn't be deliberately leaving her alone with Mr Pepys, could he?

She looked to him, 'Will, I...'

'I'm sure you'll be happy to keep Mr Pepys *busy,* won't you, wife?' The bitterness in his tone was unmistakeable.

'Will, wait—' But he was already calling Mary, and pulling a protesting Jack out of the door.

After they had gone, the silence in the room was suffocating. Bess did not dare turn to look at Mr Pepys. Will knew. Pepys must have told him. And now he'd left them alone. A great chasm had opened inside her, knowing he had left her there on purpose.

Pepys cleared his throat softly, like a reminder.

She whipped round. 'What have you done? You told him, didn't you?'

Pepys was sheepish, 'No. No, he guessed. He's a clever man.'

'I don't want him to go to sea.'

'You said, a better position. And the *Garamond* is a fine ship, and the crew well paid. He'll be happy enough. And I know times have not been easy for you both. This will ... smooth the way.' He stood up and came towards her.

Instinctively she retreated.

He shook his head sadly, 'Mrs Bagwell, good positions are hard to come by, and easier to lose. We have an hour. I wouldn't like your husband to be disappointed.'

He would take the position away, and then there'd be no hope of getting out of their debts. Will must want her to do this. She struggled to swallow this fact. He'd left them alone on purpose, and it was all her fault. She should never have started it.

'The bedroom – is it this way?' Pepys's lace-cuffed hand came gently on her arm. She pulled away, but he took a firmer hold. 'We have little time, Mrs Bagwell, to seal our agreement.'

She couldn't think. If she did this, was she being a good wife, or a bad one?

Mr Pepys had one hand on her back now, pushing her. She crossed the threshold, but was immediately struck by how untidy the spare bedchamber looked, as they passed, with all the children's clothes lying on the floor. One of Billy's socks lay in the corridor. Mr Pepys picked his way past it in his red high heels. She pulled open the bed-curtains and the imprint of Will's head was still there, crushed into the pillow.

Pepys undressed to breeches and shirt, but she didn't know what to do. It didn't feel right to undress, not here, where she'd spent so many nights with Will. Pepys jumped onto the bed with a flourish, and patted Will's side of the bed.

'Come lie down, Mrs Bagwell.'

She sat gingerly on Will's side of the bed, but Pepys snaked an arm around her waist and pulled her backwards. His lips found her neck. There was a reek of pomade and a scrape of bristles against her collarbone.

She'd done all she could to escape the whorehouses of Ratcliff, only to find the same stew here. She closed her eyes, and heard the rustle of lace as Pepys hitched her petticoat aside.

Chapter 44

Christmas was supposed to be a time of cheer, but in Flaggon Row there was little celebration and less cheer, although Bess did her best for the boys' sake, and at last the Navy paid Will's wages. Pepys must have used his influence. Will himself had refused to talk to her. Never a man of many words, she was at a loss to know what he was thinking or feeling. On Christmas Eve he had insisted on going to church on his own, leaving her to mind the children. Jack, of course, spent the night in the Old Oak drinking with Will's father.

Christmas Day dawned dry and bright, with a sky the colour of heaven. In the kitchen Mary sang as she trussed the goose, and with Will's new-found wealth, a feast of sweetmeats lay ready on the kitchen table. Bess took a deep breath. Surely, today of all days, she'd be able to make amends with Will.

After she'd laid out bread and fish on the table for their breakfast, she went to the bedchamber. She leant in, to plant a kiss on his cheek, but he pushed her away with a sharp, 'Don't touch me.'

'Please, Will, we can't go on like this. Look, I got you something.' She reached under her pillow and held out a small parcel wrapped in paper.

'I don't want anything.' But he took it from her anyway, as she pushed it into his grasp.

'Just open it,' she said.

He pulled a striped knitted hat from the paper.

'I thought it would keep you warm on board ship. I saved the wool from the caps I knitted for the boys.'

He swallowed, stared at it a moment. Then he deliberately put it to one side. 'Here.' He leapt out of bed and dragged his pouch from his breeches pocket, so the white lining was left flapping. He fumbled inside it, then threw two Angels onto the covers. 'Buy whatever you like. I suppose you've earned it.'

In the next room, Jack's snores seemed to add insult to the injury.

The rest of the day passed in icy politeness, with morning worship and then the Christmas feast. Mary and Bess slaved in the kitchen, and the meal was devoured in a few moments by Jack and the boys. Will barely touched his food, but kept up a conversation with Jack about the yards, bitterness written all over his face.

Boxing Day was equally sour. She gave the boys their knitted caps, but on seeing her gift to the boys, Jack produced three sixpences from his pocket, and in the excitement at seeing real silver, her gifts were soon forgotten.

As for Will; he spent Boxing Day in the workshop hiding from them all, despite the freezing weather and no fire below. Two days later he took his canvas carry-all and was gone to sea. So now there was no cheerful hammering from below, and the workshop was dark and silent.

His parting words to her had been, 'Do your duty and look to the children.'

Now even that pleasure was to go. Jack had been offered bigger rooms over Kite's premises, and was packing his bags. From the bedroom came crashes and bangs and scuffles as the children squabbled over who was to carry them for him.

Bess cut six thick slices of bread and buttered them before laying on slices of cheese and packing it all in paper. She had no confidence that Jack would feed his children properly.

Jack and Toby dragged the bags to the door. Billy's nose was pressed to the window. 'Grandfather's here,' he yelled, 'with the cart.'

Bess wiped her hands and went to peer out. Owen Bagwell was bulked up in a thick wool cloak and a hat with earflaps. His moustache bristled white with frost. She'd no wish to meet with Will's father, but couldn't deny he'd been thoughtful to organise transport on a day like this – cold to make your bones ache, and a brittle layer of snow to make stepping outside treacherous. Even the horse had sacking tied to its hooves to give it extra grip.

The boys whooped with excitement and her warnings to be careful of the ice rang on deaf ears. They clambered on top of the cart like monkeys, huffing their breath in clouds into the cold air. Little terrors. She smiled a smile full of tears. She couldn't resist going down to say goodbye. The number of times she'd wished them gone, and now it was happening she just wanted it to stop.

She hugged them one by one, and handed Toby the packet of provisions.

'Now you be good,' she said, her voice choked.

He shuffled away, embarrassed to be embraced, but little Hal clung tight to her. 'I want to stay home,' he wailed.

Mr Bagwell hoisted him away and shook him. 'No crying. Big boys don't cry,' he said, shoving him roughly next to the driver. Hal was so surprised to be there that he stopped immediately.

Bless him, she thought.

Jack handed her a scrap of paper. 'This is where we are. Tell Will, when you write.' She nodded. 'And call to visit.'

'Yes, I'll miss the boys,' she said, looking at the address. St Clement Danes, just beyond the city walls.

'And me I hope,' Jack said, catching her eye.

She backed away, but he took hold of her arm.

'It wasn't my idea, moving out. It was Will's. He didn't want me in Flaggon Row whilst he's away at sea. Can't think why.' His smile was full of implication. 'Quite insistent, he was. Though you can do better than Pepys.'

That phrase again. She ignored it, and shook him off; his words felt like a stab. 'It will be good for you to spend time with the boys, Jack,' she said. 'Will they still be having their lessons?'

'Lessons?' He frowned as if he didn't understand. 'No. The boys will be working with me; proper men's work. We've a stable to clean out, work to do. I'll need their hands.'

'What? Hal as well?'

'He's big enough now, too old to be in petticoats.' A pause. 'Well, my beautiful Bess, you'll have the house all to yourself. Maybe I'll call in.' His eyes held hers a moment too long, and it made her recoil.

She folded her arms; partly against him, partly against the chill. 'Bring the boys any time,' she said.

Will's father shouted a swear-word at the horse and flapped the reins. He'd not said a single word to her. The cart creaked away and not one of the boys looked back.

***

Agatha scanned through Dr Harris's leaflet with distaste, '*Certain Necessary Directions for the Preservation and Cure of the Plague*'. It was a tract revived from the last bout, but hopelessly old-fashioned. Dr Harris had given it to her, after he was summoned to an emergency public health subcommittee of the King's council.

It advised you to avoid bathing and smoke tobacco. There was a list of foods that were considered 'injurious' and to be avoided, such as cucumbers, melons and cherries. She'd never read anything so foolhardy in her life. Cucumbers and melons! Why, they were rich men's fodder, and there were no cherries to be had in London anyway – not now suppliers from overseas had heard of the contagion and trade had stopped. Weavers couldn't get silk, ostlers couldn't get fodder for their horses. Dr Harris said the King had told the College of Physicians to put a stop to the plague, as if they could just wave it away with a few pills. Fools.

She cast the tract aside, and tucked the cover over her basket which contained her precious remaining supplies of dried rue and wormwood, green vitriol and Venice Treacle, along with some cakes, four for a penny. An expensive treat. She'd tried several times to see Jack or the Sutherland boys, hoping for news of Bessie, but they were never in. She worried for them. The boys and her daughter. Today she would try once more.

As she set off, she hoped the boys wouldn't fight over the extra cake. It had been her plan to take the tract with her as well, had it been any use. She took a detour to avoid the Chancery Lane area, for the contagion had reached there a week ago. She knew that because she'd traced the path of the sickness, its deadly trail, through the Bills of Mortality. The Chancery Lane and Drury Lane area would be full of carts and horses by now, for the law students who would be leaving in droves from the Inns of Court.

Her hip ached as she walked, and the basket bumped against her thigh. It was a good few miles to St Giles. She knocked on the door of the narrow house where Jack lived, but again there was no answer. Eventually, she walked around the back of the row to peer in to the window behind. She pressed her face up to the sliver of glass, shielding the light away to see better.

The room was full of women spinning fleeces.

'Oy, you.'

She stepped away.

'What are you doing?'

The neighbour, a tanner by the look of him, in a stained smock, was blocking her retreat.

'I'm looking for Jack Sutherland and his boys.'

'Well they're not here.' He was still eying her suspiciously.

'They moved out. It's Widow Stow now and her daughters. Good thing too. Them boys were a bleedin' nuisance. Always in and out banging the doors and pinching the eggs from our hens.'

'Do you know where they've gone?'

'No, and I don't want to know. He kept some shady company, that Sutherland, despite him dressing like a fop. He was in gaol, didn't you know? Best place for him, I say.'

'You've no address for them?'

'Are you deaf? I told you, I don't know. And I don't like folk snooping around my back yard.'

He made a gesture at her, like shooing a cow into a meadow.

Agatha took the hint, and hurried away with as much dignity as she could muster. They'd moved. And nobody had bothered to tell her. She sagged with disappointment. She'd looked forward to a cuddle from Hal and telling the older ones a tale. Now she didn't know when she'd ever see them again. Of course she could ask Bessie about them.

But no. She had her pride. Bessie would have to come to her first.

***

Bess slept badly and now she chafed her hands against each other. She'd paid Mary the wages she owed her with the Christmas gift Will had given her, and then sent her on a day's leave.

With no Mary to lay the fire, she busied herself tearing paper and banking coal until a blaze flamed in the hearth. She didn't dare think; it would be too painful. She squatted before the fire, but its blaze didn't warm her. The wind was rising, and she could hear its whistle through the spires and masts of Deptford. Her back was cold, and she was aware of the empty house behind her seeming to suck all the warmth from her body.

Another gust, and the house creaked as the timbers moved, like an old vessel at sea. It put her in mind of Will. She wondered how he was faring in this icy blast, whether he still thought of her and longed for home. Her thoughts about him were complicated; she couldn't square the man of the last months with the man she'd married. She supposed she loved him, or why this tearing feeling in her chest?

She turned from the fire and surveyed the room. Now there was nobody but her to fill it, the parlour seemed huge. Under the table was one of Hal's knitted socks that he must have left behind. She crouched to pick it up, remembering the number of days she'd helped him to pull it on. She imagined his warm little toes inside it; felt her throat tighten.

Outside, the hollers of the early morning round of bread-men and milkmaids, knife-grinders and button sellers, drifted by, carried away by the wind, as haunting as seagulls. She didn't feel like sewing. Couldn't put her mind to it, somehow. She would give the house a good clean. That's what she'd do. It was what her mother used to do in times of trouble, she realised.

The thought stopped her in her tracks. Her mother. She saw in her mind's eye her mother's trembling lower lip when she told her the boys were gone and that she didn't need her. It still made her bitter, their argument, but now the hollow pain of regret gripped her. No point in thinking of it now. Briskly, she folded up the palliasse where Jack used to sleep, and gathered the bedding in a heap, grimacing at the holes where tobacco from Jack's pipe had dropped onto the sheets. Lord, they could have all been burned in their beds!

Outside, the wind increased as she worked. There was no noise now except its howl, no horse's hooves passing, just the skittering of debris in the road. Somewhere outside, a shutter banged. She peered out. The Thames was foaming with grey waves. Sleet flew horizontal across her view. No boats were passing; the watermen's craft huddled to the bank.

She paused with the pail and washcloth in her hand. She'd stay within; work to keep warm. She went through to her bedchamber to strip the bed. A rumble overhead. All at once lightning flashed, slashing the big four-poster bed with light. A picture came to mind of Will, how he used to take up three-quarters of the mattress, spread-eagled out with his legs too long and hanging over the end.

How she missed that man. For the last few weeks she'd missed him even when he was here. And now he was out on the sea, in this storm, thinking she didn't care for him. She gripped the sheets tight, absently pulling at them as another picture came to mind.

The turned-back sleeve and lace cuff of Pepys. Then his hands pressing down on her shoulders, as she stared up at the bed canopy, trying to think only of that, fixing her eyes on the gilded button at its centre, the pleated material, and not ...

Oh Will. She bundled up the bedding in an angry gesture and threw it into the laundry basket. Everything had changed the day he'd given her to Pepys. For that was what Will had done – traded her for a position on board ship. Why had he done that? But she knew. It was her fault. She was a faithless wife and it had hurt him. *You've made your bed,* was what he would say, *you'd best lie in it.*

Lightning split the sky, and a great clap of thunder. The wind roared. Above there was the sound of tearing timber immediately followed by a crash. Bess instinctively ducked, put her hands over her head. The smash of something breaking on the road outside. She ran to the window, pressed her forehead to the glass. The road was littered with roof tiles and mangled wattle fences. Up against the wall was wedged a broken garden gate that had blown clean off its hinges.

Another squall of rain and wind; too close. As if it was in the house. Bess pushed open the kitchen door. It scraped against something gritty. She forced it open and peered around the door. And saw sky. Felt rain on her face.

The whole of one corner of the roof was gone. Red roof tiles littered the floor and the cook-hearth. Rain gusted in over her dry provisions. A rook's nest, a mess of twig and bird lime, had splattered into the fallen rafters. The timbers that remained above were jagged and listing in the wind.

Hurriedly she shut the door. Just in time. Behind it a thud that shook the soles of her shoes, followed by the clatter of more falling tiles. She did not dare open the door again.

By evening the storm had blown itself out. The door to the kitchen would not open. She went down the steps outside to look at the damage. From below she saw that some of the shingle wall had also gone. The sight of it pierced her heart. The house had been perfect, and now it was as if some devil had disfigured it.

There'd be no cooking in that room for a while, that was certain. She knew instantly that it would cost her. Such repairs were tasks that Will could do, if he were here. But he was not here. She sat down at the table and pressed her hands to her head. Who could she turn to? Her mother? No. She said she wouldn't come back, '*not if you paid me*,' her mother had said. There was no-one.

Chapter 45

The wind was still high after the January storm, and Agatha clutched her canvas bag to her chest as she forced her way against its blast back towards the festering rookery of St Giles. The house she'd to visit was easily spotted by the dishevelled, windswept mourners by the door. She ducked into the front parlour, squeezing past, murmuring 'beg pardon'. Someone handed her a candle and she carried it before her, the wax spilling onto her wrist. She did not usually come at night, but Dr Harris, the physician who employed her, had insisted. He was compter for the Parish records, and responsible for the Bills of Mortality in her area. 'Too many deaths in St Giles,' he'd said ponderously, as if he'd noticed it himself, 'it could be a contagion.'

The Fraser family were poor laundry-workers, so the house stank of urine from the buck tub, and of wet linen, and the back room, where the bodies lay, was dark as a tomb.

'You don't need to see them.' The daughter of the house, Norry, a large lummock of a girl with a badly mended hare-lip, would not let her pass. 'I swear it's the bad water from the Fleet. Two others from our street died of it just last week.'

'And your ma and pa; had they the gripes?'

'Aye. Both of them.'

'The flux?'

'Something awful. But they be at peace now. No need for you to go prodding and poking at them. I can lay them out myself.' Norry folded her arms across her bosom, barring the way.

Agatha placed a hand softly on her arm. 'I'm sorry. I know it's upsetting, but I'll be gentle. I have my job to do, and I just need to look in on them, to give the cause of death, so if you'll let me by—'

'No.' The word was aggressive. 'I've told you—'

'Then I'll call the constable, and he'll have you arrested.'

This seemed to shift her, and she stood aside. The room stank of faeces and blood, but Agatha was used to this and merely made a note to herself. In the gloom she saw that one of the bodies wasn't even in the bed, but contorted on the floor.

A whisper came in her ear. 'I can pay you, if that's what it takes. I've got two babbies, Have a heart, missus.'

And neither of them in wedlock, thought Agatha, noticing the lack of a wedding band on Norry's finger. Agatha bent low over the man on the floor. His expression was one of open-mouthed terror, lips purple over yellow teeth; his fingers clawed at his nightshirt, but had turned rigid by the strangle of death. But it was what she saw on his neck that made her recoil, clapping a hand over her nose and mouth.

Black boils of pestilence.

'Please,' Norry said. 'I'll pay you.'

Agatha turned to her. 'You know what this is, don't you? And you know what you must do.'

'No!' The shout was more of a moan. 'No, not that, please, not that.'

'What is it?' An elderly straggle-haired woman came to ask what the commotion was.

'Quick,' Agatha whispered to her. 'Fetch a constable. Anyone in this house must stay here. It will need to be signed with the cross and the doors boarded up.'

Nobody said the word 'plague' out loud, but whispers of it soon cleared the house until the only sound was of a crying baby. A small girl put her head around the door. 'Ma?'

Norry did not answer. She headed for the parlour where,

ignoring the grizzling baby, she stripped the linen from a clothes-horse and stuffed it into a bag.

'Where will you go?' Agatha said.

'My cousin,' the answer was muffled as she was bending over the bag. 'Lives in the West Country. She'll take us in.'

'It's a long way. Has she family?' Agatha had to shout over the noise of the crying baby.

'Quiet, Walter! Yes, two young 'uns like mine.' The woman swept up a small pair of shoes from the hearth and was about to push them in the bag, but Agatha swiped it up and held it closed.

'What about her husband? He won't welcome you if he knows why you've come. Think woman. How will your cousin feel if she knows what you've brought with you? Would you visit this affliction on her children as well as your own?'

The thought of Toby, Billy and Hal flashed before her. Her thoughts were interrupted by the child.

'Mama, where are we going?'

'Cousin Flo's. Now fetch your warm cloak from the hook, there's a good girl.'

Bang. Bang. Bang.

The door.

Norry hoisted the crying baby onto her hip and chivvied the young girl before her. 'Back door, quick!'

Moments later she was back, followed by a constable with a sharp-bladed halberd in hand. Agatha picked up her things. 'Two dead of the plague, in the back room,' she said. And to Norry, 'God have mercy, and be with you all.'

Outside, she was haunted by the bleak look in the woman's eyes. Her first instinct was to run to Bess's house and tell her to get out of London. Once the plague took hold, there'd be no stopping it.

But she turned her back on the river, and slowly, deliberately, walked in the other direction. Her heart was as heavy as her feet, but she knew Bess didn't want her, and she had her pride, she'd keep away. As she went, she closed her ears to the hammering and split of wood as the shiny nails went in the Frasers's door. It would be a month before they would be pulled out, she knew, by which time they'd be red with rust.

***

The Bagwells's wasn't the only house in need of repair and it took another week before Bess could get the roofers to come out. Bess and Mary had worked tirelessly in the dust for the last few weeks, so the kitchen was spick and span at last, though Bess had no idea how she could pay Mary her wages next month. Her purse was empty again after paying for the roof. Would it never end, this scrimping and saving?

As usual, by the time the noon bells struck, they'd wiped down the whole parlour, and the day stretched ahead with nobody to cook or clean for, nobody to ask what was for supper. 'Bread and cheese will do for us again, Mary,' she said.

In the afternoon, when there was a knock at the door, Mary went to answer it. Bess stood warily in case it was Pepys again, for he'd been twice since Will had left, and each time she'd sent Mary on a petty errand. One time, she'd returned before he'd left, and Mary had looked on her with a pitying expression.

But no; not this time. Today it was Mrs Fenwick, panting on the doorstep, her bosom heaving. What did she want? She hadn't spoken to Bess for months. But glad of the distraction, Bess ushered her into the parlour.

'No fire today?' Mrs Fenwick said, eyeing the empty grate.

'No. Now there's only me, I leave it until dusk. It would be wasteful, otherwise, as I'm in and out a lot. And anyway, I keep warm enough, being busy.'

'Yes, I saw you had some trouble in the storm. We lost our weather cock from the roof. Such an inconvenience. My husband relies on it to predict his sailings.' She was already pulling out a chair at the table. 'Still, a good fire is so cheering. We have ours lit all the time in this weather. But I thought I'd better come by, Mrs Bagwell, in case you haven't heard the news.'

Bess sat down opposite her. 'What news?' she asked listlessly. 'Is it the plague? If so I already—'

'Plague?' Mrs Fenwick's eyes widened in alarm. 'Who said there was plague? No. Two of our warships sunk. In a sea battle in the Sea of Gibraltar, and what with your husband being at sea, I thought you might—'

Bess had stood up without thinking. Will's ship lost? It couldn't be so. 'Thank you for telling me, Mrs Fenwick, but I'm sure there's nothing to worry about, now why don't you—'

'But my dear, they were blown up!' Her face was alight with scandalised excitement. 'Cannon, my husband said. Got in the line of fire, and—'

Bess saw Mary's eyes widen. Seized with anger, Bess took Mrs Fenwick's arm and started to hustle her towards the door, but then realising what she was doing, dropped it as if it was red hot. 'Mrs Fenwick,' she said icily, 'thank you for coming, but if you'll excuse me, I have to go out now.' She gestured at Mary to hold the door open.

'My husband was telling me over dinner, and when he'd gone, I said to myself; I said, I must go and let poor little Mrs Bagwell know—'

'Thank you for coming,' Bess said firmly. 'Mary'll see you out.'

Mrs Fenwick fussed her way to the gaping door with a series of clucks and sighs of disapproval, but this time Bess didn't care.

Her heart was full of foreboding. She had to find out if Will was on one of those ships, and she knew Mrs Fenwick was the least reliable source of information.

As soon as Mrs Fenwick had gone, Bess dressed herself in her warm winter cloak and tied a felt hat over her hair. Mittens and an extra shawl armed her for the freezing weather outside.

'Shall I come with you, mistress?' Mary said, her eyes anxious.

'No. Wait here in case a message comes.'

The steps down from the house were slippery and rimed with frost and Bess clung tight to the banister rail.

On the river, the Thames's wherries jostled and clanked for position as there was only a narrow channel that wasn't frozen, and large queues of boats had formed to land at Old Swan Stairs near the Tower.

She bought a news-sheet but it told her nothing. An hour later she was waiting outside Pepys's office on one of the leather chairs in the corridor, the crumpled news-sheet in her hand. He was out. When he finally returned from his dinner he was with his clerk, Hewer, and clearly nonplussed to see her there.

She didn't wait for his greeting. 'I've heard about the ships sunk off Spain. Tell me, is one of them Will's ship?' She searched his face, but it was blank.

'Oh dear, now then. Which one was he on?'

He didn't know? She was incredulous. 'It was the *Garamond*! You arranged it for him yourself.'

'Hewer, go and find out if the *Garamond* was lost, would you?' he said, and Hewer disappeared into the offices. Pepys took her by the arm. 'Now don't distress yourself, Hewer'll be back any moment. We've only just heard the news ourselves. And mighty fine news too, seeing as we sunk the *King Solomon*, and they say she's worth two hundred thousand pounds! Think of that!'

But Bess could not think of anything except Will.

When Hewer emerged, with a paper in his hand, he was smiling. 'The *Garamond*'s safe,' he said.

'Oh, thank God.' The wave of relief made her sway on her feet. She sank into the leather chair and to her shame, burst into tears.

'Oh dear, oh dear,' Pepys said, patting her on the shoulder as if she were a dog. Finally, Hewer offered her a silk handkerchief.

'Will you be alright, mistress?' Hewer asked.

Bess nodded, unable to speak. What a fool; to cry like this. She gulped for breath.

'She needs a strengthener,' Pepys said. 'Call a carriage.'

'But what about your two-o'clock appointment, sir?' Hewer gestured at his door.

'I need to give this lady a strong drink, and then see her safely home,' Pepys said. 'She's had a shock.'

'No,' protested Bess, instantly knowing where this might be leading. 'I beg your pardon. I was just overcome. As long as Will is safe.'

'I insist. The carriage, Hewer.' Pepys flapped his hand at his clerk, who hurried away down the stairs, two at a time. He took her by the arm. 'Now lean on me, and we'll walk slowly.'

In fact she was glad of him, she was light-headed and her legs seemed to have a mind of their own. She realised she had eaten nothing that day. She hadn't felt like eating; the bread and cheese Mary had left out for her still stood on the sideboard at home.

Pepys ushered her to the big double doors at the back of the building where a carriage stood, with Hewer holding the door. 'No, Mr Pepys,' she said, 'I feel quite myself now. You can leave me be.' But he was man-handling her, pushing her in the back, and behind her Hewer was closing the door.

Panic assailed her. She shouldn't be here. She tried to climb out again but Pepys pressed her back down and pushed up the leather blind to speak to Hewer. 'Tell the driver, the usual. Cancel Mennes. And send a message to Rickard,' he called. 'Tell him I'll be late.'

Hewer's response was lost as the carriage set off. A draught of icy air made her gasp. Pepys yanked the blind shut so they were plunged into gloom.

'Where are we going?' she asked.

'A little "caberet" I know. We went there before. The Inkwell; you remember it?'

Not that place. The memory of it was like shrapnel, buried deep and festering. 'No, Mr Pepys, I'd like to go straight home.' Her words came out jagged with the jolting of the carriage.

'Nonsense. You'll feel better after a tot of rum, and a hot dinner.' He was so certain. He pursed his lips as if that was the end of the matter. The horses were increasing speed now and she was thrown back against the seat.

Her stomach growled, and her head swam. Dinner was tempting, but she knew it would not end with that. 'Mr Pepys, I don't know how to say this, but I don't wish for any further ... any further relations with you. No matter what you might think, I love my husband, and I respect him. It wouldn't be godly.'

'Hush, Mrs Bagwell. I'm merely offering to take you for dinner. Can't see why anyone would object to that.'

'I don't want dinner. Stop the carriage.' She pulled up the blind, and the bare trees of the heath whipped past her, along with a blast of blisteringly cold air. She put her head out but the road was passing frighteningly fast.

Pepys pulled her back in and shut the blind. 'You might not want dinner, but I do. The portions at The Admiral's are too damned small. I'll not survive this blasted Turkey meeting tonight without a good dinner.'

'But, Mr Pepys, I just want to go—'

He put his hand over her mouth. 'Madam, stop. You'll have a long walk home in this freeze. Stop your silliness now, and allow me to buy you a hot pie. I'll take you home once we've eaten. I give you my word.'

Though the surroundings were just as dingy as she remembered them, the dinner was good, and she felt better in herself, although she was still guilty with herself for being there. She clenched her fingernails in her palms and left the rum untouched in the glass. The smell of liquor reminded her of Ratcliff and her mother and made her nauseous.

'Will you drive me back now, sir?' she asked.

'No hurry, is there? I've cancelled my afternoon appointment, and I like your company.' His hand reached under the table for her knee. It was starting. As she knew it would.

She moved her knee away. 'I'd like to go home, Mr Pepys.'

'Soon. As soon as we've had a little fun.'

'No.' She leant towards him. 'Mr Pepys, do you not heed the Commandments? Do you not think of your wife? *Thou shalt not commit adultery.* That's what it says in the Bible, doesn't it?'

'Pish. What's so bad about a little playfulness?' He could not keep the defensive tone from his voice, so she knew she had dented him – finally.

'I doubt your wife would think so,' she persisted.

'Damn it! Elisabeth cares nothing for what I do. She is bound up entirely in household duties and gossip. She doesn't understand me, nor does she have any interest in the mighty wheels of the Navy. I like women. Especially attractive ones like you. I like to talk to them, and she will never let me talk. She never has time for me. What's wrong with a man taking a little pleasure? It harms no-one.'

'Your pleasure will not be with me though, sir. I intend to do my duty.' She stood up, but was on the wrong side of the table to leave easily, and he stood too.

'Mrs Bagwell, you talk of duty, but what of your duty to your husband?' He leant towards her now, grabbed both her arms. 'Mr Bagwell understands he keeps his position only on one condition, that his wife should be my company if I wish it, whilst he is abroad. His express wishes are that you should do so.'

'No. I don't believe you... Will never said...' But then she remembered him leaving her with Pepys, his coldness, his refusal to say goodbye.

Pepys raised his eyebrows in a knowing smile. 'There are many people who lack employment. Food and shelter too.' She wilted under Pepys's grasp. He became gentle again, lowering his voice. 'So it would be better for us both,' he said, 'and for Mr Bagwell, if I don't have to force you.'

Chapter 46

Jack hurried home, chiding the three boys, and ducking under the jetties of the houses. They had been in the old stables at an acquaintance of Will's father, Owen Bagwell, the place where he was making his potion, and dusk was falling. They'd worked on a while, but now the cost of candles would make working prohibitive, and Jack had an eye on his profits.

A cluster of women were gathered next to the bill board where the wherry plied its trade. They were gesticulating in a way that caught his attention. One of them pulled something from the board and stuffed it in her bag. Before he got there the women dispersed; but curious, he went to see what they'd been looking at.

A clutch of new notices, plastered over the other faded yellowing papers against the splintered wood. Probably more bear-baiting, Jack thought, or the plays on the opposite bank.

'What's it say, Pa?' Toby asked.

'Can't you read it?'

'Nah.' Toby lost interest and took the others to throw pebbles onto the thawing ice at the edge of the water, but Jack barely registered it. He was reading;

'An eminent HIGH DUTCH PHYSICIAN, newly come from HOLLAND where he resided all last year during the PLAGUE, and cured multitudes of people, available for personal consultations at...'

In mounting concern he scanned the other notice roughly nailed below it,

'Experienced PHYSICIAN, well-versed in every kind of pestilence for 40 YEARS, offers advice and remedy against any kind of DIS-EASE, with God's Blessing...'

The third notice was a small bill for an *'elderly APOTHECARY, treated many in the last plague of James's reign, can offer the strongest, least costly and warranted PROTECTION...'*

God's blood. So he was not the only one. There'd been others too, but only torn scraps of paper remained. He stood a moment, the words blurring before him.

The race was on. He'd have to be quick. Flood the market as quick as he could. He'd one advantage – that he'd done it before, and he was ready.

At the same time a frisson of fear made him momentarily unable to move.

The rumours were true. The plague was here.

He'd have to watch his employees, make sure there was plenty of vinegar for washing and a fire burning brimstone in the workplace. He'd seen the dead in Amsterdam, and he didn't want to be one of them, but the excitement made him light-headed.

He ripped all the other notices down and tore them into shreds. He watched them skitter across the ice like ash.

Now was his time. He intended to make his fortune.

Chapter 47

Bess stood on the jettied balcony and stared out at the sullen Thames. The wherries were full of couples laughing and talking. February, and Will was finally home, but he wouldn't talk of his month at sea, and the distance between them was like glass, a cold, transparent entity. Nowadays he did not meet her eyes and spent his time either in the workshop below or walking by the river. On his arrival, he'd been horrified by the damage to the house.

'We haven't even paid off the loan yet, and it's a wreck,' he said. Then he complained about the state of the repairs and how badly they were done, and blamed her for the cost of it. So she'd spent last evening in the cold, stitching more gloves. She'd held up the cut out pieces and longed for the touch of a real hand.

A knock below. The burring noise of Will winding the drill through wood stopped.

She leant over the rail, to hear who was visiting Will.

Bastable. She'd know that nasal voice anywhere. She crept to the top of the steps to listen.

'You've already had a week,' Bastable said. 'The bailiffs will be round on Friday. If I were you I'd sell something, or hide what you want to keep. Or have a talk with your cousin, after all it's his responsibility, but he refuses to open his purse. Says it's up to you.'

'It's not my fault. Navy pay's late again, and there was that storm—'

'That's what they all say, but excuses won't stop Kite, when he's a mind to be paid. I'm just the messenger. Friday. Don't forget.'

Bess crept back indoors. But they'd nowhere to go. His father wouldn't take them in, and her mother had only the one room in the lodging house. Jack? No, heaven forbid.

Later that night she watched Will hide the parchment from her with his arm as he scribed a letter. He was grey in the face, but would not tell her what was wrong.

Jack,

I hope the boys fare well. It is rare I ask a favour, but this time I fear I must. The Navy pay is late again. I can't tell you how much it irks me that sailors fighting for England against the scoundrel Dutch are left penniless after all their endeavours. So I was wondering if you could see fit to advance me a few pounds. I will pay you back as soon as my pay packet arrives, but Bastable's demanding Kite's damages again, and my half of the loan must be paid this week or we will be without a roof over our heads.

I'm desperate, coz. Or I wouldn't ask.

Do it for Bess, if not for me. Please send me by return where to meet you.

You cousin, William

Jack smiled, holding the letter between finger and thumb. Will's letter had fallen plumb on time. The sedan from the wherry deposited Jack near the end of Flaggon Row, and he paid the bearers. He blew on his hands and slid on his new sheepskin gloves, before wrapping his warm cloak with the rabbit-skin lining around himself to keep out the cold. Business was good. Better than good, in fact. And about time too; the spell in a debtor's cell had dented his business reputation.

Still, the elixir was shifting like the devil. Of course he didn't go to the infested areas himself, but sent his men. Paupers would always crave risky work.

He didn't knock when he got to Will's house, just pushed the workshop door open.

'Ah, Will,' he said, noting his cousin's drawn face and the fact he'd almost jumped out of his skin.

'I thought you'd send a message,' Will said.

'Not much of a welcome then.'

'Sorry, Jack. I'm glad you came. Come and sit, so we can talk.'

'I'd rather stand; my legs are cramped from the sedan.'

Will hovered then, unsure whether or not to sit.

I'll put him out of his misery, Jack thought. 'Lucky for you, I've a proposition. Business is booming. There's a panic in the city. Two more doors with the red crosses, and already my elixir is the talk of the city. And London's bigger than Amsterdam. I need warehouse space.' He gestured around the workshop, mentally filling it with crates of his elixir.

'No,' Will said, backing away from him. 'Not here.'

'Why not? It's ideal. You are frequently at sea, and I need the space.'

'I don't want that stuff in my house.'

'*Our* house. Remember? You signed half to me last October, when you were unable to keep up the repayments. Or rather, you signed it all over to me.'

Will's face dropped. 'What do you mean?'

'It was for your own good. You should always read the small print, coz. The papers you signed granted me full ownership of this house. I didn't want to upset you, but I knew you'd never be able to manage it; you just have no business-sense.'

'That's not true, you're twisting it all!' Will's face had taken on a brick-red flush.

Jack smiled at him benevolently. 'You couldn't pay, so I thought it a kindness to take it on now I'm established. Saves family embarrassment. And as we're family, I think it only reasonable I should have some use of the workshop, don't you?'

'But I trusted you! You were supposed to be helping me. I helped you often enough. The Navy are slow in paying. I just needed a bit of leeway. I was wanting a loan, not this … this … what will you be doing in there?'

'We'll try not to disturb you – there'll be deliveries, and my men coming and going, but it shouldn't disturb you. Or the beautiful Bess.'

'But I need the workshop, Jack, for my work.'

'What work? A few bowls? I'm surprised you bother any more, now you can go to sea, and Bess is keeping Pepys sweet for you.' He smiled. 'She was always a good one for that, Bess.'

He was rewarded by Will's wary expression. 'What do you mean?'

'You know, before she wanted to be queen of Deptford.'

'I don't know what you're talking about.'

'Really?' He laughed, enjoying it. Now was his chance to set Will against his wife. 'I recognised her mother. She's Mrs Allin, though she calls herself Prescott now. She had quite an unsavoury reputation. Proprietor of a bawdy house in Ratcliff.'

'It's not true. You're making it up.'

'Ask her. Ask Bess what she did before she made gloves.'

'Get out.' Will was upon him in one bound, his fists out.

Jack side-stepped him. 'You can't ban me from my own property. If you want to stay here, then you'll need to keep the repayments coming. I'm a very reasonable landlord.'

Chapter 48

Upstairs, Bess leant over the candle to stitch the two halves of the sealskin together. She heard Jack's angry voice in the workshop below, then Will's raised in argument, and a door slam.

What were they fighting about now?

She sighed and carried on stitching, determined to ignore it. Best to keep busy. The stitches were hard to see in the dark fur, but she dare not use another light. Candles were a farthing each. It ate into her, the fact that the house itself was so fine, now it was fixed up again, but she resented these sheep's grease candles that stained the ceiling with soot, because they couldn't afford better.

Bess had been forced to take on more piece work for Dashwood, another glover, but he was more demanding than Hutchinson had ever been, and kept arriving after nightfall with more batches for her to sew before morning. The quality of the fur was worse, and he didn't have a proper shop, just sold them on a market stall on the south side of the river. She supposed she should be grateful, for she still remembered the cold, the hunger and the squalor of her childhood.

Her eyes were gritty with lack of sleep and her stomach growled with hunger. There was no more coal. The fire was out, and her breath stood in clouds over her work. Will had not mentioned Bastable, though the threat of the bailiff hung in her mind. How would she tell Mary? They surely wouldn't be able to keep her on. She could hear her in the kitchen, slapping the dough on the table with her plump white hands, ready for tomorrow's bread.

The gloves Bess had finished were packed ready, but no-one

had been to collect. Reluctantly, as it got to evening, she thought she'd better take them to Dashwood's house. The money from her work might help Will pay the money they owed.

She peered into the workshop. Empty. Will must have gone out to the Dolphin or the coffee-house with Jack. She wouldn't take Mary; it wouldn't do for her to know what a pittance Bess was paid, and how close she was to losing her employment.

Dashwood's address was on an invoice for the fur in one of the boxes. Basket in hand, she set off for St Giles, walking because she needed to save the fare. The light was fading from the sky leaving a city of dark shadows and gloom.

Bess hurried, partly to keep warm, and partly to be back through the city gates by curfew. St Giles used to be inhabited by bowyers and bow-string makers, but Bess was sad to see that most of these houses were now taverns or dice-houses or, from the look of them, and those loitering outside their doors, worse.

When she got to Fore Street, she paused to rub the chilblains on her fingers. A great knot of people were gathered around the well, despite the ground around it being wet with mud and slime, so Bess asked for Dashwood's house and was pointed down an unsavoury-looking alley. She dodged past the leaking conduit that came from the well, and down the narrow passageway.

Dashwood's house was shuttered and dark. There was no knocker so Bess banged on the door with her knuckles. The shutters on the house to the next side swung open, and a woman leant out, lantern in hand.

'If you're another searcher, piss off,' the woman yelled down at her.

'I'm looking for Mr Dashwood? Do you know if he's in?' Bess called up.

'Who wants to know?'

'I'm one of his piece workers. I've brought this week's work.'

She craned her neck at the woman.

'Tough luck, ducks. He's dead,' she said. 'Two days since. Of too much heat in the heart. And don't let nobody tell you no different.' The shutters banged.

Bess was just about to leave, when the shutter swung out again. 'I'll take them gloves off you though. That fur'll be his property.'

'But it's my labour,' countered Bess. 'I've not been paid for them yet. You can have them if you pay me.'

'Pah.' The shutter closed over the black hole of the window.

As she turned away, a bedraggled woman in a filthy apron almost lurched into her, a pot of something dark swinging from her arm. 'Watch where you're going, can't you.'

'Beg pardon,' Bess said.

The woman glanced at the basket, took a step back. 'Piece-worker are you?'

Bess nodded. 'Yes. I've brought a delivery.'

'Aye, third since yesterday. I'd not be so keen to get in there if I were you, maid,' the woman said, an Irish brogue to her voice. 'He died of the pestilence, poor soul, sure as I'm standing here. Oh, I know the searchers said they found nothing at all, but I saw him before he died. Biddy called me over on account of me having some knowledge of herbs, so she did.'

'How do you know?' Bess asked. 'The woman next door said—'

'I know what she said. I'm telling you, soon as I saw him I knew. He had the tokens, for sure, and I was out of there that quick, like there was butter on my heels. I prayed for him, but I knew it was too late. The devil had him in his grip already.'

'How terrible.' Bess said. The words sounded thin and useless. 'Has he got family?'

'Wife and four little ones, or had, last I looked.' She shook her head. 'Bribed the searchers didn't they, thinking she'd get away with it. And she calling herself a Christian woman. What about the rest of us, eh? No, I've told the whole street what I saw. Not right to keep it from them all, not something like this. I wanted the lot of them nailed up, like the law says, so they couldn't pass it on, but Biddy Dashwood's only bleeding upped and gone. Did a flit in the night. There's no-one there now, but I'd be failing in my duty if I didn't warn them as'd take their possessions. You can catch it off blankets and that.'

'But what shall I do with these?' Bess pointed to the basket of gloves.

The woman stepped back again. 'Keep it away from me. Did that fur come from him?'

Bess dropped the basket on the ground. She'd been working with that fur for days. Now she didn't want to touch it. It had the stink of death.

The woman took a dripping brush from the pot by her side and splatted it onto the door with venom. Bess moved out of her range, away from the door. She couldn't believe it. Her mother was a searcher, and yet she hadn't told her. The plague was here in London.

Instinct told her to run, but she curbed it. The woman made another ragged stroke then stood back to admire the great dripping cross on his door. In this light it was black as tar. Behind her, the woman from the next house darted out into the street and within seconds, sneaked the basket of gloves inside. The sight of that cross gave Bess an urgent longing for warmth and comfort, and the familiar safety of home.

She ran, panting, back through gathering fog to Deptford, head down against the damp weather. No gloves, and no pay, and the bailiffs due on Friday. A disaster.

As she rounded the corner into Flaggon Row she was nearly knocked down by a waggon trundling at speed up the road. She yelled at it, in annoyance, but of course it didn't stop. From the top of the street, through the misty air, she could see a crowd of women gathered around her front door. Mrs Gordon, and Mrs Fenwick, with Maudie. Even the skinny figure of Lucy.

Was Will home? She speeded her step, but as she grew closer she knew something was amiss by the way they stood aside when they saw her coming.

'What is it? What's happened?'

They parted to reveal the door to the workshop was locked by a brand new padlock.

'Who did this?'

Mary was petulant. 'We couldn't do anything, mistress. Bastable came, with Kite and your brother-in-law and a bunch of men. They had a waggon full of boxes. They took out all Mr Bagwell's wood, put the boxes in, and then they boarded it up.'

'When?'

'Not five minutes ago. I tried to stop them, but they threatened us. Right nasty, they were. They had crowbars, and one of them had a billhook. They took everything that was inside.'

'All the wood? The tools?'

'They bade me take a message. On the parlour table.'

Bess glanced at the women; Mrs Fenwick and all the neighbours gathered there, all avid to hear what the rumpus was about. She braced her shoulders and ignoring them all, went inside to retrieve the letter. A glance behind showed the women still there, waiting.

Bess closed the door, shame making her face hot. She found a candle and as soon as she had light, ripped the seal off the letter. She knew what it would say. *Confiscated Goods in lieu of Payment* jumped out at her. It wasn't even Friday, and they'd come already. She couldn't bear to think of it. Will's things, all gone. *The Property 15 Flaggon Row Beneath, will be re-possessed within the Week if payment is not made to the landlord*

Mr Jack Sutherland. The words reverberated around her head. Worse, *Should the House Above Remain in Arrears, Goods to be taken to the Value, and owner evicted so the house can be sold.*

Jack Sutherland. He had something to do with this. She should have guessed.

Chapter 49

Will trudged back from the Dolphin. He had not been able to drown his sorrows after the altercation with Jack. The one half-measure of ale he could afford had left him still stone-cold sober. Jack was long gone, but his words were not. He'd been a fool to trust Jack. And how would he tell Bess?

A glint from his workshop door. A shiny iron padlock. Puzzled, he lifted its solid weight in his hand. What had Bess been up to whilst he was out? Why had she put a different lock on the door? He rattled it, but it didn't give. The shutters were closed on the inside, but he went to the window anyway and put his eye to it. Through the narrow gap between the shutters the dim square shadows of boxes were just visible. He stared a bit longer, his eyes accustoming themselves to the gloom.

The workshop was full. Piled high. Already. It could only be Jack; he'd wanted the storage.

A sound on the stairs made him turn. Bess clung to the rail.

'I couldn't stop them,' she said. 'Bastable came when I was out.'

The implications of her words took a moment to sink in. But then his heart seemed to contract into a fist.

'Who has the key?' He could barely speak.

She came down a few more steps, her hand reaching towards him through space. Now he could see her face was thinner, that she looked pale. Different from how she used to look.

'What have they done with my stock?' he shouted.

'Bastable took it in lieu of payment.'

'And you just stood by and let him?'

'No, I told you, I was out. I went to Dashwood's. But he's dead. The plague, its—' Her voice shook.

What was she blethering about? 'Have they left me the key?' Will gripped her by her shoulders.

'No. But there's a writ. It has something to do with Jack and I...'

Across the road, Mrs Fenwick came out again, brazenly watching them.

Bess glanced at her, frantically beckoned to him again. 'Come inside, Will. We can talk there.'

A loose cobble lay by the roadside, and in a moment it was in his hand. Later, he didn't remember hitting the shutter, just the noise of wood splintering and the bruising his knuckles took, as they powered through wood into empty space.

He tore at the loose wood, casting it aside like straw, and clambered his way in. All he could recall afterwards was the gasp from the neighbours, then standing in that room, a bottle of that filthy poison in his hands. *Pestdrenk*. And Bess's face outside the window, with her hand pressing a kerchief to her mouth and a pained look in her eyes.

Fury made him yank out bottle after bottle and smash them against the floor. All around was the pop and shatter of exploding glass, the dribble of green water. He heard his own grunts as he upended crate after crate. Until finally he saw what he had done.

Fear possessed him. Kite and Bastable and Jack. They would not be pleased with what they saw. They'd demand compensation, and he couldn't pay it. He turned his back on it all, and slowly climbed the stairs.

Bess was standing behind the table, her face ashen. 'What has Jack to do with this? Why is he threatening us?'

Will saw the confusion in her eyes. He was a failure. Again. 'I thought I was signing for only a few payments, and that I'd pay him back. But then I found out he'd duped me. That I'd signed the papers of this house over to him, if I ever fell into arrears with Kite.'

'What?' Her eyes filled with tears.

'It's no longer our house,' he said. 'I signed it over to him last year; I was short and he ... well, he took over the loan. I couldn't pay him. The Navy pay didn't come and I—'

'—and you hadn't the courage to tell me.'

'No. I didn't know, not until today.' He saw her sceptical look. 'Honestly. I thought I could buy him out. With Jack, money talks.'

Her eyes held his. 'Where shall we go, Will?'

'He won't want to move in. He wouldn't do that to us.'

'We don't know that. What's in the boxes?' Bess asked. Will could see her hands were shaking, and that she had to tuck them under her folded arms to still them.

'It's a potion,' he said. 'Against the plague. But it's just water and dye. Jack sells it to the Dutch, and now I guess he's peddling it here in London. It's sinful. He knows it has no healing power, yet he won't stop.'

'Are you saying he claims it will cure them?'

'Yes, but it's a deal more complicated than that. Some Dutch folk claimed they were cured after taking it. How could they? I know its only water, just coloured water. It didn't do anything. But there was a run on it and Jack made his fortune. So did we, but we saw none of it. None of the money came to us because they confiscated the ship.'

'Wait.' She sat down, head in hands. 'You're saying it's our fault? That we helped to make this stuff?'

He nodded.

'You knew, didn't you? And yet you didn't stop him.'

'I thought he was trading in snuff. I only found out later what he was doing, and by then it was too late, I'd sunk my savings into it.'

'How could you?'

'I didn't mean for this to happen; if Pepys had paid on time—'

'I can't believe you'd throw away the roof over our heads.'

'Me? Hark at who's calling. It's only a house. You threw away your good name and your reputation. If you ever had one.'

'What's that supposed to mean? What have I done now?'

'You never told me, did you, what you did before we married.'

'I took in sewing. Nightshirts and mending. You know what I did.'

'Jack says you were a whore. That your mother isn't really Mrs Prescott at all. She's Mrs Allin of the whorehouse on Fish Yard.'

She stared. How could he know about her mother? 'No. You've got it wrong. We lived there yes, and my mother was... but not me. I swear it. She wouldn't let me, said she didn't want me to be...'

She paused. He'd walked away.

No. He couldn't believe it. 'You can't think ...' She approached, touched a hand to his shoulder.

He flinched as if he'd been burnt. When he turned back his eyes were flinty and his voice choked. 'No wonder you were so keen on Pepys. You'd done it before. How many times, eh?'

'Never! You've got to believe me.'

'Never, is it? What about Pepys?'

She cringed as if he'd hit her. Her hands reached to him in entreaty, but then fell. What was the use? 'Yes. With him. But only with him. I did it for us. Like you wanted me to.'

The slam of the door. Again. It was always his way; to walk away from it, the minute his anger took hold.

She stood swaying on the empty boards.

She'd left all that behind. Lord knows, she'd tried to.

Jack. It all came back to him. He'd taken her house, and now her reputation. A blind dread rose inside her that Will might leave her. What would bind Will to her, if not the house? They had no children, and now their possessions were diminishing little by little, to be sold or pawned. The inanimate objects that had seemed so unimportant before, became huge spaces, gaps she might fall through. And if she was not Mrs Will Bagwell of Flaggon Row, who would she be?

***

When Will returned, the next morning, he was sober and grim.

'Where were you?' she asked.

'Drinking. At the Dolphin. And then I slept on a hulk,' he said.

'What?'

'The de-commissioned ship where the sailors from out of town spend their leave.'

He looked dishevelled, and a smell of the Thames hung round his clothes. She waited, a cloth in hand, for what he might say next. It was not what she was expecting.

'It's Valentine's Day tomorrow. Go and see Pepys.'

'You forbade me to see him,' she said.

'Word in the Dolphin is they need a ship's carpenter. On the *Assurance*. It's a decent frigate. I remember my father building it in the Commonwealth, in Phineas Pett's time. Before Father and I fell out.' His gaze was far away for a moment, but then his face hardened. 'Talk to Pepys. If talking's actually what you do.'

She flushed. 'I don't want to see him.'

'Do you want to keep this house?'

She shook her head, stumbling over the words, 'No! I mean yes... I want us to be back the way we were, where we weren't always at each other's throats, back to—'

'We need to keep paying Jack. Tell Pepys to deliver my pay. And I want a position on the *Assurance*.'

She blinked. This was not the Will she knew, the soft-hearted craftsman she married. This Will was stiff, like he was bound in iron, and his eyes were dark with anger. 'I can't, Will. Pepys isn't the one in charge of Navy pay and—'

'Do you want to continue to be my wife? Then you need to learn obedience, and to earn your keep by more than stitching.'

Chapter 50

The next morning was Mary's day off, and Bess was aware of Will watching her from the door as she dressed. So she was to be Pepys's Valentine, was she? Then she would do it right. And hurt Will by it, if she could.

She stepped into her best chemise, the one from the dower box she'd saved so hard for – the one with all its fine lace. It should have been pawned months ago, as should the gown, but she couldn't bear to see it go. Though Will had dropped hints, she'd hidden it away. Will pretended not to look, but the memory of their wedding night five years before burned like a hot coal between them.

Still he did not speak as she lay out her best green taffeta with the pin-pleated bodice and double row of ruffles at the low neck. It had been her wedding gown. Surely he'd stop her now? But no. He ignored her as she fumbled to fasten the points of the bodice.

By the time she was dressed he was poring over his accounts juggling them on his knee. Bess tidied her unruly curls with much fuss and pinned them under her felt bonnet, before swinging her winter cloak over her shoulders. Will's mouth tightened, but he said nothing.

She hesitated a moment at the door, gripping the brass wedding band tight with her hand so it couldn't be seen, hoping he'd call her back, but dropping his gaze, he stood and strode into the kitchen.

'I'm going now,' she called to an empty room.

At the gardens of the Navy Offices she managed to intercept Hewer, who appeared harassed when she told him she wanted to see Pepys.

'He should be along soon,' was all he'd say. 'I can't give you an appointment. Wait here if you want to catch him.'

She scanned each person as they arrived until she spotted him, walking in that precise short-stride way he had.

'Morrow, Samuel,' she said, smiling prettily at him, whilst her whole body felt fragile, as if a whisper could blow her over. To give Pepys credit, he did look taken aback by the fact she put her hand on his arm, and was not running away as she usually did.

'Mrs Bagwell,' he said. 'I thought your husband was home.' He glanced surreptitiously sideways to see if anyone was looking.

She ignored the implication that she shouldn't be there. 'It is Valentine's Day,' she said, 'so I rather hoped I would be the first to ask…'

'Oh, yes. Yes. You're the first.' He seemed distracted, pulling at his waistcoat pockets, and looking over her shoulder. 'I'm afraid I'm—'

'I thought we might have a little Valentine's celebration,' she persisted. 'At the Inkwell.'

'Did you?' A brush of velvet as he extricated his arm from her hand. 'I mean, I'm mighty busy today. I've to go to Westminster this morning, and I won't be dining in town.'

She caught a glimpse of Hewer, gesturing at him from inside the building, to come away. Pepys set off towards him.

'But I need to talk to you about Will's ship,' she said, following him into the vestibule. 'I hear that the *Assurance*—'

'Oh that. It will have to wait.' He beckoned to a lad who was waiting by the stairs, leaning over the banister with his heels off the ground. 'Boy!' he called, 'get down from there, and go fetch me a coach.' He turned to her, 'Now, I'll call to see you as soon as I can.'

'Mr Pepys, wait. The *Garamond* is an old ship. You promised him a proper position on a decent ship. With Lord Sandwich. The *Assurance* is in need of a carpenter.'

'I'm doing what I can.' His words were clipped. 'That will have to suffice. A man can do no more.'

'The *Assurance*, sir!' she called after him, as he beckoned impatiently to Hewer and the two of them hurried away up the stairs. The words echoed and fell like stones into a pond.

She stood at the bottom of the stairs whilst the world swarmed around her. It seemed that Pepys liked to be the one to do the chasing. But worse, she felt small, hopeless, at sea in this world of men. Trying to please them just so she could have a secure place in the world suddenly seemed like a task too overwhelming to do.

***

When she got home, she tried to avoid the workshop, but Will came out when he heard her arrive. He'd been sweeping and still had the broom in his hand. A basket full of broken bottles stood by the door. He appeared older than his thirty years. He looked her up and down as if she were a doll in a window display.

'What did he say?' Will asked.

'I couldn't get to speak to him long, he was busy.' She hitched her skirts and started to ascend the stairs.

He grabbed her arm. 'But what did he say?'

'That he'd try.'

'So when will I know?'

His fingers dug in her wrist. She couldn't answer him, so she stayed quiet.

Will let her go and she went up, fumbling with the key in the lock. His footsteps followed her. Angrily, she picked up the shovel and began to rake out the ashes of the fire, not caring that she was still wearing her best gown.

'Let Mary do that, when she gets back,' he said.

She dropped the shovel with a clatter on the hearthstone. 'Will,' she said, voice rising. 'We can't go on like this, in this…' she struggled to find the words, 'in this constant ill-feeling.'

'You will be rid of me soon enough,' he said. 'If I get taken on the *Assurance*, it sails in ten days, and I daresay Mr Pepys will want to visit.'

'I don't want him to visit.'

'You started this. And you're my wife. It's the only thing you seem to be able to do. If I get a position with the fleet I'll be out of this cursed house that has brought us so much ill-luck.'

'Will I be able to stop, then?'

He turned away.

***

A week later, Bess was sewing when the post boy came. Not piece-work, but repairing the elbows of Will's winter coat. Mary answered the door, though she tiptoed around them both, no doubt sensing the strained atmosphere. She placed the post carefully and deliberately before Will's plate. The table now was two planks set upon two rough stools. The other table had been sold a few weeks ago. Will did not acknowledge her presence, but gazed past her, pulling the letter towards him. She spotted the official seal as he opened it, and tried to see over his shoulder. But he flattened it out on the rough surface and leant over it so she couldn't see.

He folded it again and carried on chewing his bread and butter.

'What is it?' she couldn't resist asking.

Just then there was a noise below, bangs and scrapings.

'Jack's men again?' Bess stood up in alarm. 'You didn't tell me they'd come today.'

He shrugged. 'I didn't know.'

Bess put down her sewing and went down the outside stairs to look. Fletcher and two other men were loading a cart full of crates.

His ears were red with cold. ''Mornin', missus,' Fletcher said, spotting her watching.

She went down then and peered in. There were dozens more crates now. When Jack found out Will had smashed some of his stock, he'd made him sign a writ for what he owed. It had made her cringe to watch Will do it, without even a protesting word. The two men pushed by, scraped the crate across the top of another to push it into place. A rattle and chink of bottles. So this potion was the 'wine' Jack was exporting. It hurt her, deep in the belly. Her house was no longer a house, but a factory. She remembered Will making his beautiful chairs for Hertford; his pride, the smell of new-sawn timber and beeswax. Now there was no room for Will. Jack had pushed him out.

She ignored Will as she came back up, too full of emotion to speak.

He was already on his feet though, the letter in his hand. 'I'm to report to Lord Sandwich at Chatham,' he said.

She swallowed. 'Will you go?'

'What do you think?' His voice held the touch of a sneer.

'When?'

'Tomorrow. Soon as I can get a seat on a coach. This talk of plague's got everyone on the move.'

'You got what you wanted then.' The bitterness crept into her voice.

'What you wanted.' The words exploded from him. 'It was always about what you wanted.'

'Me? That's a jest. Don't you think you've punished me enough?'

'You were the one that was never satisfied, that wanted to make me something I'm not; you were the one that wanted to take over the bloody world.'

'And whose idea was it that I should open my legs for Pepys?

~368~

Who was it that made a deal with him; that sold his wife – his *wife* for God's sake, to advance his own career? You think I wanted that? That I should bare my crack for that—'

'Shut your mouth. There's men below and I'll not have your gutter talk in my house.'

'Gutter talk?' she hissed at him. 'If I talk that way it's only because of you! You turned me into a common whore.' She leaned towards him. 'You gave me to Pepys. What did you expect?'

His face reddened. 'You wanted him. I saw you, preening yourself, throwing yourself at him.'

She shook her head. 'No. No. It was you. You saw he wanted it, and you're so pathetic, you couldn't say no. He walks all over you, yes sir, no sir, three bags full, sir. You'd let him do it with your own mother if he—'

'Shut it, shut your mouth.' He blundered past her, his face contorted, whether from pain or anger she couldn't say.

She chased after him. 'Don't you run away!' she yelled, but he was already half-way up the street, leaving her breathless at the top of the stairs.

Chapter 51

Will was gone to sea again, and the tension of the previous weeks evaporated, leaving Bess in a deeper despair. Living alone with Jack's men coming and going downstairs made her nervous. Jack had brought a table and chairs to replace the ones they lost. She'd had to be grateful to him, but the gratefulness had stuck in her throat. After all, wasn't he responsible for most of their trouble?

A noise from below.

What now? Could she never have a moment's peace? She wrapped her wool shawl around her shoulders and went downstairs to investigate. A thick-set man in a woollen cap was just unloading crates in and out of the downstairs door. Fletcher, whom she recognised, was lifting the crates onto the wagon, where a moth-eaten carthorse was shackled. She felt a twinge of compassion for the horse, weighed down with all those crates.

'What you staring at?' the thick-set man asked.

'I live upstairs. That used to be my husband's carpentry shop.'

'Oh. Well Mr Sutherland owns it now,' he said. 'When he's paid off the loan to Kite, that is. Convenient, down here by the river. We've only to get these to the boat down yonder.'

'Hurry up,' Fletcher shouted. 'Stop yabbering and get on with it.'

She watched the older man until he'd loaded the last crate. 'God keep you, mistress,' he said. 'You've a fine spot here. The pestilence is terrible up in the city. They'll have need of this potion. Folks can't get enough of it.'

'Is it bad?'

'Twenty more houses shut up, and that's just in St Giles,'

Fletcher said, butting in, and fixing the padlock back on the door.

'And does it cure them, this stuff?'

The two men looked at each other. 'They say so. No point buying it, else.' Fletcher turned the key and pocketed it.

Over the next few days men came and went below. Their grunts and curses, the clink of bottles, the thud of crate upon crate filled her with unease. She trusted neither of these men. She slept with a kitchen knife close to the bed, such was her fear.

Worse, within a week of Will's departure, Pepys appeared at her door again. It was well after curfew. Lantern in hand, she held the door open as he bustled in. The rich seemed to pay their way past the constables who were supposed to arrest night-wanderers. It was Pepys's pattern now, as soon as Will was at sea. He seemed impervious to the darkness of the city, dressed as he was in colourful waistcoat and breeches, with a light drab silk-woven coat over it. Outside the sky was sullen with looming cloud, grey against the night sky. A few heavy drops fell as she opened the door, and he hurried inside.

'Looks like rain,' he said. 'Been devilish weather, hasn't it?'

She nodded. She was too preoccupied to make conversation with him, despite his cheerful manner. As usual, he had brought her a small pouch filled with coins. His habit now was to set it on the table without referring to it, and when she heard the chink of coin, she would wordlessly pick it up and hide it away in a drawer of her clothing chest.

'A little extra,' he'd said, the first time. How could she explain that being paid by him made her feel worse off than ever?

The rattle of rain on the new roof. Her thoughts fled to Will, somewhere out at sea. Storms always sent her thoughts scurrying to him.

Pepys patted her on the shoulder, like a reminder. She had even ceased to protest any more, but simply took him straight to the bedchamber. There, she hitched up her chemise. As he did his business, she stared at the button on the bed canopy, or the ceiling plaster, or the reflections of lights from the water that shimmered in from the windows outside. This was the life she had thought to avoid, but now she was here, there was an inevitability about it that she recognised.

He was quick that night, as if he were merely relieving himself. She had ceased to make him hot, she realised, and she had become a function, not a person. He didn't want to stay to talk. It made it seem even less like company and more like business, which was both a relief, and a worry. A relief that he expected no more, but a worry that he might tire of her and his coin would dry up. With Will away, at least it paid Mary's wage, and she did not know what she'd do without her. Just having her there was a sort of stability. She pictured her darning in her room below the stairs, stoically ignoring what her mistress was doing in the rooms above.

Pepys headed for the door. His air was apologetic, as if the thing should really mean something, but no longer did.

Chapter 52

Agatha followed Dr Harris towards Cripplegate. The way cleared before them, with folk crossing the street. It was as if they carried the miasma with them. Mind, the doctor did look grim, dressed all in his stiff black suit, with the terrible bird's beak hanging like a ghoul from his waist. The first time she'd seem him wearing it, even she was affrighted. It was the deadness of that white beak, but also the moving eyes behind it, like something living in a dead skull.

She too carried the mark of her profession – the searcher's white stick. She supposed they made a good pair.

'Look,' the doctor said, 'over there.'

The knot of people clustered around the tented hand-cart. It was the sixth such stall she had seen. And she knew exactly what it would be selling. They'd sprung up everywhere like a fungus. She wished she knew where it was all coming from. Quack potions like these were in every house she'd been to. And still the poor buggers died.

They crossed the street to head towards the cart. The youth who seemed to be in charge of it, a tall lad with ears like jug-handles, eyed them warily.

'Will you fetch the constable?' she asked the doctor.

'Let's see what quackery it is first.'

He stooped to pick up a handbill. '*Pestdrenk*,' he read aloud. '*A thousand cured in Amsterdam. One shilling.*' He screwed it up and cast it to the channel of filth in the middle of the road. 'Daylight robbery.' But already their presence had been noted and the awning pulled down, and the goods shoved back into their crates.

Illegal then, Agatha thought. No licence. More handbills fluttered to the ground as the youth and his shorter ill-kempt friend trundled the cart away.

'Quick.' The doctor hurried towards it and their presence cleared the protesting gaggle of customers who retreated hurriedly, all except two. One – a butcher by trade, judging by the state of his apron – was clinging to his bottle, but the other taller man, dressed in fine raiment of lace jabot and petticoat breeches cursed him and tried to wrest it from him.

'Leave off!' the butcher yelled. 'It's mine. I paid for it.'

'I was first in the queue,' the tall man said, and he grabbed the bottle, uncorked it and put it to his lips.

'My wife needs this! Give it back, or you'll feel the cut of my knife!' The butcher drew his boning hook from his belt.

The taller man drew his sword and keeping the other at bay, downed the liquid on the spot and threw the empty bottle back at him.

'By heaven, I'll take you!' The butcher lunged, and thrust his knife at the other. It met flesh and the man staggered back, then fell to the floor clutching his stomach.

'You've murdered him, you fool!' the doctor said.

'Quick,' Agatha said, 'get something to tie the wound.'

But the butcher was already fleeing half-way up the road.

She knelt and undid the buttons of the man's doublet to get at the wound, and raised his shirt. The wound was deep and bubbled with blood, but it was the other marks that made her drop the shirt back. 'Tokens,' she said.

He stepped back. 'Not worth treating.'

'Looks like a rich man.'

'Maybe I'll take a look. If I can mend this wound, I could apply a poultice of hog's grease and get him to discharge the

~374~

poison…' The physician shook his mask to release the herbal vapours and strapped it on.

'Fetch me a hired horse,' he said, his voice muffled through the contraption, 'I'll need to get him to his home.'

Agatha left her searcher's stick with him and did as he asked.

When she returned, leading a hired horse by the bridle, he was leaning over the body like a carrion crow. 'You're too late. Call the dead-cart,' he said, through the mask. 'He's dead. Of the plague, not the wound.'

'You'll not be needed, fella,' she said, stroking the horse on the nose. 'Lucky for you, horses can't catch it.'

***

Bess startled as the door opened. Automatically she put the table between her and the door. Jack. Again. He'd taken to visiting her whenever he had business in the workshop below.

'Jack,' Bess said. 'I'd prefer it if you'd knock.'

'Why? Will kept open house for me.'

'Will's not here.'

'Shall I go out again and knock?'

'No. Don't be foolish.' He was well-dressed in fine slate-blue breeches and one of the new light-weight coats with a cream silk waistcoat. They hung off him a little for he'd lost weight, but his boots were new and shiny, and barely worn. It gave her a pang just to look at them; they said 'money'.

Bess sat herself down on the opposite side of the table from Jack, and resigned herself to keeping the peace. 'Well?'

'Do you miss having a man about the place?'

This wasn't the sort of question Jack usually asked. She shook her head whilst she tried to form an answer. 'There's no time to miss it, what with my piece work.'

'I miss Alison.'

She was disarmed. Jack never talked of anything personal.

'And you're fond of my boys, aren't you?'

''Course I am. They're like my own.' She wondered where the conversation was going. Something about his intense look made her uncomfortable.

'Don't you want children?'

'Yes... of course we do, but... it just hasn't happened yet, that's all.' She shuffled in her chair.

'I could give you children.'

She froze. What was he saying? She was so shocked, it was as if she was pasted in place.

He was running on now, his voice urgent, 'We'd be a good match, you and I. My business is expanding, and you'd always be provided for. You said yourself, my children are like your own. And in time we'd have more—'

She found her voice. 'What are you saying? Have you lost your senses?' She made a little laugh, but it sounded weak and tinny.

He grabbed her hand where it lay on the table and gripped it tight. 'You wed the wrong man. Even his own father says so. Will's weak, and he'll never give you children. He's got no ambition—'

She wrenched her hand away and stood up. Her mind could not keep up with the conversation, her mouth had turned dry as dust. She saw him as if he were a picture in a book, an illustration of some scene that had nothing to do with her.

'But Jack... I'm married to Will, have a care—'

He stood too, and in two strides had hold of her shoulders. His eyes bored into hers, determined. 'There's no love lost between you now, is there? Any fool can see that. Think about it, Bess.'

She wrenched away. 'What are you playing at, Jack? Is this your idea of a jest?'

'Just listen. The boys need a mother, and you need children. You were born to it; anyone can see that, it's a waste, you being with Will…'

She backed away. Something of what he said had struck deep inside her like a lance. When her voice came out, it was like a croak. 'Enough. Do you want to destroy us? I'm married to Will. And I'll stay that way, d'you hear me?'

His intake of breath was loud in the silence. He cracked his knuckles together then, as if making a deliberate decision, his face took on a benign expression. He sat down, in Will's chair near the fireplace, and his voice was almost leisurely. 'That's a shame. You'll do it with Pepys, but not with me.' He shook his head wonderingly. 'You still think you're too good for me.'

'I'm a married woman, Jack. Before God.'

'You're the daughter of a whore. But I'll forgive all that, because I have a tenderness for you. I always have.'

She turned rigid as a stone pillar. A tenderness? Was that what he called it? Whatever it was, it was laced with threats. His reasonable tone sent a chill into her heart. 'Just go, Jack, and I'll pretend you never said it.'

'You forget,' he said, resting a boot casually onto the hearth. 'I own this house. Will made it over to me. Last year. October. Didn't he tell you?'

It was as if the ground beneath her feet had begun to quake. 'Yes.' Her voice was a whisper. 'I knew.' She sat, suddenly. Afraid.

'Will couldn't pay the loan, and I was doing well, so I bought him out.'

She put her head in her hands. 'No. You don't mean… you wouldn't.'

He smiled. 'I care about you. I wouldn't force you to anything. You could choose me, and this house, or you could choose to go

~377~

back to Ratcliff. But I know you'll see the sense in it and choose me.'

Against such certainty there was nothing she could say. She was numb with shock. On shaking legs she left him sitting there, went to her chamber and slid the bolt home.

Silence. She rested her back against the door.

Then his voice on the other side. A whisper. One inch away. She leapt away from it.

'I give you one month. After that, I'll take it you want to go back where you came from, and I'll claim the house.'

His footsteps receded. Below, she heard the men return, the chink of glass and Fletcher's harsh voice.

A few moments later she heard the parlour door click shut and Jack's boots on the stairs.

Only then did she realise the predicament she was in. She longed for Will, for safe, predictable Will. But he had turned against her too. If Will were to abandon her, what option would she have? How would she survive? It would be the street or the workhouse. And the boys – Jack was right, she loved them.

If Jack took the house, Pepys would not help her. She shuddered at the thought of him. He'd had what he wanted; there was no bargaining power left with Pepys. Whereas Jack ... But no. The thought of it made her shudder.

Sleep evaded her. Over the city the sky lightened into pale pearl, and the clamour of bells pealed for the early morning service. But Bess didn't want to go to church. Her prayers were over and done, even before dawn lit up the sky. *Bring Will home. Let him forgive me.*

The workshop below was silent. Gone was the rasp of the saw and the clang of the hammer, the whirr of the string from the treadle-lathe. It was as if Will had never existed. She turned the brass wedding band on her hand, but it was tarnished, and there were no words of love inside to bring her comfort.

Chapter 53

The Assurance, coast of Holland

Will struck the chisel with the hammer, bracing his legs against the timbers as the frigate *Assurance* rolled. He was making pegs to replace the ones that had broken, splintered by the strain of eight weeks at sea in a freezing northerly wind. It was May now, and no sign of any summer heat. He planted his heels against the beams, feeling the squelch of leather, his ankles six inches deep in water. It sloshed inside his boots as he worked, so that he could no longer feel his feet; his fingers were disobedient maggots, clumsy with cold.

He imagined his dry parlour at home, but the moment's inattention caught him off-guard. The ship lurched, and the chisel slipped on the greasy wood, slicing into his thumb. He cursed and sucked at it. Now it would get salt in it and sting like the devil. He rummaged through his kit, searching for a dry bandage to bind it, and finally managed to tear a strip of muslin loose and wrap it around it, staggering in the swell of the sea as he did so. He was weary through lack of sleep. He climbed up the ladder to the decks where his presence was ignored – everyone was busy belaying.

He weaved his way unsteadily to the rails, hoping for a sign of land. Nothing. Just a heaving swell the colour of mud. In the distance another set of sails battled against the wind. He was sick of this tilting deck, sick of the cold, the greyness of the sea off the coast of Lowestoft, the sting in his eyes, the queasiness in his belly. He pulled his oiled cloak tighter around his shoulders for he felt the weather more now. He'd lost weight, what with the bad diet and the worry. Not the impending battle – the Dutch were rumoured to have more than a hundred men-of-war, as well as galliots and fireships, and that was worry enough. But he never thought being wed would be the death of him.

His fingers clung to the rails, the spray splattering his face. He wondered what Bess was doing, whether she and Jack were at each other's throats, whether Jack would be laughing at him when Pepys came calling. He did not care, he told himself. Then he cursed himself, for the thought of Bess brought nothing but a raw pain. She'd be in Pepys's bed. He groaned, doubled over.

'Sick again, mate?' One of the men threw the remark to him as he passed clinging to a rope, skidding on the salty planking.

Will shook his head. He was sick, yes, but not from the sea. From jealousy, from the horrible cramping feeling that someone else might be at this very moment in his bed. Every day grew worse than the next. The longer he was away, the more it swelled inside him like a canker. He should never have let it happen. It was his fault. He'd agreed to Pepys's bargain, not realising he'd condemned himself to this – this purgatory of his own making.

'Lord, make it stop,' he said. But he'd said the same prayer over and over, and the pain still flayed him.

He'd thought they'd be back on land by now, but no. The Dutch had captured a convoy of English merchant ships off Hamburg, and so they'd been ordered to go back to sea. He didn't know how he'd survive it; not the fighting, but the torture of not-knowing. How much could Pepys do in a day? In a month? In two? How many times could a man…? He shuddered. A wave crashed over the side, soaking him, sending a stinging pain into the cut on his hand. But the pain inside him hurt more.

***

At noon on the first day of June, Evans, one of the midshipman came to fetch him.

'Look there!' In the distance the Dutch fleet was, like them, waiting for the wind.

'Christ.' It was enormous. At least twenty flagships. The rails of the *Assurance* were packed with men, all staring morosely at the grey blur that hugged the horizon.

'Thank God there's no wind,' Evans said.

'For how long, though?' Will said.

The two fleets were separated by a calm sea, but it only made the waiting worse. Will wondered if the Dutch sailors felt as he did, and whether their commander, who they called Foggy Obdam, was as foolish as the Duke of York, who was always wanting to divide the fleet and make them more vulnerable.

They jumped every time a puff of wind lifted a tarpaulin, every time a seagull cried. The tension curdled his innards so he couldn't eat.

He was sleeping the next night, swaying in his hammock when the call came.

'The wind's with us,' Evans shouted to him.

Even a ship's carpenter was expected to fight, so Will hauled himself to upright and staggered onto deck in the darkness, ready to load cannon.

Crouched in the dark he had no real idea what was going on, the fleets passed each other, taking fire as they could, until one of their lines, headed by the Earl of Sandwich, saw his chance, and broke through a gap that had opened up in the Dutch line.

The sky suddenly flashed with an orange light.

'What's going on?'

Evans, who was at the rails, called back, 'We've split the Dutch fleet in half. Hold out for your orders.'

'Fire!'

Will and Evans lit the taper and got out of range. The blast from their cannons seemed to explode inside his head.

'To starboard!' came the shout.

The ship veered to the side, just as a burning Dutch sloop came across their bows.

Shit. A fireship. An enormous blast. Timber and burning debris rained down on them. In front of him, Evans fell.

At first it was all Will could do to put out fires. The rigging trembled with runnels of flame. Hot pitch rained from the sky. Around him screaming men scurried like ants, clutching their burning clothing and stamping out gobbets of flaming shrapnel. The fireship had been close, but not close enough to sink them.

A groan. Evans was pinioned by one foot under a collapsed mast. Will rushed to try to free him, but the mast, that looked so tiny from below, was thicker than a girl's waist. Beneath it, Evans struggled and shrieked. Will braced his shoulder against it, but it didn't budge.

'Here they come!' came the yell. Will glanced over the side to see a Dutch ship drawing alongside. Men rushed to the side, swords and muskets ready. The Dutch were preparing to board.

'Help me!' Evans cried.

Will didn't stop to think. He leapt down the stairs to the cabin and grabbed an axe and his saw.

When he got back, the rails were full of fighting men. 'Lie still,' he shouted at Evans above the booming noise of cannon and musket.

Evans twisted and writhed. Fear glazed his eyes as Will hacked at the timber with the axe.

'What are you doing?' the bo'sun shouted, pulling at him. 'Leave him. Man the cannon.'

Another deafening blast that seemed to come from deep in the bowels of the ship. Almost immediately the ship began to list to the side.

'A hit. My God, we're going under,' yelled the sailor next to him.

'Abandon ship!' From then there were constant volleys of musket fire and screams. The rails were black with figures leaping into the sea.

'The boats! Lower the boats!' Will had one eye on the rail and the other on Evans as he sawed through the mast. The timber was damp and snagged in his saw; his muscles burned. The ship creaked and listed further, the mast shifted, and Evans screamed once before his face turned white and his eyes rolled back in his head.

'Hold on,' Will shouted, frantically rasping the saw.

The ship tilted again. Cold water sluiced up to his waist. Evans choked and gasped as water hit his face. He sat up, struggling for breath. The water was over his chest, the mast submerged. The ship was moving beneath them now, in a way that felt all wrong, the masts veering sideways, the cannons sliding to the rails.

For a split instant, Will thought, this is it, we're going to die. But then a dull splintering and the mast rose up in the centre, out of the water, and into a jagged peak.

Will grabbed Evans and rolled him away as the mast sheared in two, and the ends plummeted back down. The deck slid away from him and the water closed over his head. Dark, stinging salt water. He still had hold of Evans by the arm. They struggled, gasping, to the surface. Next to them a boat bobbed, a life raft crammed with men. Arms reached out to pull them on board. Evans was so white he was almost translucent.

Will ran a hand over his mangled ankle. 'Broken,' he said. 'You'll not be fit for duty now.'

'I've never been ... fit for duty. But thanks to you, I'm still...' he winced, '...still here.'

Will smiled, and squeezed his arm. Next to them the limping *Assurance* had been flanked by two more English ships, divided from the English fleet to prevent the Dutch taking her carcase away. The Dutch ship the *Hilversum* had been taken and was under their escort too.

Dawn came as they bobbed in the boat, all shivering, watching the battle from a distance; nobody seemed keen to row or to swim to join another ship. In the distance the

Duke of York's ship, the *Royal Charles* let loose their cannon on Opdam in the *Eendracht*. The men were silent, knowing that the flashes of firepowder and squalls of smoke meant more dead men like them.

Finally, after a two-hour duel, the sea seemed to shudder. An almighty flash and *Eendracht* exploded in a flower of flame. One moment it was there, and the next gone. They stared into the empty space, unable to believe it. The boom reached them a few seconds later, a deep thud in the air that shivered Will's chest. The men stood and rocked the boat with their cheering, all except Evans, who could not, but made up for it by punching his fist in the air.

'Don't know why we're cheering,' Will said. 'There were four hundred men on that ship.'

'And fuck knows what we're fighting for,' Evans said.

'We're fighting for our wives and families back home,' the sailor behind him said.

'Easy to say if you're wed,' Evans said. 'I'm not.'

'Then for England and King Charles.'

Derisive laughter from the men.

'You got family?' Evans asked Will.

'Wife.'

'She pretty?'

Will nodded. The pain in his chest was worse than before. It made him want to cry.

'She'd be proud of you,' Evans said. 'Saved my life. Bravest thing I ever saw. You cut it fine though, I thought we were goners.'

Chapter 54

Will shouldered his bag and made his way down the plank onto solid ground, though to him it felt as if it was wavering, shimmering in the grey light, like walking on the back of a moving horse.

What sort of a welcome would he get from Bess now? He hadn't written. He couldn't have put a word to paper, the way he felt.

Rather than taking a wherry, he walked. He didn't want to be on water again, and it would help him get his land-legs back. Perhaps Jack would have moved his crates out. A vain hope; but a man could dream. He wished he still had his old tools; he hadn't realised how the familiar feel of the wood transforming from rough to smooth in his palms fed his soul. He imagined the dry odour of sawdust and longed to make a few simple things, in the dry. Some bowls maybe, or a plain stool.

London was full of colour after the grey of the sea, even on this wan afternoon. As he passed St Stephen's he heard the tolling of the passing bell, and out of habit, crossed himself. He passed the yards at Deptford and stopped to gaze over the workers, milling around a large war-ship like ants. All that trouble, just to make kindling for the Dutch. He cast his gaze over the row of sheds, the bristling skeletons of half-built ships, and the pontoons stretched over the mast-pond.

His father was down there somewhere. The thought made him move quicker. He hurried away and down the main street towards Flaggon Row. His heart lifted to see his familiar house, with its wooden stairway up to the first floor, and the pea-stick fence he'd made himself after the storm had taken the other.

Would Bess be in? He paused and looked up at the window. But then something else caught his eye. Movement behind the glass. Two figures. With a jolt he realised one was a man.

He left his bags at the bottom of the steps and ran up two at a time, and threw open the door. Everything seemed to happen at once. From behind the bedroom door he heard a panicked, 'Who is it?' from Bess.

A boy, who was gouging a hole in the parlour table with a pocket knife shot up and looked frantically at the bedroom door. Will knew that livery. The boy stared at him like an owl.

'Jack?' The door opened a crack and Bess's head appeared from around the door.

It shut again immediately, and he heard her whisper, 'It's my husband.'

More scuffling. Will's head was pounding as he dumped his satchel on the table. He knew who was behind that door, even before it opened, so it was no surprise to see Pepys, red in the face, with his shirt ballooning over his breeches and his waistcoat all askew.

The boy rushed to help him retrieve his hat, but was brushed aside as Pepys headed for the door.

Will stood to one side to let him pass, his back stiff to hold in his rage. Pepys passed close enough for Will to imagine the satisfying crunch of his nose if he were to punch him. His fists itched to do it, but he clenched them tight. If he did, it would be the end of his career.

Pepys scuttled past him eyes lowered, without saying a word. Will caught a whiff of hair oil, and wanted to gag. He went to the bedchamber then, and threw open the door.

Bess's eyes were glittering and defiant. 'It was only what you wanted.'

The bedcover was crumpled and awry, but the linen and lace looked strange after all these weeks at sea. A bed fit for fornication, he thought.

Bess was fully dressed, but her hair was mussed and the laces of her bodice undone. She bent down to fasten her shoes and the sight of her bending to tie the ribbons made something break inside him.

He backed away, and was surprised to hear his voice come out like any normal man's. 'My bags are at the bottom of the stairs.' It was as if he was disconnected from his body. His thoughts went on as if everything was normal, but deep inside his world was shifting.

How much can a man endure? And yet he could not imagine a life with no Bess. Will put on his hat again, careful to walk around the back of Bess's chair, even though Bess wasn't in it.

She followed him, saying, 'I'll fetch your bags up.'

He imagined for a moment that everything was normal, that he'd just take her in his arms, tenderly, like he used to. He stretched out his hand. But then drew it back, flinching. No.

Her eyes were fixed on his shoes.

He took a gulp of air that could have been a sob. They could not bear to be in the same space, but left a yard's berth as if one might contaminate the other. Neither spoke.

When the knock came, it startled them both.

Will answered it to find Jacob, his old apprentice, standing there, out of breath from running.

'It's Hertford, sir,' he panted. 'The plague. They've locked him in. Mayor Lawrence's orders. I thought you'd want to know.'

'Is he ill?'

'Must be, sir, they've put a guard on the house. There's four houses on their road shut up now.'

'Wait.' He rushed to the table and grabbed his satchel that was lying there. It was a relief to have something urgent to do.

Bess opened her mouth as if she would speak and forbid him to go, but then she was silent. Will didn't stop to speak to her or tell her where he was going. He hoped she hadn't heard the word, 'plague'. As he shot out of the door, he glanced back to see her wiping her hands on a dishrag, staring after him. Their eyes met, and in them he saw a kind of pleading. But the moment was tiny, like a sliver of light, and there was no time to dwell on it.

At the dockside he hired a coach and bundled Jacob into it. 'Bearbinder Lane,' he yelled. 'Gallop.' They rattled through the city past the exchange and into the parish of St Mary Woolchurch. As they came down St Swithen's Lane, a crowd jostled in the road, protesting, as two constables hammered more nails into place. At the house two doors away, in Whistler's Court, a group of women wailed, besieging the guard, pulling on his sleeves to try to pull him from his position.

Hertford's front door was barred by three rough-hewn planks, incongruous against the glossy polished wood.

'Who has the plague?' he asked the overweight Constable, who was even now slathering the door with red paint. 'Is it Mr Hertford?'

'Don't know no names. Master of the house.'

'Who's inside?'

'Master, mistress and their three servants. There now.' He stood back to admire his handiwork.

'When will you let them come out?'

'Forty days, the Mayor says. It's the law. Forty days after the last one dies.' He smiled. The thought seemed to give him satisfaction.

'Can I go in and speak to them?'

'Not unless you want to stay in there with them.' He laughed, but it set off a wheeze which he hastily stifled.

'Maybe it's just a cold, like you seem to have.'

The Constable scowled. 'I've told you. Signs are clear enough. And I've got my orders. Anyone on this street with suspicious signs, they're to be shut up. You can call through the window if you like, but not too close.'

'Mr Hertford?' Will put his mouth to the gap in the shutter. 'Mr Hertford?'

A disembodied weeping voice came from the other aside of the gap. 'Who is it? Oh Mr Bagwell! Is that you, Will?'

'Yes, mistress. What's happening?'

'It's Henry. He's a fever.'

'Has he any tokens, Mrs Hertford?'

'What?' Her voice was shrill with emotion. 'What do you mean?'

'Signs. Any swellings?'

'No. No, I keep telling them, but they won't believe me. Those Frenchmen next door, it's all their fault. They brought the foul disease from Holland. One of them died last night, and now because Henry is ill, they want to shut us up. It's pure foolishness. Henry's is just a cold, just a cold, I'm telling you. Whatever shall we do? Please Will, tell them.'

'Sir, the gentleman has a summer cold, not the pestilence, his wife assures me. It's quite safe to open the door.'

'No sir, our orders are clear. This is an infected area.'

Will looked to Jacob, who shrugged.

Will shouted through the hole again. 'Give us some coin, and we'll bring you some provisions, Edith, this evening.' Then in a low voice, 'Pack a few bags. Prepare the servants and get Henry dressed. Think where you can go.'

'Where? Where can we go?' Her voice was high with panic.

'Shh. Out of London,' he said. 'Anywhere. Do you understand

me?'

'There's nowhere! What will we do?'

There was no time to argue. Will sighed. 'You must come to us at Deptford.' He did not dare think what Bess might have to say.

'God bless you, Will. We'll be ready.'

'The coin, Edith. I'll need it for the coach.'

She passed him a purse heavy with gold, and he pocketed it.

'What will we do, sir?' Jacob asked.

'Don't know. But they'll starve in there. We have to get them out.'

***

The curfew had sounded. The street was quiet, but Jacob waited around the back, with a hired cart with an old pack-horse in its shafts. It was the best Will could do. Any sort of carriage was hard to come by, and he'd had to give over most of Edith's purse to secure it. It was uncovered, which was not ideal, given that a cold drizzle was soaking Jacob's shoulders and dripping off his hat. English summers. Always the same. He surveyed the cart and sighed. It wasn't how Hertford was used to travelling, and scarcely fit for a gentleman and his wife, but it would have to do.

Will took himself to the front, heavily muffled up to his eyes and with the damp hat pulled down over his hair. He'd been home and collected the one remaining suit from the sack of clothes that used to belong to Jack. Bess had watched him do it, but they had said not a word to each other.

Now, dressed in a clerk's outfit, he strolled down the main street which was deserted except for a keening coming from a house three doors away. Outside the Hertfords' a burly yeoman with a bristly moustache was still stationed outside as a guard, his sharpened halberd glistening in the rain, and drops of moisture dripping from his helmet.

When Will reached the front door of the Hertfords' he beckoned to him.

'Filthy weather,' he said, in his best refined voice. 'Dr Bulstrode. Can I prevail upon you to help?'

'What's the trouble?'

'My coach has lost a wheel, and I need someone strong like you to help me.'

'Sorry sir, but I can't leave my post.'

'It will take but a moment, and there'll be a florin in it, if you do.'

Used to obeying his betters, the big man barely hesitated. 'If we're quick,' he said.

He followed Will obediently as he hurried away down the street.

As Will glanced back he saw Jacob lever the planks off the ground floor shutter with a crowbar. He winced, hoping the noise would not draw his companion's attention. He didn't dare look back after that, just hurried away with the sound of the watchman's heavy footsteps splashing in the puddles, and even heavier breathing behind him.

'Wait!' called the watchman breathlessly, after they'd gone a few hundred yards. 'How much further?'

'Not far. Just around the corner in Sherborn Street,' Will answered.

When they got around the corner, Will stopped. Of course there was no conveyance with a broken wheel, just rain pouring off the overhanging roofs and into the road.

'Well where is it?'

'I don't know,' Will said, acting bemused. 'They must've fixed it. Well I'll be damned. The rogues have gone off without me. In this weather! How's a man to go about his business with no conveyance?'

The watchman's face turned dark with annoyance, but Will saw he couldn't bring himself to call a gentleman a liar. 'You've dragged me from my duty, sir,' he said.

'I do beg your pardon. Here my good man.' Will drew the last half-angel from Edith's purse. 'Thank you for your assistance.'

The watchman strode away, head down against the rain. Will hoped he'd given Jacob enough time.

Soon as the watchman was out of sight, Will ran back to Thames Street, where he saw the cart ready next to the wharves, with the humps of two figures on top of it. He ran over to it, but before he could get there, Jacob saw him coming and hurried to meet him. 'We need to get off the main thoroughfare,' Jacob said, wiping the wet from his face with his sleeve. 'He's bad, Will. Didn't recognise me, and he keeps on moaning.'

'Best get him home then. Bess can take care of him.'

'The servants helped them get on the cart, but then they all scarpered. I can't say I blame them. Don't go near, sir.'

Will went over to speak to Hertford, but he wasn't prepared for what he saw. In the darkness, the figure on the cart writhed and moaned. Will barely recognised his friend. He was pale as cheese. He couldn't tell if it was sweat or drizzle that stuck his sparse, lank hair to his head.

'Mr Hertford, it's me. Will. We're going to take you to my house.'

'No, no! Don't let the Devil take me! It's my own fault,' Hertford said, twisting his head side to side, 'my sins have come home to roost. ' Edith tried to quiet him, holding him down, her eyes wide with fear. Her hands were shaking with cold, and there was a stink of excrement and vomit coming from their clothes.

Jacob backed away.

'Help us,' Edith said, her eyes full of entreaty.

Will took a step back. He knew with gut-wrenching certainty what was before him; this was no simple cold. But Hertford was his employer and his friend. He couldn't turn them away.

Jacob dragged him to one side by the coat sleeve. 'They've duped you. Don't do it, sir. You'd be risking your life. And he'll die anyway.'

'I can't just leave him there in the street.'

'I'm begging you. Don't go near. Take him back to Woolchurch, sir, there's a pesthouse. Leave him there. Think of everyone else.'

He glanced to Edith, who was watching them whispering together.

'Have mercy on us,' she cried. 'My husband called you friend, surely you won't abandon us now?'

'It's alright, Edith.' He spoke firmly, though there was a turmoil raging in his head. He turned to Jacob, 'Go on home,' he said. 'You've done as I asked and I'm grateful. You can leave them to me now. You need have nothing to do with this.'

'You're crazy. You can't—'

'He's my friend. What else can I do?'

'I'll tell the authorities.'

'No you won't. Because you know Hertford's always done right by us, and I by you, best I was able. And you're a kind lad at heart.'

Jacob's face crumpled. When he opened his mouth to speak again, Will held up his hand to stall him. 'If anyone asks, Hertford has a rheum, an infection of the lungs. Nothing more. Do you understand?'

'If you say so, sir.' Then, as if to gainsay himself, Jacob shook his head, uncomprehending. 'God bless you for a fool,' he said, and turned on his heel and strode away.

Will grasped the horse by the bridle and pulled it down the

road, his heart hammering in his chest, and his palms sticky. He called up to Edith, 'Keep him quiet. It's nearly curfew and we don't want to draw attention to ourselves. Act as if we're just going home from a day's labour.'

'I'll try,' she said, but Hertford's moaning continued.

It didn't bode well. But he couldn't leave him out in the street to die, could he? And what would Edith do, locked in a house with no-one to help her? Now was his chance to make amends for that damned potion; to help someone the best way he could. Maybe then his luck would change. But the thought of what he was bringing home to Bess made him nauseous. He just hoped she would understand.

Chapter 55

Bess had not seen Will all day and now the dark had set in and it was curfew time. Even Mary was a-bed. Bess paced the floor, wondering if she should go out to look for him. In the old days she might have done, but now she did not dare.

Voices from below made her go to peer out through the cracks in the shutters. Rain like needles slanted diagonally across her view. She squinted through it. A cart, with a coarse nag in the shafts. Will, helping a woman down from the cart, a woman she didn't recognise, but a woman of class, she could tell by the fact she wore no coif, though the rain had made rat's tails of her hair. And on the cart, luggage, and a man, curled up around himself like a baby, clutching what looked like a bundle of soiled rags.

She grabbed a lantern from the shelf, opened the door, and stepped out. Immediately the candle guttered, and her hair blew wildly about, whipped into ribbons by the rain. Hitching her shawl over her head, she shouted, 'What's afoot?'

Will did not answer; he and the woman were trying to haul the man from the back of the cart.

'Get in out of the rain,' she yelled, her eyes stinging.

'It's Hertford,' Will said. 'Help us get him inside.'

She took a few steps down, peering into the gloom. Hertford. She would never have known him. Bess stayed rooted to the spot. She stared through the rain at the man in the cart.

His legs twitched, splayed at an odd angle over the rough wet wood. His stockings were stained, his ankles thin as twigs. One shoe with its mud-stained rosette lay off to one side of the cart. The woman, who must be his wife Edith, shook the wet off it and tried to force it onto his foot. Will grasped Hertford under the arms to lug him down.

'No! Leave me be!' Hertford yelled, tearing at his cravat, eyes full of confusion.

The world seemed to freeze in place. Bess caught tight to the hand rail for support, lest her knees buckle under her. Even in the dark she couldn't miss it – his neck showed a rash of red swellings, big as plums.

Edith shot a glance her way, tried to hide them, tried to tie his cravat back in place, but he fought her off with curses.

'It's all right, William,' Edith cried, her skirts stained with rain, her hair loose and ragged hanging around her face.

No. This couldn't be happening. Bess took a deliberate step away. 'Will,' she shouted. 'Come inside.'

Will turned to look at her, but shook his head. 'We need to get him out of the rain.'

'No, Will. He's not coming in here. We can't have him here.' She heard her own voice come out with a rising edge.

'Get a spare bed ready.' Will was half-carrying Hertford now, propping him up as he staggered forward.

Bess continued to walk backwards, her eyes fixed on Hertford's lolling head.

'Please,' implored Edith, 'there's nowhere else. Have mercy.'

Just at that moment Hertford began to thrash wildly, and taken by surprise, Will let go. Hertford fell into the road, his hands like claws, tearing at his clothes, face stretched into a grimace. Fear shot like a snake up Bess's spine.

Hertford slumped, his wigless head lolling in the dirt.

'Come on, sir.' Will knelt to try to pick him up.

To Bess's horror, Hertford grabbed Will by the collar and tried to speak to him.

'Keep away from him!' she shouted, but Will's attention was

on Hertford.

'Look after Edith,' Hertford said. A quiver, like a long shudder, ran through him, then he was still.

'Mr Hertford?' Will shook him, but he lay limp and flaccid, his white hand in his velvet sleeve extended, as if reaching for help.

Edith dropped to her knees beside her husband. She shook him and shook him, but his head rolled sideways and his mouth fell open in a gape. Edith drew back, turned to Will. 'He took me to the theatre,' she said. 'Just the day before yesterday. He can't be… not so quick…'

Overcome, Bess pressed her fist to her mouth, ran upstairs and banged the door shut, ramming the bolts home top and bottom.

The noise of Will's footsteps on the stairs, then a hammering.

'Open this door, Bess.'

The door shook. She put her hands over her ears, but could still hear his voice as if it were inside her head.

'Bess. Be reasonable. We can't just leave him there.'

'You fool, Will.' One hand pushed against the door to keep it shut, the other raked her forehead to clear the mass of thoughts gathered there. 'No,' she repeated. 'We can't take him in. Not a plague corpse.'

'What about Edith?' Will's said. 'Have a heart. I can't just leave her.'

Bess couldn't think. All she knew was that she wasn't opening that door. Death was on the other side.

The banging on the door persisted a few more minutes, but then it stopped.

Silence. Just the skitter of rain on rooftops and her own beating heart.

Will's boots going down.

She took a few steps and crouched low to look through the biggest gap in the shutters. Will's broad back strained as he heaved Hertford over his shoulder, and dropped him like a sack back onto the cart.

Edith rested her husband's limp head in her lap, with a dazed expression, her mouth moving, speaking words as if he could still hear her.

Will threw off his heavy cloak and lay it over Hertford's body, trying to pull it up over his face. The words screamed in Bess's head, *don't touch him, don't touch him.*

'No!' Edith shouted, loud enough for Bess to hear, as she pulled the cloak away. 'He won't be able to breathe.'

But he's dead, Bess thought.

Will let go of the cloak, and then in his thin doublet sleeves, dragged the horse in a tight circle to turn it around. He cast a glance towards the house, and that look of suffering made a mixture of terror and guilt clutch at her innards.

She watched the bedraggled group go, the rain still lashing down over them, as they headed away from the city, towards the docks and the river.

Her husband, and she'd turned him away.

Where could you bury a body like that? The river. She imagined the corpse slowly submerging. Bess sank to her knees by the window, suddenly cold as the Thames itself, her clammy bodice clinging to her back, her hair dripping wet.

Had she been cruel? Or was she right? Would Will come home after this? She didn't know. She'd let him down; she knew that much.

A light in the window of the Fenwick's house caught her gaze, and there, silhouetted at the window, the figures of Mr and Mrs Fenwick, staring out as the cart and its grisly load turned the corner.

~ PART FOUR ~

Now the cloud is very black, and the storm comes down upon us very sharp.

Now death rides triumphantly on his pale horse through our streets and breaks into every house.

Thomas Vincent 1665

Chapter 56

Will did not come home and the night seemed to stretch into a year. Shivering, Bess boiled up water and scrubbed at her hands. The water ran clear, though she felt it ought to be tainted. She bundled the clothes she'd been wearing into a sack and lit a candle to pray. The plague had been miles away, on the other side of the city, and now Will had brought it here.

In the morning she examined herself – every mole, every blemish made her mouth dry and her heart lurch. She tried to remember what her mother had told her about the pestilence. The things to keep it away. Sage, sorrel, dandelion. Why hadn't she listened more closely?

In a panic she ran to the apothecary, but there were none of these things to be had. Just a counter piled with papers, each one offering different cures. Burning brimstone, one said. Washing all over with vinegar, said another. The relief of finding something she could do! She had vinegar in the pantry. At home she stripped herself bare and swabbed herself all over with the sharp brown liquid, her fingers stinging. But still, she wasn't sure it was enough.

At eleven there was a knock at the door and a boy stood on the doorstep with a letter. She took it from him, watched him wrinkle his nose at the smell of the vinegar. The letter was addressed to Will and sealed with an impressive Navy seal. Her first instinct was relief, that the hand was not that of Mr Pepys, but then her spirits sank. She knew instinctively what it was. Will's orders again – to join Sandwich at Harwich. The fleet against the Dutch.

She put it down on the table, then picked it up again.

'Any reply, mistress?'

Someone else was coming, she heard the latch gate and feet on the treads.

The boy, still waiting by the open door, turned.

It was Will.

A rush of something like panic made her sway on her feet. But she wasn't quick enough to shut the door. His face was haggard and his hair hung about his face. Before she could say a word he'd crossed the few yards between them and caught up the letter. Unable to help herself, Bess drew away.

'It's your orders, I think,' she said, her voice wavering.

He tore off the seal and scanned the letter, his mouth tightening. 'I'm to leave first thing tomorrow. Carriages are waiting for the crew at the staging posts.' He paused. 'Tell Sandwich I'll be there.' This to the boy who took his leave.

'So soon? But what about…?'

'Don't start. You'll be glad.' His voice was bitter. 'After all, you don't want me in the house, do you? Not since Hertford… since…' He swallowed. His too-glassy eyes studied the floor. He couldn't go on.

'Where did you…?'

'You don't want to know.'

'Is Edith—?'

He turned away, silent.

She was caught between the desire to hold him and comfort him, and the fear of the contagion, so she remained still, pulling at the fringes of her shawl.

'I'm going to pack my things,' he said eventually. 'I'll eat at the tavern tonight.'

He made to walk past her, but despite herself, she took hold of his sleeve. 'Will, I couldn't—'

'Shut your mouth. There's nothing to say.'

'Have you checked yourself—'

He wrenched his arm away. 'For tokens, you mean? And if I had them, what then? Would you bar me from my own house? Send for the authorities to lock us up?'

'That's unfair.'

'You don't care. You just think of yourself. Bess Bagwell and her big dreams. I used to think it was attractive, all that fire. But now I see it burns only for you. Everyone else is left out in the cold.' He strode away into the bedchamber, leaving her trembling in the parlour.

She heard the noise of him dragging things off shelves and the clothing trunk lid banging down. When he came out he grabbed his sea boots from behind the door, and wrenched open the door.

'Will!' she called after him. 'Wait! You haven't told me how long you'll be at sea?'

'What does it matter?' he said, pausing to hurl back at her, 'Pepys can keep you warm.'

Chapter 57

Even with the window open, the heatwave made Bess's chamber airless. The sound of vomiting woke her from her uneasy sleep.

She called down the stairs to Mary, into the servant's quarters. 'Are you well, Mary?'

No answer.

'Mary?'

Bess slipped on her shoes, hurried down the stairs in her nightgown, and warily opened the door.

Mary looked up at her with beseeching eyes. 'It's something I ate. Must be.'

'But you ate the same as I did.'

'No, no mistress. I had... I had a pie when I was out. Must've been off.' She leant over the chamberpot again and heaved.

Bess took another step back. A dark dread had her in its grip.

'I want to go home, mistress.'

'Can you walk?'

'I think so.'

'Will you need help? Because I...'

'No, mistress. I'll manage.'

Bess nodded. A surge of gratefulness coursed through her.

'Don't worry, mistress. I'll be back soon. It's just a stomach ague.' She looked up at Bess with watery eyes. 'My mother will look after me.'

Bess's thoughts immediately went to her own mother. Was she all right? Her mother had suffered a dose of the plague when Bess was a child – but as a searcher, her mother would be in the thick of it. Bess had never been good with sickness, and the thought of all those sick people made her insides flutter. Full of remorse, she scribbled a note and hurried down to the landing stage where she knew she could find a beggar boy to take a message to her mother. She needed her; her mother would know what to do.

By rights, if Mary had the plague, this house should be locked up with her inside it.

***

In her lodgings on the third floor, Agatha snored, exhausted from tramping house to house in the heat, and having to be the bearer of bad news everywhere she went.

'Mrs Prescott!' Her Irish chamber mate prodded her to waken her, and give her the message.

At the sight of Bess's handwriting, she ripped it open.

Mother,

The plague is bad in Deptford now. I fear my maidservant Mary has the disease and I have sent her home. I wonder every day how you fare, and regret the harsh words I spoke to you. Will is at sea, and I have no-one else to turn to.

I'm afraid, and I don't know what to do.

If you know of any remedy, please, think of your daughter, and pray for her. And if you have the time, you'd be welcome to call.

Your daughter, Bess

Agatha felt the blood drain from her limbs. Not her own daughter; God couldn't be so cruel, not when she'd tended folk with such charity. But she knew better than to think God could be bargained with.

She read it again. It wasn't an apology.

Could it count as one? Bess said she regretted her 'harsh words'.

She hovered a moment, folding the letter carefully and putting it in her bag, heart thudding. That was probably as much apology as she was likely to get from Bess. And anyway, her feet were already moving no matter what her head was deciding.

Agatha crammed the scented kerchief over her nose to breathe in the smell of roses and set off at an ungainly trot towards the premises of Boghurst the apothecary. She needed to fetch some more Venice treacle and a jar of leeches on the way, if she was to help.

With her white stick before her, Agatha forced her way through St Giles, past the laden wagons and carts which were emptying London of people. Now folk rushed by, in too much of a hurry to avoid her. Yesterday, the King and his whole family had fled Whitehall for Hampton Court. They'd abandoned ship, like all the other fat bullfrogs of the town.

'Fools,' Dr Harris had said. 'The same God will follow them there.'

A man with a huge bundle teetering precariously on his back, stood on Agatha's foot as another laden cart rattled by.

'Ouch. Watch where you're putting your big feet,' she said.

The royal seal of approval on running away to the country had created a stampede. Never had she seen people on the move like this. Those that were left gawping at the cavalcade of bundles and baskets and trunks, were the poor – those ragged souls who couldn't afford to leave. London was drained of wealth, becoming shabbier, more down-at-heel by the hour.

At last, the sign of the pestle by the White Hart Inn.

Agatha halted at the door. Another cross. And outside, a watchman puffing out his chest. So even the apothecary was cursed. It would be laughable if it wasn't so grim.

But maybe it would be a boon? He, of all folk, would be making money.

When he saw her white stick, the guard on the door let her in, evidently thinking she'd come to make report of Boghurst's death. A display of Sutherland's Plague Water stood right by the door, labelled a shilling a bottle.

Last week it was sixpence.

In the dim, garlic-reeking interior, Agatha swatted impatiently at the flies already buzzing over the counter. Powders and plasters, tinctures and cordials, stinking storax and blood-letting basins littered its dusty surface.

Opening the till, she expected to find it stuffed to the brim with coins and tokens, but it was empty. Someone had been here before her. She slammed it shut and stuck her head out of the front door.

'Who else has been here?' she demanded of the guard.

'Reverend Evans. He came to say final prayers.'

The bastard. Cheated by a preacher.

She peered into the choking fug of the bedroom, where the embers of a fire still glowed dully, despite the raging heat; it must've been quick if he was still burning brimstone. The corpse was cast across the bed, as if he'd fallen from a great height. Next to him, a sheaf of papers cheaply printed with grids of magical numbers.

Numbers. At last night's count there were seven thousand dead. Those were the only numbers that mattered; not these bits of abracadabra. She grasped the papers, ripped them into shreds and cast them into the fire where they flared and smoked.

Moving as quickly as she could, she stuffed everything that could be of use into her bag, then forced her way out into another press of people, their barrows and carts laden with all their possessions. So many gone, and those that were left would get poorer. Soon there would be no transport out of here. And she must hurry. If Bessie's maid Mary was suffering, God help her, Bessie could be next.

***

Meanwhile, in Flaggon Row, Bess held the letter at arm's length, trying not to breathe, before shrivelling it over a candle flame.

Regret to inform you that your servant Mary Steele passed away of the Plague last night.

How good of Mary's family to let her know; many would not have troubled to do so. After the note was reduced to ash, she washed her hands over and over.

Poor Mary. Such a young life, and Mary so willing. It didn't seem right. She couldn't believe it; she kept thinking she'd hear her shout from the still-room, 'ale's ready.'

No-one had thought the pestilence would ever come this far out of the city. Bells rang all night now for those departed and the clangour made Bess's head throb. And there'd been no news from Will since June, and then only from a news-sheet; that he wasn't dead, that he hadn't gone down with those lost on the *Assurance*. A sailor's wife had a hard life; the coming and going, the waiting for news, the feeling that the sea could swallow your husband whole at any moment. Doubly so, for those with men on warships.

Would Will ever come back to her? Was he still at sea? She had heard nothing.

The not-knowing ate into her thoughts every day. The news-sheets told her nothing of how individual sailors fared. Should she write to tell him of Mary's passing? All her letters had gone unanswered. But she still yearned for a crumb of news from him.

She'd go and ask Mr Bagwell if he'd heard anything, though she doubted he would tell her if he had. Still, there was surely no harm in trying.

The house just next door was boarded up now and a stout, elderly watchman with rheumy eyes loitered outside it. They must be short of men to employ such as him. The disease was rife in Deptford now, but she dare not leave in case Will returned. Bess averted her eyes as she passed, but the watchman shouted over to her, 'Good morrow, mistress.'

She stopped. 'Is it? I think not. I've just heard my maidservant has passed away.'

'Aye. Tis only a figure of speech. Not much good to say about most days now. Still, at least you stopped to speak. Most folk ignore me, like it's me that has the contagion.' He wiped the sweat from his forehead. 'I'm to keep an eye on this whole street now, by myself. Not enough of us to go round, see.'

'Would you watch my house for a half-hour, sir?' she asked. 'Tell me if any messenger comes, and when I return, bear me the news?'

'Can't. It's against orders. Only plague houses.'

'I'm waiting for news of my husband. He's at sea.'

'Sailor is he? Fighting the Dutch?' He sighed, stretched his back. 'Damn fool war. It's the French we should be fighting, not the Dutch. Well, I can't go anywhere anyhows, so I suppose so. You going into the city?'

'No, just to the shipyard. His father works in the sawpit. He might have news of him.'
'Good luck, mistress. There's three plague ships out by the mouth of the Thames, a floating prison for captured Dutch sailors. They say the ships are corpse ships, half the sailors dead of the pestilence. They won't let them off. They'll stay there until they rot.'

***

Owen Bagwell stood at a distance from her in the dust, his meaty hands shoved into his pockets, his belligerent stance failing to mask the fear in his eyes.

In the background the heads and shoulders of the men laboured in the pit, making planks, pulling the great saw back and forth over the huge trunks of oak.

'Have you heard from Will?' she asked.

'No,' he said. 'When they said you'd come, I feared you might be bringing me bad news.'

'It's been a month, and no word.' She had to raise her voice over the scrape of the saw.

'It don't surprise me.'

'When did you last hear?'

'Month ago, maybe. Jack's boys had a note. But my bet is, he'll stay at sea. Take his chance with the war, it's safer there than in London. And he'll want to be as far as he can from his cheating wife. Jack tells me what you do when Will's away. He'll not come home, not if I know Will. He'll hide, like always.'

The insult stung. 'Why do you have to run him down all the time?' Her voice rose higher so that the men in the pit paused to look. 'You've never given him a chance. He could have been a fine carpenter in these yards, but you prevented him. Why? What has he ever done to you?'

Mr Bagwell took a step towards her. 'Nothing,' he said in a low voice. 'He never does nothing. Never makes a decision. He's like his mother. She was a coward.'

'He's not a coward! He's fighting a war! It's not Will's fault what his mother was like.'

'She let me think Will was mine for five years. Too cowardly to tell me, that's why.'

'She's dead, Mr Bagwell. You shouldn't speak ill of the dead.'

'I'll say what I bleeding like.'

'Wait … I don't understand.' She took a step nearer. 'What did you mean, about thinking Will was yours?'

'Will's not my son.' He delivered the words with a bitter laugh.

'What?'

'Jack's my son. My conniving bitch of a wife Ellen cheated on me, and Will was the result. He's no son of mine. Of course I didn't know it was going on until her sister took pity on me and told me. By then Will was five years old. Couldn't turn them out then, could I? I'd look a fool in the yard.'

Bess turned away a moment, placed both hands to her cheeks. Long-forgotten things began to make sense. She turned back. 'Does Will know?'

'Oh he knows right enough. But he's too much of a coward to admit it to himself.'

Anger rose in her chest. 'Did you tell him?'

'He'll be stupid if he hasn't guessed. He looks nothing like me, does he? And he's too clever for his own good. Like his father, working here was never good enough for him.'

Bess suddenly saw. And it was not good enough for Will either.

Mr Bagwell was still talking. 'Ellen died, didn't she? Scarlet fever took her. Good riddance. Left me with a bastard son, so I took my revenge and bedded up with Jack's mother, Phyllis Sutherland. Jack was the result. But Phyllis, God rest her, and her whole family took bad and died in the last plague. She should never have died. That's why I took Jack in. From charity. And because he's my son.'

Jack's face swam before her. She could see it now, the resemblance. Something in the half-aggressive, half-defensive manner of the man.

'And who is Will's father, pray?' Icy politeness concealed her rage. 'Does Will know him?'

'John Ward.' He spat out the words. 'Master Carpenter in these yards. Before my time. In the Troubles. Never could abide the man. Roundhead dog. Killed he was, in a skirmish in Ireland.'

She could hold back no longer. 'It doesn't matter who his blood father is. They're all dead and gone! You brought him up, didn't you? He regards you as his father. He's tried to please you all these years, never understanding why he cannot. He worships you and you fling it back in his face. It is you who are stupid, Mr Bagwell. Shame on you!'

She saw his face drop in shock, before she hitched up her skirts and stumbled away, over the rutted ground, her knees shaking. She had reached the perimeter fence when she heard him shout, 'Oy, Bess? Send me word if you hear.'

Never, she thought. But she did not stop, some sort of fire-powder flowed in her veins. Only at the gates did she pause to catch her breath.

Beyond the shipyard, towards the estuary, three ships idled in the shimmering heat-haze, with no sail showing and no flags flying. The plague ships. If ships like that were moored here, then there might be ships like that in Dutch waters, full of captured Englishmen. She shuddered. She could not imagine what it might be like inside – stinking holds full of rotting corpses. Hell was supposed to be a fiery place, but she couldn't imagine a worse hell than that watery no-man's land. She turned for home, squinting her eyes against the sun, head full of Owen Bagwell's words.

A noise close behind her.

'Bessie.' The hand on her arm made her startle.

She turned.

'Ma.' Before she knew it she was folded into a tight hug. 'Oh Ma! How did you find me?'

Agatha pushed her to arm's length. 'You all right?' She scrutinized her with an assessing gaze. 'The watchman told me you'd come to the yards. I got your letter. About Mary being ill.'

'You're too late, Ma.'

'She's already gone?'

'She went home. But a message came this morning. She died

~414~

yesterday. It must have been quick.' She shook her head. 'She didn't deserve it.'

'Nor do most that have gone. What about the Bagwells? Still safe?'

'Seems so. I came to see if my father-in-law had news of Will.'

'Any news, love?'

'News yes.' She was still digesting it. 'But not of Will. And I'm worried. See those ships in the channel? Plague ships. I worry he might be on one of them. That the Dutch might have captured him and—'

'Wherever he is, he'd want you out of London. I passed seven doors on the way here with the red cross. Including the Fenwicks's on Flaggon Row.'

Bess stared at her mother. Surely not. But then she had taken the short cut by the brewers and hadn't passed their house. It was impossible to think that anything could have happened to the Fenwicks. They were so self-satisfied, so certain of themselves. They were like the wooden scaffolding that held up the town.

'True as I stand,' Agatha said. 'I asked the watchman. Says it started with the cook and housemaid. Mrs Fenwick passed last night. Her husband the day before. They're already in the ground along with their servants. Just that poor lady's maid shut up in there.'

'Maudie?' All alone in that big house? 'What about Lucy, the kitchen maid?'

She shook her head. 'Dead. You can't wait any longer. Everyone's leaving. There'll be no work, no food or milk. Go to Portsmouth. My sister'll take you in. Have you the fare?'

'No. I've nothing.' She was reeling from Owen Bagwell's news and the death of the Fenwicks, and Lucy. Poor Lucy.

'I've brought what I have, but it won't buy your seat on the stagecoach. They're talking five pounds now.'

'Five pounds? Surely not? But it's robbery.'

As she protested her attention was taken by a coach drawing up further down the road. The women watched as the door opened and two dark–suited men bearing satchels climbed out and held the door for another gentleman.

'Who's that?' Agatha asked.

'It's Mr Pepys.' Bess said. 'And that's his clerk, Hewer. Come to inventory the victualling yards. He often calls on me when they do. Don't know the other man, though.'

'Is he the one? The rich man you once mentioned?'

'Yes, but—'

'How well do you know him?'

'Well. Too well. We have … an arrangement.'

'Then we'll wait for him to finish his business and you can talk to him. Persuade him to loan you his coach.'

'No, Ma, not now. I'm too worried for Will. And I can't leave London. What if Will comes back and finds me gone?'

'He'll find you gone if you stay here. To the pesthouse or plague-pit. I hadn't realised it had got so bad round here. Now's not the time to shilly-shally, Bessie. You've a choice to make, and it's simple. Get out of London, or die here, with the rest on your street. Like Mary. Like Lucy and the Fenwicks. It can be that quick.' Her mother's steady gaze held hers. 'In St Giles they're casting bodies into pits. Thousands. They're throwing lime on them to rot them quicker. They can't bury them all. 'Tis hell on earth.' Agatha gripped both her hands in hers. 'Do you understand?'

Bess remembered Hertford. The gaping mouth and unseeing eyes. She didn't want to die like he had. She closed her eyes a moment. Her mother took that as a 'yes'.

***

They waited more than an hour and a half, wilting in the summer heat. More than once Bess wanted to give it up, but her mother was determined they wait for the men to come out.

All at once there was a flurry of activity at the gate.

'Now,' Bess said, as Pepys bustled out of the King's Yard, with Hewer at his heels.

They made their move, strolling by arm in arm, as if they'd just come from the wherry.

'Mrs Bagwell!' Pepys gave her a mock bow. 'Fine weather we're having, eh?'

'It is, sir. This is my mother, Mrs Prescott. She's just visiting.'

'Pleased to make your acquaintance, madam. The name's Pepys. And this is my clerk, Hewer. I trust you're well?'

'I thank the Lord for my good health every single day,' Bess's mother said.

'As do we all, as do we all,' he said, tipping his hat and making to side-step around them.

'It's devilish warm, isn't it?' Agatha said stepping into his path. 'Won't you join us for a little refreshment before you catch the wherry?' she asked. 'There's no shade on them boats.'

He looked to Hewer, who shook his head. 'Your four o'clock appointment, sir.'

'Oh, that.' Indecision played on his face.

'It's cool in my parlour, Mr Pepys,' Bess said. 'You need to get out of this heat.'

'What say you, Hewer? I've been with Andrews all morning, about the victualling. And talking of food and drink's given me a thirst.'

Hewer did not meet his eyes. 'Shall I go on ahead, sir?'

'Yes, I'll take the wherry. It will be cool—'

'Why wait for it, sir?' Bess interrupted. 'Why not have your coachman draw up alongside our house?'

'Yes, quite right. See to it, would you, Hewer?'

'Yes, sir.'

'You can have him wait on the corner.' He turned to Bess, 'Will we be ... I mean, your husband's still at sea, is he?'

'Yes,' Bess said, glancing at her mother.

Hewer sighed and wiped the sweat from under his hat before setting off towards the coach. Pepys walked ahead, whilst Agatha took her daughter's arm. As they passed by the Fenwick's house, Bess shuddered to see the red cross daubed across their fine oak door, and pictured the mousy Maudie alone and afraid, somewhere behind those boarded-up windows.

Agatha noticed her looking and turned to whisper, 'Make sure you get him to agree to the loan of a coach,' she whispered. 'Or the money for one. Nothing less, you hear?'

Bess nodded.

'And take this,' her mother said, thrusting her basket towards her, 'you never know when you might need it.'

Chapter 58

The month was well past, and Jack had been lenient with Bess because his business was taking all his time. He was struggling to cope with the tremendous demand. But the boys taxed his patience and now he could wait no longer for an answer from Bess. The sooner she was mothering them, the better.

On Flaggon Row, flies buzzed round the mouldy horse droppings in the sultry heat, as Jack instructed his men to load up his stock from the workshop. Two wagons stood by, but to be drawn by men, not horses. Horses were like gold dust in the city now. Not even a scraggy mule to be had anywhere.

Once his men were busy, Jack bounded up the stairs to knock at Bess's door. No answer. He shielded his eyes to peer through the windows, but could see no sign of her.

Out. Frustrating. He'd have to wait.

He turned his attention back to his men. 'Careful!' he shouted to Fletcher, who almost tipped a crate off the wagon as he levered it on board. Jack was about to give him a rollicking, when he spotted Bess, and her mother with her, coming from the direction of the shipyards. Damn. The mother was a nuisance. He'd have to get rid of her. And there was another man with them. Who was that? He shielded his eyes against the glare for a better look.

Pepys.

Smug bastard. He could only want one thing. At least he, Jack, was offering something of value – marriage and a future. Bess was a fortunate woman.

He watched them approach, but the mother's quickly disguised expression of hostility on seeing him did not escape his notice. He tensed.

'Good afternoon, Mr Pepys,' Jack said, forcing a smile. 'Mr Sutherland, Mr Bagwell's cousin, if you remember?'

'Oh yes.' Pepys frowned. 'Mr Sutherland, yes.'

'Don't let us hold you up, Mr Sutherland,' Bess's mother said tartly. 'I can see you're busy.'

'Not so busy I can't stop for a few words to pass the time of day,' Jack said, moving smartly into their way. 'Hot, isn't it?'

'Very warm,' Mr Pepys said, looking over Jack's shoulder to Bess who by now had got to the top of the stairs with her basket, and was opening the door. 'Mrs Bagwell there, she kindly invited me in to take some refreshment.'

'I'll join you, if I may,' Jack said, swivelling, and making a determined stride for the stairs.

'Oh, but I'm not sure... I mean...' Bess's mother was no match for his speed.

'When you're loaded, don't wait,' he shouted back to his men. 'I'll follow later.'

As he glanced back he saw Fletcher give him the two fingers, before heaving up the shafts and dragging the loaded waggon away.

Bess stood in the doorway, blocking his entry. 'This is not a good time, Jack.'

'I'd say I have perfect timing,' he said.

Pepys was waiting expectantly, so she stood aside. They both tried to go in, and he found himself shoulder to shoulder with Pepys, until he forced past him into the cool dim interior.

'I'll help you bring the ale,' Bess's mother said, gesturing meaningfully towards the kitchen.

From the kitchen Jack heard them whispering, caught his own name.

Pepys did not sit, and stared uncomfortably away from him out of the window. It was obvious he didn't want to engage in conversation, but Jack wasn't going to let him get away with silence.

'She's an attractive woman, isn't she?' Jack said, sitting down.

Pepys was startled. He blinked, cleared his throat. 'I suppose she is.'

'But married, Mr Pepys. To my cousin.' He smiled benignly. 'Are you married?'

'Well, yes ... I am.'

'It must be a great comfort,' Jack said. 'Especially in times such as these, with so many falling ill.'

Mr Pepys swallowed, searching for words. 'It is. I mean she is.'

Bess and her mother arrived bearing the ale, and a dish of oatcakes with a few slivers of sliced cheese.

They sipped at the ale in uncomfortable silence. Only Jack took his fill of the oatcakes. He took his time, feeling the tension building around him.

'Are you going back to the landing stairs, Mr Pepys?' Jack said, 'If so, I can walk alongside you.'

Pepys's eyes shifted to Bess.

'Mr Pepys will stay a little longer, as he and Bess have some business to conclude,' Bess's mother said. 'But I'll accompany you,' the mother said, standing up and giving him a steely look.

Business to conclude. So that was what she called it.

Bess blushed and it made Jack want to slap her.

'Your men will be waiting. Nice to have met you again, Mr Sutherland,' Pepys said. He too stood.

Mrs Prescott held open the door. Jack knew he'd been outmanoeuvred. He couldn't risk making an enemy of a man like Pepys who was in control of so much in the sea trade.

'Goodbye, Jack,' Bess said.

Jack curbed his inward resentment. 'I too have some business to conclude,' he said. 'In the warehouse below.'

He saw Bess's face turn stony.

Mrs Prescott led the way down the stairs. At the bottom she turned on him, the anger almost palpable. 'Keep your nose out of her business, Jack Sutherland.'

'Her business is my business. I own this house. And if I suspected you were running another bawdy house here, *Mrs Allin*, I could turn her out like *that*.' He snapped his fingers.

The old woman took a step away from him, her expression wary. 'What are you saying?'

'Mr Allin would be very interested to know the whereabouts of his wife and daughter.'

'Don't involve Bess in this. She's leaving London, and Pepys will pay for it.'

Leaving? The shock reverberated up his spine. She couldn't leave. He couldn't allow it.

Bess's mother jabbed a finger towards him. 'And if you care for your children, you would do well to leave too, Jack Sutherland.'

'My children are fine. I give them a treacle every day.'

'Not your potion, then?'

'That too.'

Bess's mother curled her lip in derision. 'You don't fool me. I've seen what your men are doing. You've no licence and that potion you're selling is worthless.'

'Who says so?' He found himself suddenly on the defensive.

'I don't need anyone to tell me. Who you are, and how you are; they tell me all I need to know.'

How dare she? He imagined throwing her to the ground; punching her in the face. It would be so easy. But he thought of Bess and took a deep breath, moving a step nearer so he loomed over her. 'You'll regret saying that, Mrs Prescott,' he said. 'Or is it Mrs Allin?'

'See. Threats. That sort of behaviour tells me exactly the sort of man you are.'

Now his fist shot up unbidden, but he stopped it, just short of her face. Bess's mother gasped and stumbled back. 'You wouldn't dare.'

'Get off my property before I throw you off.' He raised his fist again.

'It's not your property.'

'Yes, it is. My cousin sold the loan to me. And it's nearly paid off. So unless you want me to fetch Mr Allin, I suggest you leave right now.'

The name Allin seemed to crumple her. 'Don't tell that brute where she is,' she begged.

'Then go.'

She stared at him a moment, eyes full of hate, before she retreated and clutching her bag, hobbled away up the road.

Jack smoothed down his velvet coat and pressed his fingers to his moustache. His fingers shook. He'd been an inch from punching her.

A deep breath. He'd handled it badly. The woman was Bess's mother, damn it. And worse, Pepys was still in there. The thought made him tighten his mouth. He unlocked the door to the workshop and stepped inside, his ears pricked for any sounds from above.

***

Bess went into the privy to protect herself with a fennel-infused rag, a remedy against conceiving a child that her mother had taught her, not that she seemed to need it, she thought. She heard Pepys pacing in the parlour, his heels clacking on the boards. When she came out, he was distracted – impatient to get to bed, and with one ear constantly listening for the tolling of the time.

Jack's presence seemed to have made him edgy. She saw him take the money bag from his pocket and leave it on the kist at the foot of the bed as usual.

'Come, Mrs Bagwell, I'd like to make my four o'clock appointment.'

'It may be the last time you see me for a while, sir,' she said.

She told Pepys of her plans to go to Portsmouth, but it seemed to anger him. He refused her the coach, as she thought he would.

'You are not the first to ask,' he said. 'At Coombe Farm downriver I saw a coffin just lying open, the corpse mouldering there for all to see. I'd have taken it by coach to be buried, but I cannot even have the use of the coach myself, except for official business,' he said. 'It belongs to the Crown. My hands are tied.'

'Not even as a favour for a small part of the journey, sir? I could walk the rest.'

'Don't ask me again. I'm tired of people asking me, and I hate to refuse. And besides, it's perfectly safe in London, if you're careful. Look at me – picture of health.' He slapped his chest to emphasise it.

'Is your wife still in London?'

He gave her a sharp look. 'No. But it is no business of yours.'

'Do you not wish to leave London yourself, sir?' she asked him.

'Alas, you know I cannot. The Navy calls. Though it is mighty quiet with no musical gatherings and the theatres all closed. And there is so much to do, now my clerks have left. London's a graveyard.' He put his hand to his mouth. 'Oh dear. What an unfortunate expression.'

'And what of the sailors' families, sir?' she pressed. 'They can't leave. Not until their wages are paid. '

'Not my fault. There is little I can do,' he said, sighing and unbuttoning his breeches from his waistcoat. 'The King won't release more coin. And what with the war…'

He reached for her.

***

Jack stood in the middle of the workshop, unable to breathe. The sweat dewed on his forehead under his heavy wig. He wiped it away.

There it was. The rhythmic noise of the bed creaking.

He stared at the ceiling, holding his breath. The regular bang of the bed against the wall increased. A soft scatter of sawdust fell from the rafters onto his shoulders. He brushed it off. He was frozen; a statue looking up. He crushed his fingernails into his palms. The banging went on and on. Would it never stop?

All at once there was a cry from Pepys. A groan like a bellows' discordant note.

Jack shot out an arm to the wall to steady himself.

From Bess, no sound.

Anger swelled in his gut, making his eyes blur. He closed them tight, gritted his teeth, ears straining to hear what was going on over his head.

But then footsteps above him and muffled voices. The rise and fall of conversation. For some reason that incensed him. That it should be so casual, when he, Jack, had offered her everything.

Jack exhaled; gave his brow one last wipe, and straightened his silk stock. If Bess could do that with Pepys, she could do it with him.

***

Bess scrambled off the bed. Mr Pepys was already putting on his shoes, and reaching for his coat.

'Wait, sir. You promised my husband—'

'Enough. It is becoming tedious to hear of him. Your

conversation becomes dull, Mrs Bagwell.' He picked up the pouch from the kist, dangled it briefly before her, then pocketed it.

As she stepped forward to protest, he swept his hat from the chair by the door and threw open the door. When she followed him through the house, her chemise still in disarray, it was to find he had left the front door swinging open.

She had only just laced her stays when she heard a noise. She turned, expecting to see her mother.

'So how was Pepys?' Jack asked, idly turning a button on his cuff.

Bess drew her chemise closer to her chest. Something about his manner gave her an involuntary shiver. 'Get out of here, Jack.'

'You turned me down. I offered you marriage and a house and children. But you turned me down. For that puffed-up bullfrog.'

'It's no business of yours what I do.'

'Is that what you think?' He moved in two long strides until he was right before her.

She stood her ground, pressed her hands to her chest, but her heart was racing beneath them.

'It is my business,' he said, staring her down. 'I own this house and you've turned it into a whorehouse.'

She raised her chin. 'Not me. Your cousin. My husband. This was his idea.' Beneath her chemise and her skirts her knees shook.

'But you enjoy it, don't you?'

'No.' Her lips were dry. She glanced to the door. 'What do you want?'

'I want what Pepys had. If you can do it for him, you can do it for me.'

Her mouth turned dry. 'My mother will be back soon.'

'No she won't. I sent her packing. It's just you and me, my beautiful Bess.' He reached out a hand to touch her neck. Instinctively she flinched.

He saw it and his mouth tightened. 'Not good enough for you, am I?' he said. His hand came out to land a stinging blow to her cheek.

Her hands flew to her face. If she could reach the privy closet, there was a bolt on the door.

Jack's eyes were dark and unreadable. He reached out again towards her face.

She leapt to the side and ran for the bedroom door and the closet. She got as far as the bedroom before he was upon her from behind. His fingers dug into her flesh as he hurled her onto the bed and straddled over her.

Another slap to the side of the head that made her gasp. His hands pinioned both her shoulders to the bed.

She closed her legs but he forced them open with his knee.

'Let go,' she said, twisting. He grabbed her flailing arms, and his fingers dug into her flesh.

He moved his face close to hers. He was going to try to kiss her. Maybe if she let him, he'd relax and she could free herself.

She fell still, waiting.

His mouth came towards her. Then suddenly he was shaking her.

It seemed to rattle her teeth in her head. She couldn't think. His face was over hers, his mouth yelling. At first she didn't understand. Then she did. A stream of foul language.

'D'you think I want you now? After Pepys has had his prick inside you?' He flung her away from him. 'You disgust me. I wouldn't want you now if you were the last woman on earth.'

He reached down beside the bed and, with one sudden movement, upended the chamberpot over her. A drench of cold, foul-smelling water. She gasped. The sulphurous stench of piss stung her throat, before he hurled the pot away.

A crash as it hit the wall. She cringed away from him.

'I hope that was Pepys's shit,' he said.

In two strides he was at the door. It slammed shut, and a draught shivered the room.

For a while she did not move. The chamber echoed with silence. Her face was tight and sore where he'd hit her, her body shaking with fear and shock. Finally she curled into a tight ball of humiliation.

***

Later, she crawled off the bed, stripped it, threw the sheets and all her clothes into a sack and knotted the neck of it tight. As she washed and scrubbed herself all over, she searched for tokens. Just bruising on the arms, and a red weal on her cheek. But her breath was shallow and her hands trembled. She took the sack down to the Thames and threw it in. It drifted a while before sinking out of sight.

Above, the sky glimmered with a sprinkle of stars, the moon floating in a halo of light above the rooftops and spires. In the distance, sailors cackled outside the tavern. Laughter, whilst London was full of the dead and dying. She shook her head. The world was so beautiful and yet so ugly.

When she got back to the house she unlocked the door warily, fearing Jack might return. And surely he would, to throw her from the house. He'd have to get in first, she thought. Once inside, she levered the bolt from the privy door with a kitchen knife, and then fixed it to the bedroom door with a few nails found in one of Will's old apron pockets. It was a rough job and it hurt her to gouge holes in their fine wooden door, but it was better than nothing. She nailed the windows shut in the parlour. Then she went to the front door and locked herself in with the brass key. Every small noise made her startle.

But nobody came; not her mother, nor Jack's men.

She lay awake hearing only the hoots of barges on the river outside, and hating herself. Jack was right. She was a whore. And she'd blamed Will for it all. But really, she'd begun it. She'd wanted more than she had, and now it seemed presumptuous to want more than life, and love, and a safe place to lay your head.

Chapter 59

Agatha paused over the corpse she was washing, and blew out through her mouth. Worried, she had called to see Bess the day after Jack Sutherland had threatened her, and again three times since, always at dawn in case she should bump into Jack Sutherland. She'd told Bess about Allin, and Bess had locked all the doors, when they used to stand open. Jack had threatened Bess too, she feared, but Bess wouldn't speak of it. She wouldn't speak of anything – just got thinner and thinner, waiting for that husband of hers to return. All over London people protested about being shut up. But Bess imposed it on herself.

Agatha could not help but worry about her daughter every minute. She turned to the task in hand. Five dead in this house. Overturned cups on the table, soiled bedlinen roiled up in the bedchamber, milk soured in the pail.

She'd laid out a man, his wife and baby, and the two servants. She'd found their names from the clerical list and double-checked them against the rent book and the correspondence in the house. Nothing more to be done except lock it up.

Better go and tell the watchman, she thought. Carefully, she swabbed her hands in vinegar again and tied her apron closer around her waist. She wished she could have got Bess out of London, but there was no chance now. Not a pony or mule to be had anywhere for less than a small fortune, and in the city poor folk were dying of famine because bread was too dear to buy.

Agatha swept a space clear of debris on the parlour table, and was just writing the names of the deceased in her book, when there was a knock.

Whoever it was would have to wait. She ignored it and continued her writing.

The door behind her creaked open. She was about to shout and tell the intruder to keep out if they knew what was good for them, when she recognised the man standing there.

The physician, Dr Harris.

'There's a man asking for you by name.'

'Who?'

'Jack Sutherland. Third on the right, Stanmore Street. Black door. Says can you call in to see him.'

She was wary. 'What's it about?'

'Don't know. He wouldn't say. He said I'd to tell you it's urgent.'

Agatha finished writing the names in her book, with an agitation in the pit of her stomach. It could be a trick – something to do with Allin. But what if it wasn't? She'd have to go. What if it was Bessie?

'Shall I finish up here?' Dr Harris asked.

'That would be kind.'

'I hope it's not bad news,' he said.

***

The third house in the row had no cross on the door, which was surprising, because it was the only one, despite this being a solid, respectable neighbourhood. Did Jack really live here? On this street of stone-built houses? My, he'd certainly gone up in the world. She'd had no idea. A hard knob of resentment burned in her chest.

Jack opened the door at the first knock. Agatha pulled herself to upright, suppressing her dislike. He was less imposing than she remembered, and agitated, stepping from foot to foot, his face

~431 ~

scored with a deep frown.

'What's happened?' she said. 'Is it Bessie?'

'No. No, not that.'

'Then I'll be going.'

'Wait!'

She caught the hint of desperation in his voice. 'Not the children?'

'No.'

'You're a fool. You should have got them out of the city.'

'We're going. But before we go, I mean it's probably nothing, but … '

'What's wrong with them?' Her heart contracted.

'It's me. I've got a bit of a rash. I thought you could look at it for me. Probably just fleas.' He smiled ruefully, though it didn't reach his eyes. 'But just to set my mind at rest, and I know you're good with herbs …'

'You jest,' she said, and she turned to go.

'Do it for the boys. Not for me.'

She hesitated. She'd seen so many orphans these last few months. And she was desperate to see the children again. 'You'll let me see the boys?'

'Yes.'

She followed him into his house and closed the door.

'Nanny Prescott!' Billy was already clinging to her skirts.

'Now just leave me and your father a few minutes, and I'll see you later.' She prised him off. 'Is there somewhere …?'

'This way.' He led her through into a fine dining room with a slate fireplace, and a hanging chandelier for candles. Her footsteps echoed on the polished wood floor.

'Show me the rash.'

He stripped off his shirt and raised his arm. A purplish swelling right in the armpit. Even now, after seeing so many, the livid colour of it against his pasty skin still shocked her.

'Put your shirt back on,' she said.

'Is it...?'

'Nanny!' Hal burst through the door. 'Billy said—'

'Not now, sweeting,' she said. 'Go and wait in the parlour.'

As soon as she said that, Jack's face seemed to age. He knew. And he knew what it meant. That they'd be locked up here until they died from the disease or hunger.

'What can I do?' he said. 'What shall I take?'

'D'you want the truth? None of the remedies do much. All the quacks' tinctures, all the so-called cures. There *is* no cure. It's a wheel of fortune.'

He took hold of her arm. 'There must be something. Some herb or potion,' he said. 'This can't be the end. Tell me what to do!'

'Leave go. Don't touch me. You'll not lay hands on me or my daughter again, or it'll be the Constable you'll answer to.' She backed away from him. 'There's nothing to be done. Pray, that's all.'

'What will happen to us?' Now she did see the fear, squirming like a living thing, naked in his eyes.

'You need to make provision for the boys. Have you checked them today for tokens?'

'No, I didn't, I thought—'

Five minutes later she had checked them all and found Toby hot to the touch.

'Do you have a headache?' she asked him, turning his chin this way and that.

He pushed her away. 'A little bit. But it's nothing,' Toby said. 'I often get them. They don't last long.' His eyes evaded hers.

Billy elbowed his way between them. 'It won't be the plague, Nanny, because we've been drinking Pa's Plague Water every day.' He looked up at Jack with his big brown eyes. 'It keeps it away, doesn't it, Pa?'

Agatha frowned. 'What's this he talks of?'

'Nothing. It doesn't matter—'

But Hal was already running to the corner. He returned with a heavyweight glass bottle and thrust it proudly into her hand. 'You should have some, Nanny. All the other houses nearby have crosses on their doors, but not us.'

Agatha drew it up to close, squinting to read the label.

SUTHERLAND'S ELIXIR.

The only elixir proven to prevent the pestilence.

Five thousand cured in Holland alone.

Herbal relief from all agues and fevers.

Testimonials available.

She sighed. She'd seen so many of these. She uncorked the bottle and sniffed. It smelt dank and swampy. Just as she'd thought; she couldn't detect any odour of astringents, spices or herbs.

'What's in it?' she asked.

He shook his head. Then in a low voice. 'Please, take the children. Will and Bess can take care of them, Will won't mind, but Bess...' He crumpled. Put his head in his hands. 'Oh God, Bess. What have I done?'

'What did you do to her?'

He shook his head; groaned. 'You don't want to know. Please, for the boys' sake, get them out of here... take them to Bess.'

'I can't. Your elder boy has a fever. You can't expect anyone to take him in that state.'

'Stop whispering,' Toby said. 'I can hear you. I'm not going nowhere. Not without Pa.'

'Toby, you need to go, to look after your brothers,' Jack said.

'No. Why? Why can't we stay here?'

'Because... because I'm ill, and I don't want any of you to catch it.'

'Is it the plague?'

'I don't know... perhaps. But better to get you clear of it.'

'Will you die?' He was backing away now, his eyes wide and glassy. 'Don't leave us, Pa.'

Agatha swallowed. Curse it. She was better at dealing with the dead than the difficulties of the living. 'It's best you all stay together,' she said.

Jack's face was desperate. 'No. You'll take Hal and Billy at least.'

Billy took hold of his father's coat and clung on, half-hiding behind him. 'I don't want to go without you and Toby. I'm staying here.'

Jack lifted his hand and gave him a slap across the cheek. 'You're going, and that's that. Get your night things.'

Billy responded by bursting into tears and running up the stairs to the bedchamber.

Jack slumped into a chair, his head in his hands. When he looked up, his face was yellow-hued and pinched. 'I didn't want to hit him, it's just I don't know how else to make him go. He doesn't understand. Will you fetch the Constable? Will they lock us up?'

'Look, Jack, I can't take them. I live in one room with four others.'

'Will you ask Bess? Please?'

Agatha sat down on one of the hard chairs and pressed her hand to her forehead. She loved those boys. But Bess was her daughter. 'I won't let Bess take them. It's a risk to her. And I know you insulted her. I don't know what you did, but she's not been the same since.'

He moaned. 'Oh God. Please. You must. There's no-one else.'

'It would be a mortal risk she'll be taking, to take them in.'

'I'm begging you, just ask her. She loves them. They've no-one else.'

'What about your uncle? Mr Bagwell from the sawpits?'

'He straps them. He's not soft, like Bess...'

Agatha shook her head to shake off the thought of little Hal being beaten by a bully like Bagwell. Finally, she spoke. 'I'll ask, but it'll be up to her. And I'll be advising against it.'

He stood up again, swaying on his feet. 'What about Toby?'

At the sound of his name, Toby appeared at the door again.

'I'll give him something for the pain. We'll see if his headache's gone in the morning.' She stood up. 'But these things can be quick ... Have you made your peace?'

'Peace?' he looked blank. Then suddenly he said, 'Forgive me. I was angry about Pepys and I didn't know what—'

'No, not with me, you foolish man. I don't matter. You must make peace with the Almighty,' Agatha said gently.

'You mean, this might be the end?'

'Best be prepared.'

He looked at her with wide eyes, as if she was telling him a fairy story that he couldn't quite believe.

'It's alright, Nanny,' Toby said, 'I'll look to him.' And she watched the boy guide his ailing father back to the chair, as if he were the father and Jack the child.

***

Agatha limped down the street with her mind churning, and one hand clinging tight to the lucky amulet, the scrap of Holy Palm from Palm Sunday, that hung around her neck in a pouch. The sun beat down on her head, but it didn't seem right for the weather to be so fine when she'd come from such scenes of death and sorrow in St Giles. Instead of having to jostle for the wall, the streets were eerily deserted. Not a carriage was to be had, and no sedans, even if Agatha could have afforded one. All the lackeys had left. Houses were shuttered, their windows sealed. Grass poked up on the highways.

What would Bessie say when she told her that Jack's family had been struck down? Jack and Bessie had never seen eye to eye, and he was a mean bastard if ever there was one, but Bessie loved those boys. And her useless husband away at sea, and nobody to help her.

She speeded her step; if anyone was to find out Jack's was a plague house, those boys'd be shut up double quick, and Bessie would be able to do nothing for them.

After a breathless run down Thames Street, Agatha scrambled aboard a wherry to Deptford. Though the streets were deserted, the wherries were not. Every boat was crammed, with fleeing families reeking of camphor and vinegar, and hunched-over merchants with their troubled faces turned away from each other. The woman opposite her chewed determinedly on a wad of tobacco, a stained handkerchief pressed to her nose. Agatha smiled grimly. Tobacco wouldn't keep it away – if it did, there'd be no men dying at all.

She gnawed at her fingernails as the wherry crawled downriver. Nobody wanted to be the bringer of bad news. And Bessie was so awkward, blowing hot and cold – one minute pleased to see her, the next irritable and wanting her to leave.

Agatha stood up sharply and was first off the boat, but had to stop half-way down the road because the stitch in her side forced her to double over.

When she finally clambered up the stairs, she clobbered the door with her fists. At first she thought no-one would come, but then the rasp of the bolts, and it opened, and there was Bess, hair untidy round her face, and a closed-off look.

'It's Jack and the boys,' Agatha said, still clinging to the handrail and gasping to catch her breath. 'The plague ... Jack's struck down.'

***

Bess stared, unable to believe her ears. Then her first thought was, *serves him right*. But then her second one was for the boys. What would become of them? Her third thought was that Jack had breathed right into her face. Her head reeled, her stomach seemed to drop five fathoms. She could have the disease right now and not know it.

'Will you go?' Agatha asked.

'I don't know, Ma,' Bess said. She paced the room, unable to be still. Even the thought of Jack brought back the stench of piss. She didn't know if she could bring herself to even look at him. 'And you say that Toby's ailing too?'

Agatha nodded. 'He's bad, love. No sign on the younger ones, but they've all been in that house together so it might only be a matter of time.'

Bess's heart lurched. 'My poor little man. And Jack – are you sure? I mean did Jack look...?'

'He was sweating a little, and I could feel it on him. A darkness; bad blood. Like a miasma. I've an instinct for it; I've seen it before.'

And he'd breathed over her. 'Serves him right. A sinner like him.'

'No love, I've seen plenty of innocents taken. That serving girl, Maudie, they were taking her corpse out of the Fenwick's as I passed. It's not sin that does it. Take my word, plenty of babes die who haven't had time to sin. Jack's a strong man, so he could weather it, or he could die. Only the Lord knows which.'

Maudie. Dying alone. In that huge house.

Bessie clasped and unclasped her hands. 'But what will

become of the children then? If he dies?' She was stricken.

'The pesthouse if they catch it; the poorhouse if they don't. Though I'd do my best to help them, I've only the one room. I thought you'd want to know.'

'No. Not those places. Will wouldn't stand for that,' Bess said.

She paced the floor, back and forth, back and forth, unable to decide.

'You'll wear that floor out,' Agatha said. 'I came straight here. And we have to be quick. If anyone else finds them, they'll be shut in, sure and certain.'

'Shut in?'

'Let's get the little ones away, Bessie. If Jack dies first, there'll be no-one to care for them—'

The image of the three boys all alone in a house with only a corpse for company fired her resolve. She unhooked her cloak from the door. 'I'll come,' she said. 'But I'll not make any promises.'

'I knew it. You've a kind heart, Bessie. Just the younger ones, mind. Toby will have to stay there with his father.'

'Leave Toby there? I can't do that—'

'If you value your life, you must. But you've no need to come with me. I'll go and fetch the boys back. You stay here where it's safe.'

'No. I'm coming. If I'm taking in Jack Sutherland's children, I want to see him beg.'

Bess and Agatha made their way through the empty streets, until a thick soup of smoke blocked the street. A house fire? The weather was certainly warm enough.

As they grew nearer the sweet-sour smell of burning flesh made Bess crush her kerchief to her nose. Not a house fire then.

'What is it?' she asked.

Her mother didn't answer. Ahead of them blazed a huge

bonfire, taking up half the street, and surrounding it, a motley collection of carts and barrows piled high with furs. As Bess got nearer she pressed her hand to her mouth. It wasn't furs at all, but the bodies of cats and dogs, rats and moles, all piled high, and all stiff, dull-eyed and staring.

She gripped hold of Agatha's arm.

'They said they'd planned a cull,' Agatha said. 'Never worked the last time, don't know why they must. Think they just like the satisfaction of seeing something else apart from us suffer.'

'I don't want to look,' Bess said.

'We'll go around it,' Agatha said, 'but be quick.' She pulled Bess forward, up a side alley. Here, litter blew around her ankles, the windows of the houses rough with crossed planks, every door nailed up like a coffin.

A few moments later they emerged onto a broader street. 'Is this it?' Bess asked.

'Grand, isn't it?' her mother said. 'It's that one.' She pointed to the only house with no cross. 'Go on, knock.'

The door swung open almost before she'd withdrawn her hand. Her first thought was that Jack's eyes looked very bright and he looked genuinely pleased to see her. It was a look she'd never seen on his face before and it disconcerted her.

'You came,' he said. 'The boys are ready.'

It was then, as he turned and walked away, that she saw his hands shaking and the unsteadiness in his gait.

'I'm sorry…' She didn't know what else to say.

'I'll fetch them.'

Bess and Agatha stood on the doorstep, but after a few minutes the children still hadn't emerged.

Jack staggered back to them, his face sheened with sweat. Bess took a step back as he clung to the door jamb, reluctant to breathe his air. 'It's Hal,' he said. 'He won't come out. Please, he might listen to you.'

The dark interior of the house looked uninviting, and the thought of being so close to Jack, who was clearly ailing, made her shoulders tense. The consequences of going inside ran around inside her head. But she couldn't leave the boys there, could she?

'Two minutes,' she said to her mother, holding up two fingers. 'Wait here.'

Determined to get it over as quickly as possible, she dived into the darkness of the house, immediately gagging at the stench. A chamber pot full of vomit lay off to one side of the hearth, but the hearth itself was spattered. She tried not to breathe.

'Aunt Bess!' Billy was leaping up at her, and without thinking, she hoisted him up and he wrapped his skinny legs around her waist. 'Toby's been sick,' he said. 'It stinks.'

'Toby?' she shouted, putting Billy down.

Meanwhile, Jack had collapsed into a chair and was panting like an animal in pain.

Sooner she could get the boys out, the better. She hurried up the narrow stairs and into the bedchamber. What she saw there made her stop in her tracks. Toby was lying on the bed, but his shirt was rucked up his back, and on his smooth white flesh a ring of red welts seemed too bright. As if someone had daubed paint there.

She had barely time to take this in, when there was a commotion downstairs. Agatha shouting, and men's voices. Hal crying. She turned away from Toby and took a few steps onto the landing to look down the stairs.

'No, we're searchers,' Agatha protested. 'Both me and my daughter. You have to let us out. See, here's my pass.' Agatha fished in her bag and drew out a signed warrant. She thrust it towards the two guardsmen who were standing like bulwarks at the door to the cramped parlour. One of them gave it a cursory glance.

'Bess,' her mother shouted, 'Come down!'

Bess heard the panic in her voice and took two steps down towards the parlour.

'You've to come away now,' her mother said, her eyes sending frantic messages. 'We're done in this house, we've got the information we need.'

Time seemed to slow. She could see her mother's eyes pleading with her, knew it was her chance to get out, but she hesitated. The red welts on Toby's back seemed engraved in her mind. There was no-one to care for him. Jack looked in a bad way. If she left them locked up alone they would all certainly die. The world seemed to swim around her. The guards expressions were hostile; one of them held a flintlock in his hands, it pointed at her like a threat.

'Auntie Bess?' a whimper from Hal. He'd crept up behind her and his small hand grabbed hers.

'No,' she said finally, gulping back tears. 'I need to stay.'

'She doesn't know what she's saying,' Agatha said, pawing at one of the guards with her fingers. 'Let me have a word with her.' She hurried over and came half up the stairs, gripped Bess by the hand. 'Are you stark mad?' she said, her whisper hoarse and low. 'You can't do anything. Leave them.'

The noise of hammering had already begun.

'Aunt Bess! They're nailing our windows!' Billy cried from the bottom of the stairs.

Bess looked into her mother's eyes and saw the desperation etched there, but it could not budge her. 'I can't.'

'What about Will?' Agatha said.

'He won't care. We're ...' she swallowed, she couldn't find the words.

'I'll not leave without you.' Her mother's grip tightened.

The noise of hammering was coming from front and back, it made it hard to think.

'Aunt Bess!' Billy shrieked.

'Out now, if you're coming,' the big guard shouted from the door.

Bess pushed her mother away. 'Go, Ma. We'll need someone on the outside.'

Her mother grabbed her in a fierce embrace, more like a bony grip, with a strong smell of sulphur and vinegar, but it weakened something inside, something hard that had begun to melt. Bess could hardly speak, she was so choked up with tears.

In what seemed a blur, the door closed, and the last light was blocked from the parlour. From outside, she heard the split and splinter of wood; the nails going in. She slumped onto the stairs, rested her forehead on the newel post.

Only then did she realise she may not come out of Stanmore Street alive.

Chapter 60

The next day days stretched as if time itself had given up on them. Minutes became hours. The boys were hungry and moaned about their cramping bellies, but when Agatha finally came that evening she pushed some scraps of oatcake through the crack in the window. There was no bread to be had, she said. The bakers had all left London.

Inside the house the air was hot and fetid; sun crept through the cracks between the boards like needles. The light hurt Toby's eyes, and made him curse. She put a blanket over the light to shield him, and because she could see that the rash was worsening. Now it was like ripe red haw-berries surrounded by a dark bruise.

In the parlour below, Jack bellowed and moaned.

She had tried to give him some of the oatcake with a little brandy she had found in the tack cupboard, but he flung it away, and caught her a blow on the cheekbone that made her head spin.

Billy and Hal clung to her skirts, scared of this man who was alternately raving and morose. 'Don't go near your father,' she said to them. 'He doesn't know what he's doing.'

Part of her hated him, for what he had done to them, but part of her could not be harsh. The boys' fear of him on the one hand, and dread of him dying on the other, filled her with compassion. He was quite a different Jack from the man who had swaggered into her house in his new coat and wig. Skin and bone now, his head stubbled and covered in lesions, she had watched him slowly turn into a corpse.

Toby, of course, never saw him. He was too ill to leave his bed.

'Aunt Bess,' Billy said, tugging at her. 'Give him some of Pa's medicine.'

'For God's sake! It's not medicine,' she snapped. 'It's just water. It'll do nothing.'

Billy slunk away, and Bess sighed, ashamed to have been so harsh.

That night she slept on the floor next to Toby's bed, in a restless daze, hearing Toby's breath rasping, like an old man. The other two boys curled up next to her, still disturbed by this nightmarish prison they were forced to endure.

***

At dawn she thought she heard something. She woke up in a cold sweat, hurried downstairs, thinking the thump was one of the children, to find Jack at the front door, as if he already knew he was going somewhere. He was slumped there, half-sitting, like a waxwork of his former self, blood spattered his clothes, his face a mass of boils. His eyes were open, but looked like the eyes of a puppet, sightless and staring.

'Lord have mercy.' She averted her gaze. She couldn't look at him. Not like that.

But she couldn't leave him there either. What if the boys were to find him? She crossed herself.

She found a pair of hearth gloves and put them on. Trying not to look, she heaved him away from the door, to lay him flat. A winding sheet. That's what she needed. She tiptoed up and dragged a sheet from his bed. Once downstairs she rolled him onto it, trying not to touch his skin, only his clothes. She wrapped it tight round him and wished her mother was here. She knew about the dead. Should she do something else? She didn't know what. And what about his soul?

Just the effort of doing this all alone made her faint. Tears leaked from her eyes but she didn't know if it was from the effort, from grief, or from fear. She trembled, wondering if it was the start of it.

Please God, let me not be taken with it, she prayed. No, she thought. I must pray for him. For Jack. Was it sinful to be relieved he was dead? She said the Lord's Prayer, tried to stay calm.

Then she knocked and called out to the watchman on the other side of the door.

'What is it?'

'Jack Sutherland. He's...'

'Is he dead?'

'Yes.' She tried not to sound panicked. 'I can't move him.'

'Leave him then,' the voice came. 'I'll tell the undertaker to come for him with the cart.'

'What about a funeral?'

'There'll be none. Quicker into the ground the better.'

The children. How could she tell them? Toby was still ill, and the others were asleep.

As if to read her mind, a cry from above. Toby. She hitched her skirts and ran upstairs two at a time.

Toby was sitting up in bed, his face white and the bed stinking of excrement. Blood gushed from his nose and he was clearly terrified.

'Hush, hush,' she said, ripping off her coif and thrusting it to his nose.

It was soon swamped with blood, and Toby was coughing, retching, unable to breathe.

'Lord help me,' she cried.

'No... go away...' Toby's words were almost incoherent; he hit at her as he fought to get out of bed, 'I want Pa!'

She tried to catch him but was caught by surprise and he

toppled to the floor where he lay gasping, eyes full of fright. She locked her eyes on his, tried to prop him up, her fingers wet and slippery with his blood, but he couldn't catch a breath. Moments later, he slumped, his lips blue. Silence enveloped the room.

'Toby,' she whispered, shaking him. 'Toby!'

'What's going on?' Billy woke and appeared at her side, clutching his nightcap to his chest as if he could not let it go.

At the sight of Toby, head lolling in Bess's arms, he began to back away.

Then he turned and ran and the door slammed behind him.

Bess sat for a moment. She did not want to put Toby down. Did not want to accept he was dead. Yet she knew with an absolute certainty he was gone. Him and his father in one day. The fact had gone in, but she could feel nothing.

'Why not me?' she shouted to the space above her head. 'If you want a sinner, take me!'

But however hard she listened, she heard nothing. Nothing but the silence of the big, echoing house.

Chapter 61

Will clung to his holdall, his carpenter's trunk wedged between his feet to stop it sliding as the *Assurance* keeled to avoid the chains in the estuary, and limped towards what should have been the safety of London.

Instead he was met by dark spires and tolling bells. And he'd heard such rumours, about dead men in the streets, plague pits full of corpses. It hadn't seemed real. In his head he'd had the thought that Bess might catch it, that she'd be sorry for her infidelities, and he imagined her begging his forgiveness. Now the real possibility that she might be a victim had him in its grip, and his stomach felt like it was squeezing itself dry.

Apart from the rolling peal of the bells, it was eerily quiet. The ship drifted to the quay. It was badly damaged and would need repair, but there was no-one to greet them. A half-dozen empty ships and perhaps twenty stevedores on the wharf, where before, in high summer, the crowds had been hundreds. Straw from packing cases blew about; no-one had swept it up.

By the time they'd made good and disembarked, it was dusk.

To steady his nerves, he called for a drink at the tavern on the quay before going home. He passed several warehouses with the red cross slashed across the doors, and the chandler's which was boarded up, with a 'closed until further notice' sign. In the tavern the talk was all of death, of burials and of God's punishment to the city because the King was a whoremonger. Cromwell had been right, they said gloomily; they'd turned away from virtue and into sin. This was the day of judgement.

Will tried to close his ears, but it was no use. The reality of

London's plight ate into him, and with it, a desperate unease about Bess. He left his tankard half-full and, struggling with his trunk, his bag across his back, set off for home. No hackney carriages stood in the streets, and no sedans. He was forced to walk to the wherry, and then to Flaggon Row with his arms aching and the ropes of the holdall digging in his shoulders. No linkmen appeared to light his way.

The door to the workshop stood open, and when he struck a flint, the room was empty. Not a crate or a box. Not a chisel or a hammer. His foot crunched on broken glass. Trust Jack to leave such a mess. Still, it made him nervous.

He fumbled in the dark to unlock the house door and a smell of something sour made him wrinkle his nose. Once he'd lit a taper, he realised it was coming from a jug of milk. Strange how it made him queasy now, being on dry land. Though it was unlike Bess not to put the jug in cold water before she went out. He lit up more candles and was surprised to see flies buzzing round a half-eaten bowl of potage, and a piece of bread. He touched the bread with his finger. It was hard. Mouse droppings peppered the table.

He prowled the house with a candle in his hand. Bess's cloak was gone. On the floor by the mat was a note that had been shoved under the door. He must have stepped over it on the way in. It was scrawled with graphite on cheap paper.

Called to collect payment twice. You or your cousin should have arranged payment with Kite before leaving London. Stealing's a sin. You owe us.

Bastable

The threatening tone of the note did nothing to reassure him. Bess must have been gone some time. And where was Mary? There was no sign of her. He went to the maid's chamber to find it empty, and the bed stripped. The plague was here in Deptford, but there was no cross on his door.

He trawled the house looking for a note from Bess. A basket of sewing was still unfinished by the door. He picked up the marked-up pattern for a felt glove and then cast it down. Had Bess left? He knew there was strain between them, but he had not expected she would actually leave London without telling him. Where would she go?

But there was still a mystery about it that made him uneasy. Why would she leave without all her things? After pondering a while, he thought he'd go and ask Mrs Fenwick.

The Fenwicks's house was dark and shuttered. A guard was at the house next door. The Fenwicks were dead, he said.

Will found he was trembling. He went back in the house, but it seemed strange without Bess. When he slept he dreamt he was drowning.

***

The next morning he woke early. By now he was jittery. He was both angry with Bess and worried. He unpacked Bess's letters from his trunk, to read them again in case he'd missed a clue as to where she had gone, but he found nothing. He ran a thumb over her familiar bold hand-writing, and cringed. Why hadn't he written back?

Because he didn't know what to say. What was happening between them was too painful to confront. Her letters had finished with endearments he couldn't bear to read. To him, Pepys's presence was seeping between every line.

He shook off these thoughts. Perhaps Jack would know where she'd gone. He snatched up his waiting pile of correspondence scanning it for Jack's handwriting. Spotting it on one of the letters, he tore open the seal to find the current loan agreement and Jack's new address; Stanmore Street.

***

His journey to Stanmore Street only served to remind him how much London had changed. Shops closed, black ribbons on door-knockers, the smell of smoke. The only conveyance that passed him was one carrying a groaning mass of black-clad people, presumably out of the city to the pest-house.

He ran past two houses where the dead were laid out on the street, the bodies wrapped but not yet removed.

He crossed the thoroughfare, anxious to be away as soon as possible.

At the landing stairs stood a vat of foul-smelling liquid for him to wash his shoes, and another table with a bowl of herbal tincture to wash his hands. The whole city reeked of tobacco; every man had a pipe, but kept himself away from his fellows as if each man was himself the source of the contagion.

The entrance to Jack's alleyway was blocked by a cart. Even before he got to it, Will had a bad feeling about it.

'Bring 'em out. Bring out your dead!' came the cry.

He cowed away from the woman's whimper as a young girl's body was thrown onto the cart, just as if she were a butcher's carcass. What chilled him though was the teetering pile of bodies, all the limbs dangling loose from their shrouds.

The men used sticks to push the body further on, causing howls of anguish from the keening women.

He averted his eyes and squeezed past the widows, only to see a row of red crosses – one on every door. He looked back to see a red-eyed woman lay a tiny shrouded bundle on the doorstep before the door closed again.

Maybe he shouldn't have come. Jack would have left this place, surely?

'Halt,' the burly Constable said, removing the kerchief from his nose and mouth, and standing in his way. 'What's your business?'

'My cousin lives here, with his children, and I've come to see if he… if there's news of my wife.'

'Every house is locked sir. No-one goes in or out of these houses, unless by the dead cart. If I were you, I'd keep well away.' And he jammed the kerchief back over his face.

'I've just returned from sea, and I just want to ask—'

'You cannot go inside, sir. Even if your cousin yet lives, which I doubt. You must wait for them to come out.'

Sweet Jesus, not Jack and the boys? 'Can I leave them a note? Take them provisions?'

'If you want to risk your life.'

'I'll take my chance,' Will said.

The Constable stood reluctantly aside. 'Fool.'

Outside Jack's house Will paused, aghast. Like the others it was boarded up.

Until that moment he had never really believed it. Now the evidence made his knees buckle. He bent double, put his hands to his knees, took a few deep breaths. The cobblestones swam before his eyes. He looked up. At the top window he saw a blur of movement, but then it was gone. Had he imagined it?

The other houses were still, the windows stopped with shutters.

He hammered on the plank across the door. No answer. When he went to stand back again there were two small faces at the window. Thank God. Someone was alive in there.

He hammered again, 'Jack!' he shouted.

The window above opened.

'He's dead.' The woman's voice from the window was so familiar it made his stomach clench. He looked up. Bess.

Will took a step back.

'Toby too. They took them both yesterday.' Her words rolled over him like a wave.

'I was looking for you,' he said.

'Well,' Bess said bitterly, 'you've found me.'

'Are you—?' He was going to ask after her health, but the window slammed shut.

The sound of it echoed in his mind. Jack dead. And Toby. He couldn't understand what it meant. What should he do?

He stood in the street, feet glued to the ground. He couldn't go home.

Impossible to leave Bess there.

It went round and round in his head. She might die. Like Jack and Toby.

With a rush he went to the door and pulled at the plank. It wouldn't give. A rotten piece of timber, but nailed fast. He cast about for a solution. Lying on the pavement was a left-over pile of wood. He grabbed a thick spar and thrust it under the plank, levering against the nails. His muscles strained as he brought all his weight to bear until the wood around the nails splintered and with a crack, one end was off.

Working frantically, he prised off a second plank.

'Hey!' A shout from the Constable.

The sound of running feet. Will grabbed the door handle and twisted.

'Please don't be locked,' he prayed.

But it was already turning. A heavy hand grasped his shoulder but he elbowed the guard hard in the stomach and squeezed his way past the half-off plank. A rip as nails tore into his sleeves, and the door banged shut behind him, plunging the hall into darkness.

Chapter 62

Shouts, splitting wood, and the bang of the door. Bess leapt out of her chair, and Billy rushed downstairs before she could stop him. She glanced over at Hal, face on the pillow flushed pink with the fever, but he was oblivious to the commotion.

From below she heard Billy's excited shout, 'It's Uncle Will!'

No. She couldn't take it in. He should go back to sea. Safe, away from all this.

She heard his voice and it raised anger in her chest. She did not go down. She did not want to see him. Too much had changed. She did not know how to be with Will. She blamed him for being away, for leaving her in London, for Jack, for Pepys. For this.

Instead she folded the damp cloth into a pad and wiped Hal's face. She feared Hal would go the same way as his father, and his brother, but at least she'd make him comfortable. It was all she could do. If she was going to catch it, she probably would have it by now. But she couldn't concentrate, not with Will talking to Billy downstairs. What could Will hope to achieve by locking himself in here? She was just thinking that when she heard footsteps on the stairs. She froze in mid-movement when he spoke from the doorway.

'I can't believe it. About Toby.'

She did not answer.

He tried again. 'Is that why you came, Bess? To take care of the boys?'

'They won't let you out,' she said, looking at him for the first time. 'So you'd better be useful. You can find a few provisions in the scullery. And the house needs cleaning. I haven't had time.'

He was thinner and older. His eyes uncertain, full of pain.

'Don't use water,' she said. 'The conduit's broken, and my mother has to bring it from the well.'

But he nodded and went downstairs. She exhaled. She didn't want him here. It was too much extra weight for her to bear.

***

Agatha trudged along the bank of the Thames, back from the hamlet where she had been to scrounge eggs from an old farmer friend. There was nothing to be had in the city, so as dawn broke she walked the four miles past Kirby's Castle to Bleth'n 'all Green and back. She'd begged more grain to make flour too, and with luck, it would be a dry enough today to use the old stone by the harbour to grind it to make bread. It was the only way to get food to Bess and the boys. And later she'd have to go to the well.

She winced; the blisters on her feet and her bad hip made her walk more of a stumble. The thought of Toby's death kept thumping her in the guts. He'd been full of bravado that one; didn't seem possible she'd never hear him cheek her again. *What are you thinking, God?* The young shouldn't have to go before she did.

Pausing to take breath at the foot of her stairs, she rued the fact her lodgings were on the top floor. Grasping the banister, she hauled her way up. She'd get her feet up on the bed, soon as she got to the top.

A pair of dark leather shoes with iron tips stood on the top step, barring her way. She craned to look up, and had a moment to catch sight of George Allin's face before his shoe shot out to crunch the breath out of her chest. Around her the world swung on its axis, the ceiling tilting away from her, then the smack in her side as she hit the stairs, with the eggs flying.

'The eggs,' she thought, as over and over she tumbled, as if she were a bundle of washing thrown into a whirlpool.

No pain. But flat on her back. But the basket overturned, and the grain scattering like rain on the wooden steps. She was too winded to even cry out.

Allin stepped carefully down the stairs, avoiding the broken eggs. 'Get up,' he said. He was a man with a head too large for his body, and warty growths disfiguring the skin around his pig-eyes. Eyes that now glittered with malice.

Agatha tried to move, but found when she tried to rest her weight on her arm, it jagged with pain. A wave of nausea hit her. She must stand. She knew he'd hit her down as soon as she did, but it was what she always did. He expected it. She manoeuvred herself slowly to upright. 'How did you find me?'

'Jack. Sutherland.' He punched her twice to emphasise the words.

From the floor she said, 'He's dead.'

'Not when I saw him last week he wasn't.' Allin took a step back.

'Plague took him. And Bess. And I'm not feeling so good myself.'

Allin sucked on his teeth, before replying. 'Don't believe you. We followed you from the old church and you look alright to me. For a god-bothering bitch, that is. Where is she?'

'Told you, she's gone the same way as him. Both dead.' Her lips were thickening, the words came out blurred. But she'd never tell him where Bess was. She might not have been the best parent, but she'd make up for those lost years if it was the last thing she did. Even as she said this, she became aware of a noise behind her.

'Take her, boys,' Allin said.

She turned. Three of Allin's men, sailors by the look of them, with tarry pigtails and a stink of rum, grabbed hold of her, yanking on her bad arm.

The pain made her faint. *Broken*, the thought was a wisp floating past, *bad news*.

She kept up a racket, kicking and screaming, hoping someone would come. But screaming and wailing was commonplace now and no-one appeared.

'Shut your noise,' Allin said, 'or we'll slit your throat.' At this one of the sailors pressed a blade towards her face. She shrank away, but the pain in her arm made her dizzy, and soon she was leaning on her captors just to stay upright.

After that, the journey was a blur. At one point she vomited, and they let her go to the edge of the road to heave again. Where were they taking her? What would happen to Bess if she couldn't take provisions?

Ahead, the dark spires of masts and the wharf.

'No,' she shouted, already fearing the worst.

'Hold her,' Allin said. 'Where's my daughter?'

'Dead,' she croaked. Another blow to the face. She squirmed, but they had her pinioned tight. Allin swaggered before her. 'I heard you got married. So I thought I'd have you hanged for that. But then I realised hanging's a waste. So you'll fetch me a few groats in the Indies with the rest. You and that turncoat daughter. It might recompense me for the loss of a wife.'

'You were never a husband to me, George Allin,' she said, through thick lips. 'You don't know how to be a husband.' Summoning her last ounce of strength she wrestled herself free and turned to his men. 'You want to know why he runs a whorehouse? And why I left him? Why he has to use his fists on all his women? Because he can't use his cock. His cod is so small he couldn't swive a mouse.'

She had time to see the dawning laughter on the men's faces before Allin hit her so hard across the ear the world fragmented to black.

When she came to, it was to hear moans, and feel the cold weight of iron shackles around her wrists. At first she thought the moans to be her own, but then realised she was surrounded by other women, all shackled, all with wild terror in their eyes. But it wasn't their faces she was seeing, it was Bess's face at the window of Jack's house, looking out.

She wished she could send a message, longed to tell her some sort of goodbye. Her beautiful daughter whom she loved so much. But the creak of timber and slosh of water told her the ship was already underway. She blinked the tears from her eyes, prayed, *Dear God, if ever I did good in the world, send help, spare her soul.*

But she did not know if God heard her over the keening women, the pain and the slow inexorable tug of her heart over the swell of the sea.

***

Four days and Bess and Will hardly spoke a word to each other. Hal was failing, and Billy had retreated into himself and would not eat. Every day at three of the clock there'd been a loud knock on the back parlour window and when Will looked out, a cloth of provisions had been left on the sill. A pat of butter one day, two eggs the next. One day bread.

Bess would appear then, for there was always a note with it, from her mother.

Mr Shaw's gone now, and Hardwick. Even Kite. And they says now it started in Long-Acre, by goods brought from Holland. Some say it may lye dormant in the blood a good time, and that a sure remedy is faggots steeped in wine. But I know the best remedy of all is to run away from it. And failing that to wait and pray. God keep you and yours well, daughter.

Until the day there was no knock.

'What can be keeping her?' Bess said.

Will shook his head, but offered no answer. His silence spoke his fear.

***

Will was worried. The flagons of water by the scullery door were empty. Bess's mother usually brought a bucket up from the well, and he'd pass any containers they had in the house through the window so she could re-fill them with water. He was just contemplating this, when Bess appeared in the open doorway.

'Hal's dying,' she said.

'Is there nothing we can do?'

'He's full of tokens. And he doesn't know me now. Wants to push me away.'

'He knows you're there. Sure he does.'

She shook her head. Her eyes were hollow, her mouth pressed together as if to hold back words.

He longed to comfort her then, but the distance between them was something tangible, like a pane of ice.

'Do you want me to go to him?' Will said.

'No. Pass me the flask, I'll try to get him to drink.'

'We're out of water.' Will raised his arms in a gesture of surrender.

He watched hopelessly as she shook the flask. Exhaustion seemed to seep out of her clothes.

'Where's Billy?' she asked.

'In the front parlour. I set him carving faces into some wooden spoons. Thought it'd be better for him to be occupied.'

A thud above. Both of them rushed to the door and elbowed to get through. Bess got to the bedroom first. When Will arrived, her shaking shoulders told him all he needed to know. He went up behind her and laid a hand on her shoulder.

She swivelled, face contorted with tears and rage. 'Get out!'

she shouted.

He held up his hands and backed away. She was right. It was too much to bear. Bess scooped up the little body and held him close. Will bit his lip, because he didn't dare tell her not to.

When he got downstairs, he went to find Billy. He was sitting on the floor surrounded by woodchips.

'You're a good boy, Billy,' Will said, his voice thick with unspoken pain.

'Hal's dead, isn't he?' Billy said. He gathered up the spoons in his fist, but didn't look at Will. 'Here. There's Pa.' He held out the biggest of the spoons, crudely cut into a smiling face. 'And this one winking, that's Toby, and this little one's Hal. And this one with no face yet, that'll be me. And there was only four spoons in the drawer, so you'll be all right.'

'Oh, Billy.' He baulked at this child's logic. He knelt down beside Billy and put his arms around him. He was empty, he realised. His grief had turned into a hole so big he had no label for it. He wasn't sure if he was comforting Billy or Billy was comforting him.

***

Whilst she waited for the dead cart to pass, Bess swallowed to try to ease her dry mouth. She could not cry, *not even to make water*, she thought. For there was no water. Earlier, in desperation they had found brandy, which they saved for an emergency, but shared a sour half-finished flagon of wine that Jack had left by his chair in the parlour. It made her tongue furred and dull, and the liquor made her dizzy. They'd tried to make Billy drink too but he pressed his lips together and they couldn't force him. It must have made Will restless, for all morning she heard him pacing in the parlour below.

She went to the window over and over, but there was still no sign of her mother. Bess opened the upstairs window and shouted out into the street. 'Please, have mercy! We need water.'

But the guard did not reply, and the rest of the street was silent. In the distance bells tolled for the dead. She gritted her teeth and shouted again. She wouldn't give up.

After an hour her throat was sore and hoarse, and her voice a croak, but she kept on.

Will banged on the ceiling from below to stop her, but she kept it up anyway.

Finally he appeared in the scullery, 'I'll go for water,' Will said.

'You can't. It's a hanging offence, to go out,' she said.

'No matter.' He wiped the perspiration from his forehead. 'It's a beggar's choice anyway – die of thirst, or from the noose. I'm thinking of the boy. He needs water. To go that way... well, t'would be more painful than the disease.'

'They'll kill you.'

'But at least I'll be doing something. I'll have tried.'

Will strapped on his carpenter's belt. His hands shook. Was he drunk? She heard him stumble as he went downstairs.

Fear snaked up Bess's spine.

She hurried after him, as he made his way towards the scullery door. He was weaving side to side.

'Will?' Her voice was almost inaudible.

He ignored her, and headed to peer from the window, putting a hand up to the wall to steady himself.

When he opened the door from the inside, chinks of daylight crept through the barricade, but Will took the iron hammer from his belt and threw his weight behind it. A groan of frustration as he realised the blow had no force. He raised his arm again and again. The hammer rebounded.

Within four blows she was tugging at his shirt. 'Will, it's no use.'

He raised the hammer again, but by now he was panting, hanging over with the exertion. 'I've got to get out, fetch water. It's the only thing I can do now to help you.'

A pistol muzzle poked through the narrow gap between planks and a voice cried, 'Desist. Right now. Or I'll shoot.'

'Come away,' she said pulling at him.

He raised the hammer one more time before a mighty flash and a boom shook the house. For a moment she could see nothing. Smoke filled the room in a sulphurous cloud. Her ears rang. Coughing, through the rising pall, she spied Will slumped on the ground.

She stumbled to kneel beside him. 'Will?'

He rolled over, moaned.

'Are you hurt?'

Keep away from me,' he said.

'Show me where you're hurt.'

'I'm not hurt.' He spat the words at her. 'He missed, didn't he? But I'm no use to you now. Look.' He pulled the front of his shirt out of his breeches to show an ugly spotted rash.

'No,' she whispered, 'not you too. Don't you dare be sickening. Don't do this to me!' She pummelled his chest with her fists. He put his elbows up to protect himself.

'Aunt Bess?' Billy had crept in behind her, his blue eyes wide with fear.

'It's all right, Billy,' she said turning wearily, and wrapping her arms around him, 'The guard had an accident with his pistol, that's all.'

But the little figure in her arms was still and rigid as a statue, staring past her at where Will lay, curled like a still-born on the floor.

***

Will lay on top of the bare mattress, his face hot and too flushed.

Bess did not dare leave him. She did not know why she waited there, at the foot of the bed, for he would surely die, like Jack and Toby and Hal. Her gaze wandered around the room, over Jack's furnishings, so solid and heavy, wondering why it was that the wooden kist, the tester bed, could all survive, but human beings were so fragile, so easily destroyed.

She willed him to live, this long-boned man before her on the bed. Was he the man she'd married? It all seemed so long ago. And he did not know who she was; he was in a strange land inside his own head. 'I'm drowning!' he yelled, struggling to sit up. She let him yell. She kept him as clean as she could, burned the few remaining handfuls of dried sage, and tried not succumb to the dark thoughts about why her mother no longer came.

In the dark of the night she awoke from a doze to the sound of her name. Immediately alert, she lit a taper and hurried over to him.

'Don't remember me like this,' he croaked. 'When I'm gone, remember the man I used to be.'

'You're going nowhere—'

He gripped her arm. The taper shimmied in her hand, illuminating his haggard face. 'Remember when … we used to walk through Ratcliff … dream of a big house like this one?'

She remembered, but it stung to think of it. 'Hush now. Don't speak. Save your strength.'

'No. Let me speak, whilst I can. I was … a fool.' He screwed his eyes shut before opening them and fixing her with desperate eyes. 'I'm a failure. Everything I touch turns to ashes.'

'You don't really believe that.'

'Did you,' he paused to suck in a breath, 'did you love him?'

'Who? What are you talking about?' She lit the bedside candle.

'Pepys. Did you feel affection for him?'

The name set up an earthquake in her heart. 'You ask me that now? Of all times?' She stood and turned away.

'I need to know.'

'No. All I ever wanted was you. And now you talk of dying. How dare you, Will Bagwell? In sickness and in health, according to God's holy ordinance; that's what you promised.'

He was silent a moment. 'Promises are easy to make. Not much point in them... not now.' He groaned and closed his eyes. His neck was dark with a bluish rash as if from a noose. His breathing grew laboured.

She could not sleep, but sat, dry-eyed, staring at the pattern on the bed-curtains, counting the threads. A small pale hand on her arm. She turned.

Billy held out a bottle to her. Sutherland's Elixir.

'That's no use.' She waved it away.

'But it's just water, you said. Water. So I've been drinking it. You should have some.'

He was right. She took the bottle and upended it into her mouth. She choked and grimaced at the metallic taste, but it was all she could do not to gulp it down.

'Where did you find it?'

'There's more.' He held up both hands with the fingers outstretched. 'Ten whole cases. In the wine cellar.'

She was incredulous. 'What cellar? Show me.'

He went to the parlour and tugged back the big wooden chest. Behind it was a small square door. Billy pulled it open and she peered down a narrow set of steps to a low brick-lined room, barely high enough to stand up.

'In here,' Billy said, ducking in. Cobwebs brushed her hair as she stooped under its arch. But he was right. Praise God. There was an open case there.

She dragged at it, but it was too heavy for her to lift. 'We'll have to empty it,' she said. She yanked out straw and bottles, passing the bottles to Billy who stacked them on the steps.

'Clever boy,' she said. 'Carry on getting them out, whilst I go back to Will.'

She grabbed a bottle in each hand and ran back up the stairs. Will did not want to drink it, he turned his head away. He'd given up. Determined, she pushed the neck of the bottle into his mouth and tipped it down his throat. He spluttered and coughed, but was too weak to object. She dampened a cloth with some of the liquid and wiped his face.

A thud of footsteps on the stairs. Billy ran in, and her heart lurched in her chest.

'What?'

'Look!' He was holding something out towards her. It was a moment before she realised it was a loaf of bread. 'And there's more on the sill.'

She ran to the window. 'Ma!'

No sign of her. She pelted upstairs to lean out, but there was nothing to see, only the guards up the street, most lolling against the walls to keep out of the heat.

She went back and opened the bundle. It was wrapped in a piece of stiff tarpaulin cloth. Odd. Her mother usually left a basket. Bess took it down and opened it out on the table. A meat pie, somewhat squashed, some greasy pig's trotters, and a flagon of ale. A hunk of hard cheese. Relief flooded through her.

She searched the cloth again. No note. Her heart contracted in disappointment.

The emotions swirled around her. The consolation that food was on the table, and that water, however rank, was sitting in bottles on the shelves. But she ached to see her mother again, to find out what had kept her. Her words had meant more than the food, the thought that someone out there cared for her – that was what had sustained her.

Her mind went to the room upstairs. Where would she be without Will? The thought of losing him was too dark to contemplate.

***

Two more days passed, with Will worsening each day, and Bess powerless to persuade him to drink or eat. Provisions came, but still no note. Poor Ma. Maybe she'd been ill, or her fingers were bad with the rheum. At last when Will seemed quieter, Bess took a stick of pencil and scribbled a note.

Ma,

Will's been taken with it.

I beg you, if there's any remedy you know, bring it. And ask your Congregation to pray for us with all their might. We need your strong prayers, Ma.

I ache for little Billy. He's a lost soul without his brothers. It makes me angry to see him suffer. I tell Him that in my prayers to, but maybe I should be less outspoken.

I need to say how grateful we are that you come. I have never appreciated you the way I should. If I should fall sick and die, know this – I love you, Ma.

Write if you can, we are desperate for news.

Your loving daughter, Bess.

As she passed from the parlour to the kitchen, Bess glanced at Billy, so quiet now without his brothers. Earlier she'd seen him staring into space, but now he was whispering. She stopped to look. He had a wooden spoon clutched in each hand; the heads dipping and bobbing is some sort of argument. 'No Toby, that's mine,' he said. It made her sad. He was giving them all voices. Voices he'd never hear again.

Bess stood by the crack in the planks on the downstairs

window, where a blockage in the light, and the smell of tobacco, told her the guard was probably leaning there for a smoke.

'Guard,' she called. 'The woman who brings the provisions, can you take her a message?'

'Not allowed to. Can't touch anything from the house.'

'Can't you leave it for her somewhere?'

'No. Nothing from in there's allowed out here. Regulations, see.'

'Then can you tell me how's she faring?'

'Who?' The guard answered.

'The woman who's been feeding us.'

'T'aint a woman,' came the reply. 'It's your husband's father, Owen Bagwell. Thought you knew. I haven't seen a woman this week.'

Bess dropped the note she was holding, and her eyes met those of the guard through the slit in the boards.

'Are you sure?'

He shook his head. 'Not for nigh on two weeks. Only the father.'

Bess looked up to him. 'Then where is she?'

The guard shrugged. 'Hope it's not bad news.' He turned to go.

'Wait!' Bess shouted. 'Tell my husband's father I need to see him.'

'He comes early, Owen, 'bout four in the morning.'

'Wake me then, hammer on the door. And tell him to wait.'

***

In the upstairs chamber Will thrashed in pain. There was no point in trying to get him to eat, she knew that. Terrified it might be the end already, she hurried over, but though deathly pale and mottled with black lesions, his chest still rose and fell.

She did not sleep, but dozed, on tenterhooks for a noise from Billy in the next room, or from the bed before her. The knock at the shutters made her leap from the chair. In the faint light of dawn she felt her way downstairs.

A lamp at the shutters. 'Mr Bagwell?'

'Bessie?'

'Yes, I'm here. Don't get too close.'

'How is he? Guard says he's bad.'

'He's failing fast. I'm not sure … I'm not sure he'll make it. The fight's gone out of him.'

'What about young Billy?'

'He's asleep, but he's well. Grieving though for his brothers.'

'We got worried when Jack didn't come to the yard like he was supposed to. Then the guard told me … told me he'd gone.' A moment's silence.

'It's hard to lose a son.'

'I can't take it in. All these deaths. That guard – Stephen, he's called – I've known him from being a nipper. Told me about Toby and Hal too.' His voice broke and he coughed to cover it. 'Stephen said some damned fool had broken in. Tall sailor with blond hair. Didn't take much to work out it was Will. Thought I'd better bring food, if I could find it.'

'Have you seen my mother?'

'No. But maybe…' His voice tailed off.

'Will's not eating. Hasn't the desire for it. Listen, can you write, Mr Bagwell?'

'A bit. Not much.'

'Write a message for him then. Please. Give him something good to live for.'

'What shall I say?'

'I don't know. Anything. He needs to know there's someone out there who wants him back in the world. We had a … well, a falling out. But I love him, Mr Bagwell. That great lanky son of yours. It was always him for me, no matter what's gone on.'

She heard him ask the guard if he had something to write on. Then the scratching against the wood. A moment later a torn piece of paper poked through, with a short message written in graphite.

I'll bring a meat pie tomorrow.

Father.

'Is that it?' She hammered at the wooden plank. 'Is that all you're going to write?'

'I couldn't get much today. I have to go out of town; there's no food in London. It's a journey by row-boat. And I'll have to get moving, I've to be in the pit by six.'

'Wait!'

But her shouting brought no answer. She read the note again, and began to laugh, but it was a laugh that was full of tears.

'Sorry, mistress.' Stephen's eyes appeared a short distance away through the slit. 'He's gone.'

Will was barely conscious when she got back. 'Your father's been,' she said.

No response.

'Don't you dare leave me,' she begged him, but he barely flickered.

She propped the note against a bottle of plague water, and picked up his soiled breeches from the end of the bed, to take them to the laundry basket. Not that she could wash them with so little water. As she did so, something fell from the pocket and clattered away. From habit, she hurried to pick it up.

At first she thought it to be a coin, but as she stooped, she saw it was a ring. A gold ring. She weighed it in her hand, puzzling over where Will might have got it. It was a moment before she realised what she was seeing, the fancy scrolling, the chased letters around the inside. *Veritas, Fide et Amore.*

It was her wedding ring.

She staggered back into a chair, unable to take it in.

Pritchard said he'd sold it to a sailor who came in to buy a gift for his sweetheart. A gift. He'd been trying to make amends. What must he have thought, seeing it there in the pawnshop? Her face burned. So he knew she'd pawned it and had lied to him. Why had he not taken her to task? But she knew why. Because their marriage had been a sham for so long. Because of Mr Pepys.

The ring was cool to her touch. Without thinking, she slipped it on her finger. It fitted comfortably, like an anchor. Maybe if she wore it, it would tie him to her, keep him alive.

Chapter 63

Every day Bess examined Billy for tokens, and continued to pray. Until one day when she'd gone to empty the chamber pot and a shout alerted her.

'Come quick! He's sitting up.' Billy called from up the stairs.

Leaving the pot in the middle of the floor she hurried to clatter upstairs.

'Bess,' Will said.

'What are you doing? Lie down, I'll fetch you something to drink.'

When he had drunk, and settled back, she fell into an exhausted doze in the chair. When she awoke, it was to find Will sleeping, but breathing steadily.

Bess rubbed the ring between her fingers and fell to her knees to thank God.

After that, Will grew less feverish every day. One night he slept the whole night, and in the morning his face had lost its waxy sheen. But it was his eyes that struck to her heart. They were clear and direct, his gaze seeking hers from the sunken face.

He gestured to the note lying on the bed. 'Where did that come from?'

'Your father. He's been every day. We couldn't have survived without him. He brings food and fetches water. My mother ... well, we don't know where she is.' Her own eyes blurred.

'Give him some more of Pa's medicine,' Billy said, hopping from foot to foot, 'It's working. I told you it would.'

Bess blinked her tears away and propped Will up with a pillow whilst Billy fetched another bottle.

'I don't want that stuff,' Will protested weakly, 'it's bad luck.'

'You'll drink it,' she insisted. 'Drink it for Billy.' She held the neck of the bottle to his lips.

'How long... have I been bad?'

'Two weeks. Give or take. I've lost track of time. You were raving about being at sea.' He coughed as she held the bottle, talking all the while. 'We've got plenty, though it sounds like that's the last thing you want, but there's enough to see out the month, we found it in the wine cellar. Who'd have thought—'

'Bess?' Will croaked, 'Stop your blether and give a man some peace.'

She busied herself corking the bottle, but her face had split into a smile.

'Told you Pa's medicine would work!' Billy said. 'It did, didn't it?'

'Yes, lad, looks like you were right.' She bit back her scepticism, for Billy needed something good to remember his family by. And who was she to say what worked or didn't work. Who was taken, who was saved. It was all a mystery.

***

The first they knew that the boards were down, was one morning when Bess went downstairs to find herself blinking in the light.

She flung open the downstairs shutters for the first time in weeks and let the late summer sunshine and the air flood in. The light hurt her eyes. The sheer blue of the sky took her breath, though the street was silent, and weeds poked up through the cobbles. A dandelion clock released its delicate puffs of seeds in the breeze. She watched them float by, entranced. On the eaves of the house opposite a blackbird perched and pierced the air with sweetness, its orange beak wide open, thrusting out its song.

Billy clattered downstairs and pressed himself up next to her to see out.

'Can I go out?' he asked, eyes alight. 'Please!'

'Go on then. But only to the end of the street, no further. And don't talk to anyone. We don't know whether they carry it.'

He was off then, haring up to the end of the street like a greyhound. She watched him a moment, before going up to Will. When she got there she was surprised to see him up for the first time, dressed in a pair of Jack's too-long breeches and a clean shirt.

'I heard them take the boards down,' he said. 'I feel like I've just come back from sea. Shaky as a colt. My legs are like sea-legs. But I can get downstairs if you help me.'

She went to him then to prop him up as they hobbled downstairs. Before they could even get to the bottom there was a knock on the door, and it creaked open.

Owen Bagwell stepped over the threshold. 'They said it'd be today,' he said, brushing a hand over his moustache. 'But I won't come in, just wanted to set eyes on you, that's all.'

'Did you see Billy?' Will said.

'Aye. Shot past me without stopping. Grown, hasn't he?'

'Proper beanstalk, like his pa. We're grateful, Father. The food has kept us, these last weeks.'

'Well, you're family. Couldn't see you starve, could I?' Mr Bagwell shifted awkwardly, looking at his boots.

'Bess tells me you had to row six miles downstream every day to fetch it. Must've been hard work.'

'Not with saw arms like mine. It was nothing.'

'You keep in fine shape for a man your age. But take care, Father. You shouldn't be in here, you know. You might catch it.'

Mr Bagwell shook his head. 'Don't you fret over me. I had a dose of the bugger in thirty-six. Reckon that was my lot. And I had a word with Nicholson. Soon as you're fit, your Guild papers will be through.'

Bess and Will looked at each other. 'Time enough to decide once you're well,' Bess whispered.

'Will you go to Flaggon Row?' Mr Bagwell asked. 'My lads have been watching it for you.'

'Maybe,' Bess said. The thought of it was something she wasn't ready for yet. She looked tentatively to Will. 'Or maybe we'll get right away for a while. Get some sea air if we can.'

'Then I'll be off. I'm due at the yard. Send note where you're at.'

'We will. Go safe, Father,' Will called.

'And you, son.'

Bess was choked. Neither of them dared speak their thoughts.

Will held out his arms, and Bess folded herself into them. He felt thin; all skin and bone; not the muscled man she'd married. But then she was a skeleton herself. He held her tighter, and they stood there a long while, on the threshold.

'It's like everything's burnt out of me,' Will said. 'I feel empty.'

'You survived it. That's all that matters.'

'The body isn't everything, though I used to think it was. I thought if I could control your body I could control you. But I can't. The Bess Bagwell I love isn't in this ...' he squeezed her by both arms. 'I can't even see it. But I can feel it,' he said, stepping away to look into her face. 'Something wild and noisy and free.'

'We'll be alright, won't we?' There were tears in her eyes.

'Aye. There'll be no separating us now,' Will said. He pulled her off the threshold into the street outside. 'Come on, love. Let's go take a look at Old Father Thames. He never changes, no matter what goes on in this city.'

Will paused, held out his hand and she threaded her fingers into his. They took a few steps and then he lifted her hand to look at it, examined the ring on her finger. 'You found it then,' he said.

'In your breeches. But it's back where it belongs now.'

He squeezed her hand tight, and she gave him an answering squeeze. The warm touch of hands seemed to say all the words they could not find.

'Auntie Bess!' Billy came racing towards them. 'I met this boy and he said was I an orphan, and I said no, 'cos I've got my auntie and uncle. That's right, isn't it?' His anxious face looked to Will for reassurance.

'That's right, Billy. Though you've got Grandad too, remember.'

Billy grinned and took hold of Bess's other hand. 'Grandad too,' he echoed. 'And Nanny Prescott.'

'Wherever she is,' Bess said.

'We'll find her,' Will said. 'Never fear.'

And the three of them walked slowly up the silent street towards the skein of blue shining water in the distance.

Historical Notes

Pepys's Diary

Samuel Pepys is the author of the most famous and best-loved diary in the English language. Born the son of a tailor, Pepys was a self-made man who rose up the ranks to become one of the foremost citizens in Restoration London, and his diary provides a fly-on-the-wall view of life in the seventeenth century. His daily entries combine coverage of major crises, such as the Plague and the Great Fire of London, with political events, gossip, and intimate details of his many affairs. It tells us what people ate, how they relaxed (Pepys was a great musician and theatre-goer), how they spent their money, and all the minutiae of daily life. The importance of the diary to our knowledge of the era cannot be over-estimated.

Pepys began his entries on New Year's Day 1660 using Thomas Shelton's shorthand, a method he probably used in his work-life for speed. He wrote with a quill pen in standard notebooks of 282 pages, with hand-ruled margins in red ink. The diary at first looks like impenetrable code – all squiggles and dots with only the occasional recognisable word. Perhaps Pepys also used this 'code' for privacy; for he certainly would not have wanted his wife to read about his extra-marital affairs!

Pepys was Clerk to the Navy, which in the era of sail, when wars were fought at sea, meant he had enormous responsibility for the supplying of ships with everything from biscuits to cannon. He was a man who was held in great respect by the King, Charles II, and moved in scientific and intellectual circles as well as patronising the arts. He continued his diary for a little over nine years, to May 31st 1669, when he had trouble with his eyesight, and regrettably, stopped writing it.

Fortunately for posterity, Pepys left his diary to Magdalene College Cambridge, where he had been a scholar, and his whole library can be seen there too – some three thousand books, still in the original shelves Pepys commissioned for the purpose.

Several of my novels have been set in the seventeenth century, and for all of them I have used Pepys's diary as an integral part of my research. In the process, I became fascinated by the women who appear as vague figures in the background, between the lines, always overshadowed by Pepys's ebullient presence. Mrs Pepys is referred to by Pepys only as 'my wife' and not by her name, so as a sort of revenge, I started to imagine what the women in the diary might be doing, when he was so to speak 'out of the room'. The first novel *Pleasing Mr Pepys* was told from the point of view of his wife and maidservant, but there are plenty of other notable women in his diary – as Pepys ruefully confesses; '*Musique and women* I cannot but give way to.' I chose Bess Bagwell for this book because it has always been a mystery why her husband seemed to encourage her affair with Pepys.

The Bagwells

Mrs Bagwell is Samuel Pepys's most mentioned mistress. She is mentioned almost fifty times, from 1663 onwards, and even beyond the Bagwells's brush with the plague, she appears to have still been in Pepys's life a month before the end of the diary. In this novel I have called Mrs Bagwell 'Bess', the diminutive of Elizabeth, though her first name is never mentioned in Pepys's diary. No marriage record has yet been traced which positively identifies her maiden name, but William Bagwell's will of 1697 refers to 'Elizabeth my well-beloved wife'. Marriage records for the Interregnum period often didn't survive and the Bagwells's marriage could have taken place at that time. From baptismal records, it appears they had no natural children.

Elizabeth Bagwell died in 1702 and was buried at St Nicholas, Deptford on 14th August. Her occupation then was given as Gentlewoman, so it appears they did eventually become a prosperous household, and Mrs Bagwell's liaison with Samuel Pepys, as recorded in his diary, seems to have been instrumental in her husband's promotion. William Bagwell held prominent shipbuilding positions in Chatham and also in Bristol, Plymouth and Portsmouth, becoming a Master Shipwright in 1696. William also fought on board the *Providence* in the Four Days Battle against the Dutch in 1666.

A novel must, for the benefit of the reader, be limited in time, but surprisingly, Pepys's letters when he was Secretary of the Admiralty show that Mrs Bagwell was still soliciting his advice about her husband almost twenty years later. So some consensus of agreement must have been reached between all parties for their mutual benefit. Following this story, the affair between Mrs

Bagwell and Pepys continues. In my imagination, Bess and Will would have gone to Portsmouth for a while to recuperate before returning to Flaggon Row. Pepys states that the couple went to Portsmouth but not why.

On 13th June 1666 Pepys says: 'returned and walked to Mrs. Bagwell's house, and there (it being by this time pretty dark and past ten o'clock) went into her house and did what I would. But I was not a little fearfull of what she told me but now, which is, that her servant was dead of the plague, that her coming to me yesterday was the first day of her coming forth, and that she had new whitened the house all below stairs, but that above stairs they are not so fit for me to go up to, they being not so.'

As for the rest of the Bagwells, Owen Bagwell, William's father, was foreman at the Deptford Shipyard. I took his character from mentions of him in *The Secret History of His Majesty's Ship-Yard*, where he seems to have been most unpopular! Although William had a younger brother John (or Jack), the life I have given him is purely fictitious, as are his children.

Morality

Our views on morality and sexual conduct have moved on since Pepys's day. What was considered perfectly acceptable in the seventeenth century is totally unacceptable now, and we must seek to understand Pepys's behaviour as a product of his time. Pepys in my novel could easily have been a monster, but he is regarded everywhere with such affection (rightly or wrongly), that to paint this view of him would have caused great resistance in a reader who has turned to this novel because it features him.

From Pepys's diary we can read that, just like today, a simplistic view cannot suffice, as within the diary itself we see conflicted views of what constituted moral behaviour – Pepys's remorse and feelings for his wife when he has strayed, his initial reluctance to approach Mrs Bagwell because she seemed so respectable. Whether or not I have successfully picked my way across this quagmire of sexual abuse versus the historical mores of the time is something I hope my readers will discuss between themselves.

Selected Further Reading

Samuel Pepys; The Unequalled Self – Claire Tomalin
Inside Pepys's London – Jonathan Bastable
Journal of the Plague Years – Daniel Defoe
The Great Plague – A. Lloyd Moote & Dorothy C. Moote
1666 – Plague, War and Hellfire – Rebecca Rideal
The Time Traveller's Guide to Restoration Britain – Ian Mortimer
Restoration London – Liza Picard
A Survey of London – John Stow
Transformations of Love (about John Evelyn & Margaret Godolphin) – Frances Harris

Pepys's Diary Online: https://www.pepysdiary.com/

About Deborah Swift

Deborah used to be a set and costume designer for the theatre and for the BBC. She is the author of ten historical novels, and lives on the edge of the English Lake District, close to the mountains and the sea.

You can find out more about her research and writing process on her website www.deborahswift.com

Deborah is always happy to chat to readers on Twitter @swiftstory

Meanwhile, why not try one of Deborah's other books:

The Lady's Slipper
The Gilded Lily
A Divided Inheritance
Past Ecounters
The Highway Trilogy for Teens

In this series
Pleasing Mr Pepys
A Plague on Mr Pepys
Entertaining Mr Pepys

Acknowledgements

My thanks to all at Accent Press, and especially my editor Jay Dixon.
Special thanks to my husband John who is the invisible support behind all my books.

And thank you, the reader, for reading.

If you have enjoyed this book, a review would be much appreciated.

Praise for *Pleasing Mr Pepys*

'Deb Willet, Elizabeth Pepys's maid and the object of Samuel Pepys's attentions, is finally given centre-stage after 350 years, and her tale was worth waiting for. This is exceptional story-telling.' – L. C. Tyler

'Laced with emotional intensity and drama, Pleasing Mr Pepys... (has) an intricate plot that features red herrings, unexpected twists, and surprises that will take readers on a very delightful ride.' – Arya Fomonyuy

'The novel provides us with a new view of the Pepys's household through the eyes of a young woman who steps into the limelight from the shadows of history.' – Jean Briggs, Historia Magazine

Proudly published by Accent Press

www.accentpress.co.uk